M_____ ____N is the a_____ _____ ___cli___ng *Off Keck Road*, which was a finalist for the PEN/Faulkner Award and won the Heartland Prize of the *Chicago Tribune*. She lives in Santa Monica, California.

ALSO BY MONA SIMPSON

MONA SIMPSON

CASEBOOK

corsair

Constable & Robinson Ltd.
55–56 Russell Square
London WC1B 4HP
www.constablerobinson.com

First published in the US by Alfred A. Knopf,
a division of Random House LLC, New York, 2014

First published in the UK by Corsair,
an imprint of Constable & Robinson Ltd, 2014

Extract from *The Shape of a Pocket* © John Berger, 2001,
Bloomsbury Publishing Plc.

With gratitude to Alexander Allaire
for the drawings used in *Casebook*.

A copy of the British Library Cataloguing in
Publication Data is available from the British Library

ISBN: 978-1-47211-245-3 (paperback)
ISBN: 978-1-47211-257-6 (ebook)

Printed and bound in the UK

1 3 5 7 9 10 8 6 4 2

For Gabriel

Everything that deceives can be said to enchant.

—PLATO

Do we not dream of being known, known by our backs, legs, buttocks, shoulders, elbows, hair? Not psychologically recognized, not socially acclaimed, not praised, just nakedly known. Known as a child is by its mother.

—JOHN BERGER, *The Shape of a Pocket*

Yours, always, always.

—ELI J. LEE

CASEBOOK

NOTE TO CUSTOMER

The book you now hold in your hands is our first venture into the old long-form technology that our pay-to-print machine in the back room has made possible. The manuscript for this experiment was delivered to me by hand from an employee I first met when he wore board shorts and flip-flops and came into the store to read for free during the long afternoons of summer vacation. He and his pal, you've probably by now guessed, are the creators of Two Sleuths, *the first breakout seller of Emerald City, our then-fledgling publishing concern. With an advance run of three hundred, the comic book was reprinted ninety-one times and is still shipping at a rate of a hundred copies a month. It has attained the status of a classic. Needless to say, I asked, no, begged, for a sequel. I envisioned a whole series of these called* Spyboys. *Letters still come for the authors, care of Emerald City Press, and from those even more industrious, to the store, Neverland Comics, asking, What became of the Pet Delivery Boys? Did they grow up? Go to college? Did they find happiness as veterinarians? When the shaggier, pudgy one delivered this thick sheaf of papers, he explained that it was more like a prequel, made by the two of them again, but in a different kind of collaboration. It was written by one, then amended by the other, who brought it here with his Track Changes still fresh. He said he added footnotes and changed the heroine's name. Given pay-to-print technology, it's unlikely that this will be their last pass. The original author intends to read it again someday, if he can bear the experience. So it may go back and forth between the two—who don't live in the same city anymore—writing over each other, changing names to allude to private jokes, adding scenes and taking them out, until they get their story straight or until they grow up, whichever comes last, or never.*

In short, you may not be reading the final version. You're holding what we have as of today, May 1, 2014.

HERSHEL GESCHWIND
Neverland Comics
Santa Monica, California

1 · Under the Bed

I was a snoop, but a peculiar kind. I only discovered what I most didn't want to know.

The first time it happened, I was nine. I'd snaked underneath my parents' bed when the room was empty to rig up a walkie-talkie. Then they strolled in and flopped down. So I was stuck. Under their bed. Until they got up.

I'd wanted to eavesdrop on *her*, not them. She decided my life. Just then, the moms were debating weeknight television. I needed, I believed I absolutely needed to understand *Survivor*. You had to, to talk to people at school. The moms yakked about it for hours in serious voices. The only thing I liked that my mother approved of that year was chess. And every other kid, every single other kid in fourth grade, owned a Game Boy. I thought maybe Charlie's mom could talk sense into her. She listened to Charlie's mom.

On top of the bed, my dad was saying that he didn't think of her *that way* anymore either. What way? And why *either*? I could hardly breathe. The box spring made a gauzy opening to gray dust towers, in globular, fantastic formations. The sound of dribbling somewhere came in through open windows. My dad stood and locked the door from inside, shoving a chair up under the knob. Before, when he did that, I'd always been on the other side. Where I belonged. And it hurt not to move.

"Down," my mother said. "Left." Which meant he was rubbing her back.

All my life, I'd been aware of him wanting something from her. And of her going sideways in his spotlight, a deer at the sight of a human. The three of us, the originals, were together locked in a room.

My mom was nice enough looking, for a smart woman. "Pretty for a mathematician," I'd heard her once say about herself, with an air of apology. Small, with glasses, she was the kind of person you didn't notice. I'd seen pictures, though, of her holding me as a baby. Then, her hair fell over her cheek and she'd been pretty. My dad was always handsome. Simon's mom, a jealous type, said that my mother had the best husband, the best job, the best everything. I thought she had the best everything, too. *We* did. But Simon's mom never said my mother had the best son.

The bed went quiet and it seemed then that both my parents were falling asleep. My dad napped weekends.

Nooo, I begged telepathically, my left leg pinned and needled.

Plus I really had to pee.

But my mother, never one to let something go when she could pick it apart, asked if he was attracted to other people. He said he hadn't ever been, but lately, for the first time, he felt aware of *opportunities*. He used that word.

"Like who?"

I bit the inside of my cheek. I knew my dad: he was about to blab and I couldn't stop him. And sure enough, idiotically, he named a name. By second grade everyone I knew had understood never to name a name.

"Holland Emerson," he said. What kind of name was that? Was she Dutch?

"Oh," the Mims said. "You've always kind of liked her."

"I *guess* so," he said, as if he hadn't thought of it until she told him.

Then the mattress dipped, like a whale, to squash me, and I scooched over to the other side as the undulation rolled.

"I didn't do anything, Reen!"

She got up. Then I heard the chair fall and him following her out of the room.

"I'm not going to do anything! You know me!"

But he'd started it. He'd said *opportunities*. He'd named a name. I bellied out, skidded to the bathroom, missing the toilet by a blurt. A framed picture of them taken after he'd proposed hung on the wall; her holding the four-inch diamond ring from the party-supply shop. On the silvery photograph, he'd written *I promise to always make you unhappy.*

I'd grown up with his jokes.

By the time I sluffed to the kitchen he sat eating a bowl of Special K. He lifted the box. "Want some?"

"Don't fill up." She stood next to the wall phone. "We're having the Audreys for dinner."

"Tonight?" he said. "Can we cancel? I think I'm coming down with something."

"We canceled them twice already."

The doorbell rang. It was the dork guy who came to run whenever she called him. He worked for the National Science Foundation and liked to run and talk about fractals.

Later, the Audreys arrived, all four of them standing clean, like they'd just taken showers. It was strange to see Hector's hair ridged by a comb. His sister had a snub nose and freckles, but at least there was only one of her.

She looked at my two sisters for about a second, and then they all ran to the Boops' room and slammed the door. When they had a friend over, the first thing the Boops did was go to their closet, strip, and exchange clothes. Jules Audrey was a grade older, so the

Boops would be vying for her attention. They were all in there now, trying on every single thing the Boops owned in front of the mirror. I'd told my mom a jillion times she should take that mirror down.

"You're wearing out the glass," I called as Hector and I skidded past their door. "Mirror mirror on the wall, who's the stupidest of you all?"

"Hard call," Hector mumbled, hands in his shorts pockets.

We ate quickly and got excused. Later, we asked for a ride to Blockbuster.

"We're just eating dessert," my mom said.

They had ice cream with espresso poured over. She said we could have some without the coffee. She gave Hector the larger portion. Hector was skinny, as sidekicks to fat kids usually are. He wore flip-flops and shorts, even in winter, and his legs looked like bug feelers.* She gave him two scoops and me one made to look like two. My mom had liked Hector ever since the time she'd driven us to the Wildlife Waystation when we were seven and he'd pronounced Slobodan Milošević correctly. That same ride, he'd said from the backseat, "My aunt could never drive these turns. My aunt is an alcoholic."

The adults sat at the table with coffee cups and the strange-smelling bottles of liquor, the three girls screeched in my sisters' room, and from the shipwreck of dishes on every counter in the kitchen, Hector and I stood forking pasta straight from the big bowl.

My mom had strategized, inviting the Audreys. She wanted Hector and me to be friends. She thought I didn't talk enough to boys at school. Since we'd played chess tournaments at the LA Chess Club above the Men's Wearhouse in first grade, the Mims had set her sights on Hector. By fourth grade, I liked him, too. That night, I told him about the walkie-talkie under the bed, with

---

* *Don't think just because you've jumbled up our looks I don't know when you're really talking about me.*—Hector

rubber bands and electrical tape holding the button down. I wanted to show him, but my dad stayed in their room all through dinner. The Mims had told the Audreys he wasn't feeling well.

"How was it?" my dad asked, holding the remote, when everybody finally left.

"This is the hundred and twenty-sixth day this year we haven't eaten dinner together," my mother said. "And it's only June."

2 · A Walkie-Talkie

The walkie-talkie didn't work. I could hear my mom but not the other person. I hadn't thought of that. And in a lot of conversations, most of what she said was *mm-hmm*. I hadn't thought of that either. With us, she said a lot. I had to be completely still so she wouldn't hear noise through the device. Most of the time, I just heard her moving in her room, singing Joni Mitchell songs, off-key.

Hector had seen an old phone in his garage. He wanted to try hooking it up as an extension. He liked the idea of spying. He couldn't watch *Survivor* either, because they just had an old TV that was broken. His only hope was my house. I held the bottom of the ladder while he reached for the black rotary from behind rusted paint cans. The Audrey garage held treasure. We hauled the heavy phone in his backpack to our place and found a painted-over jack under my bed. I had to pick out crud from the opening, but then we plugged it in and heard a dial tone! We covered the mouthpiece with cotton balls and duct tape. Then Hector thought of Silly Putty. We tore the stuff off, filled the holes, and brushed over it all with my sisters' nail polish. No matter what, my mother wouldn't be able to hear us through that. Then, for hours, the phone didn't ring.

Finally, we heard talking from her room. The phone still hadn't rung; she must've dialed. I slid in my socks down the hall, lifted the jangly box from under my bed.

Maybe I don't inspire love, we heard her say, through static. *I've never been beautiful.*

I didn't want Hector hearing that. I wanted my mother to be beautiful.

We're as good-looking for women as they are for men. That was Sare, Charlie's mom. I loved Sare. I'd have recognized her certainty through any static. "Maybe you and I just aren't great marriage material."

That stumped me. I didn't know what she meant. My parents were better than other people's parents; I believed that in a way so deep I didn't think of it as a belief. It seemed a fact. My dad made everyone laugh. My mom stood apart, quieter, with her arms crossed. That was how they fit. The Mims didn't tell Sare that she'd asked if he felt attracted to anyone else and that he'd named a name. Did my parents not have good sex? The thought streaked through me. I supposed they'd had it twice, at least. (My sisters were twins.)

I felt miserable, sitting cross-legged, the heavy black receiver leashed by its coil on top of the bed between Hector and me. Sare said that Dale relaxed her. His heart rate was very, very slow. Even though my dad worked long hours, he was beginning to be successful, Sare said. *Doesn't that thrill you a little?* My mother thought a moment and then said no, not really. I knew that was true, and it scared me. Why didn't it thrill her?

"I think your mom's pretty beautiful," Hector said.

On that August evening, in the year two thousand nothing, those two Los Angeles mothers talked for another hour. About what? Nothing we cared about.

Where to get the best thermos? Target! Music: Josquin des Prez, Mahalia Jackson, and Lucinda Williams. My mom listened to gospel, but she didn't believe in God. More hikes, they both agreed they were going to get us to take. Putting on pumps and walking to church every Sunday? Not until those nuns got unshackled from their *fucking vows of poverty.* Sare said *fucking!* She was way cooler than my parents.

Sare was a very smart person who'd never tried anything too hard for her. She had that confidence and that boredom. Charlie had been my first friend. We knew each other through our mothers. The Mims was in awe of what Sare could make: for years, Charlie had a sandbox that took up their whole backyard, with boys crouching all over, running trucks and hoses. My mom wanted to learn from her the how-to of family life. My dad couldn't understand. *Sofia Kovalevsky wasn't Martha Stewart,* he kept saying. I heard that a dozen times before I learned that Kovalevsky was a dead mathematician, not someone they knew. But Sare had some wisdom about ease, an understanding of moving life, the warming and the holding. That never seemed to me unimportant. We were different from other families. My dad had chosen to be. The Mims just was. She couldn't help it. She probably would rather have been more like everybody else.

"Well, the answer is . . . ," Sare said. This seemed to be her refrain. The answer to sex was once a week, in the morning. "Get it over with," she said. "I always feel better after. It's just before. The *dread.*"

I pushed the tonsil-like buttons to disconnect, as if by accident. I didn't want to hear my mom talk about sex. It was bad enough to have heard Sare. I started to think about Sare without clothes on and had to stop. I hadn't understood that people their age—like our parents even—kept on doing it. Or maybe I'd known, but I hadn't thought about it.

"The answer," Sare was saying, when I let the tonsils spring up, "is gratitude every day." To our lunches, paring vegetables all at once and decanting them to glass jars in the refrigerator. Decanting seemed to be the final answer.

But I hadn't breathed dust balls to hear about vegetables. I didn't like picturing Sare nude with Dale, Charlie's bookish dad who wore wire-rimmed glasses. Did he take the glasses off when he undressed?

More than an hour and the moms never got to *Survivor.*

I'd heard the Mims complain once to my dad that they should be having an endless conversation. "And what would that conversation be about?" he'd asked.

This was an endless conversation.

I did the cut-my-head-off sign and set the extension down on its cradle.

3 · Faking Sleep

While I rummaged in my mom's drawer, I heard my parents laughing as they came up the steps outside. I dived under their covers when I heard the crunch of them unlocking and I made myself completely still. They walked in and hangers in the closet cymbaled. My mom kicked off her shoes.

"He has a crush on you, all right," my dad said. A crush! Crushing was what girls did, I thought; every day it was on someone different. At the end of the bed, my father flicked on news. Through eyelashes, I could see him rubbing his socked foot. "Did you hear him stammering, 'I'm besotted with your wife'? He practically couldn't get the words out." My dad laughed. "I guess he really liked your paper."

"I'm surprised anybody noticed." My mom had published one paper, about animal locomotion. When two copies of the journal came in the mail, my dad had brought home flowers and they'd gone out to dinner. The dork guy had been at UCLA, making a site visit for an NSF grant to the department, and he'd picked out my mom to be friends with. He said he'd read her paper, but she thought it was because he wanted a running partner while he was in LA.

"I'm not worried," my dad said. "He's a less-good-looking version of me." In general, my dad only minded taller men. "It's not an ugly baby they've got. Not like some potatoes we've known."

What baby did they think looked like a potato? Would my dad call his own daughter a spud?

"His wife asked me to talk to him. She said, *I tell him he's smilier than other babies*. She thought he'd come around because he's good with the cat and the dog. So I told him, 'You'll fall in love with him. Everyone falls in love with their own children.' And he said, 'Well, with *your* babies, sure.' "

"Miles *was* the most beautiful baby," my dad said. "And Emma! Those curls!"

Boop One! Beautiful? A startling idea. I was alive when the Boops were born and I had eyes. Two lumps that wailed was more like it.

"The wife's kind of a dishrag," my dad said. "What's with the Heidi braids?"

"You know what she said? After that whole thing about how he didn't love the kid, she told me she was planning to get pregnant again right away. I asked if she thought that was such a good idea, given how he'd taken to this one. She said, in that little-girl voice, 'Well, if he's unhappy with everything *any*way . . .' "

"Still, it can't hurt for you to have a friend at NSF."

My dad cared about the Mims's position in the math world, where she felt she was still a beginner and too old to be. She'd made a miscalculation. She'd tried to solve an open problem and not published anything for five years. Now she had to teach more and didn't get paid her summer ninths. I pretended sleep. They had a little scuffle then over whether to let me stay. "But *she's* always in here," my dad said, meaning my sister.

"So let him this once."

My dad sighed. But he didn't move me. And I slept beautifully, between them.

4 · Eavesdropping

My mother went running late at night, after we were supposed to be in bed. She loved for us to sleep. She could do things then without missing time with us. One night, I happened to be sitting in the crook of a tree when I heard voices rise from the street.

"That proved to be irresistible."

"But this is?" she said. "Resistible?"

You could tell from the sound of the wind in the leaves that it was no longer summer.

"I'd probably leave everything," the male voice, not hers, said.

"It would never work," she answered. "We're allergic to animals."

It took a moment longer than usual for the words to line up into sentences. Possible meanings assembled, like a puzzle that could be put together different ways but that still left extra pieces until the real form used every one of them. Was it the dork guy offering to leave his wife for the Mims and her letting him down easy? I didn't think it could be that. But the words pressed on me, like sharp cookie cutters.

One Sunday, I saw my dad pacing on the porch and climbed up to the roof. "I could get away for a long weekend maybe," I heard him say. There was no one else there. He was on the telephone. "Not a month. She wouldn't want to either. The last thing she'd want is a beach with me! When I get a night off, she doesn't elect to go out. She has me take the kids so she can work. And I get that. I really do."

A sweet dark twirl of air floated up to me. Thinking he was alone, my father had lit a cigar. He didn't suspect I was above him. We weren't supposed to know that he smoked. My mother had found some statistic that children of parents who smoked were more likely to smoke themselves. The Mims loved a good statistic.

That night, I stood outside their door. They were talking about the new chairman of the math department, who'd come from MIT after her husband died. "I worry about her," my father said. "She's just not attractive enough." Then he burped. "Great meal."

I burst in and said I needed a tuck. She followed me to my room and put her hand on my forehead. I loved that. Her hand was always cool. It erased my thoughts and let me fall asleep.

Then, it happened: the permanent thing.

When they told me, my lungs went out of sync. I lost the rhythm of breathing. I had to remember, *Suck in*, *exhale*, the hunger for oxygen no longer automatic.

My father went to the sink to get me a glass of water.

My mother told me to breathe.

"Drink," my father said.

"I never thought you two" was all I could whisper, my face in his shoulder.

5 · Guessing Who Left

My father moved out a month after 9/11. Even that didn't keep him home.

In school, we drew pictures of the Twin Towers to send to far-away New York City firemen, and during Life Skills, when the rock came to me in the circle, I said my parents were separating and that made me sad.

My mom got up early now. She fixed our lunches, the same as before, but she moved stiff and fast, like a general, dragging us up.

I taught the Boops to say *Jawohl*. And *Heil Hitler*.

"Who do you think left?" Hector asked.

I really didn't know. "They said they decided together."

It was the worst thing that ever happened to me, after the Boops being born. Even with all my sleuthing, I'd never suspected this. A day in October my mother sat at the kitchen table staring at an index card where she'd penciled the numbers of our friends' moms. I watched her make herself dial. I learned from the conversation she had with Sare later that Simon's mom had asked, *Did you guys ever think of doing some counseling?*

"Yeah, right," Sare said. "You ever think of that?"

They laughed frighteningly. So my parents had gone to counseling. I hadn't known.

But Hector's mom, Kat, had said, "I'm about six weeks behind you."

I counted. Six weeks passed, then seven, then eight. Nothing happened. Hector didn't know his luck. I felt bad, but I wanted it to happen to him, too. I thought it would make us better friends.

6 · How Do You Solve a Problem Like Maria?

My father told me we were going to see *The Sound of Music* as a family.

We'd never done anything *as a family* before. "Do I have to?" I said.

They made me. Hector went, too, with the aunt who paid his school fees.

"My family," I said to him at Intermission.

He shrugged. "My mom says your parents get along because it *wasn't* about sex. No one had an affair." Meaning, I supposed, that sex was the dangerous element. I acted as if I'd already known that. "Simon's mom says you have the best divorce."

"We're not actually divorced. We're here *as a family*, remember? My dad's gunning for an A in Separation."

When he picked us up Saturday mornings, he called ahead from the car to say, *Put Emma in the black headband.* He still cared about our hair. He usually ran late so we had to wait on the porch with our hair combed and then run down to his car. My mom came out in socks. He'd open the passenger window and hand her something—a cup with a straw, takeout containers, crumpled napkins—and say, *Could you throw this out?*

She took it. And we beheld our handsome dad, the distant ocean unrolling behind his profile, framed by the window of his new, heavy car.

"Your dad moved out," Hector said. "Maybe *he's* the culprit."

My dad *would* be the one to fall in love. He walked into walls, pratfalling. He said himself he was the stupider of the two. He didn't say he was also the better-looking one. Neither of my parents was especially romantic. I remembered the way they said *in love*, with spin, as if it were pathetic or a joke. My mom saw love as a trap to catch females. "You don't really believe in that romance stuff, do you?" I'd asked her once, after a Disney princess movie with the Boops.

"I think it's more or less stuff and nonsense," she'd admitted.

Maybe my dad had left her for the Dutch.

Hector looked at me with pity.

You don't even know how close you came, I thought.

His aunt walked over, balancing two supersize Cokes and a popcorn. His aunt was the age of our moms, but she wore boots and scarves because her boyfriend was married and she didn't have kids to spend money on.

Boop One had moved three rows down to sit with girls she knew from school.

"I want to go home," Boop Two whispered. "I'm homely."

"Lonely, you mean. You're lonely. Not homely."

"I just want to go home."

"Me, too. But we can't."

My mom waved to the Bennetts on the other side of the aisle. Sare had draped her leg over the movie-chair arm, onto Dale, as if to prove separation wasn't contagious.

Out on the sidewalk, we met Holland for the first time, straining at the leash of an enormous poodle. She was tall and Brentwood-looking.

I asked her if she was Dutch.

She said, "No, just American," and looked as if she had no idea why I'd asked.

I couldn't have been the first person to ask that. More like the eighty-third.

7 · A Kind of Suspense

For a long time I woke up abruptly. At attention. I lived in a kind of suspense. We come into the world whole, all of us, but we don't know that, don't know that life will be taking large chunks out of us, forever.

Over a year after she said she would, Hector's mom moved out of their house, to a cottage in Topanga. A week later their dog ran away. Hector and I stapled up signs with Rebel's picture and the offer of a fifty-dollar reward.

I told Hector, "The worst part is finding out. After that, they buy you things. I have to say, this year hasn't been as bad as I thought." Mondays and Tuesdays Malc, my dad's assistant, picked us up after school, Green Day blasting in his Honda. We stopped for takeout from Jerry's Deli. My dad ordered us the same thing every night: chicken, broccoli, and baked fries. He made it home in time to eat with us, something my mom had tried to get him to do, but she never succeeded. A sense of tragedy flitted over his face as he surveyed the takeout boxes and plastic forks, as if we were enduring hardship together. But we *preferred* this food. Every Monday and Tuesday, we ate layer cake. When we used to have Sunday-night dinners in our house, our mom had said, *Napkins on laps*, and he'd put his on top of his head to make us laugh. But now he remembered each of the dishes she cooked and spoke of them solemnly. When he called us there to say good night, he asked what we'd had for dinner. *With the shrimp?* he'd say, or *That's the salad with the beans in it?*

Before, my parents had fought about which one of them would *have to* go to the class picnic, who'd show up for the teacher conference, back-to-school night, blah blah blah. Now they still fought, but over who would *get to*. Had to or get to, the Mims always did. Since the separation, she seemed in constant motion. Like Avis, the second-biggest car-rental company, she tried harder.

Sometimes, I woke up at night and heard her crying.

"The worst is when they tell you," I said again to Hector. I didn't like remembering that. Everything had gone granular. Then, for months after, I kept wondering when the real horror would begin. In the middle of the night, I'd jolt and think, Here it is. But most days, it was as if we'd gotten another life but an okay one.

I guess I'd been waiting to tell somebody all this.

"But it's not like my parents are separating or anything," Hector said. "She just found a house in Topanga for the summer."

8 · We Try Harder

Hector and Jules never knew where they'd sleep. Often, they ended up one place and a book or a sweater, in the case of Jules, who lived for her clothes, would be in the other. We were separated, but at least we had a schedule. The Audreys decided day-by-day. Hector's dad, Philip, stayed in the bungalow where they all used to live, with the one bathroom that now never seemed clean. Hector slept over at my house most Friday nights. We never went there because he shared a room with his sister.

The Mims bought a pizza stone. As soon as she walked in the door those June Fridays, she changed into sweats, made a fire, mixed dough, and set it to rise. I liked seeing fire while it was still light out. Hector and I sluffed to my room, hauling backpacks.

This was all part of the Mims's We Try Harder campaign. She

made us regular pizzas, but for herself and Boop Two, she sliced pears and spooned on wet cheese and finished with a kind of bitter lettuce. Marge Cottle, the math department chair, brought over poisonous-looking mushrooms.

"Malted barley in the crust," the Mims said, biting down. She loved her own cooking.

"Your house smells like excitement," Hector said to us.

9 · How We Felt

"So I'm dating someone," she said, in the car. "How do you feel about that?"

Sare must've told her to ask that. The Mims looked at me and swerved. She was never a great driver.

"Watch the road, please."

The year before, Sare had made her assistant a partner in her real estate business, and now she drove twice a week to classes for her MSW. Since she'd started, there'd been lots of asking how we felt. Not that how we felt made any difference.

"Seriously? I guess I'm kind of relieved."

My dad had had Holland awhile already. I was okay with her. I just didn't want her snively runt moving into my room. I liked my room at my dad's. It felt like a tree house, with a glass wall and a loft bed built in by a famous architect in 1967. So the Mims had met someone now. Her hands stayed on the steering wheel; she faced forward. I hadn't noticed when she'd stopped crying at night. I'd thought maybe I'd just stopped waking up.

"Who is he?"

"Eli Lee," she said, as if that were a name I was supposed to know. And I did, kind of. Someone named Eli called. Was he the dork guy? I wondered but couldn't ask because I'd never called him that to her face.

"Eli. Yeah," I said. "So, is he going to start coming over and stuff?"

"Well, yes," she said. "But he lives in Washington, D.C."

I remembered Sare asking once, *What happened to that guy you run with?*, and the Mims saying they didn't live here. I pictured a wife with her hair parted in the center and braids on each side, carrying a potato baby. What did he do with her?

The Mims seemed about a hundred percent looser. She was probably dying to call Sare to tell her I felt relieved. But even so, we didn't see the guy for months. Still, he called, and I liked yelling through the house, It's *hi-im*! *Eli!*

I really was relieved. The nights we went to our dad's in the canyon, I thought, she had someone to talk to.

10 · Behind a Door

Eli Lee finally walked up our steps on an October night, and he *was* the dork guy! I'd thought he was, but his really being who I'd guessed still shocked me. I was used to being told I had a big imagination. Not in a nice way. He stood no taller than my dad and he had weird hair that stuck up on top like an artichoke gone to flower. Boop One asked to touch it. "Was it always like that?" she asked. "When you were little?"

"It used to be just awful," he said. "It grew out like a mushroom. A stylist in DC developed this cut." His head was shaved on the sides. He wore a white button-down shirt, khakis, Converse low-tops, and no socks, even though it was winter cold. He had ears I kind of wanted to pull.

Walking to the restaurant, he put his hand on my mom's back. That seemed wrong. She's ours not yours, I thought.

Then, in the restaurant, my mom ordered a glass of wine, and he ordered a Coke. When my mom and dad ordered wine, they both did.

He turned to me. "So who do you think . . ." He motioned with his hands; he seemed to have trouble getting the question out. He stammered, "What, what bands do you listen to?"

"Green Day," I said. "Coldplay." I hadn't meant to rhyme. I blamed his stammer. I hated speech impediments. Twice a week, Boop Two got driven to speech therapy, and I had to go along and sit for an hour in a room full of dirty toys.

Eli signaled the waiter. "Could we please have red *pep*per flakes?"

My mom liked hot pepper on pizza. But before, she'd always asked for it herself. An old couple stopped at our booth then, and my mom introduced us. "We've noticed them," she said, after they left. *We've?*

"Why don't I know them?" I asked, thinking, If *he* does.

"See the way she's looking at him, folding her hands?"

"Yeah," I said. "So?"

"They seem eager to talk to each other. As if they're expecting . . . fun."

"They have a nice . . ." Eli flailed, his hand flapping. "A nice . . ." He never finished that sentence. He seemed to have trouble with sentences.

Watching old people: I didn't like that. And I hoped she didn't get all *we*-ish with Eli. *Ask for your own pepper flakes*, I felt like saying.

At home, he wanted to see photo albums. Maybe my dad wasn't the culprit, I thought, maybe the Mims had left him for the dork guy. It didn't seem like it, though. My dad *was* better-looking. For that matter, so was Holland. A couple times, I skidded in socks down the hall and lingered behind the door to hear the Mims and Eli. She kept laughing. He said, "I love them already. They're your children."

I stayed slumped against the wood, my leg falling asleep.

He whispered, "Did I kiss you all right?" He sounded scared, like I would be, and I'd never kissed anybody yet.

So the culprit must have been my dad. If this was the first time Eli had kissed her.

The next morning, I found a picture on the table of my mom when she was a kid pulling on bike handlebars that had streamers. I didn't think of Eli again until weeks later, when a package arrived for me in the mail: two volumes of Sherlock Holmes stories.*

11 · Another Failed Christmas

A guy in cleats dangled from a safety belt strapped around our neighbor's fishtail palm. He was winding a string of multicolored bulbs around the trunk, to make it look like a candy cane.

My mom shouted up, "Hey, could you put lights on our roof?"

Women in Uggs and down vests followed leashed dogs while we waited in the car to be driven to school. The mountains felt close; we could see their brown ridges. Winter in Santa Monica.

The Mims bargained. "Single mom," she shouted up. "Math teacher." Sometimes she said *professor*, sometimes *teacher*. *Teacher* when she wanted a discount.

He agreed to staple on lights and set them on a timer for a hundred bucks. "Might be a lot for one socket," he said. "It shorts, you have to push the little button and reboot."

I used to love Christmas. My dad, in his glasses, carrying a tree over his shoulder, saying, *I like having a shiksa wife.* The Boops only got that for a few years. And Christmas didn't happen anymore. Last year my dad came over and gave my mom a bracelet I never saw her wear.

"It's snowing in the San Gabriels," Hector told me. They were leaving three days before vacation on one of their epic drives to Glacier National Park, on the Canadian side. "Nineteen sixty-two was the last time it really snowed in Los Angeles."

* *What was* that *about?*

The weather I think of as winter in LA has to do with stillness. Monterey pines don't move; the sway of palms is so slight as to seem imaginary. Everything sparkles. You could see snow in the distance down Pico, if you squinted.

After school let out, my dad took us to see his family in New York. My father's family—I don't know how to describe it even now—but you bent through a small door and entered a world where all of a sudden you were better. We became straight-A children, even though our school didn't give grades. We moved inside a snow globe. A waitress told our father we were the politest kids she'd ever served. Those things happened with our dad. I've spent half my life wondering how many of them were true.

We returned home Christmas Eve and tore into the FedEx boxes my aunt Mab had sent from Montecito, and Boop One swallowed a Frito of packing Styrofoam. At least she said she did. No one saw. First she said she did, grinning with her pointy teeth; then when my mom went apoplectic, she denied it, crying and choking out that she'd been *just kidding*, all the way to the emergency room. We had to wait on plastic chairs while the movie we'd planned to see was starting its music and titles. "Merry Christmas!" I said, looking at a wall clock decked with foil tinsel above the nurses' station.

The Mims called my dad and got his machine.

"Why don't you try Eli?" I said.

"He's back East. He has a brother who—" She stalled.

"A brother who what?"

"Well, he told me about his brother years ago. It was the first real conversation we ever had."

"Well, what *about* the brother?"

"He's ill."

"With what?"

"I don't know if it has a name. Anxiety, I guess. The worst thing is, he doesn't have friends."

"Not any?"

"Last year, there seemed to be a woman he talked to at work. We hoped that might turn into something. But now he's lost his job, and he's tired all the time. He lives in New Jersey in the apartment where their mother died."

"That's sad. That their mother's dead," I said. "But, at least, no mother-in-law!"

Just then, a nurse pushed through swinging doors. The X-ray hadn't found any Styrofoam. Boop One had been telling the truth that she was lying.

"It was a *joke*," she mumbled.

"Don't ever lie like that again!" I said.

"You're not the boss of me!"

We rode past the Aero Theatre, dark already, where people had laughed, eaten popcorn, and gathered on the sidewalk after to talk some more. Another failed Christmas. We passed decorated houses on our street; one roof had six lit reindeer.

"Next year, can we get *colored* lights?" Boop Two asked.

"Colored lights," my mom repeated, not saying yes or no. A trick Sare probably learned at MSW school.

But even our white lights had shorted out. My mom stomped up to the plug she couldn't see in the dark. Under a crescent moon a coyote trotted down the middle of our street. The Boops had never seen a coyote before, but even they could tell right away that it wasn't a dog. Its long tail draped the pavement and its gait carried something wild. The Mims had told us about four-legged-animal locomotion and hidden symmetries. She'd said a dog is math incarnate: when it walks, its footfalls are evenly spaced in time, and when it trots, diagonal pairs of legs, right front and left back, hit the ground together. This was connected to the fact that when you see birds on a telephone line, they end up evenly spaced. I'd forgotten why.

We followed the coyote half a mile down the road.

12 · In a Drawer

The next morning, we lunged onto our gifts, and then, after the savagery, there was that fizzy holiday feeling of *Now what?* The Boops had received an Easy-Bake oven and sat bickering about which recipe to make. Cake or bread. Bread or cake.

"There's one more for you. Outside," my mom said to me. I stepped onto the porch with bare feet. It was cold, the sky pale, almost colorless. Still so early. A hawk coasted. We both stood watching. Then she put a hand on each of my ears and turned my head. "You like it?"

It took a long time for me to see: a tree house built into our live oak like one of those pictures you find inside another picture. I ran over the wet grass, my ankles prickling, and then climbed the rope ladder. From inside, I could see the neighbors' yards and beyond. I knew I was going to like it up here.

When my father walked in hours later, he was carrying a pyramid of store-wrapped presents and a waxy crumpled to-go cup with the straw still in. My mom had put out the good plates, but my sisters and I cut slices of the warm coffee cake and just ate them off our hands.

He gave my mom earrings. She put them on, and they looked pretty.

I wondered, then, if she'd gotten anything from Eli. I hadn't. You'd think from a guy who said he loved her children, the gift boxes would tower. No presents had arrived, though. I led my dad to see my new place and he climbed up with me. "Not too shabby," he said, hands in his pockets as we stood looking out over the world. My dad was here just for a visit; he could leave anytime he wanted, any minute. We had what we'd had before, but less of it. And we never knew when it would end. Our family couldn't reassemble; even I understood that whatever held people was fragile and, once broken, couldn't be put together again. But we weren't yet something else.

A week later, rummaging in my mom's drawer, I found a card with two names and long phone numbers, the handwriting tiny, like little spiders. *These London tailors make bespoke men's suits for women's bodies. I want to take you and have them make one for yours.* I compared it with the note in my Holmes book. It matched.

She hadn't said anything about London. I didn't want her leaving the country. Where would *we* go? For a few weeks I made a point of checking that drawer for plane tickets. I never found anything until one day, a torn corner of graph paper.

I guess I'm not good at love, it said in her handwriting.

This is not bad luck was scrawled in those tiny black spider letters.

O-*kay*, I thought. Maybe Eli was for her alone, without us. London.

When I thought things like that, I just stopped. I could still stop my thinking then. But not for much longer.

13 · From the Roof

A day in January, when carpool dropped me home, I found Eli crouching in the front yard wearing a catcher's mitt. Boop Two was practicing that complicated round-the-world fast pitch they do in softball. My mom stepped out to watch. Eli had driven them to my sister's piano competition three hours east and back. My dad could never do that. He was always working.

IT'S NOT THAT I'M SO SMART, IT'S JUST THAT I STAY WITH PROBLEMS LONGER—A.E. was chalked on the ancient standing blackboard my mom and Sare, looking wind-tossed and pleased with their loot, had once hauled into the kitchen from a flea market.

At the table, we told Eli the story of the not-swallowed Styrofoam Frito, the emergency room, and the horrible Christmas lights that kept shorting out.

"I can put up lights for you next year," he said, reaching for my mother's wrist. I wanted to slap that hand.

"Maybe you can help him, Miles," she said.

"Sure." And with that a future was pledged: us on the roof with big staplers, bales of wired lights looped on our arms. The Mims and my sisters could watch from below as we lay on our bellies stringing lights on the edge. That was the first feeling I had for Eli. We could be men who did that shit. I liked the idea of putting up lights ourselves.

After dinner he left. I didn't wonder, as I should have, if I'd been old enough to care about other people when they turned the corner beyond visibility, if he flew back to DC or just stayed in some cheap hotel here, but the next night he turned up again to take my mom out. Hector was over, Simon and Charlie were coming, and we had our best babysitter, our cleaning woman, Esmeralda, who didn't speak English and let us eat what we wanted. My mom emerged from her bedroom looking different.

"What's that stuff on your face?" I asked.

Eli stood the same as always—the white shirt again and no socks. He looked my mom up and down and said, "Wow!" I'd read *wow* in the bubbles of comics, but I'd never heard anybody actually *say* it. I did a spit take. His lips opened, a bottom and top tooth just barely touching, as if he wanted to eat her. I'd never seen my dad like that.

They left, and I read "A Scandal in Bohemia" out loud while Hector sketched on my floor.* Hector could draw any *Simpsons* character exactly. Bart and Marge heads cluttered his homework.

After Simon and Charlie arrived, we took over the upstairs and had a marathon night of *Fawlty Towers* while folding paper air-

---

* *This is where I got the idea to change a name or two. I'm thinking maybe I should make every single character in the book a redhead.*

planes. I forgot about the whole bottom of the house until the girls pranced up shrieking. They'd messed around in my mom's closet and had bras on outside their clothes and underwear as hats. Makeup smeared on their faces. I'd once used a bra for Mickey Mouse ears; maybe they remembered that. But the stuff they'd found was *shiny*. Black ribbons with what seemed to be miniature mousetraps hung down over Boop Two's face. I didn't want to think about my mom wearing those.

"Put that back!" I yelled.

You knew your mom's underwear, everyone did, from before. I never went near that dresser now. She had only one desk drawer where I still rummaged. I'd picked through all her things when I was smaller, but that just stopped, the way once she'd come into my bath with me and now not, and it hadn't seemed like the end of anything until my sisters dressed in her underwear made me remember what had changed. My mom and Eli were having sex probably. That was a lower, threatening world.

My sisters, in their stupid ugly costumes, had no idea.

Hector stroked my nose with his finger, from the top, where glasses would go, to the tip. "I've been told this calms a lobster,"* he said.

We waded out onto the roof and flew our paper airplanes down under moonlight. Hector told a story about his aunt. She'd started to bake a cake and the recipe called for vanilla extract, so she borrowed a tiny bottle from her neighbor. Then, after she didn't answer her phone for three days, the police found her passed out in her car, on the shoulder of the Pacific Coast Highway. They took away her license. She'd have to walk now to AA meetings. The architecture firm had arranged a driver to take her to and from work.

* *You did give me most of our good lines. I suppose you had to so as not to appear arrogant. As arrogant as we in fact were.*

"Wait, vanilla extract has alcohol in it?"

He said all extracts did and told us his mom was moving from Topanga into his aunt's house in the Palisades, to help her.

But then, when Hector went to the bathroom, Charlie whispered, "Aren't his parents getting divorced?"

I don't know, I mouthed.

Simon blurted, "My mom said they were."

When the bathroom door opened, we shut up. Hector stepped back out onto the roof. "What were you guys whispering?"

We said, "Nothing."

He said, "Come on," and finally we said. So we were the ones who told him his parents were breaking up.

"I thought it might have been something like that." He shrugged. "Don't know why they didn't just say it."

That night, Hector invented mutants. We snuck downstairs and stole stuffed animals from the Boops and found the sewing kit. Simon had gone to Waldorf School until third grade, and he knew how to sew. We amputated limbs, jabbing our hands with the needles, trying to attach them to other sockets. We scissored off heads. We worked for hours and only completed the kitten with a pig's head and lobster claws. The Boops were out cold. After midnight, as we sprawled half asleep, *Airplane!* flickering over my friends' faces, I heard tires. I knew the sound of our tires. I stepped onto the roof.

"Your holiday weight," he was saying.

She made a *moo-ey* sound.

"Oh, come on. I love your tummy. Your tush and your tummy are the only overtly sexual parts of you."

I went inside. I didn't want to hear more. I felt unsafe, all of a sudden, as if wolves were biting at our walls. For a long time, I turned on one side, then the other, bumping into Hector; I couldn't sleep. In the morning, though, it was just our house, sun on the kitchen cupboards, my mom whisking eggs, Hector and Charlie already at the table drinking OJ. The Boops played jacks on the floor. Eli must have left in the night.

"The girls said they heard a stampede on the roof. And this morning, I found the front lawn covered with paper airplanes." She got out the camera and was taking photos when Sare drove up.

"Better get the picture before the sprinklers go on, 'cause that's going to be one mess." I could always charm my mother. But nothing about me was magic to Sare.

14 · The Year of the Mutants

Dante, Max, and Miles G. wanted to get into mutants, too. From then on for a year we had blowout Friday nights with five or six guys sleeping over. We named ourselves the Jocular Rabid Rabbits and sewed mutants in the tree house, which we called the Jocular Rabid Rabbits' Pad. Simon taught us all to sew. To this day, I'm the only one in the family who can mend with an even stitch or reattach a popped button. That was the most social time of our childhoods, Hector's and mine.

One night, Boop Two screamed, seeing her former toy headless, ragged-necked, with fluff coming out. After that, the Mims informed us that we had to buy our own animals to mutilate, with allowance money.

"How many *millions* do you need to borrow?" Eli asked on the phone. "I have money, too, Reen. I'm not going to let that get in the way." How could he have millions? I wondered, with a shiver. My parents talked about other people's money. Hector's aunt paid his tuition. Charlie's grandfather paid. My mom and dad felt like they were the only parents at the school who were actually writing checks out of their own salaries. But none of the families we knew had millions.

This was how I learned we needed money. Could Eli really give us some? He worked for the NSF, but I thought we got mailings from them asking for donations. My mother sent in checks, once for twenty dollars, another time fifty dollars to their Youth Foundation. And to the Smithsonian, too. In the morning, there was a new Albert quote on the blackboard: A TABLE, A CHAIR, A BOWL OF FRUIT, AND A VIOLIN; WHAT ELSE DOES A MAN NEED TO BE HAPPY?

Not to contradict a genius, but I could think of plenty else.

15 · The Room Not Chosen

The un-Dutch Holland wanted my dad's floors to be darker, so he moved into my room for a week. He made me take the top bunk, and I couldn't sleep right; the ceiling loomed too close.

I was never a kid who had nightmares, like my sister who woke up tangled in my mother's bed, their female legs all over each other. But the last night my dad slept in my room something woke me. A scrape at the back of the house.

I climbed down the bunk ladder. The noise seemed to come from the room off the kitchen. In its life in our house, that room had never been chosen. My mom wanted to fix it up so each twin could have her own space, but so far they liked sharing. All the unused furniture ended up there with a rack of old clothes and boxes with diplomas. From behind the dark clutter came a heave. It was hard to make out words but a melody rose. *You told me we'd be together*, it said, again and again.

This could have been from the yard next door.

You said I could be with you—

A window banged. I made myself walk through the towers of clutter, to latch the open window. But when I stepped in, a force repelled me. I knew not to go farther. So I turned back and edged toward what had once been my parents' room. Behind me, a noise choked outside. *How much time!*

I put an arm out to steady me in the hall. I was trying to decide if I should wake my mom. But only Boop One slanted across the sheets, the covers flung aside. So was it true: Was my mother in that room off the kitchen, listening to a person outside? I wondered all of a sudden if my dad knew about Eli. I felt like waking him, but then I bumped into the Mims in the hall, wearing a white nightgown. "Did you hear that?"

She put her hand on my forehead. "You're warm. Do you want a glass of water?"

I said no. She went one way; I went the other and climbed the ladder to my bed.

Just before I woke, something spat in my ear: *If you got pregnant, we'd have the baby!* Baby! I hit my head awake on the ceiling and then sat there on the top bunk. Simon's parents had had a baby, number four. He thought his whole family was an embarrassment now, and it kind of was. Plus they'd named it Theodore.

I heard the familiar scrabble of Gal. The extent of my parents' capacity to provide a living creature during the years of their marriage, despite our pleas for a dog, was a tortoise named Gal, who lived in a terrarium on my floor. They'd meant to get a smaller turtle, a sort my father recalled buying in a slim cardboard box at the circus in Madison Square Garden that afterward resided in a plastic pool with its own plastic palm tree. Gal scrabbled on wood chips to the top of a rock in her terrarium.

My father slept through it all.

16 · Were You Ever Going to Tell Me?

Hector's mom, Kat, took a job working for Sare, and he hated it. He referred to her as *Sarah Bennett's gopher* and *Charlie's mom's slave*.

Now that she worked, Kat wanted us there Friday night because she hadn't seen her kids all week. Hector and I walked his aunt Terry to her AA meeting at the YWCA. She gave us sixty dollars to rent a movie, and so we bought megacandy and rented *God-father I* and *II*. My dad had said we had to wait till we were fifteen, but we thought maybe with Kat we could get away with it. This would probably be our only chance for years. Kat stuck in her head and said, "You guys hungry?" without even asking about the rating. She looked at the candy wrappers all over the couch. Then she brought us each a bowl of pasta and told me she'd seen my mom and Eli in a restaurant. "They seemed happy. He was feeding her with his fork."

"He was what?"

"He held a hand under. It was sweet."

I had a spasm. "Yuk."

But we watched both *Godfather*s. I kept expecting someone to stop us. Terry came in and sat with us a moment. "I love Brando as an old man in that garden," she said.

"Which do you like better," I asked Hector in the dark, "your mom's or your dad's house?" Now it was our dad's or our mom's. It wouldn't ever be our house again. But we were maybe getting a dog, I reminded myself; we couldn't if my dad still lived there. He and Boop One were allergic. Boop One wanted a puppy anyway. My mom said Eli would help us find one.

"My dad's house," Hector said.

The next time Eli visited, dogless, he wore a big-shouldered jacket. An Eisenhower jacket, he told us, from the Korean War. Boop One reached up again to touch his hair.

"Marine cut," he said. "High and tight." But hadn't some stylist made up his hair? I could have remembered wrong. Was there such a thing as a Marine stylist?

That night the Boops wanted Eli to read them a book before bed. "You should feel good," I said to the Mims while he was in their room. "He's a handsome guy. He looks like Lyle Lovett, and *he* was married to Julia Roberts."

Later, they had her computer open on the table; Eli was explaining how to take money out of her paycheck for medical savings. "We're making a budget!" she called.

"Woo-hoo!" I yelled back.

The next time I came in, he was calculating on a legal pad that if she stopped going to her coffee shop, over a year she would save fifteen hundred dollars. Next to them was the wooden bowl she served popcorn in, filled with the frilly baked kale she always tried to make us eat. He picked up a papery clump. If he ate that, maybe they were meant for each other. When you subtracted the cost of beans, he said, you'd still save nine hundred. I wasn't going to like this. Sunday mornings with my dad, we ambled in and out of stores and stopped, after not very long, for what he called a restorative cup of hot chocolate.

On the other side of the wall, my mom said, "I don't have thousands of dollars to buy a new sofa." Movers had carried our couch to my dad's house. We'd kept the table.

"Well, I do," Eli said.

We hadn't known him for that long. *May*be it was nice that he'd offered money. And there was something normal about them making budgets. I didn't think you could be the way I'd heard in the unused room that night and then, like other people's parents, sitting at the table, talking about money.

It seemed as if he was turning down a job because of the Mims.

"No, sweetie. Whoever takes that job has to stay at least five years. It's a huge responsibility. I wouldn't be able to spend the time with your kids."

"We could make it work."

"I'm not going to risk that. A lot of the problems you had with Cary were from him not being home enough. I think we should go away together once a month. And every Friday night, we'll take the kids out for dinner. It's good to build rituals."

"All that time when we were friends, were you ever going to tell me?" *Tell her what?* I wondered.

"I thought I'd tell you on your fiftieth birthday," he said. "Because by then you really would be too old." Too old for what? My mother was forty-three.

She sighed. "How's your divorce coming?"

"Done."

The next day, I found three watches and old snapshots on the coffee table. Eli's mother, presumably, in a belted coat, his shovel-faced dad, and him with his brother. Eli was bowlegged, not a pretty kid. I couldn't decide if I admired him or pitied him for showing her that. He was gone again. Back to DC. Maybe this was the solution to divorce. My dad had Holland, and now my mom had Eli. They were both people I'd heard about when they were married. Sometimes I thought one had tilted the boat over, sometimes the other; most of the time they canceled each other out.

A PERSON WHO NEVER MADE A MISTAKE NEVER TRIED ANYTHING NEW, on the blackboard.

My mom put the watches in a Baggie to bring to the repair shop. I didn't remember my parents doing errands like that for each other. Maybe they did before they were married. Or at least before they had us. A few nights later, I heard Eli through the extension phone. "Honey, remember, I'm in a room waiting while you're with your kids in your million-dollar house." I felt dropped down a well. I didn't know what we'd be allowed on his budget. If he had so much money to lend her, why was he alone in a room? But did our house really cost a million dollars? If it did, then we were richer than I'd thought. I fell asleep listening to her tell him her worries about Boop Two, until his shrill voice woke me. "I need a timetable! People are waiting!"

"I know," my mom said. "Why don't *you* move here first and then bring out Jean and Timmy?"

"I really don't want to live in California if we don't end up together," he said. "If they're there, I'd be stuck."

"May I keep your pictures?" she asked. "Or should I send them back?"

"They're the only ones I have. Get me, get my photos." He laughed. He seemed to think they were some draw. Those sad little pictures.

17 · The Receiver on My Bed

With Hector's old phone, I listened in on the Mims and Sare. I was hoping that they'd talk about me getting a GameCube. Charlie had one. But the conversation turned out to be about Eli. He'd mentioned running when they first met at UCLA, with a lot of people around. Then, on their very first run, he'd said he was seeing an old friend with whom he'd been close once but wasn't anymore. My mom had asked why. He'd said, *Oh, well, it's a long story. I did something I shouldn't have done, and he lost respect for me.* Why didn't my dad ever talk to her like that? She'd probably asked herself every day of her marriage. But I knew why: he didn't have to! They were already married.

My mom niggled Eli. People gave her their secrets. Everyone except my father. He wasn't holding out on her. The man had nothing to tell. But Eli had some jangling around in there, and my mother shook one out. He'd had an affair with someone he worked with. The man who'd lost respect for him knew the mistress, and he'd also met the wife.

She was really beautiful, Eli said about the other woman, named Lorelei. It turned out to be irresistible, he said, and I knew I'd heard that before.

I shook my head, to make liquids go clear; I had to think of Eli a different way. I wouldn't have guessed he'd even had the *chance* for an affair. I didn't understand yet the part that pity could play in love.

"He shouldn't have told you that," Sare said to the Mims.

"He didn't want to. I kind of dragged it out of him."

"He still shouldn't have," Sare said.

"You're the only person I've told, besides Cary," my mom said.

"What did Cary say?"

"I don't know. I always thought our generation didn't have affairs. We're too busy fussing over our children. Fighting over whose job it is to do that fussing." She sighed. "Cary said, *An affair! Sounds like fun.*"

"*On*ly at first," Sare said.

So neither of those women had had an affair. They talked big. But in real life, they devoted themselves to, well, *us*. Eli had cheated on his wife. *This is not bad luck* was written on a corner of paper. On the other side, *A chance to put a lot of things right.* That scrap was still there in her drawer but like a coin less shiny.

18 · Speakerphone

The place I grew up didn't feel like a beach town, except for a few bright afternoons of flash and mirrory reflection. Most of the time we lived cushioned in fog. Sare talked my mom into being on the committee for our end-of-year beach party. My mom didn't do that kind of thing often. I treasured the day, for her; she loved being one of the moms.

Sare ordered Charlie and me to open the folding legs of rented tables and stake them into the Malibu dunes. My mom hung close to Sare. She turned shy and tentative here, a mystery.

The ocean had a film on its surface over the deep mess. Hector and I stalked in, letting the water adjust our legs to its temperature, the liquids inside and out the same. Twenty feet south, people from our class drifted, girls wearing bikini tops, their arms stretched out over the surface, and guys just in shorts doing lazy tricks, kicking water.

We didn't have a chance with girls, and we knew it. Hector's limbs still looked like antennae, and I could feel my fat. Tan fat was better than white fat, at least. I had dark skin. Charlie didn't have a chance either, but he walked toward the girls, hands in his pockets, looking as if he were studying the glassy waves. Everyone got married eventually, even fat people, I thought. Marge Cottle was married until her husband died on her.

Philip Audrey stood laughing with my mom. A fan of hair blew over her cheek; I wondered if he thought she was pretty.

Hector could stand up on a surfboard. The waves always pulled me under. I had a catch of salt in my throat. This was one of those rare days I knew I'd remember later: *our western childhoods.* The fucking eternal boom of the surf. The Boops pranced at the fringe of foam with other little kids, their shrieks mostly lost in wind. I noticed my mom on her phone, pacing in the sand. She had a red phone then, big enough to see from a distance. Who was she talking to? I wondered. We were all here.

Most of the kids in our class bobbed in the water. Ella knelt on a board. She was known for having a beautiful older sister, but I thought Ella was cuter. I was the only one who thought that, and it occurred to me that if she knew, she might be grateful. But I couldn't figure out how to ever tell her. Simon swiveled Ella's board, tipping her into the water, her T-shirt getting drenched. Maybe it was okay that we weren't them. We would be later. We would be in college. The Rabid Rabbits had started liking people, and now everything was messed up. Charlie liked Estelle, but she stood motionless like a deer by her mother. Zeke liked Leah, but today she'd declared herself in love with Simon. I liked Ella, but I wouldn't tell anyone because I knew I didn't have a chance. Nobody liked who liked them.

I ate a lot but still had that scooped-out feeling from being in the water a long time. I felt skinny, but I wasn't. I loved soft cupcakes. I ate three. Hector liked the tougher kind.

Boop One stood at attention at the table for henna tattoos, arms straight at her sides, while the woman pressed the patch on her arm. Ella lifted her blouse, and I saw she'd gotten a belly. That seemed terrible and sad. My mother stood with Sare, their hair wild. The Mims had gotten a tattoo on her ankle, a navy-blue chain of flowers. Sare had an anchor on her left shoulder.

Hector rode shotgun on the way home. The Boops fell asleep; a head bored into me. Then my mom's phone went on speaker by mistake. It did that sometimes, in those early days of the technology.

"Just so if anything happened," I heard Eli say, "she could tell Timmy."

"I love you," my mom said, in front of us. I blushed for Hector to hear. The Boops were out cold. I wasn't shocked, it wasn't that; if someone had asked me I would have said she probably loved Eli, but I'd never heard her say that out loud to anyone besides me and my dreadful sisters. Not even to my dad. They hadn't been that kind of couple. I always liked that about them.

After the phone snapped off, she said that Eli had had an emergency operation. To take out a tumor in his pituitary gland.

"In DC?" I asked.

"Isn't the pituitary gland in the brain?" Hector said.

"Yes, but it went well, and he's recovering. His ex-wife is there."

"Where does she live again?"

"Wisconsin. With Timmy and her parents."

I wondered if my mom would go to Washington. We generally went to the hospital. Esmeralda's son had had an operation from a pitching injury, and we drove in traffic to bring him a Game Boy my mom would never have bought for me. Eli was in the hospital for *brain* surgery. She probably had to go, but I didn't want her to.

It was the kind of summer night I loved. At four in the morning, I heard my mom bounding up the stairs. She stomped out onto the roof where we were and woke us, her face not jolly. "Do you know how dangerous this is, Miles?"

We'd set up sleeping bags on the flat part of the roof and brought up pillows and a box of graham crackers. It didn't feel dangerous at all. From up here the curve of beach looked small, like a fishing village. Feathery tree boughs touched us.

Kat picked up Hector the next morning. She was wearing shorts and her legs looked the way legs were supposed to, tan with dips where you wanted dips to be. I didn't know how I knew what legs were supposed to look like, but it surprised me how few did. Boop One's did. Boop Two's no way ever would.

The Mims didn't go to Washington.

I felt bad for the guy. Eli loved her more than she loved him.

19 · Silence

I woke up the first day of vacation and found this on the blackboard:

BENIGHTED:

IN A STATE OF PITIFUL OR

CONTEMPTIBLE INTELLECTUAL OR MORAL

IGNORANCE

"That's one I can think of some uses for," I mumbled. "Two uses."

The Mims had a will to improve us. Summer Sundays were going to be cleanup days, she announced. She chalked a quote on the blackboard: SOME FRENCH SOCIALIST SAID THAT PRIVATE PROP-ERTY WAS THEFT. I SAY THAT PRIVATE PROPERTY IS A NUISANCE— ERDOS.

She did battle with our closets. She bribed the Boops for try-ons that the other three hundred and sixty-four days they did for fun. Hives of clothes grew on the floor. She swacked open black gar-bage bags and made me twisty them and haul them to her car. At the end of the day, she asked, "Now, doesn't that feel better?"

"No," I said.

The Boops chorused. "No. No. Nooooooo."

"Well, *I* feel better," she said. "Next week, Miles, we'll start on your shelves."

But the next week, our dad took us to the pier. He loved bumper cars as much as we did and bought us ice cream at five o'clock. The light was just jelling when he bounded into the house, sniffing and scanning the kitchen. "What's cookin'?"

My mom had the table set. The way Eli had looked at her, my dad looked at the food. But our parents laughed together. People don't talk about how weird it is when your separated parents get along. They were still sharp and funny. My dad had seconds, then thirds, before shoving his chair out and saying good night. We hadn't seen Eli for a while. While we loaded the dishwasher, I asked the Mims how he was.

"Better," she said. "Definitely better."

"He's home from the hospital?"

The way she said *Mm-hmm* made me think she didn't know. I wondered if they'd had a fight. Maybe because she hadn't gone when he'd had that operation.

20 · Behind the Futon-Sofa

Then one day he showed up holding flowers. My father was usually the flower sender. I'd never before seen Eli with a bloom. My mom wasn't expecting him, I deduced; she was wearing sweats, her hair up in the clip she wore at home. He just stood there with his flowers. They didn't say anything to each other. They stared. Then his face fell onto her shoulder, his neck like a dinosaur's. Bent. Dark. He might have been crying.

"Do you want to sit down?" she asked, and they sat on the futon-sofa Sare had lent us.

I happened to be hiding behind that. Not to spy. My camp duffel and all my gear were spread out on the kitchen floor, and hide-and-seek even with my benighted sisters had seemed more appealing than starting to pack. I'd hid. The Boops were seeking me. Then Hector was coming to get me for a movie.

I'd have to pop up like a jack-in-the-box behind my mom and Eli.

"I'm s-sorry." The stutter again. "I had my first session with Dr. Wynn, and I told her I'd been crazy. I knew I was being too hard on you. She had my medical records, and she asked for a blood test. She suspected pressure from the tumor was causing the anxiety. She called me an hour later and said we had to do emergency surgery. I promise to do better. I'm going to keep seeing her. Sweetie, are you afraid to get divorced?"

Afraid to get divorced? Was it still possible they wouldn't? I had a queasy feeling: I remembered the boy to whom those words would have fallen like the deepest balm. The gold of recovery. I could almost reach his feelings, but not quite; I was no longer that boy. I wasn't sure I wanted my parents back together. I was used to things the way they were now. I'd already begun to be the man I would become. Halfhearted. About my parents getting back together. About Holland. About Eli. And the other side of half-heartedness was greed.

"I won't push you so hard anymore," Eli said.

The Boops ran panting into the room, saying they couldn't find me. My mom and Eli stood to help them look.

I gave them a head start and then snuck up behind, shouting, "Boo!"

The doorbell rang; it was Hector and I had to go. His mom had started dating their surf instructor and he and Jules hated him. The surf instructor had a dog called Scout, and they didn't like the dog either. We ran down to his mom's car, late for *Batman Begins*. Bo, the Surfer, rode shotgun and Kat drove. I guess all VWs have those little vases, but Kat was the only person I ever knew who always kept a flower in hers. That night it was a sprig of rosemary and one lavender stalk.

"Didn't Eli just have surgery?" Hector asked. He had freckles on every inch of his body from surf camp and wore a twine ankle bracelet. "Did they have to shave his head?"

"His head's already kind of shaved. The sides, anyway."

"Is there a scar?"

I'd forgotten to look. Hector stayed at my house, and the next day my mom let us sleep, which was odd since it was the Sunday she intended to go through everything I owned. But when I blinked awake, I could tell it was late from the way the sun fell on the lawn. Gal scrabbled.

"Your mom let us sleep in till noon." Hector jumped down from the top bunk. He slept in the top bunk at home, too.

"Wowza. That's a first."

We ventured out through the rooms, still in yesterday's clothes. The kitchen looked itself. I heard thunks and rustles from my mom's closet. We sauntered in and found a huge pile of clothes on her bed and my mom standing in sneakers and a dress before the mirror. Eli knelt there, tugging at the skirt of it.

"We're cleaning out my closet," she said.

I rubbed my eyes. "Does that mean mine gets a pass?" She surveyed the pile of shoes on her floor, sweaters melting on a chair arm.

Eli pinched the back of her dress like a seamstress. "Honey, this'll take most of the afternoon, and then we should do something fun with the kids." He pulled the shoulders of the dress in. Then he shook his head. "No, take it off. Giveaway."

They spent all day in that closet. I stuck my head in; she was trying on a ruffled shirt. A huge clown face was Eli's response. She pushed him back onto a pile of coats.

Later, we stepped in to say we were going out on our bikes. My mom had on white jeans. From the floor, he grabbed her ankle.

We took a long ride. Hector said, "I didn't see any scar."

"Ask him." I shrugged.

By the time we got home, they had k.d. lang singing "The Air That I Breathe," a song about cigarettes, and both of them were lying on the floor. "Guys, look at my closet," the Mims said. "It's a thing of beauty."

"It's a thing of empty, anyway," I said. "What happened to all your clothes?"

She pointed to three ginormous garbage bags, marked THROW, GOODWILL, and SEAMSTRESS. Her closet had yards of room. A cluster of empty hangers. Not only that, the top of her dresser was bare.

Eli drove us in my mom's car as the sun went down. He took the 405 onto a road that wound around a mountain, cutting into brush, where each dry leaf cupped gold. We ended up on a street that looked halfway between a mall and a ghost town.

"I love this," my mom said, stepping into the dusty light. The restaurant was known for dumplings, just the kind of thing she liked, full of odd vegetables. We preferred dumplings that were fried. But Eli ordered a Coke, and so she let us, too. "Okay, it's happened. I love LA now," she said, walking outside after to a store that sold cream puffs. You could pick your own filling and sauce. The Boops chose ice cream inside; Hector and I made ours into warm éclairs. We were almost to the car when she shrieked. I thought she'd been stung. But it was only Eli; he'd pinched.

Eli didn't seem—I don't know—maybe as *special* as my dad, but he made her looser. I tried to explain. "You know why I like him? I can say it in one word. *Coke*."

"He's better than Surferdude,"* Hector muttered.

After that day we didn't see Eli for the rest of the summer.

My mom bragged about him, though. She told me he'd had a teacher in eighth grade who made him read a book every day.

* *At least Surferdude should have red hair. He pretty much does.*

"Sounds like a site," I said. "Book of the Day."

She laughed, which was good, because I had no intention of reading a book every day. The Mims wasn't such a reader herself. She liked papers with equations.

One night in August I found her computer screen open to Dalmane addiction.

"What's Dalmane?" I asked, my skin going raw chicken. Could my mother be an addict without me knowing? I made myself say, "So who's addicted?"

"I told you Eli's brother lost his job."

"Oh, yeah. The brother." Relief hugged me, enough to make me care a little about Eli's brother. "What kind of job did he have again?"

Their dad had been a professor who made a lot of money in the stock market. Hugo had inherited that talent. He'd considered business school; Eli thought that had been his last good chance. But he'd only worked in menial positions in financial services. "His new doctor says that he's on way too high a dose of this drug. I guess it's very addictive." She put the top down on her computer. "You want tea?"

I did want tea. She made tea then that tasted like a bowl of spices. We brought our handleless mugs to the porch and sat looking out over the canyon. That was where my dad lived, in a multi-level house hidden by trees. We couldn't see many stars. Most of them turned out to be airplanes.

The next time I asked about Eli, she said his brother was in the hospital for Dalmane withdrawal. Eli had moved into his apartment in New Jersey to help.

I don't think I remembered to ask again.

I was a pretty selfish kid. But I didn't love Eli yet.

21 · A Trip to the Other Economy

That fall, my class moved to the Upper Campus, and it was a city. Over the summer, kids had grown. All of a sudden, Hector and I were short. People sold great food from carts. But my mom refused to pay for hot lunches. My allowance covered one a week; the other days I had to bring food from home. She packed leftover pasta and farro salad and carrots and shit. And she'd gotten to my dad before I tried. Some Tuesday mornings he didn't have food in the house and gave me a twenty, saying, "For just this once, Miles. It's not going to be a habit!" Then we had to rush to Whole Foods, because the Boops, who were still in elementary, couldn't add on lunches by the day.

The noodle soup cart and the burrito guy had the longest lines.

A Wednesday, after school, I saw Esmeralda eating the same kind of noodle soup at our kitchen table. I said, "I buy those for lunch."

"How much?"

"Two fifty."

She spurted giggles. "Near my place, I pay one dollar for ten pieces."

I gave her my allowance and skipped my hot lunch that week. She'd buy soup and bring it when she came to clean the house again the next Wednesday.

I started selling soup from my locker. At first I waited until I saw people in line for the cart, then I told the ones at the back that I could give it to them for a buck twenty-five. Kids worried about finding hot water. It didn't seem right to ask the cart vendors for their water if you didn't buy their soup. But I figured we could get it in the chem lab.

In two weeks, I sold out and gave Esmeralda thirty dollars to buy more. Upper Campus bustled with opportunity. I asked Esmeralda about other deals. I started to watch what people bought. I threw out the organic Whole Foods crap my mom packed and bought a burrito and a soda every day. Money piled in. I bought Hector lunches, too. Esmeralda delivered eight bags of new soup and she still had cash left over. She was happy because I gave her a twenty, as a thank-you. She didn't know how big my profits were.

"You are gaining weights," she said.

I looked at her and thought, *You* should talk.

But I'd put on fifteen pounds by Thanksgiving. My legs felt packed into my jeans, and my stomach bulged out over the top.

I wanted to investigate other products. I asked if I could go home with Esmeralda one day; she seemed happy with the idea. But I couldn't figure out how to explain to my mom.

Then my progress report arrived. Cottonwoods only gave letter grades starting in ninth grade, and they were going to be a problem: I got a C in math. My mother sat with her reading glasses on, scanning the paper report. She didn't say anything. That was bad. She would definitely notice a C in math. She disappeared to her room to talk on the phone. It had to be either my dad or Eli. Or Sare.

"Miles?" she said, coming out. "There'll be no television or video until your next report card."

"What? You're taking away TV for two *months* because of a grade?"

"We both know it's not your best."

"What if it is? No, really, Mom. What if it *is* my best?"

I called my dad to fight, but he interrupted. "I agree with your mother one hundred percent. One hundred percent, Miles." Then he had to get off the phone. Dickwad.

With no electronics, I had time, so I hitched a ride home with Esmeralda the next Wednesday. She took me to Lucky supermarket, where her son, in his baseball uniform, showed me all his favorite stuff. Chips I'd never seen before—fried pigskins! No shit!

They were good, but I didn't know if I could move them. I bought Mexi-Crisps, prepopped caramel corn, and two different chips, all cheap, and a yellow soda I wanted to introduce. I bought one bag of the pig chips for Hector. Right before I left, I saw Cokes in bottles; they turned out to be Mexican Coke and cost more than regular, even here, but I bought five six-packs, for a luxury item. Esmeralda drove me to the bus stop. When I finally got back, I left the bags outside under the windows of my room to sneak in after dark.

The Mims wasn't pleased when I walked in at nine twenty, but I'd told her I wanted to see Esmeralda's home. She couldn't say anything to that, even though we both knew she'd rather have had me copying algebra problems a hundred times and showing my idiotic work.

22 · A Basement Below a Doctor's Office

When Boop One made the dance team, our schedule turned wack. Thursdays didn't work anymore. Esmeralda could pick us up from school, after cleaning Charlie's house, and drive Boop Two to speech therapy on her way east; I had to go along. Then the speech therapist took us to the dance studio, where we'd wait for Boop One's carpool. But I couldn't read in a place that smelled like feet. Finally, we figured out that Esmeralda could drop me off near UCLA; I could work in my mom's office and then ride back with her. "But I see a doctor Thursday after work," the Mims said.

"O-kay," I said. "Just this Thursday?"

"Every Thursday."

"What kind of doctor?"

She paused. "A therapist."

"You see a *ther*apist? For what?"

She shrugged. "Just everything, I guess."

Once, after I'd been torturing my sister and repeating *gobble gob-*

ble, the Mims said if we couldn't get along better we'd have to see a psychologist. I said back, "Dad doesn't want us going to therapists," just guessing, but I turned out to be right.

So I sat with my mom in the waiting room doing homework while she watched. A tall woman, my grandmother's age, opened the door halfway.

"This is Dr. Sally Bach," my mother said. "This is Miles."

"Hello, Miles." The woman's smile seemed halfway to laughter.

My numbers on the page marched up in a slant and I needed to pee. A guy in the lobby pointed me to the basement. I found the bathroom and then, next to it, another door to a low-ceilinged unfinished place. I climbed around under hanging pipes to a spot I thought was below the doctor's office. And I could hear the old doctor laughing! They sounded like two women having tea. When you're trying all the time to glean information, sometimes it just falls onto you. That's when it felt sweet.

"Eli's pressuring me to hurry," the Mims said.

Hurry and what? I wondered.

"Some mathematicians have spouses who follow them," she went on. "Marge called Stanley a Trailing Spouse."

"Cary not only didn't follow you, he suggested you quit," the doctor said. *He did!* That was news to me.

"He didn't really want me to quit. He just didn't like me to complain."

"Or to ask him to help with his children."

"He never wanted twins. You've got to give him credit. He knew his limits."

My dad didn't want the Boops! A smile crept onto my face as I felt the wind knocked out of me. I was surprised how much they were talking about my dad.

"The truth is, I think I'm happier now," the Mims said.

That made it seem like she was the one who left. I was never sure. I didn't know when my dad had started up with Holland.

But it was hard to believe my mom left. My dad admired her; she seemed to him rare and valuable, but he didn't *need* her. She needed him, not for the complicated things but for the easy ones. She forgot to lock the door and she ruined enough kettles for him to buy one that shrieked so she wouldn't burn down the house. But then he moved out. I guess he didn't worry about the house burning with just us in it. I thought my dad had loved my mom more than she'd loved him. Eli loved her more, too. I felt a twinge; she hadn't even visited the guy in the hospital. I felt guilty remembering that; I hadn't wanted her to go.

"You're happier without him and *with* Eli," the doctor said.

"Eli's coming with me to the Kovalevsky thing. No, I'm happy with him. Everything's just . . . even bobby-pinning Emma's bun. Doing ordinary things, I feel more . . ."

"Is he going along with you?" Bells rang in the doctor's voice. She was merry. There were girls in my class like that. Hector called them the goofy good-time girls.

"Do you think he'll always be getting mad at me?"

"We'll have to find a way to make him feel secure."

"I'd never leave him," my mother said.

The doctor laughed again. She seemed like a party girl, just a very, very old one.

It wasn't until we were driving west to the smelly upstairs studio that I realized they hadn't mentioned me once.

23 · Business

I opened bags of the new chips for people to sample. Mexi-Crisps were catching on. Three girls bought the prepopped caramel corn. Salsitas were a hard sell, even though they were way cheaper than the brands we knew. And nobody touched the yellow soda. I was surprised to learn that Cottonwoods kids were so prejudiced.

But even with resistance to the new merchandise, business grew. Kids asked me in the halls if I sold soup. We had a regular line now in the chemistry room. Hector and I both stashed thermoses in our lockers to keep things from getting overly conspicuous. We had bat-shit crazy lunch periods. I stayed by my open locker while Hector went to buy us burritos from the cart. We were sick of soup. I was waiting to introduce the Mexican Coke. I still had to figure out pricing.

"What are we going to do with all the Inca Kola?" Hector asked.

"Starting next week, I'll cut it to half price. If that doesn't work, I don't know. We may have to actually start drinking it."

Hector loved the spicy pig chips. But then, he'd eaten bugs when he was little.*

24 · Einstein Was a Great Romantic

We were standing in front of Cottonwoods waiting for carpool when Eli showed up on foot. No one *walked* to carpool. He said hi to my friends—he knew the Rabid Rabbits' names, even Simon's, and he'd only met him once, and they nodded, not the least surprised to be remembered—and asked me if I wanted to take a walk. I said sure, and we headed to a supermarket parking lot, where he put his hand on top of a rusted Volvo. The car wasn't as neat as I expected from what my dad had since dubbed the Closet Caper. A dirty toy slanted on the backseat. "My friend Mark lets me borrow his mother-in-law's car," he said. "She doesn't use it. I pay for the long-term parking." He drove south to a tract of land with a miles-long duck pond and a dusty road. There were old half-neglected parks like this all over LA. We started to roam.

* *I always did have the more refined palate. That became clear later, with the older version of Coke and bath salts.*

"Your mom told me about the math teacher," he said. "She sounds frustrating."

The Mims never thought I had the right to be frustrated. No matter how horrible a teacher, my parents wanted me to make myself the little favorite. "It kinda is. I mean, before this year, I actually *liked* math."

"Well, what, wh-what did you like about it?"

Again, his question surprised me. Everything my parents said about math directly pertained to my abysmal grade and my manual lifting of it. "It was always kind of easy."

When Eli listened, his hands dug into his pockets, and his head turned down. He had a funny-shaped head and a long neck, darkly tan with a bump. "When I was your age, I was just getting to understand that I couldn't do math. I loved it, I could *see* it, but I wasn't going to be good enough to *do* it. My math test scores were so low compared to my verbal, they thought I'd cheated. I made myself learn. I'd go over every page six times. The next year my scores jumped two hundred points. Then the people from the College Board wanted to study me because I was such an anomaly." He must have been able to tell I didn't know the word because he said, "*Anomaly* means 'oddball.' "

I couldn't imagine my dad ever calling himself an oddball. And he wasn't one. "Do you mind being short?" I asked all of a sudden, thinking of my father. Height never strayed far from my father's consciousness. Eli was short, too.

"You know, I never really knew I was short, I didn't know until—" Then he stammered. I was aware of some problem. Like dust on a CD.

"Until what?" I said, to help.

"Well, when I was getting married, my in-laws complained. That's how I first heard I was short."

"Nazis," I said—the kind of joke that made my mom tense up.

But Eli laughed. "They actually *are* German."

"Did they like you?"

He paused. "Not really. The night before the wedding, I sat with Jean on their dock—they have kind of a compound, on a lake—and I apologized for taking her away from all that. She didn't deny it. I always thought that was good. Honest." He spoke about his ex-wife kindly. That troubled me in some way I didn't understand. I wasn't being fair. When my parents talked about each other in those same tones, it seemed natural and right. We walked for a long time. I thought of how he listened on the phone at night for hours to my mom and how, when she called my dad, he rushed her off. My dad didn't do that to me as much.

"I always tell your mother that math, math makes what I do ornamental. Whereas an equation"—his arms were going—"an equation is permanent."

She'd written on the blackboard: EINSTEIN WAS A GREAT ROMANTIC. Eli was, too, if he could go on this way about *math*.

I felt his hand on my back. "You know, I'm deeply in love with your mother."

"Oh," I mumbled, wondering, Should I have said *Thank you*?

"It's, it's the most important thing that's ever happened to me. Even more than my mother dying."

"Oh, good," I replied automatically, then thought, Duh! Like I wanted her to beat his mother's dying! It wasn't until later that I remembered he had a kid. The Mims would say having us was the most important thing that ever happened to her.

I felt sorry for Eli all over again. It didn't occur to me then to feel sorry for his kid. I couldn't even remember its name.

25 · Angeldog

When we returned home, a dog stood sniffing in our yard. Eli coaxed it with the voice some people try on children. "This is a stray," he told me. "See, no collar. And he's dirty. He's probably been homeless a few weeks already." He cooed, "Are you hungry?"

"Should I get him milk?" I asked. Cats liked milk.

"Do you have any canned pumpkin?"

"I don't *think* so." Canned pumpkin! It wasn't Thanksgiving, and the Halloween jack-o'-lanterns had already caved in and been hauled out back to compost. Eli carried the dog into the house, where the Boops fell onto it. Boop One went at him with a pink brush. "Can we give him a bath?" she asked. "He stinks a little."

Eli found our rice and some kind of broth in a box, and he was unlatching cabinets, looking for a pot. "He probably hasn't eaten for a few days. So we want to give him food that won't upset his stomach."

Both my sisters knelt over the dog. "Can we keep him?" Boop Two asked.

"First, we should put up signs and try to find his owners, if he has any."

"I feel like he's supposed to be our dog," Boop One said. "He came to our yard. He found us. Maybe he's an angel. For our family."

By the time my mother walked in and noticed every cabinet door hanging open, rice fanned on the floor, and Eli stirring a pot on the stove, Boop One's eyes had swelled almost shut. My mother screamed, then looked at me, accusing. I don't know why I hadn't noticed: her eyes were horizontal slits, and what showed was red, not white. On her arms, bumps pushed up from below the skin like marbles, growing. "Oh my God," my mom said. "We can't keep that dog here."

"She was brushing him," I said.

Eli squatted, murmuring to the dog. He poured the rice gruel into a bowl and blew to cool it. The Mims steered my sister into the bathroom.

"Should we be driving her to the hospital?" I called.

All the while, Eli baby-talked the dog.

I went to the Boops' bathroom, where all three females stood in steam.

"Can you breathe, sweetheart?" my mom asked, hysterically calm.

"A ball is swelling in my throat."

"Wait in the kitchen, Miles," my mom said.

I scuffed back to where Eli seemed to be overpitying the dog.

"Honey," he called. "Do you have Benadryl? Should I go buy some?"

"I've got Claritin, if it's not expired," she said.

He opened drawers until he found the medicine, then held the little bottle up. "It's okay," he said. He didn't seem *that* worried. Did he think my sister was faking it? I couldn't see how you could fake bumps coming up beneath your skin.

"I'm going to make a call," he said.

My mom, who'd just come into the kitchen, looked up at him.

"A woman I know in Malibu," he said, "she once helped me rescue a bird."

The Mims looked away. She'd thought he was calling someone about her daughter. She took ice out of the freezer and said, "Miles, grab the thermometer."

"I'm going to drive him to the shelter," Eli yelled.

"Miles can go with you," she hollered back. I didn't appreciate being volunteered. I brought in the thermometer. "Can she breathe?" I asked.

"The bumps are going down," my mom said, shower water still running behind her.

Eli carried the dog. "I don't know how long I'll be. I'm not going to leave him there if it's not the right place." I followed him to the car. I thought I had to. "I really don't know what time I'll be able to get you back."

"I can take a bus," I said, but I didn't know where the pound was. And I had to read two chapters of a book for World Civ. In the car, you could really smell the dog.

Why did I have to go?

We drove through clouds of fog and finally parked in front of a low, flat building. He lifted the dog out of the back. I just followed along. After whispering to the dog, Eli talked to a man behind the desk. I still wanted a puppy but not tonight, not with my sister all allergic. I needed our house to go back to the way it was before. With the flip of a latch, the man opened a swinging door, and we followed him through a maze of cages. Dogs howled, pushing against their wire doors. I saw one of the kind my sisters wanted: a white fluff ball. The man shoved our dog into a cage, poured food, and filled another bowl with water from a hose. Our dog curled himself up in a back corner.

"How long do we have?" Eli asked.

"We're just under capacity now. Not bad. At least three weeks."

"We'll check in every day," Eli said.

I stayed quiet riding back. He parked in front of the house and turned the engine off. I didn't know whether or not he was coming in.

"When he said three weeks, that's for what?" I asked.

"That's how long they can keep him before they'll put him to sleep. A thousand dogs get euthanized every month in Los Angeles."

I had a flash of the fluffy dog with a pig's paws. But that real dog we'd just seen would most likely die. Sitting in the car, I thought of the things I'd read about lab animals and eating meat. We ate meat. Except when Eli was here.

Eli came in that night after all. My mom had pasta waiting, covered with a striped towel. Boop One was breathing again, the bumps down. For the first time in hours, Eli smiled, watching my mother move around the kitchen. Then she stood behind his chair, her hand on his neck. "You're not using that sunblock I gave you. You're burned."

"I was using it. I ran out."

He left that night carrying a tube of sunblock in the front pocket of his white shirt. "Now, listen," he said to me. "Here's the number for the shelter. You should call every day." He gave me the slip of paper. I liked it that he trusted me with this.

After a week, it seemed I was the only one who remembered. Boop One, who'd thought it was an angeldog before it'd made her allergic, didn't ask at all. I thought of his face and the dirty tufts of fur. Then, on a Thursday, Boop Two asked, "Did they find the owners yet?" She stood there while I called. They told us he was eating, but no one had come for him. After that, Boop Two called every day; I heard her in their room on the princess phone. One night, she asked my mom for a ride to the pound. We went, the three of us, and when we came to the dog's cage, he pressed up against the wire, rattling it, and making a noise from inside. "He remembers us," my sister said.

It was two weeks now. I thought of Eli's question. Boop Two asked the woman, who had hairy legs, if they took volunteers.

"You have school," my mom said. "And speech therapy. And piano."

"And weekends," said Boop Two.

26 · A Letter Under My Father's Door

In the car one day I asked my mom what ever happened with Eli's brother.

"Well, he's at home," she said. "He was in the hospital eight weeks, but unfortunately they were only able to reduce the Dalmane a small increment."

"So what happens now? He'll keep taking it forever?"

She didn't answer. We were at a stop sign, and her short nails drummed against the steering wheel. I'd recently noticed that a lot of other moms' fingernails were different. The girls in my class were beginning to do that, too. I preferred my mom's hands.

"Will he look for a new job?" I asked.

"I found a placement agency for people with disabilities. I've got to remind Eli. I keep thinking we should hire a student to at least get Hugo out for a walk every day."

That *we* again. I didn't think *we* could afford to be hiring brother-walkers, even student brother-walkers. There were lots of things *we* couldn't afford anymore.

She sighed. "I need to keep on Eli about that."

Later that night, I thought about what it meant that Eli's brother had been in the hospital all summer to be weaned from a drug they hadn't been able to get him off of.

I googled Dalmane. It seemed to be a drug for anxiety. So when they made the dosage lower, what—he got convulsions or foamed at the mouth? I finished the sentence three different ways and hit a wall. What she meant but wasn't saying was that when they didn't give him the amount he needed, he went suicidal. There'd been nothing like this in my family before that you had to steer around thinking about. I felt it settle in my chest. A tightness. A tender spot. A nest. It made us different. I felt older.

Hector was still obsessed with Eli's head. He thought it should have a scar.

"Maybe his hair covers it," I said, though only the top part of his head had hair.

"Does he ever say anything about the operation?" Hector asked.

"Not to me. Maybe he did to her. It's been a while."

Hector wanted to check her e-mail. I didn't say he could, but he opened her computer and the program popped right up, no password or anything. She didn't erase messages, apparently. He easily scrolled back to June.

From: elilee@nsf.org
Subject: in way of apology, not exoneration
Date: June 17, 2004 12:26:59 PM PDT
To: iadler@ucla.edu
something the neurologist showed me on encephalitis

The classic presentation is encephalopathy with diffuse or focal neurologic symptoms, including the following:

Behavioral and personality changes, decreased level of consciousness.

"I'm not sure what that proves," I said.

"Listen to your mom," he said, and read out. "*I'm feeling so happy and myself in this. You've given me a life.* July eighth."

That went through my body like a shock. "Stop," I said. "I mean, she likes him, maybe she loves him, I like him, too, but it's not like she didn't have a *life*."

I pushed the lid of her laptop down.

"Wait. I found you a nice one."

There's nothing so deeply consoling as sitting in my children's music lessons.

But she meant my sister. I'd quit piano years ago. "Enough already!"

I yelled that, startling us both.

Espionage had a life of its own. Secrets opened to me when I wasn't even looking. My dad took us to dinner at a place that served Mexican Coke in glass bottles, the same ones I had in my closet! "It's the old formula," the waitress told me. "Made with cane sugar." My dad asked if they came in diet. When the bill was set down, I asked to see: six dollars each! I'd been right to hold off; I had to convince people that Mexican Coke had added value. That night I stayed up late researching, with a bowl of cereal at my dad's steel counter. In an early hour of the morning, while I read about MexiCoke, a letter shot under the front door, and through the glass, I saw the back of a short trench coat dashing across the lawn. It wasn't Holland, I didn't think. A letter under the door after midnight! I held it up to the computer glow. The envelope just said *Cary* in turquoise ink. No *Hart*. I put it back on the concrete floor for him to find. He'd jam it in his desk drawer or mix it in with the pile of bills and scripts on the counter. I'd have to read it after it was open. But the next night, we were back at my mom's house, and so I couldn't check.

While my dad was probably ignoring the letter, we sat at the table, on the other side of Santa Monica. Boop Two, who'd always lived on chicken tenders, announced that she was going to stop eating animals, including birds. "I decided not to eat anything that has a face," she said.

"What about Thanksgiving?" I said.

"I'll just have pie."

A few weeks later a woman phoned for her. I was finding a pen to take a message when the woman said, "It's Dorie from the shelter. Could you tell her Hunter's been adopted?"

I started hopping on one foot. I should have asked more, but I was embarrassed at how happy I felt with this stranger on the phone. Later, Boop Two called her back. She sat down after, her hands underneath her butt. "He got a good home, a family with five kids. One is developmentally disabled. So Angeldog is somebody else's. I thought if nobody adopted him, we'd get him."

All of a sudden, I was mad at Boop One, who'd made such a fuss that first day and then forgotten, and even at the Mims. We agreed not to tell them until they asked. They didn't ask.

Dogless, our lives went on. Angelless too.

I looked everywhere at my dad's for the envelope with the turquoise writing. It gave me something to do at his house. But I never found it. He must have thrown it out.

27 · Are You Still in the Same House?

Up until then, my dad had come to all our holidays, but this year he was going to Hawaii. My mom tried to talk him into leaving the day after Thanksgiving, but she could never get him to do what he didn't want to. I was beginning to see that we were better at talking him into things than she was.

Then, the Tuesday morning before vacation, when we were racing around his house, Holland appeared at the sliding glass doors wearing cutoffs and combat boots, carrying a small orange suitcase, and holding the *New York Times* in its blue bag. Her legs were tan, with little yolks for knees. I opened the door. She handed me the paper. My dad and the Boops pressed up around me. My dad gave her a look; I was more fluent in his looks than in Latin. This one meant accusation.

"No traffic." She shrugged.

Boop One crossed her arms and stuck her head down and said she wasn't going to school. Chin on her chest, she shook her head, saying, "You can't make me." My dad pushed her into the den, which wasn't so far, and we could still hear.

"Why do you take *her* to Hawaii and not take *me*?"

"Dad, we're late!" I yelled, aware of Holland standing there, looking down at her miniature suitcase.

My dad finally quieted Boop One, but she didn't say a thing all the way to school. She looked out the window, mad and proud. A tiny queen.

The last day of school, it seemed a lot of the kids were leaving for somewhere else. Everyone asked, *Where're you going?*

Just staying home, I said.

And some people asked, *Are you still in the same house?* That was how I could tell they'd heard about the separation. I mean, as if you say to a normal person in a normal family on a normal day, *Are you still in the same house?*

I couldn't stop thinking about money.

Eli wasn't coming to Thanksgiving either—he was working in an animal shelter. He liked to volunteer holidays, the Mims said, because that gave the people who worked there a chance to be with their families. This was admirable, I knew, but I kind of wished he were just coming, since Dad wasn't. Charlie's family was supposed to eat with us, too, but then his older brother wanted it at their house with just the family. Sare called my mom the day before to explain, not apologize—it went without saying that what Reed wished trumped us. The Mims cried without making any noise. She hung up the phone. She'd invited them a month in advance to make sure we had a full house. Postseparation, holidays became obstacle courses. We weren't enough by ourselves.

Marge arrived, carrying in a bowl of warm nuts with rosemary, trailed by three Chinese mathematicians. My mom hadn't had friends like Marge before. Marge wore cotton pants and T-shirts, like what they put on little kids, and those same colors. Pastels. Not a good look on a woman of a hundred and eighty pounds. I supposed none of that had mattered when she'd had a husband. She'd solved one of the world's open problems when she was twenty-nine. Only a handful of people in the world ever do that. My mom didn't think she could. Marge's mind, the Mims said, was incredibly elegant. And she turned out to be an amazing cook. She fried Japanese peppers on our stove and slid sunny-side-up eggs on top, because Boop Two wouldn't touch the turkey, which had once had a face. Marge said she'd tasted this in a restaurant, then pushed through the swinging doors to the kitchen and badgered the chef into teaching her to make it.

The day felt easy, light, and impersonal, the way it can be in a packed movie theater with all those people you don't know laughing at the same time. I was glad when everyone finally left.

"Marge is thinking of Internet dating," my mom told me as we cleaned up.

I didn't think that had much chance.

"Remember, she can read a demographic chart, and she's decided it's promising. She's looking into one called Science Connect."

My sisters were in bed by the time Eli's cab pulled up in front of our house. He didn't have his borrowed car. He walked in carrying a suit and a white shirt on a hanger.

Later on, I heard them talking. They sat on the porch steps, a blanket over their knees.

"I never asked why you had the affair."

"I, I didn't tell you this, but, at the time, Jean and I weren't having sex."

"Not much or not at all?"

"Not at all. She'd always said she wanted to be a virgin for her husband. But then, by the time, by the time we got married, I knew there was a problem."

"Did you work on it?"

"She was seeing a therapist. We always made that a priority. I assumed they were working on it. But then, I found out later that she'd never even mentioned sex. She said it was too icky to talk about. I tried to get to know her other ways. I didn't want to hurt her."

"It sounds like a case of serious abuse."

"I thought that, too, but it wasn't, apparently."

"What was it?"

"I guess I wasn't her type. Later on, when we were in therapy, that came out."

"So you were married, but you never had sex?"

He didn't answer that. I guess it didn't need an answer. Now the Mims asked if he'd been in love with Lorelei.

"It wasn't like that. I told you. It was an affair."

"You never said you loved her?"

"No, honey, it wasn't like that." She didn't read, he said. After a year, he ended it. "She'd started to say unpleasant things about Jean," he said in a prim tone, as if that had offended him.

I mean, duh, I thought.

Eventually he told Jean what had happened, and he moved out; he'd thought he should. But Jean didn't want anyone to know. Then they started sex therapy.

Sex therapy! I hadn't known it really existed outside of British comedy. But he and my mom talked about all this as if there'd been an illness.

"What do you do in sex therapy?" she asked, in a serious voice.

He stood up and started pacing. "It's just such a betrayal." He sounded angry. "I'll tell you, but it's a serious betrayal." He breathed a few times before continuing. "We did exercises. At first we had to undress and lie with a book covering my penis. She put her hand on top of the book."

Like swearing on a Bible, I thought. Gross.

The next week, they took away the book. My mom asked him how long until they had actual sex. Five years, he said right back. I almost laughed out loud. I calculated: He married at twenty-three, and I remembered the affair happened when he was thirty and that it lasted a year. That would make him thirty-one. Then five years. So they had sex when he was thirty-six, after thirteen years of marriage.

"What made you stick it out?" she asked. Maybe she'd done the calculations, too.

"I thought, I thought who else was she going to be with? Jean always wanted children. I thought she should be able to have a baby the normal way. And she said if we broke up and she dated other people, they'd know she'd been married and think it was strange that she'd never had sex."

They'd think it was strange all right. A married virgin. That was a type I'd never known existed. Even in British comedy. Now I wondered how many of them there were.

I sure didn't want one.

"And then once you'd finished the therapy, what was it like?" my mom asked.

"Once a fortnight," he said. "I always initiated. She never said no."

"And did it feel like real sex?"

"No," he said. "Not really." I wondered what real sex felt like and what the alternative to that was.

It was an odd story. Like the brother. A lot of Eli's life seemed weird. Sad, too. I felt that even then. But sad in a way that had no poignancy. More like a disease I hoped wasn't contagious. The opposite of my dad's family. Just then, I wanted to be a Hart, not a hyphen-Hart.

A little while after that, they came in, and my mom gave him a piece of her pie made from a real pumpkin, which tasted too vegetal. Like squash.

28 · A Double Agent

Upper School was sweet until my mom walked into my room without knocking one December night in her UCLA clothes. Somebody had told her that I'd been selling soup. She said she'd noticed me taking grocery bags to school. "You don't need to sell soup," she said. "We give you ten dollars every week."

"Wait. You object to me selling soup to my people who willingly buy it?"

"You're allowed to sell soup if you get the dean's permission to sell soup."

This was a problem; I'd already checked the Cottonwoods handbook. In the twenty-page Rules section, it said you couldn't sell anything on campus unless it was for a chartered club. Clubs had to register with the community service woman. And the way the community service woman saw matters, I already owed her nine hours.

"Okay, okay, let me get this straight," I said. "I understand you don't want me to continue. So I'll just sell the rest of my inventory, and then I'll stop."

"How much *inventory* do you have?"

I opened my closet and bags slumped out.

Her mouth tightened. "You're to stop completely as of now. Unless and until you get permission from the dean."

"Well, what do you suggest I do with all this soup?"

"I suggest you eat it. Bring one a day for lunch." She glanced at the bags again. "Share some with your sisters."

I had to find out who told her. What was the good of surveillance if you missed the call that determined your life? Hector and I spent hours speculating about who snitched. We had to come up with better methods of phone tapping. The only conversation I'd heard through the extension that week was Sare urging my mom to switch her credit cards from mileage points to cash back. "Blah blah blah," I repeated to Hector. "Gobble gobble gobble." That night, my mom complained that Esmeralda had taken me to buy soup. Sare said to tell Esmeralda that that could never happen again. Sare could be medieval. She believed in castes. But Esmeralda, who cleaned their house on Thursdays, revered Sare. Pretty much everyone revered Sare, impossible as she was.

I couldn't sleep. I knew I was going to be letting people down.

For once, the Mims didn't have to keep waking me in the morning.

"You really won't let me sell just until break?" I said. "It's only two weeks!"

"I really won't."

I slammed my door. When I came out, I gave each of the Boops two bags to carry. I hauled the other five.

"What are you doing, Miles?"

"I'm giving soup away, Mother. Since you won't let me make a profit. And I really wanted to get you all good Christmas presents."

That was true. I'd wanted to buy a necklace for her.

I felt literally dreadful all morning. At lunch, Hector and I waited until people formed the line. Then Hector asked, Who wants soup? And we handed out the cups and walked down the line pouring water from our thermoses. Whoever tried to pay us, we said no. We passed out chips and crisps and popcorn and the yellow Inca Kola. We didn't announce that we were giving food away, because we wanted to thank our regulars first, but people heard, and by the end of the period, we'd distributed all but one bag of Mexi-Crisps. "Closing down shop, man," I said. "On the house." I wished Happy Hanukkah to all the Christians and Merry Christmas to the Jews. I'd brought a six-pack of Mexican Cokes. I gave a bottle each to Charlie, Hector, and Ella. I felt a little better. I liked Ella. I liked giving her something.

"We should have kept more for ourselves," Hector said.

We counted the cash in my locker. I split it with Hector, even though I'd laid out the seed money. The alley, where we ate our lunches, was just a parking lot. The other private school in our neighborhood had been started as a military academy, and their founders bought up Los Angeles property in the first decades of the last century. Cottonwoods still rented and spent its money on scholarships. Our founder was still a hippie. Inscribed over the gate were the questions: IS IT TRUE? IS IT KIND? IS IT NECESSARY? DOES IT IMPROVE UPON THE SILENCE?

When Eli called that night, he suggested I look at the existing clubs and see if one might partner with us. So I looked around for a club that would let us sell soup in its name. The gay and lesbian club was sponsoring a movie night, it said on the library wall bulletin: *Midnight Cowboy*, Coke, and free pizza.

"I'd stay for the pizza," Hector said. His dad usually took them to a greasy Thai place near their house for dinner.

So we stayed and ate and then signed up. Maybe we could get permission to sell soup. I called my dad for a ride. We waited for him outside the admin building.

"So what club is this?" he asked as we climbed in.

"FLAGBT," I said. "Freedom for Lesbians and Gays. Bisexuals."

"And Transgendered," Hector said.

I liked watching my dad's lip wobble. He was a Hollywood liberal, way Democrat, in favor of gay rights, but his mouth went like a rope when you shook it. Then, on Venice Boulevard, we passed the Thai dive where the Audreys ate. It was an old storefront with a sagging blind.

"We get our food there most nights," Hector said.

"Yeah, right," my dad said.

"They do," I mumbled. They really did.

In front of Hector's place, I lifted up his hand and kissed it.

"Does Hector like any girls?" my dad asked, driving away.

"He may like some, but he doesn't have a chance."

Soup sellers, the girls called us, not in a friendly way.

29 · By the Heating Vent

My mom and Eli talked about budgeting time the way they talked about budgeting money. We seemed to have neither to spare. Since my dad moved out, leisure ended. The Mims didn't roam anymore with Sare through aisles of junk at flea markets on Sunday mornings. They used to return while we still slept. (Sweet! They got to do something they liked without missing one minute of our waking lives! They'd probably decided about *Survivor* there, where I couldn't even eavesdrop.) But the second Sunday in December, they drove to a swap meet to buy Christmas presents. I woke again to the sound of them moving around the kitchen. A blessed return to normal.

"But I don't want to ratchet things up," the Mims said. "So he feels he has to spend that much on my present. And I can't do it again, for his birthday."

I walked in, still in jama pants. "Can I have a bagel?"

"Sure." She stood to make it, and I turned back to my room.

"Wait, you can get that, Miles, can't you? And put it in the toaster?" Sare nodded to the Mims. "Sit down. He's *four*teen!" The woman was a nuisance.

I found the bagels. Since my dad moved out, the Mims *had* brought us breakfast on white trays—a wedding present they'd never used. (Separation had its perks.)

"Plane tickets are expensive," Sare continued. "And he's been doing all the traveling. I think it's important to keep it roughly even."

"How many minutes do I put it on for?" I asked.

"Three," my mom said. "If it just seems too much, I could save it for Miles."

"Oh, just give it to Eli. You bought it for him. It's a beautiful watch."

But I liked the idea of her saving a watch for me!

"Hey, what ever happened to that suit?" Sare asked.

"We never went to London."

"Where's the butter?"

"Bottom drawer, next to the mustard you like."

"He should have just bought you a suit here." Sare's voice changed. "Do you think there's some reason you're taking it so slow?"

Taking *what* so slow! I wanted things to stay the way they were. Separation had made me conservative.

The Mims sighed. "He called me up last night and said, 'Don't you want to just go to the movies with me?' And I do. But I have to think of the kids."

Oh, just go to the movies, I felt like saying. "I can babysit" is what I did say, and took my bagel to my room. I'd burned it.

The year before, we'd had blowout Friday-night sleepovers with six or seven guys every week. This year we'd dwindled to Hector, me, and sometimes Charlie. Several of the Rabbits were hanging out with girls. Charlie was obsessed with Estelle.

I still wanted to find out who'd snitched, but no matter what I said to my mom about not trusting her anymore, she wouldn't crack. I planned to bring it up with Eli. He'd already told me his ex-in-laws were Nazis.

Hector and I walked a lot that December, speculating about the other people in FLAGBTU. By then, we'd lobbied to get the U added, for Undecided.

I jumped into Charlie's arms just to see my dad's face tumble. I was beginning to enjoy this. I said, "You're against DOMA, aren't you?" I had to explain that DOMA was the Defense of Marriage Act. He knew that DADT was Don't Ask, Don't Tell. My mom shocked me by recognizing the term NAMBLA. One of the things my parents still shared was an irrational fear of pedophiles.

Eli had read in an English novel that a man paid his grandchildren to memorize poems, and the Mims offered to give us ten dollars a sonnet, fifteen for longer poems. Since I'd lost soup selling, I needed income. We kept buying lunches—it was hard to go back to the stuff my mom packed. So I memorized "Annabel Lee." But the Mims turned out to be a stickler. One line off and she sent me back to my room to try again.

30 · The Game in the Front Seat

I hunted for ladders to put up lights. We had two in our garage, but neither was tall enough. I left a note for our gardeners taped to the hose—we had mow-and-blow guys like everyone else we knew in LA—asking to borrow a high one. I got no answer, so I had Esmeralda translate my note. That worked. A tall rusty ladder appeared.

I kept asking my mom when Eli was coming. I hauled the lights from the basement, ran them along the living room floor, and plugged them in to make sure the bulbs all still lit.

Eli finally walked in carrying his suitcase, late the Sunday before Christmas. The tree had been up for days already. My mom warmed his plate, and he ate on a chair by the fire. The Boops, in pajamas, turned marshmallows on long retractable forks our father had once bought. With everyone there, I said, "So, Eli, our dog got adopted."

"Angeldog!" Boop One cried out. "When? Is it a nice family? With girls?"

My mother looked at me strangely. "Tell Eli when, Miles."

"November twentieth," Boop Two said. No one but us had remembered him.

"That's just great," Eli said. Then the Boops had to go to bed, and they wanted him, so I followed the Mims to the kitchen, where she whisked milk on the stove with sugar, vanilla, grated nutmeg, and some cardamom. She brought the Boops each a mug with one star anise floating on top.

I lurked around all night, listening in on my mom and Eli, half bored.

The first thing I heard that seemed to matter was my mom saying, "I could have worked harder." At what? She was a pretty hard worker. Way more than me.

"I don't know, sweetie. If he'd been there with you, you would have rubbed your hands together and blown it into something. You, you and your family romance." I'd actually *seen* my mom rub her hands together. "You haven't had the experience of being married to someone you got along with."

But my parents did get along! I knew. I was there. I lived with them.

"You had that. Why weren't you happy?"

"Jean's like a sister to me. I haven't had a life with a woman. It's not just sex. It affects everything. Still, I'm the one who should be guilty. I knew before we married."

"Why did you, then? Twenty-three is so young. I think of Miles."

I perked to my name. She'd probably want me to marry Maude

Stern, a hand-raising, butt-lifting-off-the-chair, call-on-me type. I would never marry Maude Stern.

"When I found out Jean wanted to get married, I thought she was pretty *enough*, smart *enough*. My mother knew I wasn't in love with her. But I did it. I even proposed."

"Did you get a ring?"

"No. Not then. Once, later, on Telegraph Avenue in Berkeley, she saw a ring she liked at a street vendor and said, 'Buy this for me.' It cost ten dollars."

"I wouldn't want Miles to marry someone he wasn't in love with."

"No. You want them to do it right the first time."

I peeked around the corner. They were sitting on the floor, her hand on his ankle.

My mom shook me awake and gave me a mug of hot chocolate with coffee. I sipped; it was wild in my mouth. "Eli's taking Jamie to the shelter. She wants you to go along." I hadn't even peed yet. My mom gave me two twenties. "Donate this. And throw some clothes in a backpack. Your parka. We're going somewhere right after. I'll bring toothbrushes."

"Where?"

"I don't know. It's a surprise. Eli said to bring warm clothes."

I didn't want to go anyplace. Why weren't we staying home today to put up lights? I seemed to be the only one who cared about our lights, but I really did care!

It was still dark. At the shelter, I hosed the cages and blasted the animals' bowls before filling them with new food. We squirted a green liquid in the water for their teeth as the sky lightened. "Your sister has an amazing rapport with animals," a woman who worked there told me. Weird. Boop Two had a life away from us, apparently. Eli patted a whimpering dog, and it quieted. I guess he had good rapport, too.

I liked cleaning the cages, one by one, down the aisle. I got into it. Finally, I wound up at the shed in the far corner, where Eli stood over a cardboard box filled with straw. Inside, cats tangled together. He lifted one. "You poor thing. You been brave."

"What's wrong with it?" I asked.

"FeLV," the woman who worked there answered.

"Cat leukemia," Eli translated.

He handed me the warm throbbing thing and lifted out another. I held it. After a while, I gave it back and asked the woman for a different job. She fitted a sack of vitamin pellets into my arms for me to mix in with the dogs' kibble. The shelter differentiated between three sizes of dogs. I started with big dogs and worked my way down. I had one more aisle to go when Eli tapped my shoulder.

I didn't ask, but I knew that the cats were dead. "Where did you put them?"

He exhaled. "In that box. At the end of the day, they'll probably incinerate the bodies."

"They can't get better?"

"It's incurable. When I see this, at shelters, I just try to give them a good death." What was it about this guy? I felt an attachment from the part of my chest that was where he'd been holding the cat. It was still so early the air felt thin. We washed our hands with disinfectant.

Outside, my mom and Boop One waited in the running car with the heat on.

"Where are we going?" I asked after I stopped recognizing turnoffs.

"Pine Mountain," he said.

My sisters and I fell asleep, and when I half woke and heard my mom and Eli in the front, their voices sounded different from altitude. While we'd slept on one another's bones, they'd driven into snow. A glance out the window showed mountains.

Eli finally parked in front of a shack where a bearded guy, dwarfed by the landscape, fitted us with boots and skis. Hats covered a Peg-Board wall, some fleece, some knit. We each got to pick out one, and Eli bought us gloves, too, working them onto our fingers. Then he gave us paper packets you unwrapped like candy bars and put into your socks to radiate heat. On our skis we followed the bearded guy in two grooves made from packed-down snow. It felt stiff, like walking on stilts. After a while, he said, "Arms opposing. You get the idea. Use your poles." Awkward and graceful, like a bird with open wings, he turned around in an elastic rectangle and skied back toward his shack.

The Boops got the knack of it right away. Boop One tried to pass me. A very irritating person.

The world felt quiet. Snow slipped off pines onto other snow, but you registered that in the chest more than heard it. Eli's skis crossed over each other, and he tripped. Boop One shot ahead, Boop Two scooting in behind her. I hadn't fallen yet, but it was hard work heaving uphill or else terrifying going down too steeply. Eli landed again, and my mom's ski caught on his. I got split like a V, rolled to the side, and then shoved up. The fresh snow stung at first, then melted cold and wet in my clothes.

Still, it was beautiful for hours. We saw a stiff owl, two families of deer, and comic rabbits tracking the drifts. We fell into a rhythm of numbness, pain, and occasional glory, absolutely alone. We each found a way to do it—the slide exhilarating, as in a dream—only Eli kept falling. He made jokes, brushed snow off, and snapped the toe clasps into place once more and started over again.

By the time the shack came into sight, he and my mom were far behind us. She'd slowed down for him. The bearded man took our skis back and, a few minutes later, passed us scrambled eggs on flimsy paper plates and then sweet chai lattes. He was making it all on a two-burner hot plate. It had just started to snow when my mom and Eli stomped in. Flakes stuck on Eli's stubble. "Snow-flakes are hexagonally symmetric," Boop Two said. "Like viruses. The symmetry, I mean."

"How?" the Mims asked softly.

"I forget."

"Dodecahedron. And how many symmetrical crystals are there?" my mother quizzed. We didn't know. She and Eli took their chai lattes to go because we had a long drive. In front, they studied a folded-out map. Later, they shook us awake and told us we'd carry our stuff in a wheelbarrow. We followed them under enormous sycamores. We'd entered different weather. Now it was night cold but without the freeze in it. A cabin stood at the bottom of a hill, and Eli shoved the door open. We slept with just our pants off in tightly made cots that smelled cold while Eli pushed the wheelbarrow up to the car.

In the morning, they already had a fire going. Leaves of the forest waved outside windows in patches of sun. Eli stumbled in with an armful of branches and stuck marshmallows on the ends of the longest ones. He pulled a box of graham crackers and chocolate bars out of a grocery bag to make s'mores.

"For breakfast?" I said.

"It's vacation," he answered.

The Mims stood making coffee in the wood-paneled kitchen.

"You're down with this?"

She smiled. Everything tilted.

We hiked (the Boops whining "Are we almost there?" every fifteen minutes), and Eli showed us things through his binoculars. Beaded ferns. Geometric moss on the trunk of a pine. He and the Mims began to talk about mathematical patterns; were they really present in nature or did we invent them?

I said, "I mean, they *seem* to be everywhere."

"But our visual system creates illusions," Eli said.

"Of a seamless world, for example," the Mims continued. She said that because electrons are the exact same and interchangeable, the universe holds potential for incredible symmetry. Fractals are shapes that have detailed structures on all scales of magnification, like ferns, she said, and mountains.

"Symmetry's a better illusion than God," Eli said. "It's elegant, deep, and general."

They were talking mostly to each other. I heard my mother vow to become a bird-watcher. They said if everything worked out, they should really start going to church. Church! (What about those nuns and their *fucking vows of poverty*!)

"I'm so grateful," she whispered. I wondered if religion was a result of love. That and brain mush.

Eventually, they took out pb and j sandwiches, wrapped in wax paper, and we ate by a waterfall. I felt blurry from not sleeping in my real bed. The cabin had just one bathroom. For number two, I needed comic books and a Boop-free zone.

I had no idea what time it was. Then my distracted gaze landed on a watch on Eli's flat wrist. Was that *the watch*? "I like your watch," I said.

"From your mother." He looked at her. "I've never had a watch like this before."

Sare had told her to give it to him, not me. All of a sudden, I thought Sare must have been the one who'd ratted about soup selling, too. Charlie was a traitor.

"You did Christmas presents already?" I said.

"What did he get you?" Boop One asked.

The Mims looked down. He hadn't given her anything. I just knew.

"I sent, I sent a box that hasn't arrived yet," he said. "I'm glad my gift is kind of elaborate, too." He said *gift*, no *s*. Did that mean there were no presents for us in the box he'd sent? When we returned to the cabin, we fell back onto our cots around the dwindling fire. Eli turned on the old-looking television, fiddled with the antenna, and switched channels until he found a movie starting. *All About Eve*. My mom made popcorn in a big pot; we heard it thumping against the lid. Miniature fireworks noise. When the movie finished, Eli suggested we take a drive to look at Christmas lights. He drove our car again, to a street lined with pine trees that must have been a hundred years old, their thick boughs draped with lights. My mom looked at me. *Here, you have your lights*, she meant, but even under this wattage and the dark canopy of fir, I still wanted *our* lights.

We ate at a Mexican restaurant where they served Mexican Coke in bottles. After, Eli said we could drive to the city to shop.

"What city?"

"Pasadena."

"We're near Pasa*dena*?" I'd thought we were someplace remote. And Hector was supposed to be in Pasadena! His mom had a job planning a party there. I tried to call them, but the Mims's cell phone had no reception. Eli drove us to a district called Old Town, and we walked on cobblestone streets, he and my mom bumping into each other on purpose. They veered us into a tiny bookstore, where we scattered in the aisles. Boop One found a collection of old Nancy Drew mysteries. Boop Two sat cross-legged on the dusty floor in an aisle of sheet music.

Eli seemed to be compiling a small stack of books.

"Do you have this?" he asked my mom, holding out an old hardback called *The Man Who Loved Only Numbers*.

"No," the Mims said, "but you met him, right?"

Eli opened the book to show me a picture of an old man. "I knew him a little when he lived with Ron Graham." They told me about the guy. He was the most published mathematician who'd ever lived. After his mother died, he was homeless. He traveled from one mathematician's house to the next, carrying his belongings in a plastic garbage bag. He won prizes, and he gave away all the money. He put out contracts for whoever could solve certain problems. It turned out that both the Mims and Eli had sent money so that those contracts could still stay open after he died. He called God the Supreme Fascist and referred to children as "epsilons." He was a drug addict—amphetamines (the Mims shot Eli a look when he said that). He collaborated with so many people that mathematicians assigned themselves an Erdos number according to whether they'd ever collaborated with him, or collaborated with anyone who'd collaborated with him. The Mims had an Erdos number of 3, because she knew Marge, who'd written a paper with someone who'd coauthored with Erdos. He had no interest in food, sex, or art. He didn't bother with anything but math. He left ten notebooks when he died. He used to say that God kept a book of all the best proofs. "God's proofs," Eli said. "He'd arrive at Graham's place with his pillowcase of clothes and say, 'Is your brain open?' " Eli asked the Mims, "You know Graham, don't you? They're in San Diego now."

A little bit later, at the counter, Eli showed me another book, called *The Man Who Knew Infinity*. This was about a guy who'd been a twenty-five-year-old uneducated clerk in India who wrote to the best living mathematician in the world in 1913. That guy was named Hardy, and he was at Cambridge. Hardy and one of his pals went out to lunch to study the Indian clerk's letter; they thought he was either crazy or brilliant. They decided he was a genius and brought him to England. But the isolation from his family plus the work killed him within seven years. He was dead in his thirties. But for Hardy, the collaboration was the one truly romantic incident in his life.

Eli offered to buy it for me. I shrugged. I didn't want a book.

Eli debated between the two hardbacks for Boop Two, but in the end settled on a used paperback called *Letters to a Young Mathematician*. I was surprised he didn't buy her all three. In our family, neither parent stinted on books or music. Eli found a green hardback for the Mims called *A House for Mr. Biswas*.

He paid for it all, packing the twenty-six Nancy Drews in a box. After a trip to the car to put the books in the trunk, they found another store of old things. There, Eli plucked a set of German binoculars in a leather case from a jumbled shelf, and as I was wishing I'd spotted them first, he looped them over my head, saying, "You need a pair." Later, I wondered about the fact that Eli had sent me Sherlock Holmes and bought me binoculars. Does everyone finally want to be caught? The Boops hated the smell of this store; they asked if they could go across the street to Patagonia. The Mims sent me along, and in a good mood from the binoculars, I said they could each pick out something from me. Boop One found a black fleece hoodie. Boop Two chose a birdcall. In line for the cash register, we started petting the fleece. I told Boop One to go get another for her sister. But the Santa Claus feeling froze when I saw the total. How much would you think two miniature sweatshirts plus a birdcall could cost? A fucking fortune was what. But, with my sisters watching, I handed over the last of my money.

Boop One skipped outside the thrift store. I didn't see the Mims at first, and then I heard something near the back. "Are you the personal shopper?" someone asked. The Mims stood in front of a mirror in a dress like a dress in the old movie we'd seen. The store lady was kneeling on the linoleum with pins in her mouth. I lingered behind a rack of musty clothes. Eli draped his arms around our mom from the back. They looked at themselves in the mirror. I wasn't used to seeing my mom look at herself.

She had never been beautiful before. But she was—there, then, in that mirror. And what my father had once called Eli—a less-good-looking version of himself—that seemed a little off now, too. My dad was best in profile, still. He was a great-looking man. You saw Eli's handsomeness only in movement. "Wow," he whispered, eyes stretching, looking at her in the mirror. "We'll take it," he said to the woman with pins in her mouth. "Merry Christmas."

At the counter, the woman showed us a label in the dress's collar. HATTIE CARNEGIE. "This was a thousand-dollar dress, once," she said. Our great-grandmother Hart had worn thousand-dollar dresses during the Depression, we'd been told. The woman wrapped the dress in a long plastic bag, tying the end in a knot.

My mom's phone finally worked, and I called my dad. My sisters huddled together, ready to leave, while I paced the brick street, gossiping about the weekend's releases and how they'd opened. Some things I said made my dad speed up. Questions about his work, about the studio executives who drove him crazy, unrumpled his voice and slowed him. I had him pausing now, for emphasis. My sisters kept staring at me. But this was a good talk, the first time I'd really figured out how to be with him on the phone. It was okay to make them wait. Then, as an afterthought, I called Hector. He turned out to be a mile away, where his mom was supervising the cleanup after a party for the Southern California Realtors Association. They invited us to come over.

We parked in front of a huge old wooden house. The night had turned colder. Both Boops wore their fleece. They looked good. They should, I thought, for that price. Crossing the wide lawn, Eli and my mom started singing. Horribly.

Eli was still the dork guy. He was turning her dorky, too.

> *I'm a-gonna wrap myself in paper.*
> *I'm gonna daub my head with glue.*

"I've never been to the Gamble House," she said.

In an old-fashioned kitchen, Kat was supervising kids in aprons who were packing up plates. Both boys and girls had ponytails. About fifty glass cups of what looked like chocolate pudding waited next to a metal bowl of whipped cream.

We found Hector and Jules sitting on a huge staircase. Eli started explaining Japanese influences on the wood joining. My mom smiled a way I didn't like. Hector and I lagged behind on the tour. In the big rooms the furniture looked spindly and uncomfortable. We ended up in the kitchen; Kat gave us each a chocolate pudding, with a cap of whipped cream.

My mother never seemed happier than on that day, eating chocolate pudding in the cold. She shivered and smiled. A mother's happiness: something you recognize and then forget; it didn't seem to matter much at the time, though it spread through our bodies.

How did I know a moment like that was something I'd collect and later touch for consolation?

We waited while Kat checked doors and lights and turned down thermostats. We heard a train moan. When it had passed, Eli squinted and recited:

> When we pulled out into the winter night and the real snow, our snow, began to stretch out beside us and twinkle against the windows, and the dim lights of small Wisconsin stations moved by, a sharp wild brace came suddenly into the air. We drew in deep breaths of it as we walked back from dinner through the cold vestibules, unutterably aware of our identity with this country for one strange hour, before we melted indistinguishably into it again.
>
> That's my Middle West—not the wheat or the prairies or the lost Swede towns, but the thrilling returning trains of my youth, and the street lamps and sleigh bells in the frosty dark and the shadows of holly wreaths thrown by lighted windows on the snow.

"That's a *lot* to know by heart," I mumbled. So Eli was a memorizer. Now I knew why I'd scored thirty dollars from poetry. My mother beamed again like a moron. *He's not your kid*, I felt like saying.

"Are you from the Midwest?" Hector asked him.

"Yes, the flyover," he said. "I lived in Ohio until I was nine."

"Where in Ohio?"

"Where am I from in Ohio, Reen?" Eli asked. The Mims looked down and swung her foot. Oh no! She didn't know the answer! My heart dropped, but I was also happy. "And when is my birthday?" He elbowed her side. He was smiling, but there was pain in it. Poor guy.

"I have it in my book," she said, halting.

"Mom!" She knew our birthdays! What was the deal?

"I grew up in a suburb of Cleveland called Lakewood," Eli said, looking at Hector, specifically avoiding her. "And my birthday is November tenth."

I pushed Hector out the back door so we were alone and said, "I'm beginning to think she's the bad guy. He remembers *every*-thing about us. What's up with her?"

"Maybe she's got the 'tism," Hector said. That was our new thing. The 'tism.

"See those sweatshirts?" I pointed to my sisters, one of whom was cartwheeling on the grass. "Eighty dollars each. I'm broke. Eli got the Mims a dress. We're sleeping in a cabin, and yesterday we went skiing on Pine Mountain."

"You went to Mount Pinos?" For years, in elementary school, his dad drove him to Mount Pinos to look at stars. It never occurred to me it was the same mountain.

"What have you guys been doing?"

"Just helping here. We're going home tonight."

"Us tomorrow." It was almost time to leave for Boston with our dad. In the car, driving back to our cabin, we heard a train again.

"I love that," my mom said.

Eli had those sticks you break to make light. We drew on the dark with those wands, leaving brief trails as we trucked down. Right before we went inside, Eli pulled my head back so I'd look up. Millions of sharp, small stars; it was dizzying how far the sky went back. The smell of the pine pressed close to us. This was a different kind of vacation than we'd taken before. I asked my mom if I could recite my poem for ten dollars. I was cleaned out. She told me sure, then had me turn around while the Boops pulled pajama tops over their heads.

I tripped through "The Lake Isle of Innisfree."

"Tea and Waffle Maid?" Boop Two said, from inside her top. The Boops lived on frozen waffles.

I'd made two tiny errors. My mom told me to practice more.

"Oh, honey, I think articles are fungible," Eli said. "May I pay him?" He gave me a twenty and said, "I have another Yeats for you."

> *When you are old and grey and full of sleep,*
> *And nodding by the fire, take down this book,*
> *And slowly read, and dream of the soft look*
> *Your eyes had once, and of their shadows deep;*
>
> *How many loved your moments of glad grace,*
> *And loved your beauty with love false or true,*
> *But one man loved the pilgrim soul in you,*
> *And loved the sorrows of your changing face;*
>
> *And bending down beside the glowing bars,*
> *Murmur, a little sadly, how Love fled*
> *And paced upon the mountains overhead*
> *And hid his face amid a crowd of stars.*

He was sad, I thought, because she didn't remember his hometown. She loved him, though; I could see that. I used to count on being able to enchant her: with chess, the suspenders I snapped against my shirt when I was small, the night of paper airplanes. But now, Eli could. More. Even with his twenty in my pocket, I didn't like that.

My sister whispered to me in the dark, "If Mom married Eli, would he still bring presents or would he get like Dad, not wanting to spoil me?"

"Like Dad," I said.

The next day, on our way home, we stopped and wandered through the grounds of Caltech. On the highway, Eli said to the Mims, "After you drop them at Cary's, I'll take you somewhere you can wear that dress. To a place where we'll hear trains at night."

"What are you doing, Mom, while we're gone?" Boop Two asked. She never liked being away from the Mims.

"Eli's staying."

They were playing some game in the front seat, handing back and forth my mom's small graph-paper notebook. She wrote something, and then he did.

Keep your hand on the steering wheel, I felt like saying.

"Thank you, sweetie," he said after he read her move. "I won't hold you to it."

31 · A Graph-Paper Contract

Then we flew to Boston. On my dad's side, we had traditions, too. Each year we met in a new city and shopped. We all loved the great American malls. We ate in restaurants my aunts and uncles had read about; though they didn't cook, the Harts appreciated food. My sisters and I talked about the cabin among ourselves, but we liked this, too. For Hanukkah we each got eight presents. We didn't light the candles and receive one every night the way Simon's family did. We skipped the candles altogether and got the presents all at once. I missed Hector. But he wasn't home either; they'd gone on another epic road trip.

By the time we returned to LA on Christmas Eve, Eli had vanished. He was working in the DC shelter again, my mom told us; he'd fly to Wisconsin in the morning. What about his brother? I remembered all of a sudden. Was Hugo just alone? Why didn't Eli go there, instead of to the shelter? For that matter, couldn't he have brought Hugo here? I hoped the Mims had invited him. Maybe she hadn't. She should have. But then she'd forgotten Eli's birthday.

The doorbell rang, and Charlie stood there, buttoned into a

dress shirt, holding a ridged glass canister filled with roses, holly, and pine. Every year, Sare gave presents with one flea-market component and something else she made. Last year, she delivered alcoholic eggnog in antique jugs. I preferred that. For the obvious reason.

I set my alarm for a predawn hour and pushed myself out of bed to make sure stockings were stuffed. I walked through the house, the only one up. Croissants the Mims had sent away for had risen under a white towel. On the mantel, our stockings bulged. I could have gone back to bed, but I liked waiting alone at the kitchen table. I wanted to hear people wake up. My sisters talked among themselves in their room, then they went to the porch and brought back the plate where we'd left cookies. They still believed! They really did. I tried to make them let the Mims sleep, but she came from her room, tying a long robe around her waist.

"Kind of old Hollywood," I said, fingering it. "A gift?"

But she shook her head.

After the riot of tearing, we sat around the tree. There seemed to be too few of us again. Our dad would come but still not for hours. My head hurt behind my eyes. The Mims stumbled around in that robe stuffing crumpled wrapping paper into a garbage bag. She was always moving. I wanted her to sit still. She set up the Boops squeezing oranges, each with her own old glass juicer from her stocking. (Just what every eleven-year-old girl dreams of: a citrus juicer!) I opened a drawer in the kitchen for no reason: matches, pencils, a small notebook.

On the last page I found:

CONTRACT:

I, Irene E. Adler promise to move to Pasadena.

I, Eli J. Lee promise to love the above forever.

They'd both signed their names. *Move to Pasadena!* I wanted to ask, but I knew I shouldn't have snooped, so instead I held up a rectangular thing from the drawer, a stack made of squares of cloth. "What's this?"

"Oh. Eli bought a suit. Or had one made—but I guess they didn't do it right. So they're giving him another. He wants me to help pick the fabric."

"Does he get to keep the first one?"

"I think so," she said.

"Two for the price of one. Like Dad's hats." The first present the Mims ever bought my dad was a hat, a Borsalino, the brand Humphrey Bogart wore. But it didn't fit his head. My dad took it back and came home with two different hats.

I remembered the card with names of London tailors. What was it with Eli and suits? Suits and animal shelters clashed, didn't they? I tried to picture him in a suit, holding a dying cat.

"Can I have a cookie?" Boop One called from the other room.

"Have you had any yet?"

"I had a star but it had two arms broken off."

A car stopped outside. Our dad walked up in jeans, smoking one of his little cigars, stopping for a last drag, then dropping it and smashing it out with his shoe. In front was an old dark blue convertible with a wreath tied on the grille. I ran outside to see. "A guy at the studio garage let me borrow it." He turned on the radio: Frank Sinatra singing "Fly Me to the Moon."

"Get your mom and sisters."

We drove on the Pacific Coast Highway beside the beach, wind batting our faces, riling our hair. The sky was clear, the ocean dark blue, and palm fronds were going totally wild. Air came so fast into your eyes they ached on the edges. We jammed our hands in our pockets. It was a quiet thrill to be in this car, with our handsome dad driving! At times like this, I thought of Simon's mom saying we had the best everything. The whole feeling was what people in LA know when they eat in a restaurant with a movie star but don't indicate by any word or movement that they recognize him because they understand that actors and actresses live among them and have to have real lives, too. We ended up at the Getty. "I booked a corner table," our dad said, standing in the open-air train. He carried two bags of shiny store-wrapped presents. The restaurant on top of the hill looked over miles of our city. The air felt thin, prosperous, with a stable, old sacred-day light. It was a museum, after all. We laughed without stopping all through lunch.

It felt like the first good Christmas since I'd been old enough to understand there could be any other kind. My father bent down to kiss my mother's forehead when he dropped us back, brushing a piece of her hair behind her ear, the jewel earring he'd given her hanging next to her cheek. That's how I remember it, anyhow. I realize, it probably couldn't have been that jolly. These were people going through a divorce. From what I know now, they must have been almost done.

The Mims made a fire inside, threw on a log, saying, "Another Christmas."

It was only afternoon, but we each went to our rooms. I pulled my shades down; I liked the lush, dark privacy, like a movie theater, with the scrabble of Gal.

32 · The Sex Diary

I'd been watching for the UPS truck. Eli had sent the box *before* he knew he was going to buy me binoculars. I knew it was greedy, but I hoped he'd put in something for me. The day after Christmas a truck parked in front of the house; it turned out to be a moving van. Men carried chairs, tables, sofas, and—in a moment of poetry—a pool table into the house next door. On New Year's Eve day the people came. They had kids, my sisters reported. Four maybe. Or five. Hector and I climbed to the Rabbits' Pad with my

German binoculars. We saw only an empty backyard. Even so, it was peaceful there. Hector read a thick book. I flipped through my dad's old Richie Rich comics. After an hour, Hector sprang up. On the balcony of the house next door was a perfect girl: blonde, wearing white short shorts, with tan legs. "She's a fox. Wait. There's more. Binoculars!"

I'd adjusted them before to look at a bug. People were a different setting. Once we had her in focus, we spied. There seemed to be three of them, different sizes, all blonde. A wooden fence separated our yards. We could make a trapdoor.

"You have the best house," Hector said.

We traded the binoculars until the girls retreated deep inside the house. Then we went down to ask about renting a movie.

My mom and Marge Cottle sat at the kitchen table, with papers spread out and a tin of almond brittle open. The widow and the soon-to-be divorcée. Neither looked that great. Hector's mom, Kat, was definitely the poster single woman. The Mims had her hair in a bun held together with a pencil. Marge said she was starting a diet, which seemed like a good idea, but then again, she'd brought the almond brittle. "I think it's really fitting that Eli's willing to forfeit the big job and come out here. Stanley moved four times to follow me." They paused. Stanley was dead. You couldn't just put him in a conversation and gallop on.

"Eli's grateful for the teaching," my mom said. "He said we'll use the money to take the kids away somewhere every month."

"He's thinking about it all," Marge said. "I like that."

I figured I'd have to write down his birthday and remind her next November. I tried to remember again where it was that he grew up. I'd have to write that down, too.

AS SIMPLE AS POSSIBLE BUT NOT MORE SO—Uncle Albert was on the blackboard again.

Boop One slid in on her socks. "What are we doing tonight?"

"Eli's coming. Maybe we'll make resolutions."

"We're not doing *any*thing? What's Dad doing?"

"*You're* probably going to bed," Marge said. "New Year's Eve is not a classic eleven-year-old's holiday." Marge believed our mother spoiled us, although she fed her dog hormone-free sirloin from Whole Foods.

"I'm going to call Daddy to pick me up," Boop One said. We heard her side of the conversation. "But you're *always* going out with your friends. You'd rather go out with your friends than be with your very own daughter." She kicked the floor.

"Chillax," I said. "Most parents go out New Year's Eve."

The Mims told us we had to walk to Blockbuster, but Marge offered us a ride in the small back of her car. The dog perched on its own plaid cushion in the passenger seat.

She parked in front of Blockbuster and said, "I can swing you on back."

"You don't have to do that," I said. But she waited. She had a sweetness that got lost in the volume of her face.

"She's really nice," Hector said as we bounded back up our steps. "I'm glad she has that dog."

I hoped my mom had invited her for tonight; I had the feeling Marge was just going to be home with her mutt.

Hector and I put on a movie until we heard fireworks booming outside. Then we strayed down to watch. The foxes from next door stood with their parents on their new front lawn. Boop One had fallen asleep, but Boop Two crawled onto my mom's lap. During the finale, Eli stepped out of a taxi, carrying a suit by its hanger.

"He looks like a spy," Hector whispered. "And he travels all the time."

"I don't think the National Science Foundation has spies."

The Mims tried to lift Boop Two over her shoulder, but my

sister was too big now. It looked like the Mims was dancing with a rag doll. Boop Two was sucking her third finger; she'd done that ever since she was born.

"Where's *he* gonna sleep?" I asked our mom.

"The futon-sofa. Or, if you guys want to go upstairs, we can give him your room."

We called upstairs. He could have the bunks. Like my dad did that once.

Eli opened a bottle of champagne from the refrigerator. They offered us each an inch. It tasted like pee.

He clunked around the kitchen barefoot, with adult knobby feet, opening oysters in our sink with a small knife. They seemed to work together without talking, like married parents, as boring as anybody else's. The oysters quivered like eye gel.

Hector and I finished *About a Boy*. After that, we watched *Annie Hall* for the third time, the plaid comforters from my bunks pulled up to our faces. I got up once to piss and heard them.

"You know what I want from you? Your memory. Will you keep a diary? Can you even remember all the times?"

"I think I could reconstruct them." His memory again—to her it was this great pile of coins. Some beautiful empty library.

"That would be my perfect gift," she said. I remembered the box that hadn't come yet. Had I just not seen it? Four books I hadn't noticed before were stacked on her desk. James Newman's *The World of Mathematics*.

I fell back onto the couch and repeated the conversation to Hector. He looked like he felt sorry for me. Diane Keaton flickered in front of us, our same LA but with everyone in outdated clothes. Then I bolted up. Sex was what Hector thought my mom was asking him to remember. A sex diary. I shook him awake. "That's not what she's talking about. She means like when we went to the cabin. And cross-country skiing."

"How do you know?" Hector mumbled.

I ventured out to the top of the stairs, but it was quiet now. I crept down and looked into my bedroom; sure enough, there was Eli, tucked in alone. Comforterless.

Unlike my dad, Eli had taken the top bunk.

In the morning, I heard water in the pipes. I sat on the landing again.

"Rosenfeld says he could get three days," my mom said, from the kitchen.

"Even though he has Malc drive them to school and comes home late?"

It took me a minute to understand: they were talking about custody. My parents must have been fighting over us! That started a feeling in my chest; our dad wanted me. I'd suggested a million times that I stay with him while the Boops were with my mom. Then we could switch. I'd never have to live with the Boops again.

"I suppose it's good for them to go there. He gets home later than I do, but it's a lot earlier than he did when we were married. Rosenfeld says divorce makes better dads."

Our dad wanted us! My hopes flew wild. I liked the idea of being tugged between them.

"Can I read your divorce agreement sometime? You've seen everything of mine."

Eli said, "Sure."

33 · A Fight About Colors

He stood in my doorway after Hector left, a sagging hour. The checking-on-her-son talk: I expected it to last less than fifteen minutes. School started Monday, he reminded me, then squinted and recited my schedule, what I had each period. The Mims couldn't have done that. My dad, oh my God, my dad. Then Eli started arranging my books on the shelves. He asked me whether I wanted to sort by authors' last names or by subject. We alphabetized. He hauled a ladder from the garage and washed the top of my bookshelf. The ladder reminded me of the lights. He'd do them next year, I was pretty sure, if he'd do this.

"Where do you read your comics?" he asked.

He must have noticed my floor. I knew the guy was neat, but I'd never seen anything like this. He'd bought me cardboard boxes the exact width of comic books. We decided to store them by publisher—Marvel, Dark Horse, or DC. He found a basket for the latest ones. He got a cup from the kitchen for pencils and made a place for every small object until you could actually see my floor. Did I know how to run the washing machine?, he asked.

"Kind of," I said.

He tilted the hamper. It was full. A little more than, maybe. "It's time for a load."

"I mean, I'm not sure I remember exactly how."

He took me down to the basement, and we separated whites from colors. He showed me where to put the soap. "Next time I'll teach you to iron a shirt." He told me he'd started wearing white shirts in high school. He'd bought them in thrift stores.

The last thing he did was sweep my floor. "I had an art teacher who'd been in Vietnam," he said. "He told us that one New Year's Eve he got so plastered that he threw up all over himself and woke up in a ditch. When he opened his eyes the next morning, the villagers were hanging out clean clothes to dry and sweeping their huts. Their tradition for the New Year was to clean. So he made us clean the clay room."

I let him go through my backpack, take out the balled assignments, and spread them on my desktop. (Now I had a desktop you could see.) We threw away old papers, then put my wet whites into the dryer and started the darks.

He suggested we walk to Neverland to reward ourselves. It was hard to keep thinking of things to talk about. I felt a gust of relief when I was finally back in my room, with a bag of fresh comics. I thought of my father's house. I liked the way Eli kept close and remembered everything, but I was exhausted, too. I needed my dad's house, those empty hours when Malc sat at the kitchen counter reading the trades, and we were left to ourselves. The architect had designed the house so different shades of green slanted in through windows. It was like living in a three-story tree house.

The Mims knocked. She and Eli were going out with Marge and some out-of-town woman named Penny who did mathematics of light. I was supposed to babysit Boop Two.

"Will I get paid?"

"No, you're a part of this family."

Eli raised his eyebrows, but she didn't relent.

When I put my sister to bed, I asked what she was reading. She had to read before bed every night now. She'd learned to count to a thousand before she could really read. "Berenstain Bears," she said.

"That's way too young for you. When I was your age, I was reading Philip Pullman, *The Phantom Tollbooth*, E. L. Konigsburg. *Harry Potter*."

"I know." She shrugged. "You're a much better reader."

I went to my bookshelf to pick a Dahl. All the Dahls stood straight in a row now. Hector's favorite was the story where the wife kills her husband with a frozen leg of lamb, then bakes the evidence and feeds it to the police.* But I thought that might be a little gruesome. I took *Charlie and the Chocolate Factory* and read to her until she said, "I think I have to go to sleep now."

She was different than Boop One, a less annoying person.

I woke up when Eli and my mom came in, fighting.

"You said she looked like the young Audrey Hepburn." Who looked like who? Whom? Could this have been a mathematician of light? "You said you'd memorized her face!"

* *Still my favorite.*

"But I've never been attracted to Audrey Hepburn!"

They kept fighting. I faded in and out. They seemed to be arguing about colors, then. My mom didn't like bright blues or greens; she only liked them mixed with gray. I knew that. But it seemed absurd: Did people *care* about colors?

"You just see things your way," Eli said.

They sounded like my mom and dad; it was weirdly consoling.

I woke up again later, in the middle of the night, to someone, a guy, yelling, "What about all those hundreds of times I've gone down on you! Happy fucking two thousand and four!" When I sat up in bed, though, the house was still. It must have come from the alley. All I could think of was that Simon Levin got a blow job, and he was a Rabid Rabbit. He still looked the same. The next morning I woke up with an ache in my neck, and Boop One returned home cranky from her sleepover.

"Where's Eli?" she asked, and I noticed he was gone.

The Mims shrugged. "He left." I looked at her, her chin in her palm, sitting at the kitchen table.

She was no longer young.

34 · Our House Had Problems

One day after school the Mims, still in her teaching shirt, crossed her arms and said she'd found us a new house.

What? Since when did we *need* a new house? This was like a wall opening to wind. *Pasadena*, I thought, with horror. Those signatures had counted. Now I felt tricked by Eli, who'd cleaned my room and bought me off with comic-book boxes.

She said she wanted to drive us over and show it to us. "Now? I have homework," I said. "We have a Latin test tomorrow. I wanted you to quiz me."

"I will," she said. "After. Come on. Let's all get in the car."

She drove toward our school and slowed six blocks from our

house, near where Marge Cottle lived. Then she stopped. This wasn't Pasadena. It was our same neighborhood. We all three sank down into the back. My leg swung by itself, hitting her seat. "I don't want a new house," Boop Two said.

"Let's just look," our mom said. "Come on."

I was still reeling from the geography. So Pasadena didn't seem to be the explanation. This actually looked like a place she would like: white-shingled, old, on a corner, with a porch. Roses. Not my dad's taste at all. But it was way smaller than our house, only one floor. There seemed to be two normal-sized bedrooms and one minuscule one, without even a closet. There was also an attic over the garage.

"I call that one," I said.

"You'd live with us in the house." The way she snapped, I got it all of a sudden: Eli's schizo brother would move into the attic. I sure as hell didn't want that minuscule room with no closet. But I knew not to say anything. The Mims seemed to peer into our faces.

"I don't want three houses!" Boop One whispered. "I don't even want two. I want one house! Everybody else has *one house!*"

"You guys, we wouldn't have three. She wants this one *instead* of ours."

"No, she doesn't!" They both looked up at her for proof.

"Great fireplace," she said, then, "Let's go home."

Nobody said anything in the car. In the house, she took off her button-down shirt and hung it on the doorknob and put on sweats. She had her teaching clothes and her clothes like ours: cotton, tending toward fleece. That night, I loaded the dishwasher. Boop Two helped. For days we strenuously behaved. But the Mims brought up the house again on Sunday. She said if we had a smaller house we could take more vacations.

"I hate vacations!" Boop One cried.

I was getting the feeling that this wasn't a choice. It must have been money. Maybe it had already been decided.

My mom pounded a FOR SALE sign into the front lawn.

"I hope nobody buys it," Boop Two said.

But the Mims loved our house. At first, when I thought it was Pasadena, I'd blamed Eli. Now I kind of blamed our dad. Why didn't I just ask her the reason? I knew not to, the way I'd known not to go into that room off our kitchen the night I'd heard the noise. She'd acquired a nervousness. She seemed to be hesitant in her steering of us, and we weren't supposed to notice.

"What about the Jocular Rabid Rabbits' Pad?" I said.

"We'll see about moving it."

"We can't move it, Mom. It's built around a tree! Forget it. It belongs here. It should stay. Somebody else's kid can use it." More than the separation, this seemed the end of my good life. She was selling the house that smelled like excitement.

Sare sat at our kitchen table with a notebook, listing our house's problems. I'd never known our house *had* problems. But apparently a potential buyer had complained that there was no guest bathroom.

"Guest bathroom!" Hector said.

Sare shrugged. "People want to give parties."

Why did you need a guest bathroom to give a party?

"Couldn't they put one in?" my mom asked.

"But where?" They walked through the house, opening closets. They couldn't seem to find a place.

I opened the back door. "Porta Potti."

Only Hector laughed. "Your house has three bathrooms," he said. "How many do they *need*?"

"People don't like to have to go through a bedroom. And there's no coat closet."

Our house had problems because we didn't have a coat closet?

I really didn't understand life.

"If your house has problems," Hector whispered, "maybe no one will buy it." I just then remembered: he loved our house, too.

35 · A Vent Above the Doctor's Office

Every Thursday, at Dr. Bach's, or Dr. Sally's, as I thought of it, I took the stairs to the basement, but now the door to that huge underworld of boilers and ceiling pipes was bolted shut. So I had no clue what they said. After, my mom walked out as if she'd spent an hour at the beach. Then one Thursday I noticed painters leaving with buckets and rollers as we entered. Once my mom went inside, I slipped out of the waiting room and ran upstairs two steps at a time. The apartment above Dr. Sally's office was unlocked. I pushed the door free. The rooms smelled of new paint; the windows were staked open. I lay on the floor, my ear to the ground, and only heard faint mumbles.

I found a heating vent, but it was painted closed. With my key, I worked a line around the edges. I could probably get in trouble for this, I figured, though whoever moved here would need to be able to open the vent, right? Then I remembered the Swiss Army knife the Boops had given me at Christmas. I carried it for the tiny ivory toothpick. I had to run down to get it from my backpack. The knife worked. I picked away at the paint and got a corner loose. Below me, the women were laughing. I heard bits:

unglamorous people
Marge
set theory
if I could do
he likes that I'm friends with people like Marge
Eli a class
spring
fly out every week?

I heard words but not enough to make sense. I had the top-left and bottom-right corners free. I used my shoulder and shoved the thing. It sprang open.

"Marge dressed up," my mom was saying. "She hopes to meet someone. Eli said, 'What exactly is she trying to preserve? It isn't as if there's any beauty there.' "

She asked if Dr. Sally thought that was bad.

I didn't hear an answer. I just heard laughing.

Once on the blackboard had been: MATH = BEAUTY.

But what Eli said did seem bad. My dad had worried that Marge wasn't attractive enough. It was probably why she was alone. That was no joke.

And Marge said nice things about Eli. I'd heard her.

I liked Eli, but there were shards of something else, too. Maybe that's how it felt when you grew up. Why would my mom try to sell our house? I thought suddenly. They didn't talk about that at all. There were so many holes in my knowing her.

36 · On the Other Side of the Trees

Kat stepped out of her bug at carpool, hair blowing across her mouth.

"Your mom's a MILF," a kid said to Hector.

"What's that?" I asked.

"Mother I'd like to fuck," the kid mumbled, ending in low laughter.

Everyone looked at the ground. My mom was single, too. Nobody said she was a MILF. You didn't want them saying that about your mother, but you felt kind of bad when they didn't, too.

Hector went home, but I stayed. Winter practice for tennis had started, and my mom had found the coach for the Santa Monica Specials and volunteered Charlie and me to help. I was way behind on community service hours. So after team practice on Mondays, we hit balls to the Specials. It was weird at first—these people were grown-ups, even if they were . . . whatever—but after a while you forgot. They ran after balls they missed, clumsy but grateful seeming, and it was fun being out on the courts just hitting the balls easy down the middle. I made up things to remember their names. Arthur had spiked hair. Like a crown. King Arthur. Ralph had a belly and incredibly pale legs. I tried to remember to think of him as Mountain, because *Alp* was in the middle of his name.

One Monday in February, I was teaching Arthur to put spin on his serve. We'd just hit a bucket and I was leaning over, picking up balls with my racket against my ankle, when I heard my mom and dad on the other side of the trees. They'd come to Open House for my sisters' class. "I'll walk you to your car," she said. What were they trying to prove? *You're separated, people*, I felt like saying. But I didn't want them to know I was here. I liked being outside this late and sweating. Since my report card, home was a penitentiary. Everything good was banned.

I heard my mom's rasping heels. My dad always walked ahead. "What?" he said. "Why are you looking at me like that!"

"Well, you were forty-five minutes late to the teacher's conference!"

"Okay, I was late to the teacher's conference. And because of you, I didn't have sex for a decade during my thirties!"

I turned back to the steady lines of the court, listened to the *thwock* of the ball. The sun was lowering. I loved the liver-colored rectangles and clean yellow lines, even the hazy poor-park trees, where dim light settled a jewel on every branch. I pictured my mom's earrings—all gifts from my father—flung up in the air and landing in the cupped leaves. So I guess my parents hadn't had sex. That neutered me somehow. Maybe that was why I was fat, I thought, my reasoning zigzagged, looking down at myself. People in my class at school, some of them, they were having sex already. We all knew exactly who. Simon told us. What was sex, even? I'd seen it in movies since I was eight or nine. I'd watched porn on Charlie's brother's computer. But was it hard to have? Why didn't they? I had a flash again of Charlie's parents, old and naked. It was jarring to hear my parents fight. Usually they got along.

My parents' divorce became final on February 27, 2006, although I didn't know that then. I never asked, and they didn't tell. DADT. When people presumed my parents were divorced, I still said, "Actually, they're just separated." I'd made certain deductions. I'd heard Eli promising my mom he wouldn't pressure her anymore; his voice dropping when he'd asked, was she afraid to get divorced? In a shrill tone, he'd said, "I'm alone waiting in a one-room apartment and you're with your kids in your million-dollar house!" and, in a calmer mood, "I'll pay half when I move in. If you ever let me." Our house wasn't worth a million dollars. I knew that by then. One incidental proof that I'd grown up since my dad moved out was that I now understood the prices of real estate in our neighborhood. I'd heard Dr. Sally's laughter. I assumed my parents had their reasons for taking their time. But then, in March, in the car, Boop Two asked my mom, in her dyslexic way, "Are we divorce?" and my mom said, "Yes, honey, but we're still a family."

My head whiplashed. *When had that happened?* But I still didn't ask.

"Can you get a divorce if one person hates the other, but the other one doesn't want to?" Boop One asked, on that same ride to school.

My mother was bad at explaining. They both were. Half of what the Boops heard about divorce came from the driver's seat, with them in the back. "Well, you wouldn't want to stay with someone who doesn't want to be with you," my mother said.

"But you and Daddy hate each other," Boop Two said.

"We don't hate each other," she mumbled.

That night at dinner, she asked, "How do you feel about our being divorced?" She'd probably talked to Sare.

"It's okay," my sisters said, looking at each other, then down.

"You can tell me how you feel."

"I feel horrible when you say I can't watch *American Idol*," I told her.

"I can live with that," she said.

37 · My Sisters' Question

Boop One asked me what our parents had been like together. My two sisters sat huddled next to each other, waiting for my answer.

"I guess you don't remember much."

They shook their heads. I pitied them.

"Were they ever in love?" Boop One asked, her round face brave.

I rubbed my eyes. Once our dad told me that he'd taken her to hear Ella Fitzgerald in her last public concert at Carnegie Hall. They went for drinks after in the Rainbow Room. He'd said that as if I knew what the Rainbow Room was, and I hadn't asked. But now, my sister did. "I guess kind of a famous place in New York."

She nodded, somber, absorbing the information as if it were important. "So then what happened?"

I didn't know how to answer. I mean, what ever happens? And what was love, if not Ella Fitzgerald and Rainbow Rooms? These were our family myths. Was there more to it? Sex, I remembered, with a drop in my stomach. But I couldn't say that to the Boops. "Well, you know. They got married and came out here. He wanted a different kind of law, and there was the long-shot job for her at UCLA, and then they both got lucky." Before, she'd worked in the New Jersey woods, where an ancient emeritus mathematician had walked across a field to lift her hand, saying, "I heard about *the Ring*." Our dad liked being the man who'd given her *the Ring*. I liked him being that, too, though after the emeritus mathematician, she'd only worn it sometimes. I wondered where that ring was now. One of my sisters should probably eventually get it.

"Were they really in love?" Boop One asked. "Because if they were, they would never stop being."

"Well, yeah. They were. But you know them." I couldn't really handle this. *Guys*, I felt like saying to my folks, *this is your job*. The truth was, I couldn't see the two of them together anymore. They once upon a time fit a way they didn't now. "He's kind of like, going out late at night in Hollywood. And she wanted pictures on the stairway wall. A piano in the living room." *The family romance*, Eli had called it. *You and your family romance.*

"But we *have* pictures on the wall and a piano," Boop Two wailed.

We did. It was true. I'd flubbed up, explaining. "I mean, they were in love, but—" We were in the Boops' room, on the floor, and I picked up two Rubik's cubes. I held them together so they touched only on the blade of an edge and explained, "They connected on a corner." That didn't go over either. Boop Two was right; we did have pictures and a piano. They never went out late in Hollywood. Why hadn't they? That was a bad thing to remember, too. Probably they hadn't because of us.

"I don't believe they were ever really in love," Boop One said.

"Did one of them like somebody else better?" Boop Two asked.

"I don't think so," I said. "I mean, I love Eli, but . . . compared to Dad? And Holland, I don't know. She seems like a rebound." They both seemed consolation prizes.

"Why did they have kids then?" Boop One shrieked. "What's the *point* of love if it's going to end! There is no point!"

By then, both Boops were crying. Their faces caved in like apples rotting before my eyes.

"Hey, but wait. They're close. They're friends. You know that. They still love each other."

"But not romantic," Boop One spit out.

I had no answers. Last night, when he'd dropped me off, our dad opened the car window and said to the Mims, "Hey, Esmeralda tells me I need new pillowcases. I guess sheets, too. I don't know where to get them."

"Should I send you a link?" she said, leaning on the car top.

"Could you just order them for me, and I'll pay you back?"

"But, Cary, I don't know what color you want. And there're different fabrics."

"I'll like whatever you pick. You know more about these things."

"Romance can be overrated," I finally said, as if I knew. That set them off more.

Females. They flopped on their beds to cry it out. I wondered: What was so-called romance? It seemed a lot like friendship, but with a fleck of sparkle. What was that sparkle? Hope, maybe. But hope for what? A better life. Some future.

After their department meeting, my mom and Marge blared in, wearing their serious clothes. Marge settled herself at our kitchen table. I was hoping she would leave so I could get my mom to talk to her daughters.

"So you know who came to see me?" Marge said, nodding hello. "This woman from the executive committee. She's supposed to be the number one scholar in the world on the medieval Bible. And she lost her husband, too. You know what she said? She says if you put on the form that you're open to men under five foot five, there's this whole wonderful population of grateful short men. So I did it."

"Did what?" I said.

"I sent in the check to Match.com. I heard if you gave them your credit card, you never get rid of them."

"Where do you hear these things?" the Mims said.

"From the students."

I lingered. "Can I ask you something?" I said. "What did you do to your hair?"

They both started laughing. Marge's hair was definitely different. It seemed more . . . *out*, a new shape, maybe even another color.

38 · A Move Without Reason

I heard no more about guest bathrooms or coat closets, and I hadn't seen Sare tour-guiding strangers through our house, so it began to feel like we could stay. Tennis started for real. We had practice every

day after school; Sare stood with her arms crossed, watching Charlie. Cottonwoods didn't have its own courts; we practiced at a park
strewn with crack vials where homeless men picked through the
Dumpsters. Not the fastest player or the most agile, I could usually
psyche out the other guy, tap the ball over the net when he expected
a slam. But I was on probation for throwing down my racket.

Then, one April Friday, the Mims picked me up from a match
I'd won against a Harvard-Westlake guy twice my size and said
she'd sold our house. My heart dropped three inches; I felt it clear-
ing a trench. Without the place where a bunch of guys slept over,
what did I have?

To staunch the Boops' hysteria, my mom told them we'd get a
puppy.

"You're overpromising," I mumbled.

"I don't even want a dog!" Boop One shrieked. "I'm allergic,
remember!"

Even in her depression Boop Two couldn't say that. But she
stretched her arms out and kissed the outside of our house and
got a splinter in her lip. This time, we drew a young doctor in the
emergency room. Boop Two dug her nails into her twin's arm as
the doctor pulled out the splinter. He gave it to her in a jar to keep.

I wanted to blame someone. Both my parents seemed guilty.
Or Eli. To make the move easier, my dad took us to Houston, and
we shopped with cousins in the biggest mall I'd ever seen. While
we were there, my mom packed up our house by herself. Or with
him, I supposed. I wanted to talk to my dad, but I couldn't get him
alone until finally, in the airport, he allowed my sisters to go to the
newsstand to buy candy.

"Miles, it's not my decision." He shook his head.

"She can't afford it, Dad. And she probably doesn't feel great
about that. Do you think she *wants* to move?" I was winging it; I
didn't know for sure the reason was money. But the Mims loved
our house. Of all of us, she probably loved it the most.

"Miles, when people get divorced, everyone has less income. We're supporting two households now. Everyone has to make choices."

"Well, what choices is she making? I mean, I don't see her out buying fur coats!"

He just shook his head. And Eli! He'd once offered to lend us millions. Where was his checkbook now? I remembered that box he was supposed to have sent for Christmas. I sure never saw it.

We went straight from the airport to the new place. My dad parked the car, and none of us moved to get out. I counted nineteen boxes on the wraparound porch. Finally, my dad led the way up to the door. My teeth chattered. All the boxes on the porch turned out to be empty. My sisters' room and mine waited—beds made with our sheets and their animals, my bookshelves alphabetized with the Pez collection, coin jars, marbles, and Legos. She seemed to have tried to make everything the same. Two of my Legos had come apart. Even arranged as much like our old rooms as spatial geometry allowed, these rooms looked off. It was our same stuff, body-snatched. I heard my dad oohing and aahing in the Boops' closet. I opened the door to a cabinet they must have built into my corner: mutants in a Vons bag, next to a six-pack of Mexican Coke.

The kitchen had our pans and utensils, but when I checked the refrigerator, there was only a new carton of milk. I sat on a sealed box. The doorbell rang; Eli walked in, holding bags of takeout. My mom looked up, a way she wasn't usually with him, hair in a clip, her cheek smudged. He was the one to blame, I thought. But this wasn't Pasadena. It must have been money.

"We're going to the beach," she said. "We'll have a picnic."

My dad scooted out, head ducked, smaller with Eli there.

The smell of food spread from Eli's bags. He slung a blanket over his shoulder, and he had a football tucked under one arm. It must have been his. We weren't a football family, or a beach family either, for that matter, even though we lived in Santa Monica. People were trudging back over the sand to the tunnels that ran under the highway, returning to their cars as we walked toward the water, none of us in a good mood. The sun was already setting. We were way late for the beach. My mom would make us take showers. The thought of that new bathroom made me queasy. What about our house? Would we never go there again? Eli looked like a beach bum, his legs dark in frayed khaki shorts. He must have gone to beaches in Washington, if they even had them. Or else how did he get tan?

He spun the football at Boop One.

Behind us, waves roared. The heads of surfers bobbed far out in the ocean. At the pier, the Ferris wheel, still closed for the season, stood frozen. My mom and I sat on the blanket, eating from the white cartons. If you ever want to corrupt me, use Chinese food. Nasturtium shoots were apparently a favorite of Eli's. The indistinct food was warm, spicy, and really oily, the kind of thing the Mims rarely let us have, but she ate it now. That eased me. I liked to see her eat. Sare had said that Dale had a very slow heart. He calms me, she'd said, as if it were an excuse. My mom cared what we ate, she cared what we watched, she cared she cared she cared. It was a burden how much she cared. Now her hair blew. The salty food tasted wooden from the chopsticks and hours spread unbound. Without her worrying, I felt a pang. I had a Latin quiz tomorrow. We were at the beach. I could have loved this, I thought, if only we still had our house.

Then Eli threw the football at me; I caught it in my gut and staggered up. Eli's shirttails flapped. This was what men did, I thought, and forgot everything. It felt good to run. He put my fingers over the lacings, to teach me how to send long spiraling passes. I caught the ball to my chest and fell back, wiped sweat off my forehead with a sleeve. He tackled my mom to the ground, and they stayed there a moment, him on top of her. I saw the crescent of her face under her hair, his arms a cage, and my stomach lurched.

She looked not herself. She looked *under*. He had something to do with all this. Hector thought my mom wanted Eli to write a sex diary. What would he even remember? Positions? The idea of my mother in positions made me heave.

I held my belly, felt it undulate. Once, I couldn't remember when, Eli had said, *I'll pay half when I move in. If you ever let me.* At that time, it had sounded like they'd bought something he'd pay half of. Now I thought maybe it was the whole house he'd been talking about. Maybe he would have paid for half if she'd let him move in. I wanted to go back, let in Eli and even his kid if we could get back our house.

Why didn't she ask me first? I hated her for a moment.

But then where was I?

Down by the surf two dogs bounded into waves, rascaling each other. The sunset was a too-bright yolk. "Watch," my mom said the minute it spread to a line, then sunk. It was going to be a new, worse life; I was sure of it.

Had she tried hard enough to keep our house? I'd always defended her. *She does her best,* I'd lectured my sisters, *she tries hard to make our lives right.* But this new house—this *wasn't* for *us.* I'd never before thought anything she did was for someone else. That gave me a dark feeling in my head, as if there were a hole and air getting in where air shouldn't be. I guessed this was what people called a headache. My first. When I think of my life as a boy, it ended there that night, while the Mims stared out at the Pacific with its barreling waves, the world indifferent to our losses.

My sisters played on the lacy edge. Then they ran to us, wet, smearing me. Eli and my mom wrapped towels around them, and we started the long trek back. I lagged behind, hauling the bag of stuff, and looked back at the mirrory water. Even after sundown, it wasn't dark. The sky had turned a deep clear blue, impermanently beautiful.

Eli was telling the story of his dog. In Texas, he'd rescued or stolen a dog, depending on how you saw it. The dog had looked scared. He'd been abused. They'd found him tied up in a small West Texas town. "I picked him up, he was trying to bite. I got him in the car and drove away. That was how I got my dog."

"You and Jean," the Mims corrected.

"She would have just walked by." You could tell he thought that was treachery.

"You *stole* a dog?" I said, remembering Rebel, Hector's lost pet.

"I suppose I did."

I shot a look at my mom. This didn't bother her? He *stole* a pet.

Before the sand ended in a parking lot, there was an old playground, the metal equipment now faded and peeling, the colors worn to plain steel on the monkey bars in places where hands held on. In its corner stood a concrete-floored shower. Eli turned the knob and leaned under the spurt of water so his hair flattened on his forehead like Herman Munster's. With the ancient cracked soap bar from the public dish, he soaped his whole head: hair, face, ears, eyes. The Boops screamed when he soaped his eyes. He did it again, getting his shirt wet. I lagged back; Steve Martin the guy wasn't. I missed Hector all of a sudden. I couldn't whine to him about this, though; he'd already moved twice to not-as-good places.

I held the football on my lap in the backseat. We'd ended our game without a winner. Like in Cottonwoods Elementary, where we'd never been allowed to keep score. A thousand games and nothing mattered. Then, all of a sudden, this year counted. Grades that would go on our permanent records. Divorce. Moving. Everything was ending.

I felt like secret scores had been kept all along, and I'd lost and never known.

My mother drove the long way around, not to pass our old house.

Our first night in the new place, Eli slept on the futon couch.

Late at night, I heard the Mims say, "But she's allergic."

She sure was. We'd all seen Boop One's body go reptile with bumps the size of golf balls, gunk streaming out of her nose. No one would want her kid to be like that.

"She can get shots," he said. "They *do* work." Was that all he could offer us?

I kept my hands at my sides that night in the strange room. The walls came so close, it felt like a ship's cabin. From my bed, I could reach out and touch almost everything. A chalky light fell onto my comforter; morning, and I hadn't slept at all.

I heard the noises of beginnings: water in pipes, the kettle whistling. Then my mom laughing, again and again, as if she couldn't stop. Happiness! I bolted up. Hers, not mine. I pulled on sweats and went out. Eli was flat on his back on the floor, her head on his chest. He seemed to be tickling her.

She choked out, "Oh. Oh."

It seemed so easy for them to laugh. She didn't used to be happy when we weren't. They didn't startle when they saw me. They looked up, sweet-faced. I thought they owed me guilt. What happened to his *million dollars*?

"Hungry?" my mom asked.

"Not yet." I went into the kitchen and opened the refrigerator. Just then, it came to me, why he wanted my sister to get shots. He planned to move in his dog! The dog he'd stolen! Would that kid roommate with me because it was male? I still hadn't ever seen it. I'd met Haskell, Holland's kid. A little nightmare. Way worse than the Boops. And from what my mom said, this kid didn't even sleep through the night.

Eli finally stood to go, and my mom said "Wait" and ran to the bathroom. She returned with her electric toothbrush. She tucked it into the pocket of his shirt. But that was expensive! She'd gotten me one already, because I had braces, but the Boops didn't have one. She spent too much money on him! That watch. Also, she'd given him sunblock before. Little useful things. Not that the toothbrush was so little.

39 · Will You Melt?

But nothing terrible came true. Eli didn't move in with his insomniac kid and hive-inducing dog. He said good-bye that day and flew back to Washington with our toothbrush, leaving us to ourselves in the new house. That was a relief. The next weekend, we took a hike with Hector's family, and my mom broke off a branch of sycamore on the trail and hung it on the wall with small nails when we got home.

Marge, who lived around the corner, came over carrying a bowl of batter. The smell of baking found me in my room.

"I can only have one," she was saying in the kitchen, spreading a muffin with whipped butter and spun honey, both new delicacies to us. "I'm on a cleanse."

"What's a cleanse?"

"It's what they used to call a diet."

My mom shot her a look. We didn't talk about dieting in our family. After their mutual terror of pedophiles, my parents' second-worst fear was anorexia.

Eli returned every week to teach a class Marge had arranged for him. He and my mom washed walls and painted, the days we slept at our dad's. With a sander, they stripped the windowsills down to wood.

When I walked in after tennis one day, a stranger was kneeling in the fireplace. He was an electrician, he explained; my mom had talked the landlord into letting her install a gas pipe so we could turn on fire with a key. "Oh," I said. He showed me how it worked. That was when I learned that we were renting. Another yank.

We could lose this house, too.

But we made fires every night that spring. Saturdays, she assigned us chores. Because the house was smaller, she told us, Esmeralda would come only once a month now.

Sundays, we hiked with the Audreys. The Mims found a papery wasps' nest and set it on our mantel.

The first time Sare visited, she walked backward. "This sure came together fast! Think of how we agonized in the old place. Here, it's all turning out right." She went from station to station, where my mom had hung things on nails in the wall. A fire broke over itself. There was nothing on the mantel but that branch with the nest.

"Well, I was intimidated there."

"That was the great house," Sare said. "And you were the glamour couple."

They both laughed, a bad way.

Once, my mom was driving us home from school through a huge storm when Eli called and it went to speakerphone. You could hear rain pelting the car on all sides, like drums.

"It's really pouring," she said. "I don't know if I can run."

"What will happen?" he said. "Will you *melt*?"

But I didn't want her running in this. My father never would have suggested that any of us go out during inclement weather. This guy wanted my sister drugged for allergies and my mom to run through a storm while pieces of trees fell, clumps of palm wood, and she could get hit by lightning.

40 · The Double

We had tennis matches Tuesdays and Fridays. My mom learned I was playing first court when Sare called her from our second game, at a school that looked like a country club.

The Friday of a week we'd already been whupped by Brentwood, we took a bus to Polytechnic, leaving early for the long ride. The bus went through an old WPA tunnel into Pasadena and finally stopped under ancient trees, their thick roots running above the ground. There was nothing public-looking about this park: the benches were ornate, new-painted green, and in the distance, old men in white shorts and caps played bocce ball.

Pulling on a sweatband, I started against their third-court player. Here, you felt the heat. My hair dripped water. I should shave my head, I thought as I beat their guy easily, trying not to run. Then I had a break and watched Charlie and Zeke. Our team looked bendy, our timing slightly off. We played close, tight matches, and it all came down to me, playing against their number one, and he stood a foot and a half taller.

On our fourth game, it was deuce; I got a point off of him, and he asked for a break. The air felt powdery, hot but settled. A brown line smudged the horizon. There were mountains here, backing the view. He went to get a towel from his bag. The sun began to pull in as I watched him pour a bottle of water over his head.

My scalp itched and I wondered if I had lice, as I did every time my head itched. Lice liked my hair. I'd forgotten to pack water. Every morning, in the rush to the car, my mom yelled, *Remember sunblock* and *Did you put a thermos of water in your racket bag?* I always mumbled *It's all good*, sitting in the car stony, half awake. So now I wandered off toward an old drinking fountain outside the courts, held the lever down, and let the little arc of water splash my face. Water from water fountains has the same pipe smell everywhere, and that weird mineral taste. The identical stain on the porcelain. When I pulled my head up, I saw a guy in the distance who looked like Eli, with hair like that. This guy was with a woman and a little kid between; they were going *one-two-three-swoosh*, the way all parents do, I guessed, with all little kids, and then I thought, Well, no, not all parents with all kids. Like a bell ringing in the distance, I remembered the Boops. They didn't get that. And then, *It couldn't be Eli, he lives in DC.* But it really kind of looked like him. That weird square hair, the white shirt.

I broke into a run, following them, but they were pretty far ahead. I stopped when I started hyperventilating and saw them in the distance, bending down to put the kid into a car. Then I jogged back to my team. My friends stood waiting. "Two minutes more, and they were gonna call it," my coach said. "Bus gets here, we have to forfeit."

I served. Their Number One guy returned. We rallied, and then I hit the ball long. I served again and double-faulted.

I couldn't recapture my concentration and I lost the game for us all.

That night I jumped to answer the phone.

"Are you in DC?" I blurted, when it was Eli.

"Yes. And, well, you, you had tennis today. How was your game?"

"I lost," I said. I had the strange feeling of something vibrating, like the floor before an earthquake. I handed the phone to my mom.

"You know Eli's brother?" I asked when she got off. "Are they twins?"

"No," she said. "The brother's older."

"Do they look alike?"

"Not especially, Eli says. Why are you thinking of Hugo?"

The rest of the season, my tennis was for shit. I choked up, even though I kept my eyes trained on the green rectangles. The coaches never knew why their first-court player lost it. The last day of school, I stayed to clean out my locker. At the bottom, old lunches still in their bags had seeped and grown into something like soil. I had to get paper towels to carry clumps of the gunk to the trash can.

"Aren't you tempted to just close the locker door and leave?" Hector said.

"Yes." But I kept returning and transferring the gooey slime. I had a foot and a half to go. I hadn't told Hector about Pasadena yet. This was the first thing I hadn't told him since his parents' divorce.

By now I was pretty sure it hadn't been Eli. Anyway, though, I wanted to tell him. About Eli stealing the dog, too. I just remembered that.

Charlie and I still hit balls to the Specials on Mondays. They kept improving, but now there were new Specials, beginners. The coach told us people had heard about the team because we were doing a good job. But the new Specials didn't know anything. Their wrists wobbled with the weight of the rackets, and they chased after the dropped, wiggling Day-Glo balls like kids going after a faster puppy.

"Retardeds," Zeke's nanny whispered.

We hit balls to them and chased down the ones that looped over the high fence. One night, I was hunting down a ball that had gone into the park and I saw a guy who looked like Eli from the back: the white shirt again, that hair. I sped up, ran, huffing; I caught him this time, tagged the papery back of his shirt. But when the guy turned around, it wasn't him at all. "Oh, I'm sorry," I had to say. "I thought you were someone else."

Eli called that same night from DC when my mom was out taking food to a geometrician in the hospital. I'd met the guy; he worked on fractals. Ferns and mountains, as I thought of them. Later on, when she got home, she and Eli talked for hours. Or I should say, he talked. She *mm-hmmed* the way she did when Boop One whined. When I picked up the extension, he was saying if he wasn't jealous, he'd feel like he didn't love her well enough. I tried to remember what the fractal guy looked like. He'd seemed pretty old.

My dad hadn't been jealous. Did that mean he didn't love her well enough? I thought of the time something had been outside our back window. It had sounded like an animal dying.

Eli couldn't bear to lose her; I didn't know if that was good or not.

My dad had lost her and my dad definitely had not died.

41 · Overhearing My Own Business

One morning when I blinked awake, I saw Eli on a ladder in the backyard, hanging the tire swing from our old house. The tree here was better for it—it had a thick branch and clear space around. I stayed in bed, reading comics, and every once in a while, a sister flew past my window, higher than we'd gone before.

My mother knocked maniacally at eleven.

"Stop raping my door."

"Get up. We're going out. It's late."

"Where you going?"

"We're shopping for silver." They thought it would be nice to have silver forks and spoons, she said. Eli was going to buy us a set to use every day. He was big on the everyday thing. *Your life with your kids is now*, he'd said.

"Eggs in the ref," she told me, "and there's bread for pb and j."

I batted my eyes. "You're not going to *make* breakfast for me?"

"Miles, you're fourteen. We're dropping Jamie at the pound."

Batting had always worked before. I blamed Eli. They gallivanted out to shop. It no longer even seemed weird that Boop One had friends and Boop Two volunteered with animals by herself. I blamed Eli for her having that job, too.

I was still in bed when they returned. The store carried five types of silver, and they hadn't liked any, they said in the kitchen. I was sure that wouldn't be the last I'd hear about it. A smell came under my door. Toast. All of a sudden I felt starved. I heard the *thwack* of a knife. I expected my mom to open my door, a sandwich on a plate in her hand. But she didn't. I had to force myself up.

". . . not only reading," my mom was saying in the kitchen, "it's more than books. Emma and Izzy are going to the movies, and she doesn't want to go along. She says movies are boring. Everything's boring or scary."

I knew all this. My mom had talked about it with Sare. I'd overheard Sare say, *Boring or scary! That pretty much covers the world.*

"I don't know if she follows the plots of these movies."

That wasn't the problem, though. It was a social thing, I was pretty sure. Boop Two knew that Izzy really only wanted her sister and that they had to invite her along.

I walked in, took a sandwich, and headed back to my room as Eli asked my mom question after question. He loved her, I supposed. I couldn't stand to hear more of this, and it was my sister.

Once upon a time, I remembered, my father had been able to calm her. She called him even now about Boop Two. His refrain was *She'll be fine. I was a late reader, too.* And *I was a National Merit Scholar.*

"You still don't read," she'd say back.

"But I *can* read, Irene. I can."

Eventually, I supposed, she'd figured out that everything would be *fine* not because there wasn't a problem but because my father wanted to get off the phone. When I was older I understood that he couldn't take anxiety. He seemed to be trying to talk her into the idea that everything would be fine, but really he was talking himself down. One of my discoveries from the extension was that she still called him four, five, sometimes six times a day about us. He seemed in a race against himself, to see how fast he could get off. One Saturday, I timed him. Thirty seconds. Why answer at all? If you're just going to say, *Can't talk now. Got to call you back.*

The douche. He did it to me, too, but not as much anymore. I'd learned how to talk to him. Why hadn't she?

Eli must have been more selective about when he told her not to worry: she still believed him. The next time I went to the kitchen, she was saying, "She doesn't seem ADD to me either, but maybe I should have her tested. Sare thinks so."

Eli was silent, then said, "Well, if *Sare* thinks so." He said if she had so many people to talk to, he wouldn't spend all the time he did thinking a problem through with her to give her his best advice. Then he lit into her about *retailing* the story. (Did he mean *retelling*?) I realized then that he didn't know about all the phone calls to my dad, even if their average length was under a minute.

"I saw your friend in Philadelphia," he said. "We had dinner."

"But you said you wouldn't see her. You promised."

"I'm teasing you, honey. We didn't have dinner. I talked to her on the phone."

"That time we went out, you said she looked like the young Audrey Hepburn! You touched her stomach!"

"I didn't touch her stomach. I touched *your* stomach."

We still avoided the neighborhood where we used to live. We knew all the routes and took long ways around, just not to see our old house.

Then I went to camp. Inside the echoing clomps of guys, I forgot all we'd lost at home. Portaging canoes through the swampy banks of a freezing Maine river, I thought only about keeping up. It was hard. We climbed Mount Katahdin on hands and knees in a hailstorm. Ten times every hour I wished I'd let my mom order the water gear I swore I didn't need when she tried to make me put it on at REI. My stomach grew fur inside it. We ate Chef Boyardee from the can. I waited for the other guys to go to sleep before I braved the woods to shit. Back at camp, I found a clean facility, off the cafeteria, and hiked there with comic books sent from home. I'd gotten into superheroes that summer. I'd put in orders at Neverland and Malc picked up a batch every week and FedExed them with notes and treats from my dad. Hector sent me postcards. His dad had him reading his extension students' *Merchant of Venice* essays, separating them into batches of acceptable, horrible, and even worse.

When I got home, it felt strange to be clean again, as if I were a smaller self. I roamed loose in my clothes, slept in late, then woke up to the smell of good hot food. Boop One could do side splits now. Boop Two had grown taller, but despite new glasses, she still didn't read. She'd developed math talent, though. "I can tell you a trick for squaring numbers that end in five," she said. I couldn't do that in my head, I told her. I was more patient, partly because they felt less like my sisters, after six weeks away, partly just from something shed by the old trees. Trees in Maine had a smell. *Petrichor*, Hector wrote in a postcard. Here, August was dry. You didn't smell the trees, but you heard them at night, like string instruments.

When my dad came to take me out for dinner, I saw the first gray in his hair.

I overheard Sare trying to talk my mom into the swim team for me. *The swim team? Really, people!* The annoying thing about wiretaps was that you couldn't talk back. Then I learned that my mom had signed me up for cross-country! I'd never run in my life! Philip had joined Hector, too. It was all his doing.

I'd have to get out of it, of course, but I couldn't start arguing until I officially knew. This was a huge downside to reconnaissance. And Hector wasn't even home yet.

He finally returned from surf camp taller and tan. They'd made bonfires on the beach and heard waves boom and crash over and over, all night long.

"You like Surferdude better, then?"

"No. I still hate him."

Hector had gotten to be an even bigger reader over the summer. Or at least he read bigger books. He was in the middle of *Moby-Dick*. I'd gone the other direction. Floppies, superhero comics. I followed ifanboy.com. Hector had a bracelet tied on his ankle, woven from string that looked like it had already been wet and dried a lot of times. I kicked it. "Where'd you get that?"

"A counselor," he said. "College woman."

If that bracelet had been on the ankle of any other Rabid Rabbit, I would have teased him, but Hector was the last of us to show any interest in sex. Other Rabbits wondered if he was gay. I didn't know. It seemed the one thing from his parents' divorce; he just didn't have that yet.

He kept the string on his ankle all that year. It was the most romantic I'd ever seen him and ever would, for almost a decade up till now.

42 · A Full House and a Borrowed Dog

It was the Mitzvah year, Bar and Bat, for the Boops, and so far Boop One had received thirty-six invitations and Boop Two five. Hector and I hadn't been invited to many either when we were in seventh grade, just to Simon's and the ones that included the whole class, but what mother would allow her brat to invite one twin and not the other?

Apparently, quite a few of them.

Our whole family got invited to Simon's sister's, and the Mims decided I had to wear a suit. She trudged me through department stores and appraised me in mirrors, where, even after climbing the mountain Emerson called a "vast aggregation of loose rocks," and someone else famous said was the most treacherous in America, I still appeared stout. As opposed to pleasantly plump, which is how I liked to think of myself, or even as *about to shoot up.** All through that miserable afternoon, the Mims called Eli. This is what she'd always wanted with my dad: a running commentary on her life with us. *An endless conversation.* "It's all good," I said to the first two suits, but she trucked me halfway across town to Brooks Brothers. Eli's idea, probably. We wore the salesguy out until he produced a suit that made her shoulders drop when she surveyed me. She took a picture on her phone, and Eli called back in about ten seconds. "That's the one," he said from Washington.

* *In both senses of the cliché.*

"Let's pin it," my mom told the salesguy.

She hadn't even asked me! And I was there! In the store! In Los Angeles!

I had to admit, though, when I glimpsed myself in the mirror pinned, I looked taller. Slim. Nineteenish. She put Eli on with the tailor. They talked for a long time about sleeves.

My dad loved the suit, too, when I modeled it. He clapped a baseball cap on me backward and told me to put it on with sneakers. My dad wore a baseball cap backward after he washed his hair; he'd figured out if he put one on while his hair was drying, it went a way he liked. "That's great," he declared, looking at me. My mom agreed. She seemed happier now with him. He gave her the same attention he'd always offered, but now she had Eli talking her through the rest of the day.

Boop One insisted on wearing Uggs with a borrowed black dress, and the Mims said, "You are not attending a Bat Mitzvah in Uggs, young lady," and she said back, "Then I'm not going!" and I said, "Don't be such a brat," when she stomped into the kitchen and the Mims said, "Oh, that's adorable. I was wrong." Boop Two had on tights and the Doc Martens Eli had bought for her that looked leather but weren't, a plain dress, and her hair in one thick braid. Then Eli showed up, carrying a suit on a hanger and a dog on a leash in the other hand. "Your dog!" Boop One said, but he said no, it was a friend's.

"Are those leather?" Boop Two whispered, looking at his shoes.

It may have been the first time I'd ever seen him in hard shoes.

"Yes. I already owned these, so the damage is done. I keep getting them resoled. They're going to have to last me the rest of my life." They looked wrong. Square-toed. Even now, I don't understand how fashion gets to us. Why did I think those shoes looked wrong? I'd certainly never picked up a fashion magazine.

In the beach club I severed myself as quickly as I could from them all and found Simon, sucking a Coke. Hector hadn't been invited. "Hey, dude, you hear what happened?" Simon said. "Zeke got kicked out."

We'd been in school with Zeke since kindergarten. Simon told me he'd been caught with a joint in the parking lot. One joint. Zeke played tennis, too. On the team.

"Suspended or expelled?" I said.

"Like forever after."

I jammed my hands down into the pockets of the new suit pants. "Hey, man, you didn't tell your mom about me selling soup, did you?"

"No, Miles, for the ten millionth time."

We took egg pies on napkins from a tray. Girls huddled outside, their dresses blowing up in the wind, so they batted them down not to show too much. I made myself stop staring at their legs. Simon said his sister had learned *two hours* of Hebrew. My parents had decided before we were born no Christenings, no Bar or Bat Mitzvahs. Because we were half. But people hauled in thousands of dollars at these things! I thought about that money during the long, long service. Almost all my friends were half, too. Simon and his sister were just half. But their parents were still married.

After the candy throwing, they showed a montage and Boop One was in a bunch of the pictures, Boop Two not in any. The grown-ups ate outside, where wind snuffed out their candles. Only the girls who took dance every day after school danced.

At ten, I went to ask my mom if we could go home, and just then Eli came and put his hands on her shoulders. "Would you care to dance, Ms. Adler?"

They went off to the windy dance floor where my popular sister hopped around. My mother couldn't dance. Eli moved strangely, too. He kind of jumped up and down. They matched. Before my parents had gotten married, my father had arranged for ballroom-dancing lessons, probably worried about how they'd look at the wedding, dancing their first dance. He'd given my mom the lessons for Valentine's Day. (A joke in our family was that she had one big talent and none of the small ones. He had all the little ones. And they came in handy!) My dad was like Boop One; he'd been popular all his life. Boop Two and I were like her, bad dancers.

I wished I were more like my dad.

Walking to our car, my mom held on to a pinch of Eli's sleeve. Which suit was this? I wondered out loud. "The second suit, or the one they gave him for free?"

He looked at my mom keenly. "This is the one they made right," he said, in a weird way, faltering. Eli drove our car home, and she leaned her head back and started singing "Blackbird." The Mims couldn't drink. She couldn't sing either. At home, she kicked her shoes off and flung herself down on her bed. Eli dabbed a wash-cloth to her forehead. When Hector arrived, Eli was pulling a T-shirt down over my mom's head, like she did for us when we were young. She sat, lifting her arms. Seeing her arms stick up like that, I remembered the feeling of a shirt pulling down darkness over me.

"Do we own *Rear Window*?" I said, flipping through the pile of DVDs on her dresser. Eli flopped onto the bed next to her.

"Okay, I can die now," she said, banging her head against the headboard, happy but drunk. She might have been the happiest she'd ever been, but she wasn't the smartest. With our dad, she'd been sharper, her wit chased by his lower knowing laughter. A ter-rier circling under a cat in a tree.

A few minutes later, Eli appeared at my door holding *Rear Window*. He showed me where he'd alphabetized the Hitchcocks, and then he went outside to feed the dog. That was the first night Eli slept in the Mims's room. When I went to get chips from the pan-try, I heard him stammering. "But maybe you don't want to, maybe this is enough for you, one or two nights a week; the rest of the time you can run your little empire."

Her voice unrumpled itself. "I want to be married! Don't you?"

"You know I've always wanted to marry you."

Eli's kid wasn't there, but his friend's dog was sleeping under the tree with the swing; it was a small full house, and everyone had somebody. I had Hector. He'd sunk into my beanbag, where he always slept at the new house.

"Was it fun?" he asked.

"What?"

"The Bat Mitzvah."

"Oh, I gue-ess, kind of."

"Good," he said. He sounded wistful, like he wished he'd been invited. But the only reason I was, was that Simon's mom thought the Mims had the best everything. It wasn't 'cause of me. I told him that. He was quiet then and it occurred to me that, even divorced, probably my family seemed better-off than his. I tried to share whatever I had with him, but there were things you couldn't share. "It wasn't that fun," I said. "You know."

Maybe I really was gay, I thought, like I was always hinting to my dad, because the world tonight seemed complete. Hector was there. For a moment before sleep, I imagined saving Eli's dog, his real dog, rescuing him in the ocean. As I finally fell down the dark chutes, I thought that Eli's kid could live in my room, I'd make a tent with a blanket. Once, when my mom was pregnant, I was in the bath and I reached out and touched her hard belly and said the baby could live in my room. I knew that was the best thing I could give to her. She'd asked a hundred times if I wanted a baby sister or brother, and I'd said, *No, just a wooden one.* And then they went and did it anyway! We hugged that night over the tub, me from inside, her kneeling on the mat. I remembered that darkening swoop of feeling.

But that was before I knew there were going to be two of them.

The next morning Eli and the borrowed dog were gone.

43 · The Story of Eli

The move was turning out to be like the divorce. Not as bad as I'd thought. I'd kind of expected Eli to come more but felt relieved that he didn't. Even though I liked him. I understood that was strange. He left behind traces, though, the days he taught while we were at our dad's. One Wednesday I picked up a receipt from the floor, for a sofa bought with Eli's credit card from a store called Moderne in Pasadena. Pasadena again. Maybe she was renting our house temporarily but still planned to move us there. Where *was* the sofa? You couldn't hide a couch! He seemed to have purchased it days ago. It was like cross-country; when was she going to tell me? I thought as long as she didn't, maybe everything could stay the same and I could continue the way I was, unrunning.

But Hector's parents, who agreed on nothing, and mine, who concurred about everything, particularly the insane, all loved the idea of cross-country and wouldn't let us out of it. So Hector and I had to pound dirt two hours after school every day for a coach who was a dick. We lagged behind and that made him hate us. He had to wait for us at the end when he wanted to go home. My ankles jilted me; my knees hurt; I felt fat. I was fat. Clomping at the back, the rest of them no longer visible, Hector said four words:

Stupendous
Tremendous
Horrendous
Hazardous

"Those are the only words in English that end with -*dous*."

Guys waited at the Coffee Bean when we staggered in. We ordered ice blendeds with whipped cream and gulped them. I had to buy Hector's. The next day, I had two words for Hector that the

Mims had written on the blackboard. *Sedulous* and *seditious*. They sounded the same but meant the opposite.

"But they don't have the *d*," he said.

The next time Eli called, I told him Hector's words. He called right back. "Check your e-mail. I know you've gone text only."

Paludous = of marshes
Apodous = footless
Rhodous = of radium in lower valency
Voudous = another spelling of *voodoo*

I passed footless, of marshes, and the alternate voodoo to Hector in class.

Usually, I kept the receiver of the extension off the hook on my bed at night and listened to my mom in the background while I did homework and switched screens every few minutes to ifanboy .com. One night, I'd been lulled into minor attention by their endless discussion of Boop Two's aversion to *The Secret Garden* when I heard, "You never wore a wedding band?"

"I want to this time, though," Eli said. "And I want you to, too."

This time! Were they getting married? What about his kid? Would it live with us? Would we have to move to Pasadena with the new sofa? I wanted things to stand still.

He asked her to hold then. He was picking up takeout soup for dinner. "Thank you," he said in DC to someone giving him change.

My mom and dad used to play with their wedding bands. We're a family of fidgeters. My dad spun his on the table once, and it fell down a heating grate, in our old house. So the people who bought our house bought that, too, I guessed.

"What kind of soup?" my mom asked.

"Lentil."

She asked Eli if he'd ever given his wife jewelry.

"No!" he said, as if, *Why would I!* Then: "I bought her a pin once."

I heard wind outside, or maybe it was in my own ear. *I'd* bought my mother jewelry. When I was thirteen. And I didn't give her just a pin either.

"Cary gave me jewelry," the Mims said, "but I can live without that."

"The Irene and Cary Show," Eli said. That seemed mean. But my mom did talk about my dad a lot and her engagement ring was no ten-dollar trinket from a Berkeley card table covered with an Indian bedspread. It was an emerald-cut diamond with triangular baguettes my father's grandmother had worn. I wondered where that was now. "I shouldn't have said that, but what I should have said is, that's the easy part. Don't you think I want to pamper you?"

They'd joked about marrying that night of the Bat Mitzvah, but in a somewhere-over-the-rainbow way. This sounded serious. Nothing stayed still enough for me.

"Are you done with the dishes?" Eli asked.

"Mm-hmm, I'm in bed now," she said, "falling a little bit asleep."

"Why don't you get me off first?"

I banged the receiver back on the phone. Maybe they heard that. And then I just sat on my bed, looking at the boxy machine as if it were contaminated. I crawled underneath the fabric and unplugged it. Him saying that to my mother made me feel ugly, as if my body was wrong-shaped and no one would love me. No girl. I wrapped the wires and put the whole boxy telephone under a blanket in my closet. I felt limbless—just a torso.

I wanted to be a man like my dad, safe and indoors, who padded around the house in sweats he called his cozy pants.

I didn't want to get near the extension, what I'd heard burned, but I couldn't easily stay away. It took discipline not to listen! It felt virtuous and, like everything virtuous, hard. Still, I had superstitions; maybe resisting temptation would stave off Pasadena. Then one weeknight I went to my mom's room to ask for her credit card;

the answering machine was playing, and a woman yakked on about carpools while my mom rummaged in her bag. Then, *Hey, Reen, it's Penny. I had a nice dinner last month with your friend Eli—*

My mom punched the machine off and handed me her credit card. She usually asked me for what and how much. "It's for a book," I volunteered. "For Core." So Eli *had* seen Audrey Mathematics of Light Hepburn. Like he first said he had.

The Mims's face stayed tight. The Boops did the dishes after dinner without being asked. We just knew. Then she closed her door, and all night long the phone rang. I thought about re-hooking-up the extension. But she never seemed to answer. The phone rang and rang, and five minutes later it would start again. I began counting. Twenty-nine times, he called. The last time, I flopped over to look at my clock. Ten to four.

The next night, Marge Cottle and Sare arrived.

"He's a nut. He called *me!*" Marge said. "I told him, 'This is between you and Irene.' "

"He called me, too," Sare said. She didn't seem to think this was at all funny.

They saw me then, and stopped. In a while, they went out to the porch and talked in low voices. And after that, we didn't see Eli. He'd been around for three years, and now, all of a sudden, he was just gone. Vanished. He didn't seem to call anymore either. After a few weeks of no Eli, I asked my mom how he was. "Oh, fine," she said. The next week, I came out and asked if she was still seeing him. She said, "Of course." I didn't know what to think. If they broke up, at least we wouldn't move to Pasadena. I wondered if we had enough money by ourselves, though. I'd noticed that he'd left a suit in my mom's closet. I wondered if it was the perfect one or the freebie that could never be made right. I felt like calling him myself, but I couldn't decide if I wanted him back or not.

One morning during that limbo time we were dashing, getting ready for school, and Esmeralda arrived in a fluster, landing a bag of cleaning supplies on the kitchen table. "Mr. Cary has new girl-friend. Yesterday I saw her. She is there! In the bed!" Both Boops' heads snapped and looked at the Mims.

She kept making lunches. "Cheese or peanut butter?" she asked Boop One.

"Cheese."

We'd met Holland. There might have been others, too. I didn't really want to know.

Marge called one night from the bathroom of a restaurant, asking my mom if she could walk out on her date: she'd just found out he was a libertarian. My mom told her she had to stay for the entrée but not dessert.

I was reading to Boop Two about mice. "Night," she said, at the end of the short chapter.

"I can read you more," I said.

"It's okay."

I bent down and kissed her gummy forehead.

Every time I thought of plugging in the extension again, I stalled. But I allowed myself anything that didn't involve wires. And even that way I found out stuff I shouldn't have known. Lying belly down on the roof, I learned that Boop Two had a diagnosis now. There was really something wrong. She didn't even know herself. That old-fashioned eavesdropping gave me respect for moms. The Mims and Sare talked about educational therapy almost an hour. At the end the Mims mentioned that I wasn't loving cross-country.

She got that right. Sare of course thought the answer was swim team. "He needs the exercise," she said. "He's heavy. And they don't like that now when they're beginning to think about girls."

Hearing her say that, I was ashamed of myself.

....

We went another month with no Eli. I was beginning to think that was a good thing. Esmeralda came again in October just as we were leaving for school. "Miss Irene," she said, out of breath. "Mr. Cary asked me to cook for a party. He says you will tell me what to buy."

"What to buy? But I don't know what he's serving."

"That is what I said to him."

We called my dad in the car.

"Well, you know I'm no cook!" blasted out of the speakerphone.

"But it's your party. Maybe that fish with the vegetables?"

"Some people don't eat fish."

"I don't eat fish!" Boop Two said. "They have faces."

"Not clams," I said back.

"Ask are we invited?" Boop One asked.

"It's an adult party," he said.

"What about mom?" Boop One yelled into the speakerphone. "She's adult."

My mom clicked the phone off speaker and held it to her ear.

"It's against the law to drive talking," Boop One said.

"Well? What did he say?" I asked, climbing out.

"That's none of your business."

But I gleaned that though he used her recipes (I found leftovers in his refrigerator—the salad with beans, pasta with eggplant), she'd stayed home with us that night.

Finally, on a rainy Friday in November, an odd ring came from the kitchen. A cell phone, not my mom's. I shouted *Esmeralda!*, thinking she must have been hiding somewhere, though I thought she'd already come this month. So I answered it.

"I'm looking for Eli Lee," a man said.

Eli! But I was alone in the house. "Oh, he's not here," I said.

"Could you please tell him Ellis called, in Custom Men's at Nei-man Marcus? I've spoken with my manager, and we'll remake the suit. He can schedule a fitting." Another new suit! What was this, his fourth? My mom hadn't even told me he was coming. I thought they hadn't been talking. I went to her computer and checked her e-mails. I found one, dated three weeks ago—days after the phone rang all night long.

Can we unbreakup? he'd written.

So I guessed she'd forgiven him for seeing Audrey Math of Light Hepburn.

I sat in the kitchen doing nothing.

SOME INFINITIES ARE BIGGER THAN OTHERS was on the blackboard. What the hell did that mean?

An hour later, the Mims and Eli clomped in from running through the rain. *Will you melt?* I remembered.

"Hi, Eli." He opened his arms and I fell against him, surprised how good it felt to close my eyes. Underneath the sopping shirt, his chest was hard. My dad, even trim, was softer. When I lifted my head Eli was looking at me, with a gaze that seemed long, sad, and important. But "I'm sorry I'm wet" was all he said. He pulled his shirt off and wrung it out in the sink.

"You got a call," I told him. "From Neiman Marcus. Somebody named Ellis. Are you here for a while?"

"No, unfortunately, I have to leave tomorrow. But I, I want to measure your room for shelves."

That night the three of us hung around. Every hour, Boop Two called to say she was going to be a little longer at the shelter. Boop One was out, of course. Eli and the Mims put together dinner. I just sat at the heater grate reading comics. At first I listened to them. I wanted them to talk about the fight. But they knew I was here. Then I kind of got into their conversation. They were talking about his childhood. His cat was sick, and illness reminded him of his mother. By the time he left the next day and from what I'd overheard before, I knew the whole story of Eli. Like a book. I could tell it to Hector, who didn't come that night for the first Friday in a long time. He'd had to see his aunt.

Eli's parents had fought bitterly, but they'd had an agreement to stay together anyway, until the boys grew up. Then his father met somebody else. They told the boys they were getting a divorce when Eli was nine. That same year, his father took a job teaching at a New Jersey law school. They'd had to leave Ohio. His voice had a sweetness, saying that his mother had loved being a mom. You mean a stay-at-home mom?, the Mims asked. He nodded. You could hear his love and something else, too—embarrassment, maybe?—as if he knew he indulged his mother further than his beliefs should have allowed. But he was glad she'd had the luxury of being a woman who stayed home, happy her children could walk to a good public school. I didn't get his sheepishness. I mean, of *course*, you wanted your mom to be happy. He seemed to think that because she'd managed to have a little more luck, a little more ease, than so many people in the world, she was robbing some other child's ability to walk to school. I didn't buy that that was true. Maybe it was, though. Injustice already loomed, an insoluble problem. You wanted the people you loved to have good lives. You just did. And it was hard to imagine that a woman with a life she liked in Ohio changed things one way or another for a person suffering somewhere in the world. In Rwanda, for example. But I was just beginning to understand that we were all connected on something like a teeter-totter, and our up depended on someone else's down. Our teachers wanted us to believe that. You had the feeling that that was because they thought our parents' up was their down.

Eli and his mom and Hugo moved to an apartment in New Jersey. *The fall.* It was a mean life, he said. (Meaning the other meaning of *mean*, Hector interjected.) They bought everything generic. Generic soap. Generic food. After she died, Eli found a letter from her divorce lawyer. *As your adviser, I cannot condone your decision to accept this settlement.* She wouldn't take money. Eli's father had done well in the stock market. If she and her boys lived on her salary, her thinking went, he could invest the money, and in the end there'd be more for Eli and Hugo. She made the father promise that the money would all go to her sons. Not to the mistress.

"But your childhoods were then," the Mims said. "Once."

"It was her decision, sweetie."

The move changed Hugo. Ohio was the last place he ever had a friend. And their mother worked as a legal secretary in the city; she didn't get home until nine or ten at night. Their dad came over sometimes in the afternoon but left before supper. The boys fended for themselves. They ate from cans. When Eli's father did take them to restaurants, for their birthdays, their mother came. Not the mistress, who'd moved to New Jersey, too.

The Mims asked Eli if his mother ever *liked* working.

But Eli's mother hadn't. A partner at the law firm noticed her reading a history book once and tried to promote her to be a paralegal, but they couldn't, because she didn't have a college degree. So it made her proud when her sons went to better universities than the partners' kids. Eli's father eventually married the mistress. And Eli had to admit, he was happier then with Joyce, just better. His father kept his word, and the boys inherited his estate. By then, though, their mother was dead, and they split the money with Joyce.

The Mims asked him if his mother had ever met anyone else. Before she died.

She'd joined Mensa; where else could she meet people in the suburbs? Once, in the hallway of the quote unquote mean apartment, Eli passed a chemist wearing only a towel. "Maybe that wasn't so good," he said. But the chemist really loved her. He'd wanted to see her when she was ill. Eli was twenty-three years old when his mother died of metastasized lung cancer. His voice dropped when he said those three words. He'd been in England the year she died. Hugo had been taking care of her. When Eli flew home, she asked him to wash her housecoat. Hugo hadn't thought to, even though he could see she wore it every day. I made a mental note. I wasn't sure that laundry was something that just occurred to me either. I wondered why their father hadn't helped more. My mom and dad would always help with something like that, even divorced. Hector agreed with me. For sure they would. His, too.

Eli's father came over to see her, and at the end of the visit, he bent down and kissed his mother, and he had a—Eli stammered, saying this—a certain smile. They had laughed a little. His mother and father. Eli remembered thinking, That's what's left.

You could tell that memory was his treasure. He was probably making more of it than it was. I'd seen my parents kiss like that pretty many times. "And that turned out to be the last day my father saw my mother," Eli said.

"Where was Jean during all this?" the Mims asked.

"Well, that was the question," he said. "Where *was* Jean?"

"She stayed in England?"

He didn't answer. He was quiet for a moment, then said that his dad had died completely unexpectedly—of a heart attack—six months later.

When Hector heard that, he shook his head, grim, as if he was seriously concerned.

"What?" I asked, but he wouldn't say.

When Eli left to go back to DC, he gave me a sideways hug, pulling me hard against him. I stood with my mom on the porch, watching him get into the taxi. Things had finally settled. I'd gotten used to the new house, the creak of the tire swing outside my window. I wanted everything to stay. And for a while longer, it did.

44 · Friends of Dorothy

Hector and I stayed after school for FLAGBTU and learned the phrase *friend of Dorothy*. I loved code. Kids talked about how their parents spied on them. One girl's dad had a program he put in her computer to see every IM. A guy said his mom listened in on his phone conversations.

"How?" I asked. "I mean, technically how does she? Can't you hear her breathe?"

He told me she'd bought a device for thirty bucks at RadioShack.

Just then, Maude Stern broke into the meeting room and, typical her, raised her hand. "Is this FLAG?" she asked, looking around when no one called on her.

My mom was clueless. I could so never marry Maude Stern.

"BTU," Hector corrected. "FLAGBTU."

We were running a winter clothing drive for teenage gay kids. I had grocery bags of coats in my locker. I reported the statistics on homeless gay kids compared with every other kind of kid. Maude volunteered to help. What was this about? Could Maude Stern be gay? Oh, I hoped so. I hoped so so much. I'd love to inform my mom that Maude was a lesbo. She had an older brother and he was perfect, too. They both had that bright red moppy hair like Annie and were all-star athletes in two different sports. He was at Princeton now, where he sang in a choir called the Tigertones.

"So tell me what to do, 'kay?" She smiled at me, her mouth full of iridescent butterfly-wing-colored braces. She liked me. Maybe that was all; she was joining to get to me.

I suggested that we start selling soup for FLAGBTU. People went for the idea. I said we'd need to take a cut. I'd have to give some percentage to Esmeralda, too.

"That seems fair," Maude said. We voted. Everyone was down with that.

45 · The Hollywood Spy Shop

Eli showed up one Thursday and took me with him to pick up Boop Two from the pound. As we waited for her in the small office, a tall man in a suede jacket and loafers dragged in a recalcitrant dog. "We can't keep him," he said, out of breath. "He attacked our five-year-old! He missed her eye by an eighth of an inch!"

"Did you ever train your dog?" Eli said.

The ponytailed guy behind the counter lifted a hand, like, *Yo. Chill.*

"What did your *five-year-old* do to *him*?" Eli said.

The tall man turned and seemed to notice us for the first time. He had a friendly, majestic air. Eli bent to pet his dog. The pony-tailed guy behind the counter hopped over the swinging door to usher us out. "It's cool. I'll handle it. Guy's upset. His kid almost lost an eye."

"We're here to pick up my sister," I had to say. I felt bad for Boop Two. We'd embarrassed her. We waited outside by Eli's borrowed car. It was a cold December night.

"Fucking North of Montana people," Eli said, kicking a tire not even his.

But North of Montana was where we lived. We didn't even own a house there anymore. We rented, just to stay. What if he wanted us to move away from everyone we knew? Eli seemed less whole to me after that. I couldn't shake that phrase, *Fucking North of Montana people*. He must have meant us, too.

When we walked in the door that night, my mom looked happy and looser, the way she did around Eli, but our life didn't feel as pure as it had been last year at this time, the way Christmas wasn't after you learned it was just your parents, and almost nothing felt as right as at Little League when you were nine and the ball landed hard in your mitt.

I just blurted it all out to Hector, what I'd seen or not seen in Pasadena, up to Eli yelling at the pound. Hector's jaw literally dropped. I'd never seen that before in real life. "He doesn't have a scar," he finally said, and I realized that I'd been ambivalent about Eli for a while. I told Hector about the phone ringing all night and Eli calling Marge and Sare.

"He met that Audrey Hepburn woman after he said he didn't," Hector said. "First he told your mom the truth, and when she was upset, he lied."

"He got caught. And promised never to do it again." I'd gotten caught and said the same thing. Now I wondered if he really had touched the mathematician of light's stomach.

Hector just shook his head. "Remember that time he had his friend's dog? Who loans dogs? I mean, really, think about that. We're friends. But you never borrowed Rebel."

Something woke in Hector; he came alive with suspicion, energized in a straight line like a dog tracking. He read about the Hollywood Spy Shop, and once he'd decided we had to go there, the best I could do was stall, saying we had to save allowances, meaning mine. He didn't get an allowance. I was the one with money. I could memorize poems. We had to get permission from the community service woman for selling soup through the club. Finally, when he wouldn't let me put him off any longer, we took a bus after school on a Friday—the only day of the week we didn't have to clomp on a trail.

People who didn't look like us filled the bus. Mostly women. Many seemed to be holding grocery bags on their laps, housekeepers going east, home. I thought of Esmeralda, then of Eli's mother having to work. We stood holding the pole. The address was on West Sunset. Los Angeles was big! You forgot. We passed ugly cheap hotels, the kind of nonarchitecture that gave LA a bad name. Except for the night I'd come home from Esmeralda's Lucky supermarket, I didn't have experience with buses. Forty minutes later, we still swayed, now holding straps from the bus ceiling on Santa Monica Boulevard, long past Santa Monica. An old-fashioned brown sign said HIGHWAY 66. "Santa Monica Boulevard is a *highway*?"

"My mom grew up here," Hector said. "Before LA got glamorous."

My mother grew up in Dearborn, outside Detroit, and she took classes at Wayne State during high school. She played violin. She was good at math. I'd once visited there and saw the weedy, chain-link-fenced fields she walked past every day with her violin in its violin case. She was no beach girl, ever. "Is it glamorous now? I didn't know."

He shrugged. "It's a place that puts up signs for its own old highways. What does Eli do again for work?"

"The National Science Foundation. They give grants. Marge says he deals in prestige. And survival."

We rode past the address for the store and had to get off and walk back. We couldn't find the place. Maybe it went out of business, I said. The number belonged to a brick building, with a billboard on the western side that said PAINTBALL. We went to the door, which was closed with a metal diamond-patterned grate. Inside, a sign said PAINTBALL and then, in smaller letters, HOLLYWOOD SPY SHOP, and gave the hours as eleven to five. Through the spaces in the lattice we glimpsed two rooms: the bigger one had guns, ammo, and camouflage gear; the smaller had items in glass cases I couldn't make out. I rattled the cage. "Hey, you open?"

A thin Asian guy came out of a back room in sneakers with the heels stepped down. "I just waxed the floor," he said.

"You're s'posed to be open." I pointed to the sign. It was only four forty.

"I can let you in, but you can't walk on the wet part." He slowly unlocked. We meandered to the paintball cases, waiting for the other floor to dry. The army masks looked real. A lady minced in, holding her purse under her arm.

"I can't let you go in there," the guy said.

"He did some shit to the floor," I said.

"What are you looking for?" he asked her.

She glanced at us and then looked down. "I want something that records, maybe video. I think my husband is cheating on me, and if I had it on tape, he couldn't deny it."

I squatted down and touched the floor with my fingers. "Pretty dry."

The guy made us take off our shoes. Hector was barefoot without his flip-flops.

They had video cams and recorders built into sunglasses. The guy opened cans that looked like real Cokes and Pringles but were actually safes.

"What if someone threw it out?" the woman said.

The guy shrugged.

Everything was a fake something else. Pens that digitally recorded, also thumbsticks and an ugly tie. "I like the pen," the woman said, stepping in carefully on the balls of her feet. "How much is it?"

"We're out of the pens. They're on order."

"Oh," she said. "I'd buy it."

"Everyone wants the pen."

"Not much of a salesman," Hector whispered.

They installed security systems to keep people from breaking into your house and carried devices to help you invade other people's lives, take their pictures, and record their conversations. And they had stuff to detect bugs. A picture of two black guys behind bars hung on the wall, with a caption that read: ONLY STUPID PEOPLE TRY STEALING FROM A SECURITY SHOP. "Racist assholes," Hector whispered. Three additional grates were folded behind the diamond-patterned one. This was the most secure store I'd ever seen, and to paraphrase Eli, what exactly were they trying to preserve?

"When will the pens come in?" the lady asked.

"Two weeks. Maybe three," the guy said. "What kind of cell phone do you have?"

She took it out of her purse and showed him. A blue Nokia.

"You can do it on your phone." I looked at Hector. *Some salesman* all right.

"Would the pen have a better-quality recording?" she tried.

"Gonna be about the same."

Hector looked at me. *Man.*

"You probably don't need anything," he said. "If you think your husband's cheatin' on you, he's probably cheatin'." Even we could see that that wasn't what she wanted to hear. When she looked down, her face bent. She was pretty that way.

I wondered if Eli really was guilty of something. Hector thought so. But of what?

The lady tied the belt of her coat tighter and left without buying anything.

I told the guy about the device from RadioShack that we'd heard about at FLAGBTU.

"Sound is probably better on that. 'Cause it hooks directly into the line. These'll pick up the area noise. But they're camouflage. Just depends what you need."

Hector seemed disappointed. And we had a long way back. By the time we got home, supper was over. My mom looked like she was going to be mad, so we had to say we'd already eaten at Hector's. A lie like Eli's, I thought. Except he had had dinner when he said he hadn't. We hadn't eaten and said we had. And I was hungry.

Then Hector and I each had a setback. FLAGBTU sponsored a doctor from Cedars-Sinai to speak about sexual preference. After his talk, Hector went up and asked him what kind of medicine he practiced.

"I'm an endocrinologist. This isn't my field. I'm here as Casey's dad." Casey was a kid I hadn't talked to in FLAGBTU. A freshman.

Hector said, "Well, we know someone who had brain surgery

for a pituitary tumor. But he doesn't have a scar. Is that possible? They didn't even shave his head. He still has his hair."

"It's not really brain surgery. The pituitary gland is below the brain; it's separate. Those pituitary tumors aren't usually dangerous."

"But wouldn't they have had to shave his head?"

"No, it's endoscopy. They go in through the nose."

I had to keep myself from smiling.

But then I got mine. After the doctor left, people stayed to sort clothes. Maude, who'd appointed herself secretary, said, "Bad news. We're not allowed to sell anything that competes with school-licensed vendors. Only homemade food. Like a bake sale."

Where *was* Eli, anyway? I had a better feeling about him now that the scar question was settled in his favor. I wondered why it was taking him so long to move. I didn't want him here necessarily yet, but for all the talk of wedding rings, I hadn't seen him much this year. That night I asked the Mims if he was coming for the holidays. I was thinking of lights again. But our roof on this house wasn't pointed. Lights wouldn't look as good flat.

The Mims said she didn't know. Eli's cat was sicker. I hadn't remembered it was sick.

"He has a cat?" Boop Two asked.

"He and his wife did. The cat of the marriage. He's in Wisconsin now, nursing it."

On a call I'd listened to long ago, he'd said that the cat was the great unrequited love of his life. "Oop," my mom had said. "And I thought I was that." He'd answered, "I'm hoping you'll be the great requited love, sweetie."

"Doesn't he have a dog, too?" Boop One asked.

"Why does she get to have both?" Boop Two said.

"Well, their son lives with her, and so I suppose it's nice for him to have his pets."

We were quiet then. Of course, the only pet we had was nocturnal and mine. Gal slept most of the day. This year I'd spent more time in my room, and so I knew her habits.

46 · The Yellow Pages Detectives

If $x + y = 3$ and $x - y = 5$, then $x^2 - y^2 =$

A. 4
B. 8
C. 15
D. 16
E. 64

Boop One pushed her pencil so hard it made a hole in the paper. She bit the end of her hair. I grabbed the pencil and started working, but Boop Two skidded in, squinted at the problem, and said "Fifteen" before I finished. I checked. It worked.

"How did you just do that?"

She shrugged. She didn't know.

Friday nights, Hector reread Sherlock Holmes out loud to study induction techniques. But I didn't care just then if Eli was a spy or a bum. Hector's rabid suspicion took away mine. I just wanted to haul my grades up to where they belonged. Hector was doing way better without working at all. He wanted to buy the RadioShack device. I balked at spending the money. We could always just hook up the extension again. What was the difference, really? But Hector figured out the difference: I had to be here to pick up the receiver and listen in real time for that old phone to work. The RadioShack thing digitally recorded. Late one Friday night, we heard rustling in the garage. In the barely lit cavern, I found my mom and Eli bent over our old bikes.

"Hey, Miles, do you know where the pump is?" the Mims asked.

I found it in a cobwebby corner, in a box we still hadn't unpacked from our old house.

"He probably wouldn't like pink," she said, yanking out Boop One's old bike. They settled on Boop Two's Sting-Ray with the banana seat. The Mims asked me to fill its tires. She knelt down to wipe the fenders with paper towels. Then Eli shook his head. "Maybe I don't have to rub it in her face at Christmas," he said. "I'll just buy him one."

My mom straightened up. "Whatever you think."

The Boops didn't know their old bike had been almost donated to a kid they'd still not met. I was glad Eli didn't take it. I always liked that banana seat. And was there anything the Mims wouldn't give him? She'd saved her favorite of my outgrown clothes. She had a bagful waiting clean and folded by the door, my childhood red hiking boots on top. In our old house she'd kept that stuff in the basement in a trunk for our kids. I didn't like her robbing my future son.

Hector looked up from Sherlock Holmes when I returned. "Have you noticed discrepancies in Eli's stories?" Talking about this with Hector was way better than being scared alone. The only thing was, once Hector got going, I couldn't slow him. And by now, I'd pretty much decided I'd made up most of the bad stuff. I remembered when I'd jumped up to tap that guy's shoulder; he'd turned around and wasn't Eli.

I couldn't think of discrepancies. Only small things I might have remembered wrong. Once, he'd told my mom he married his wife because *she* wanted to, that he knew he wasn't in love. Other times, he sounded more patient with his younger self. *We'd started this relationship we both wanted and I was going to England . . .* The facts weren't different, really, it was the way he said them. But that was probably normal.

"Think harder." Sometimes Hector drove me bat-shit.

The main discrepancy concerned Eli's wife's geographic location when his mother died. *Where was Jean?* my mom had asked him, and he'd said, *That was the question. Where was Jean?* Which made it sound like she wasn't *there*, where his mother died, in an apartment in Montclair, New Jersey. Another time, though, he was talking about cleaning out his mother's place after. Jean went home to Wisconsin for the holidays. He couldn't go. He was in no shape for Christmas. Which sounded like Jean actually *had* been there when his mother died but then left. *Is that what you meant when you said Jean wasn't there?* the Mims asked. She was coaxing him to the truth, feeling around for it in a bag full of things she couldn't see. He'd murmured *Mm-hmm*. Maybe she'd broken his code and could decipher him.

He'd said his wife had wanted a baby. He said that having a kid was like *You dig a hole to fill a hole*. He said if they had to have a kid, he'd wanted to adopt. But his wife researched and found all these problems with adopted kids.

Hector shot me a look. You couldn't say a thing like that in our school. Our class had three adopted kids. We'd been taught to believe that adopting was noble. And we did believe that. I still do.

But then, a different time, Eli had been talking airily about if his mother had lived; then, he said, he would have had children earlier. Because there would have been a purpose. But how did that jibe with digging a hole to fill a hole, and if his wife was still a virgin, how could they have, even if he wanted to? When his wife *had* a baby he didn't like it. Back when they were married, his wife had asked the Mims to talk him into loving it.

"Varlet," Hector said. "Feckless mountebank."

"It's getting so I need a dictionary to be your friend."

The next morning we biked to RadioShack. The thing wasn't thirty dollars, like the kid had said in FLAGBTU. Forty-nine with California's steep taxes. And then, when we got it home, it took a long time to set up. We had to hook the recorder to the place the phone line came into our house. We couldn't find that. I wasn't going to ask my mom. I'd have to get Esmeralda to show me, but she wouldn't come for a while. So we prowled around, with no success. Three weeks later, Esmeralda led me. *The back of the basement. Here. Phone and electric.* I snuck down and used the knife my mom peeled cantaloupe with to shred off the plastic on the wire ends. I twisted the copper strands together and sealed the joint with duct tape.

But then it worked. And after all that, we heard only bits of things.

Why don't you just sleep here?
I'm not sure that's the best thing for your children.
We did it once. They didn't mind. I loved that night.
I know, sweetie. I loved that night, too.

The problem seemed to be cell phones. We were hearing the ends of conversations. They'd talk for an hour, and when her juice ran out, she'd call him back on the landline. We seemed to have always just missed the best part.

Sweetie, if you had a deformity that didn't get in the way of the rela-tionship, if you had a limp or if you were missing a leg, that would be fine. That wouldn't prevent our having a relationship. But this does.

"What's *this*?" Hector asked.

"I don't know." I shrugged. "She forgot his birthday that time."

"So, she forgot his birthday. Does that prevent their having a *relationship*?"

"Not more than his wife not having sex." But then I remem-bered my dad screaming beyond the tennis courts. "Maybe sex isn't that important, though."

"I think it is," Hector said.

"No offense, dude, but how would you know?"

"Movies. Books. That woman in Pasadena, did she have both legs?"

"Of course. Anyway, that wasn't Eli, I'm pretty sure."

Our landline seemed to be getting worse. It carried a ticking sound, sometimes bad enough that the Mims said, *I'll call you back on my cell.*

I love you so much, we heard him whisper once. Then nothing else. Just breathing. I turned it off before any sex talk started. I'd still never told Hector that.

We had finals for the first time, and this year's grades, I kept remembering, would go on our permanent records. Hector pulled A's out of thin air. A bad premonition sunk into me, of a frozen, menial future.

I woke up hearing my mom and Sare moving in the kitchen. Boop One had called my dad the night before; he'd driven over and taken them both. Her crying worked, sometimes.

IT'S MUCH EASIER TO PROVE SOMETHING YOU ALREADY KNOW IS TRUE was on the blackboard.

I put my bagel in the toaster and went to sit at my spot by the heating vent.

". . . Not just that they do something but that they do it with care," I heard Sare say. "I mean, we put our best into this."

The toaster dinged, and I skidded in on socks. They had the Christmas assembly line going. Baskets covered every counter. In each, they'd put a red-netted bag of walnuts, a jar of quince jelly, and now they were baking little loaves of pumpkin bread. After the baskets were full, they'd wrap them with red cellophane and raffia. Boop One hated our homemade baskets. "You're supposed to give a candle," she complained.

"Do you have the yellow pages?" Hector asked. "I'm buying you a present." Then he found what he wanted on that flimsy paper, the one time in my entire life that I saw anyone *let their fingers do the walking*. He called three private investigators. Two agreed to meet us that very day. The first was far away in a neighborhood Hector thought would make him be cheap. On bikes, it took us almost an hour to get there. The old building had three traffic schools, Jewish Social Services, and him. We knocked on number 207.

"Who is it?"

"You don't know us," I said. The door creaked open to a square room with a nine-foot American flag covering the far wall and a suit in dry-cleaner plastic hanging on the back of the knob. I had to lift a Dopp kit from the chair before sitting on it, and I tipped over a bar of deodorant at my feet. A toothbrush and razor stuck out from a pencil jar. The guy's hair was shaved on the sides, like Eli's, though this guy's was light brown. There was a picture of him in a Marine uniform. He stood up to shake our hands. He was wearing shorts and had the meatiest calves I'd ever seen. Like two footballs.

"What can I do for you?"

"We're not sure." Hector and I looked at each other.

"I thought I saw someone," I said finally.

"Saw someone what?" The detective stole glances at a sandwich, mayonnaisey egg salad oozing out onto its wax paper on the desk.

"It was my mom's boyfriend. He lives in DC, but I thought I saw him here."

"It's a free country. Maybe he was visiting."

"But I saw him with a woman and a kid. He has a kid, but *that* kid's living in Wisconsin." We told our story in bits that didn't make sense, even to me. The PI said the first thing he'd do was run a criminal records check. Hector and I looked at each other again. "I kinda doubt he's a criminal," I said.

"You never know with these guys. A lady came in here with credit card statements; her husband'd been charging lingerie, every month five hundred, six hundred bucks, sometimes once a week. All different stores. She's crying, she thought he was having an affair. I had to tell her, 'Lady, that's no mistress. A guy spends that kind of money on lingerie, it's not for a woman. It's for himself.' "

I looked down, then at Hector. We started making excuses. I

stuttered like Eli. As we shoved up to go, the guy couldn't stand it anymore. He lifted the messy sandwich and took a bite.

That was enough for me. I wanted to go home, but we had another appointment. Hector had told the second guy we could ride our bikes to his office, but that PI had suggested a public place. "A suspicious detective," Hector said.

When we got to the Starbucks, Hector took a tiny notebook from his pocket.

"What's that?"

"Kat bought it for me to write down homework assignments." He was calling his mother Kat now. I flipped through the pages; they were all blank.

I've often thought back to that afternoon and what we must have looked like to him: two kids in shorts, bikes mangled at our feet. He was a good-looking guy wearing jeans and a blazer, sunglasses—glamorous in the sheer December light. He seemed about our parents' age, a little younger or a little cooler. I thought he resembled Tom Cruise.

His name was Ben. Ben Orion.

Hector and I told him the whole story, interrupting each other. This time, we made sense. It felt exhilarating to spill it out as Starbucks piped Christmas music onto the sidewalk. I'd been alone with this a long time. And then it had just been me and Hector.

We told him about all our devices. He laughed out loud at the story of the walkie-talkie that had to be on all the time and then ran out of batteries. He looked at us strangely when we described rigging the extension with Silly Putty and nail polish. That seemed like a long time ago now. I said that through that phone I'd heard Eli say he'd lend us a million dollars to keep our house, but that later, he and my mom signed a joke contract to move to Pasadena. And Eli was like a prophet because we really did have to move. Not to Pasadena, though. To a non-million-dollar house we were anyway just renting. And where we'd hooked up the RadioShack digital-recording machine.

Then Pasadena was where I saw Eli, or thought so that time.

Eli loved animals, but he stole a dog and told us. He went bat-shit crazy once in the shelter, but the other time he held dying cats. He hung a tire swing at our new house, but he lied about taking out to dinner a mathematician of light who looked like Audrey Hepburn.

"A mathematician?" Ben Orion stopped me. I had to explain that my mom and everyone she knew were mathematicians, the worst-dressed people on the earth. I told how Eli said that Marge was unglamorous but that she'd gotten him a job.

Eli lied and they fought and he called her friends and then he vanished. Eventually he came back, carrying flowers.

Hector recounted other details. The box that didn't arrive.

"Or at least I didn't see it," I corrected.

The two suits. (I hadn't told Hector there was another call, another suit made. So Eli was up to four now, that I knew about.)

Eli borrowed a dog once, and slept over.

Hector talked about his brain operation and how he didn't have a scar.

I reminded him that a doctor had said it wasn't the brain exactly. And that they went up through the nose. Listening to Hector, I wondered what made him so rabid. Only a few things really bothered me about Eli.

I just wanted those irritants explained away.

He had an affair on his wife.

But the worst ones I couldn't say: him asking my mother in that voice to get him off.

"He wanted to *drug* your sister," Hector was emphasizing.

"Well, because of the animals. She's allergic."

He was jealous of an old man who taught fractals. He was a neat freak. He wanted the Mims to run outside in storms.

I didn't know how to explain about whether his wife was there when his mother died. Or if he really did or didn't ever want the baby he already had.

The PI posed a lot of questions, maybe to calm down Hector.

He perked up when we told him we'd gone to the Hollywood Spy Shop. He knew the guy who owned it.

Hector said that the Mims had asked Eli to keep a diary of every time they were together.

"People do that kind of stuff," the detective said. "Couples." He told us about a case where a guy wanted him to spy on his girlfriend. He thought she was cheating. The girlfriend was some thirty years younger. Ben Orion's guys tailed her for five weeks. She wasn't doing anything. She went out to dinner once or twice with her girlfriends. "Cost him forty-five thousand dollars," Ben said. He shook his head. "Silly case."

The figure stunned me. We had to get out of there, I thought. Would he charge us? I kicked Hector under the table. He looked at me, not knowing why. We'd just assumed he'd help us. We were used to people helping. I was only beginning to understand that hidden from us, somewhere behind a curtain, people were being paid. We had saved money from my allowance. But less than a hundred dollars.

"What is it you really want to find out?" Ben Orion asked me.

We both stayed quiet. When he said it that way, I came up empty.

"I feel like the guy has a secret," Hector finally said. "And Miles should know it."

"Do you think that, Miles?"

"I mean, he's odd. I guess I want these things that seem weird to be—understandable."

"He could be an impostor," Hector said.

"Are you afraid he might be a con man?" Ben asked. "Do you think he's after your mother's money?" He addressed these questions to me.

"She's a math professor. We're not rich."

Hector looked down. "You're kinda rich."

My neck blotched hot. I never knew he thought that. I guessed it made sense, but we weren't. Not now, anyway. "Maybe my dad is, more."

"Must be really smart," Ben Orion said. "Mathematician." He shook his head. "The main thing that set you off is you thought you saw the guy with another woman?"

"I guess," I said.

"You know it could be that he's married and planning to leave after the holidays. People postpone things like that till the new year."

"Wait, you think my mother is the other woman, the, the mistress, like Eli's dad had?" Eli had a mistress once, too, I remembered. "My mom's not a mistress."

"My aunt is," Hector said.

I knew she was, and now I felt bad for saying it this way. "She's not really. I mean, it's different." When Hector's aunt Terry was young, she fell in love with her boss. They'd worked together every day for more than twenty years, but he had a wife and family, too. That's why she bought really expensive clothes. He had a cell phone for just her. She was the only person who knew the number. They traveled together all over the world. They were architects. "No offense to your aunt, but that's not at all like my mom and Eli."

Ben Orion kept biting down his bottom lip. The first time I'd recognized pity was after the divorce. Then I'd hated it; sometimes now, I was beginning to use it. But if Eli was married—and he wasn't, I just knew he wasn't—my mom had no idea. I said that, my leg swinging up against the middle bar of the table, so Ben Orion's by-now-cold latte spilled. Hector was looking down like he felt sorry for me, too. "If he *was* married, it would be better," I said. "This way, she's counting on him. For years already."

The PI's head whipped around sharply. "How many years?"

"I'm not sure. Pretty many," I said. "I think he's okay, it's just . . ." I thought I had to prove my case. But I didn't know where to start. It felt unfair. Anything I could say would sound wrong.

The detective had a nice way about him, though. "Let's just get through the holidays and then see. You guys have my number."

"Hey, you believe me, don't you, man?" I said to Hector as we lolled on our bikes past Maude Stern's house. On the corner, three Brentwood girls stood in shorts. I made my eyes look up to the branches of a tree, and they slid back by themselves, and I had to do it all over again. The girls pretended not to notice.

"I believe you," Hector said. But I could tell when he was just being loyal. Eli said to my mom once, *I don't lie to you. That way when I say something's okay, you can know it really is.*

"I lost seventeen pounds," Marge announced at dinner. She did look a little different. Still, she wasn't *thin.* "Next I'm going to have to find a trainer." She looked straight at me, saying that.

"Oh, *don't.*" Philip groaned. "Waste of money. I'll get you running with Miles and Hector. You won't have to pay anything." I saw her looking at me and thinking she wanted more results.

"I'll give it a try. If it works, I could spend the money instead on a personal shopper."

"Didn't the lady in that store think Eli was your personal shopper?" I asked the Mims. This year, I didn't hear anything about gifts for Eli, but my mom sent presents to the kid that I still worried would end up in my room. She bought it a rainbow maker and two baseball gloves, a father-and-son set.

That night, we got a tree, an eight-footer. Once we cut the ropes, its fronds sprang out to cover a good portion of our living room, touching chairs. We'd always bought big trees for our other house. Our rooms smelled uplifting, even though we had to press against the wall to get out the front door.

47 · Scraps of Paper in the Dresser Drawer

Our dad took us to Hawaii that year and it rained for four days out of five. On the pad of paper next to the telephone, he kept calculating the room bill. One day, we went to the most depressing JCPenney's in the world, and in the diner, he said, "This cup of coffee is costing me two thousand dollars," and that became a running joke. Later, he told me it wasn't really the money. He'd been terrified that his one vacation with us was going to be a bust. No beachside dinners near torch-lit waves, no smoothies by the pool, and no lobby life, either, because everyone had fled to the mall just for something to do. So he was worried about that and thought he was wasting thousands of dollars. Boop One didn't care about the weather. She hung on our dad's arm the whole time. Boop Two roamed outside looking for sea turtles that came up on the rocks, also not minding the rain. For me, it was just fine. I didn't like the beach much anyway. We had one at home. Inside I could watch movies, and since it was vacation, I watched them from the bathtub.

We flew home a day early. My dad came for dinner Christmas Eve.

Nobody even mentioned lights.

Philip had their car packed up outside our house—he was driving Hector and Jules to Canada through the night. Marge and the Mims packed them sandwiches and a thermos of coffee. My dad went home first. Marge and my mom cleaned the kitchen, swilling champagne and listening to what Hector had called angel music. Eli didn't make it for Christmas—because of the sick cat—but he sent gifts: sweaters for my sisters and, for me, a pen and a book called *How to Draw Comics the Marvel Way*. I planned to pass that along to Hector.

Christmas morning, the Boops hung rainbow makers from their stockings. They really did bounce colored arcs all over the walls. At noon, there was a knock at the door: two guys with a clipboard. "Delivery," one said. "You're working on Christmas!" the Mims said. I figured somebody had sent us flowers. My dad, probably. He was the only flower-sender we knew. But they came up the front yard, hauling in a sofa. We had to move Sare's futon couch to fit it in the living room. "It's from Eli," the Mims whispered. She sounded shocked. "We saw it once in a store." I ran back to my room to find the receipt.

The Alvar sofa. The paperwork they left matched the receipt. So there was no house in Pasadena! Only a store called Moderne. We wouldn't move. But why had it taken so long to come? Eli had bought the sofa on August 19, according to the small paper. The Boops and my mom were already sitting on it. Happiness really may be just a form of relief, I thought.

I had to remember to tell Hector.

The Audreys returned five days after school started.

"I didn't factor in a blizzard," Philip told my mom. I could tell she was appalled.

On their trip, Hector had found a book in a cardboard box at a library sale in Idaho about the guy who'd invented criminal profiling. "He's better than Holmes," he said. From a corpse, he could tell the age of the killer, that he lived with his parents and had a stutter. "A lot of murderers have speech impediments, it turns out."

"Eli stammers," I admitted, because Hector already knew. He was beginning to make me nervous. Sometimes I wished I hadn't told him all this; Hector got so into things. In kindergarten he'd eaten bugs with an insane relish. Right away, this minute, he wanted to haul the RadioShack machine up from the basement and hear what it'd recorded.

From two hours of listening, our ears to the tiny speaker, all we learned was that Eli had returned the father-son mitts my mom had sent for Christmas. "I could never use leather mitts," he said. The animals! Of course. "Keep them for the twins. But Timmy really likes that rainbow maker." We still hadn't met his kid.

"Does he know it's from me?" she asked.

"I tell him it's from my friend Irene."

They talked about his sick cat, its medicine, and his trips to the veterinarian.

I kept reminding Hector, he'd bought us a whole sofa. It was expensive.

"So on our trip," Hector said, "I learned to drive."

"Cool," I said.

"If you consider a frozen highway cool. My dad miscalculated where the hotel would be. If it weren't for the food your mom and Marge packed, we would have starved to death. There was nowhere to stop. One night, he skidded on ice and almost killed a moose. That was when he taught me to steer."

"But he was right next to you, right?"

"When he wasn't asleep. Can we go to your basement?"

I didn't want to reattach the wires in the dark; I reminded him that the line came in in a corner.

"Can I wash my clothes, though?"

"Oh. Sure." I didn't ask why. But I went to my dresser and opened the bottom drawer. He took some sweats and a pullover and changed in the bathroom. My clothes were enormous on him. Then he pulled a bunch of crumpled-up underwear and T-shirts from his backpack. He never wore socks. I didn't ask about the washer/dryer at his house. It must have been broken. I didn't ask that night or the next time it happened. It became a thing we didn't talk about. I knew how to do laundry, thanks to Eli, but just as I was about to show him, Hector started setting the knobs. He sprinkled on detergent. All that year Hector brought over his clothes and washed them in our basement.

....

The next Friday, Hector wanted to check the Mims's drawer. He found scraps of paper mixed in with her treasures: my sisters' baby teeth and my childhood suspenders. By now I recognized Eli's penmanship.

I want to get you a tattoo, administered by a hip lesbian, with your metric.

I have known you, Irene Adler.
Yours is the last face I'll see.

I was glad to see she'd kept my suspenders; they hadn't gone to the little Lee.

Timothy, its name was. Timothy Roy Lee.

"But did she get a tattoo?"

"What do *you* think? You've seen my mom."

"Maybe it's somewhere private."

My stomach lurched, an involuntary gulp. I didn't want to even go there. "No," I said. That would be like branding a person. It would hurt. Why would she endure that? I was pretty sure she wasn't branded. I hoped not. The worst feelings I knew at that time came from momentary glimpses of humiliation in my parents.

"He doesn't have a scar," Hector said, "and she doesn't have a tattoo."

"Enough about the scar. You heard that doctor. *They go in through the nose!*"

"But aren't you worried about her?" Hector asked. All of a sudden, I saw again: he loved her. He always had. I pitied him, because my mom loved Hector, I mean she *loved* Hector, he was her favorite Rabbit, but it was nothing like the way it was for me.

The Mims must have found some obscure guy in rural Canada who made 100 percent leather-free baseball mitts. I was sure they were also 100 percent more expensive than Wilson and Rawlings, but she must have ordered them anyway because they arrived in a box on our porch one day. She sent them off to DC. And that time they didn't come back.

48 · An Open Laptop

Hector wanted to call the PI again, but the sofa, large and so clean-angled that it made the room look modern, satisfied me. The house seemed intelligent now, the way a face could change with the right pair of eyeglasses. Before the couch, I'd never noticed our windows; they were square-paned, cased in dark metal. Often, when I walked in, a book lay tented on the sofa with a laptop open. I caught Hector reading on the Mims's screen.

I really do love you, Eli had keyboarded, on January 11.

And from her:

I want to be married by the time I'm forty-five.

She'd told me she wanted to be married again someday. She'd said that barefoot in the driver's seat, holding her knees. Her music— *I've got secondhand blues, I've got secondhand blues*—on the CD player. "She turns forty-five this summer," I said. Marriage again. I supposed that was when people bought presents like couches.

"He can't be after money," Hector said. "Does she have anything else? Like something she invented?"

I shrugged. "No. Marge is the one with all the patents."

Then Hector told me that his mom had gone to Baja with Surferdude and come back with a ring. It was an old ring, but it wasn't Surferdude's mother's or anything. He'd bought it used in a shop on Via De La Paz. So it probably came from the finger of somebody dead or divorced, he said. I wondered again what had happened to my mom's ring. One day when she was out, I'd have to check her jewelry drawer to see if it was still there. I didn't want to do it now, in front of Hector.

Those months of the New Year, I was happy. This house seemed like our house now. The Mims and Eli might have been talking about marriage, but that still seemed far in the future. Hector stayed over more. He slept in my beanbag chair. We were getting to be like a couple when it came to money. I paid for everything, and I was the one who worried. Hector could be frivolous. I noticed, though, that he seemed always hungry. After dinner at our house, he sometimes stood with the refrigerator door open just looking at the food. My grades needed help. I made him slow down and show me his Latin declensions and the steps of his math. It was a patient time. He read his book about criminal profiling while I copied his homework. After school, we worked at FLAGBTU, where I was becoming the de facto leader. Once, the doorbell rang and flowers arrived for the Mims—not from Eli, though, from my dad.

All that time, Hector wanted to call Ben Orion but I staved him off. The couch had tamped down my doubts. I couldn't get why Hector was still antsy. Nothing new had happened. Eli wasn't even around because of his cat. But Hector called the guy again anyway. He couldn't help himself. This time, the PI said that he worked at home, and we could come there a week from Friday. When Hector told me all this, we had our first real fight. I felt like I'd end up having to pay. I always did. The PI was supposed to be my Christmas gift, but Hector didn't have any money. I didn't blame him for that, but he had to be more realistic. We fought for a long time in my room. I was winning. He had no logic. Then finally he said, "You don't think your mom seems depressed?"

And that was like the sound of a distant bell ringing. He told me she didn't seem herself anymore. It rained the next day, and the Mims went outside for a walk. I glanced at her tying on her scarf, knotting the triangle under her chin. Her face looked wrong.

So that Friday we rode bikes to the PI's house, Hector on mine, me on my sister's Sting-Ray, standing-up pedaling, pulling the wobbles into a straight line. Ben Orion lived in our neighborhood. That seemed weird because by now I understood what male work resulted in which LA zip code (sorry, Mom, wherever you are, I know you hate me saying it, but it's true, it actually is), and our neighborhood, near the beach, backed by mountains, was the geographic consequence of the Industry. Our old house stood on a street all Industry or family money. Where we lived now had younger people. Our pediatrician had moved in two streets over. Ben Orion's address belonged to a wooden condominium, a block below our main street. His unit was on the ground floor. By his door, he had a wooden box planted with neat rows of lettuces and a thin-branched, white-flowering tree.

He showed us into his living room and offered Cokes. This was exactly the way I wanted my house to be when I grew up: a tight couch, a coffee table, and two chairs. It felt *male*. I heard wind in chimes somewhere we couldn't see.

Is he gay? Hector mouthed.

Ben returned with our Cokes in glass glasses, each with a straw, the paper scrunched on top, like in a restaurant.

"So your office is here?" Hector said. "On the Internet, it gives an address on Montana."

"That's just a mailbox," he said. "My car's my office."

"I like your place," Hector said. "How do you make so much money?"

Only Hector could get away with saying that. I flashed on his laundry. This house was better than his.

Ben Orion grinned. "More than half my business is background checks for reality TV shows."

"They want the real people to be actually real?" I said.

"No actors, no liars. No one who's going to embarrass them."

"Do they pay a lot for that?" Hector asked.

"Depends on what they need. If it's *The Bachelorette* and they're marrying him, they need more than a show where they're just competing for money. Some just need to know that they're not criminals. But figure it's two hundred ninety-five times a year, three hundred eighty dollars to six hundred a pop. Adds up."

"Do you get to go to the shows?" I asked.

"I've gone to a couple over the years. When we started with *Big Brother*, we used to be on the set."

"Do you have a partner?" I asked, since he kept saying *we*. Hector kicked me. He thought I was asking was he gay. But I didn't mean partner-partner; I meant for work.

"My sister. She lives in the Valley. She does most of the background stuff from home, on the computer. And then I hire part-timers when I need them."

Maybe he'd hire us. Then we wouldn't have to pay him.

The PI took out a notebook. His front teeth overlapped in a handsome way.

"So, what can I do for you?"

Hector talked this time. He talked about how Eli hadn't been here for months because of a sick cat. Hector said he hadn't been calling as much either. I hadn't thought of that, but when he said it, it was true.

"Animals are his thing," I said. "He says they're what he cares about most."

Even as I was saying that, though, I thought, If his cat is dying and he loves his cat that much, why doesn't he call all the time about it?

"So, Eli Lee is his name," the PI said, writing it down. "Do you know his birthday? Or his middle name? And how about the ex-wife?"

I knew Eli's birthday. November 10. I said I could find out his middle name. (I knew the initial was J.) Though my mom hadn't remembered where he was from, I did. *Lakewood.* The ex-wife's name was Jean. Jean Lee. I'd listened to some talk once about her having taken Eli's name because she was making airline reservations and realized how much easier it would be with one name, not two. The Mims had snorted.

She and Sare had both kept their original names.

"Do you know what state they divorced in? I can run that check pretty simple. Course, all that'll tell us is when he divorced. Not if he's some kind of womanizer."

He sure didn't *look* like a womanizer. Wouldn't you have to be taller for that? I told them I'd overheard Eli asking if he kissed her okay, after he kissed her for the first time. It was like what I would do. If I ever kissed someone.

Ben Orion said, "That doesn't square with his having had an affair. Didn't you tell me he'd cheated on the wife?"

I hadn't thought of that. It *didn't* square exactly. But Eli was a nerd! I remembered him in a turtleneck and her in her math-teacher clothes, *caroling.* The word *womanizer* didn't square with that activity either.

"Maybe you guys ought to trust your mom to handle this."

"Do you ever find out people are innocent?" I was remembering the guy with the young girlfriend, who went out to dinner with *her* girlfriends.

"Lot of the time," he said. "We have a client, a celebrity, lives out in Malibu. A gay man. Around fifty." I looked at Hector. A gay man wouldn't say *a gay man.* "There's a woman dentist in Glendale who thinks he's the father of her kids. And these kids are one hundred percent Asian."

"The Malibu guy's not?"

"Jewish," he said.

"So she's cuckoo bananas," Hector said.

"Well, about this one thing. She's a successful dentist, on the faculty of USC dental school."

A breeze swept through. I felt calm in this room. "Did she ever go out with the guy? Like, before?"

"She's never met him. We've tailed her; she doesn't drive west of the 405. I've told him that. But she e-mails him three a.m., four a.m."

"And he pays you?" I said.

"Jeez, we've got an actress who was in an abusive relationship with a guy nineteen years ago. He went to jail in Arizona for a drug charge. When he got out, he stayed there and started a construction business. He married, had kids. But she's scared he'll come back looking for her. So we fly out three times a year. We're watching his kids grow up. They're teenagers now."

"Do you think he's on the up-and-up?" Hector asked.

"Oh, yeah, this guy is clean, we pull his taxes, everything. He turned his life around. Every year, I ask her, Do you really want to keep doing this? I don't like to take her money. Sending people out there, putting them up in hotels, it's expensive. Three hundred an hour per car. Two cars. We gotta rent the cars. Two shifts a day."

"You need two cars to follow somebody?"

"Well, the FBI uses seven. Her career isn't . . . you know, actresses, as they get older. But she always says one more year."

These stories depressed me. Love ruined people's lives, the way our parents said drugs could. I didn't believe it about drugs. Before we left, Hector took out money. I didn't know he had any. Forty-two dollars: a twenty, a five, and crumpled ones. I gave mine: I had eighty, not half the amount it would have been if the Mims had let us sell soup. I started to say he should just do a hundred and twenty dollars' worth for us, but he pushed the curled-up bills to our side of the table.

"Keep your money. I'll run a few checks. I've got the software. Most of these databases don't have fees. Plus you've got me curious. More will be revealed."

See? Hector looked at me. People always did want to help Hector. I wasn't the only one. Why did the PI bother with us? Hector didn't wonder, and the attention felt natural, even to me, although we'd rarely gotten it before. That was the thing about attention when it finally came: it never seemed amazing. It felt, if anything, maybe just a little *late*. We mostly stayed under the radar at school. Ben Orion didn't have kids; that was pretty obvious. He wasn't married, he said when I asked him. He grinned. *Not yet.*

Then he complained about women. "This younger generation now is so antipolice."

"But you're not a cop." That was Hector's way of reconciling the fact that we were antipolice, too.*

"I was a reserve officer. You go through the academy; you just don't get paid. Five months. Twenty hours a week. You learn all the criminal justice stuff. Self-defense. Firearms. Driving a police car on wet tracks."

"Do you have a gun?" I asked.

"I do."

"What kind?"

"Glock nine millimeter."

"Have you ever used it?"

"No," he said. "I've never had to use it. If I'm going out at night, I'll have it in the car with me. But I got a whole lecture the other night from these two girls at R+D Kitchen. They hate cops. And all those same people love the firemen. Everyone loves the firemen."

49 · Not Looking

But I didn't google for Eli's middle name. I didn't ask the Mims in what state he filed divorce papers. I tried to forget the whole thing and stay on the lit, apparent side of my life. The rest had been my twisted imagination, I decided. Hector asked me about it a few times, and I blew him off.

All that spring, I strained toward simple pop melodies: I kept my earbuds in, listening to *Pet Sounds* while my mom and Sare complained in the kitchen. Simon's dad had enrolled in a pastry-making

---

* *Though not nearly as antipolice as we would get. Then it was just style. The substance(s) came later.*

class, Sare said. Now he baked all the family's desserts. "*That's* the kind of thing I'm talking about."

These were notes I'd heard all my life.

They lowered their voices to talk about Philip. Marge had gotten him a class to teach through UCLA extension. He was really trying to finish his dissertation now, the Mims said. He'd started running with Marge, but she'd hired a trainer anyway. Philip was offended; he couldn't believe what the guy charged. "But the trainer gives me little head rubs when he stretches me out!" Marge had told my mom. Sare asked if Kat still had the boyfriend the kids hated. My mom said yes, but she didn't know why they hated him so much. Even I thought they hated him too hard.

Marge had asked my mom to collaborate with her on a complex system model. The math of crime. My mom had said she'd try it. She'd never worked with someone else like that before. She thought it would be good to talk to someone about the steps, though. It might help her confidence.

I heard them like a chorus.

And tennis started again. On April 1 I poured fake blood in the bathtub and lay head askew. The Mims came to find me because I was late for school and yanked open the shower curtain.

Once, Hector was over when Sare said, "Is it my imagination or is Eli coming less?"

"The cat's still sick," the Mims said. "I think it's dying."

"Can't it hurry up?" Sare said.

The Mims didn't laugh.

I knew Hector's expressions. Sometimes it was hard to believe what I thought, without him seeping through. I started to sit at the big tables at lunch, so I wouldn't be alone with him. I invited other guys, too, Friday nights, but in the few years since we'd had the Jocular Rabid Rabbits' blowouts we'd become less popular. The other guys went to malls now where they met up with girls and they didn't invite us along.

I found Boop Two curled up on the floor. "What's up? You okay?" I nudged her with my shoe.

"I finished a book, and they didn't even notice or get me anything."

"Well, they probably noticed."

"You ask Daddy. He couldn't even guess the name of the book."

What could I say? She was probably right. "I'll give you something," I offered.

"That's okay," she said. "You don't have anything I want."

"Yeah, I do, come here." I pointed to my shelves. "You can pick any book."

"They're all too hard for me." She looked like she was about to fall off a cliff, so I opened a Coke can I'd bought from an online spy shop and took out a twenty.

"Really?" she said. "Thanks."

That save reinforced my already-strong belief in the universal language of money.

At my dad's house, I found another letter slid under his modernist wall-sized glass doors late at night. After Holland, we never met the women he dated or even learned their names. But he took us out to dinner with guys he worked with.

"These are the stages of a Hollywood career," he said while we studied the tall menus.

Who's Harrison Ford?
Get me Harrison Ford!
I want someone *like* Harrison Ford.
Get me a *young* Harrison Ford!
Who's Harrison Ford?

He said his career was at the *Get me a* young *Harrison Ford* stage. One of the other guys had to go in for a pitch on a thick book. The producer had had it for years; he'd never read it, but kept it around because it was the perfect size for calf stretches.

. . . .

My mom answered the phone. "We're just sitting down to dinner, may I take a message?" If she'd been a dog with ears that shot up, it couldn't have been more obvious: the pedophile terror. She asked, trying to sound offhand, "Who's Ben Orion?"

"A guy at our school." It was the first lie that big I ever told her.

I was furious at Hector. How did the guy get my number? Hector must have called him without telling me. "We can't have a detective!" I yelled at him. "There isn't even anyplace he can call us back without getting me in trouble. We don't have money!" Hector thought maybe we could give him Dylan Land's number. Dylan Land was a kid who had two cell phones because his parents gave him everything he wanted. Maybe he'd lend us one.

"Your parents are divorced, man!" Dylan told us in school. "They owe you guys phones. You go to a psychologist, tell him you're getting a divorce, and the first thing they'll say is *Get the kid a cell phone*. Your parents probably went to divorce shrinks."

"I highly doubt it," Hector said.

I tried that on my dad Monday night, his night. I said, "You owe me a cell phone."

"I beg your pardon," he said. My dad made a point of not spoiling us. And except when it was convenient for him, he really didn't. Hector knew better than to try Philip. Philip thought cell phones were one of the many things wrong with the modern world.

When tennis got rained out, I sat in Dr. Sally's waiting room again, reading my homework as the Grateful Dead crooned in my ears. I remembered how I'd once heard the two women giddy, laughing as they plotted to placate Eli, when he was in such a hurry. When did that stop? Maybe it hadn't. Maybe I just wasn't letting myself listen. I didn't believe that, though. Something had changed. For a long time, I hadn't wanted Eli to move in—not yet. I'd been not wanting it, not wanting it, and then *poof*: all of a sudden, he was gone.

Because his cat was sick.

The guy with shoulder-length gray hair who sat at the desk in Neverland Comics offered me a summer job. I told my dad on his night. He stood up from the table and made a call, then returned, saying, "Your mother and I have decided it isn't a good idea."

They were actually insane. When I pressed him, he said, "It's not the healthiest environment. I've seen a lot of lone, sad-looking men in there." He actually used the word *lone*. I had to call Hector. In eighth grade, Hector had dragged around saying, *I'm a lone lorn creature. And everything goes contrary with me.*

"What are you laughing about, Miles?" my dad said.

I knew how this would go. When my mom picked me up, they talked for a long time, standing up in his kitchen.

"You're such homophobes. I mean, come on, guys, I'm fifteen years old. No men at Neverland are going to *molest* me. I can politely decline."

"Well, we didn't mean only men," my mom fumbled. "You could be approached by a woman, too."

This was so lame.

"And this woman, what would her measurements be?" I rounded my hands over my chest. My mom started laughing. She couldn't help herself. But they still said no.

Finally, Hector ambushed me. "Eli *James* Lee. November tenth, 1963. I found him in the American Academy of Sciences. Now we just need the divorce state."

I felt a headache starting, a small pulsing growth at the back of my neck. "Can we give this a rest? We're leaving in a week." For the first time, Hector was going to my camp. Last November, we'd put down that we wanted the same cabin, but now I yearned to be by myself, with guys I didn't know. "We might even see Eli," I added. Every year, one parent and I flew east, stayed overnight, then rented a car and drove up to Maine. This year was her turn. She'd probably invited Eli along.

The next morning, my camp stuff was spread out over the kitchen floor. The Mims stood checking off a list.

I felt poignant for life passing. A Boop swung outside on the tire. Summer came full on, and even in our happiness, all of us home, there was a quality of waiting. The Mims's contentment rested on a belief that Eli was coming, coming with a dog, coming with time for family walks after dinner. *You and your family romance.* Could she go our whole lives like this, waiting, believing in something sweet? Was it so different from all those people who went to church once a week and maintained a precarious faith in heaven? I didn't know. I really didn't know. My eyes hurt on the back, inside my head.

I still had that message from Ben Orion I hadn't returned. As the Mims ironed labels into my T-shirts, I said, "You know how I put down to be in the same cabin with Hector? I kind of want to be on my own now."

"Don't you think he might need you, his first year there?"

I assured her Hector was fine, and she made the call.*

But even while I was avoiding Hector and the PI, I harassed her. Why was I busting her balls? I'd always been a know-it-all. Now I didn't want to know and hated not knowing and took it out on her. I asked if we were going to see Eli in the East, and it turned out that he didn't plan to be home. He was bringing his son *here* on vacation.

I picked a fight between them; I knew, because I heard part of it. "But I told you the dates months ago," she said. "Why did you plan your trip for then?" It was true: he knew her schedule. He'd memorized *my* schedule, for crying in the bucket. Unlike certain fathers.

Eli told her it was the equinox, and he loved that, he loved that light. That was when he'd wanted to take his son to the Monterey Bay Aquarium. So we'd miss him in both the East and California.

* *I never suspected.*

....

The day before we left, Ben Orion called again. That time I answered. He said Hector had found something. I felt ganged-up on. I was still ringing from the luck of my having been near the phone when it was him. And all Hector had was a middle name, I thought. But I rode my bike over to the PI's place anyway. He answered the door in sock feet and led me to a room full of file cabinets my height and a computer. Hector was sitting on an old crushed-leather couch. *What was he doing here before me?* I wanted to think about other things. A petition was circulating to get a proposition abolishing same-sex marriage on the ballot.

Hector handed Ben Orion a sheet of paper. "We still don't know the divorce state. Probably Virginia, though, right? That's where DC is?"

Ben Orion scribbled a note. He had glasses on, and I saw his eyes sketch over the paper with finicky hunger. He looked at us. "Hector found an article the other day. Eli's ex-wife or whatever she is . . . there's a Jean Lee who writes *romance books*. I went to the bookstore to buy one of her productions, but they didn't have any. I ordered her latest one, and it just came in." He handed over the package. "She probably makes some kind of money with these."

I slowly opened the bag and took the small paperback out. It was called *The Other Woman* and had a drawing of a lady in a long dress in front of a castle. I turned the book over. There was a postage-stamp-sized author picture, and it was her, the woman I'd seen in Pasadena. I'd only seen her from the back, but it was this same hair, flipped up at the bottom. I studied the expression in the tiny photo, the thin eyebrows lifted, frantically friendly like a clown. I didn't tell Hector or the PI.

I turned to the dedication page. It read: *For C, who made writing less lonely.*

"It's not dedicated to Eli," Hector said. "I guess that's good."

"I'll run the background check," Ben Orion said. "Maybe we'll have something by the time you get home. Just forget about this and have fun at camp, 'kay?"

"Did you go to college?" I asked him.

"Yes. I have a degree in criminology from Sacramento State," he said. "It's a pretty easy major. It's all retired cops, telling stories."

I wondered if Sacramento State was an okay school. Maybe I could go there. Questions jumped in my mind. If it was a decent college, then why didn't Ben Orion have women falling in love with him the way my dad did? I couldn't say that to Hector, though, because I was pretty sure Philip hadn't had a date since Kat moved out. He might never have a date again in his whole life.

"Did you always know you wanted to be a PI?" Hector asked.

"It's all I ever wanted to do. I used to say, '*Mannix* is responsible for my career.' "

"Do you have lots of cases like this?" I asked.

"Not really. These marital problems, boyfriend-girlfriend cases, they're not my thing. Too messy. And I don't take cold calls usually. We don't advertise."

"So what kind of cases do you like?" Hector asked. "Besides reality shows."

"I like the security stuff."

"What's that?" I asked.

"For me, a legitimate stalker, that's a good case. We do threat assessment. Some celebrities keep us on retainer. They have fan mail services. And the fan mail company will send something over if it looks suspicious. They'll say, 'This guy says he's coming out to LA in two weeks.' For a few people, we get all the fan mail directly here." He pulled open a file drawer. "These are all fan letters. The great majority of fans are not a problem. They'll just send letters. Only a small percentage are dangerous. It's the ones that just got divorced or lost custody or were fired from their job. They tell you a lot in their letters. Sometimes they write up and down in the margins. Ninety-nine percent are just pen pals. But a few are mentally ill."

"And what do they do then?"

"Well, they come out here and try to meet the person. They'll go to a hotel; they'll rent a car and drive to the celebrity's home."

"How do they know where it is?"

"Well, we try and make that hard, but these days you can find the addresses pretty easy on the Internet."

"And what do you do then, call the police and arrest them?"

"You can't arrest them yet. Unless they're actually trespassing on the property, they haven't done anything. You usually don't want to go with a restraining order. We increase the security on the celebrity, and we follow the person. The goal is for them to realize *I can't reach my star* and go home. Then we keep on them. Every six months we check to see if they're back at work. If they have a relationship. If they have friends. If they're a loner and go into gun shops, then you worry."

"Wow."

"Have you heard of Gavin de Becker? De Becker's office has almost four hundred people. At any given time, they're working on three hundred stalking cases. LAPD has less. De Becker's time is billed like an attorney's. No one knows where he lives."

I hadn't heard of this guy, but I could tell Ben Orion looked up to him and envied him a little. My dad had a few men like that. I knew their names. I only had Hector. I looked up to him, but I didn't envy him, really. I knew, even though he was way smarter than I was, I'd still rather be me. I pinched a roll of my fat.*

As we left, I looked back once at Ben Orion's neat living room. There was one framed picture of buildings and a woman in a

---

* *You say that even fat, you would have still rather been you. Well, I would have rather been you, too. That was one of my problems then. I wanted your house and your mom who cooked and plenty of money.*

kimono walking over a bridge, holding an umbrella in slanting rain.

Hector carried *The Other Woman*. "I suppose we should read this," he said. "You want a crack at it first? It probably contains evidence."

"You're the reader," I said. He and his dad had listened to *The Odyssey* on the car ride back from Idaho.

"Ben's a good-looking guy," I said when we were alone.

"I gue-ess."

"Have you ever heard of Sacramento State?"

"No," Hector said. "I've heard of Sacramento."

I remembered Eli's hand on my back when he told me he was in love with my mother. Did he sneak his ex-wife and kid to Pasadena for a visit without telling us? But why? I was still wondering that when Hector's dad picked him up. He told us about collaborations in Shakespeare. "A guy would say, I'll do acts one and three. Why don't you do two and four?" There was one guy, he said, who just wrote clowns. Philip taught at extension, but he didn't get benefits and earned less than two thousand dollars a class. "I asked the students, If Juliet was your friend, what would you advise?" he said. "And they all shouted, *Go for the Other Guy! Go for Paris!*"

Then, after they left and I was alone, I thought our life was over, though I couldn't have said why. I took out the garbage without being asked and just stood in the alley. It was a tender evening sky, blue with gray clouds, the way skies were supposed to look but didn't most of the time here. Something I'd believed in more than I knew was over. My mother's hope. Our good future. The happy ending, but to what? I'd thought Eli would help us afford our life. He'd said he would. Now what? So much we'd imagined and counted on . . .

All of a sudden, it seemed our family had been lying. We'd been trying to be this great divorced family when really our lives, like the lives of any kids who were the products of failure, were coming out worse. Like being illegitimate. Or adopted. We'd been churning fast, trying to convince people. Probably nobody believed us anyway. That's why the Boops were so obviously disturbed. Everyone knew it was better not to be a *divorce kid* or a bastard or adopted. Schools like Cottonwoods existed for us. People like our parents sent kids there to be educated in the art of pity. IS IT TRUE? IS IT KIND? IS IT NECESSARY?

I tried to conjure my dad as an antidote. Sare had once called him my mother's Prozac. Maybe he would get remarried, I thought, and have a whole nother family. An unbroken one. His way of dealing with divorce had been comedy.

You can see my progress on my Amazon bills, he'd said. *In October, when I moved out, the bill listed eleven self-help books. By April, the statement had no books at all.*

Only a 52-inch plasma television.

Still, as starkly as night lurched, morning rang back morning in our house: the scrape of the whisk against the bowl; the Mims calling, *Come on, slugabeds;* Boop Two's eager-to-please *I AM up, Mommy.*

We'd received a Belgian waffle maker from Marge, and my mom stood pouring batter, the glass jar of maple syrup knocking against the pot of boiling water.

I tried again what I'd tried before: to forget. I thought, Even if *this* Jean Lee is Eli's ex-wife, what does that prove?

I left it all in California: my sister's reading, our funny, abrupt father, our potentially dismal future, and, unfortunately, the thing plugged into the jack downstairs. I'd meant to dismantle the machine but I forgot. I thought of those wires a few times on the way to camp. I considered drawing a diagram for Boop Two to take it apart but that seemed risky. The Mims could intercept the letter.

She talked on the phone with Eli as we drove through New England. He directed us to a place that had great caramel ice cream, saying, Turn right, now right again. He stayed on the phone until we found it.

I thought of things. "Do we *invite* Eli's brother for Christmas?"

"Yes," she said. "But Hugo won't travel."

"They put us in separate cabins," Hector said when I finally saw him at camp, sitting on a top bunk, his legs swinging. He jumped down. We were the only ones there. From under clothes in a cubby, he pulled out the book. We flipped through to find sex scenes. There weren't many. Raoul "entered his wife tenderly." He "made love wildly." That was to the mistress who, in a hilarious touch, admired the wife. Everyone admired the wife.

"Artistic license!" Hector said. "But the mistress has a misshapen head. Your mom's head's normal."

"Anyway, this was probably about the affair he had. Not my mom," I said. It seemed to be about a woman the husband worked with. That was like Eli's affair.

I wished then that we were in the same cabin. Hector seemed disappointed. He assumed the camp had just separated us. I didn't tell him I'd asked. And he didn't make friends, really, with the guys in his cabin. I saw him alone, walking around or sitting against a tree trunk, reading. Maine camp wasn't really his thing. That was the only time he went.*

The Other Woman was a strange story. The husband loved the wife but he was in an affair, like a drug addiction. He wanted to quit. He tried. Then one day he and his mistress got attacked by

* *I didn't know until I read this thing that you were why we didn't end up in the same cabin. That was pretty sucky. And you got away with it. But you didn't have to feel sorry for me for not making friends with those thugs. I didn't mind being alone. I liked reading.*

a gang. He handed over his wallet and she gave her purse, but she wouldn't take off her grandmother's necklace. He tried to defend her, and they both ended up injured. On the pavement, in pain, he wanted his wife. Only his wife.

Malc sent us a package of fifteen big Milky Way bars. We sat on Hector's bunk, eating them. Fifteen was enough for one cabin, not quite for two, so we kept them for ourselves, hiding them under Hector's clothes.

"What are we going to do when we go home?" Hector said. It seemed like a big question. I told him we had to get through my mom's birthday. Sare had planned a party.

On our last day of camp, Hector wanted to wash his clothes. I helped him sort stuff. We had the whole laundry room to ourselves, and we used all four machines. We folded and hunted down every sock's wife. He was probably the only kid in the camp who was going home with a duffel full of clean clothes.

Mine stank so much my dad had the camp UPS it.

50 · Wiretapping

I was home two days before I remembered the device. When I did, I shot up from the table and skidded to the basement, where I found the thing making a ticking noise. I shoved it into the old file cabinet where my mom kept extra school supplies, like muffling an about-to-detonate bomb.

"Miles?" she called from the kitchen. "Come back. We're starting!"

I carried it up late at night after everyone was asleep and hid it under my bed. But I couldn't keep Hector off of it for long. He played it and turned the volume up when he heard Eli's voice.

I never thought I'd have a fifteen-year-old stepson.

Eli made that sound like an important responsibility.

We heard the Mims sigh. A jewel in her hand. A great hope for her, a correction.

Maybe he meant it. I wanted to forget the whole business, I thought wildly, and throw the machine out.

Eli complained that Sare had assigned him to bring a cheese platter to the party. He kept saying *expensive* cheese *platter*, with spin on the word *cheese*. But it was her forty-fifth birthday. Shouldn't he be bringing *at least* a cheese platter? It was a joke, I supposed, but also mean, something my mom accused a lot of my jokes of being.

Sentences got cut off on the machine, as if we were listening to bits of conversations.

Eli said, *Call me back.*

Is this better? she asked. *I've got to get somebody out from the phone company.*

The phone *company!* I mouthed to Hector, forgetting that this was a recording and that they couldn't hear us.

Are you really moving here?

Yes, he said. *You know that.*

Every night I fall asleep imagining my head on your shoulder. Could you please hurry?

I'm trying to, he said.

Another time, she asked, *How much can you contribute?*

He paused, then his voice sounded squeezed. *Between five and seven thousand a month*, he choked out. Between five and seven thousand dollars! More than all the *I love you*s, that convinced me. The thing about the cheese platter must have been a joke. Even though he kept saying it. We could stop, I decided. No more spying. Eli turned out all right in the end. Relief coursed through my body. Then, as if there was a God, the Mims said, *I can barely hear you. I made an appointment with AT&T.*

"We can't use this anymore!" I said to Hector. "The phone guy's coming. For all we know, our machine caused the static."

That night I thought more about *The Other Woman*. It seemed like the truth was that Eli had cheated on his wife, and then, eventually, he'd left her. She was probably sad. She'd written her book how she wanted it all to have turned out. I felt sorry for her. I didn't like that. I didn't like it that he was with us now but that first he'd hurt someone else.

The next morning Hector talked to my mom in the kitchen while I took a shower. When I emerged, he had a strange face. He'd found out the divorce state. The Mims had asked how his mom was doing and he told her okay, except his parents were having the longest divorce in American history and that they blamed it on the state of California. Then he asked her if she knew people who'd gotten divorces in other states, and she told him Eli was divorced in Wisconsin. Hector had IM'd Ben Orion from my computer.

I groaned. "No! I'm done with this. Eli's okay."

But Ben Orion IM'd back: *Glad to hear it. I ran Virginia and came up dry.*

I didn't let myself think too far. When Philip picked up Hector, he told me that in Shakespeare's time, tennis balls were stuffed with beard hair.

I want to be married again someday.

Now she was forty-five.

Sare had sent out a group calendar; they'd scheduled the party around Eli, delaying because of his cat's grave condition.

"Maybe he'll propose the night of the party," I said to Hector.

I had my first full headache; my brain alive and throbbing, a thousand worms growing inside, pushing through one another.

The party would be easy to crash. We planned a sleepover at Charlie's. But then, at the last minute, he called to say that we had to do it at my house; his mom decided we'd be in the way. We couldn't wheedle Sare. And I didn't want to tell Charlie much. He was the prime suspect for ratting about soup selling. And without explaining, we couldn't make a big case for his house, except for sisters.

"They're pretty harmless, aren't they? I mean, what do they even *do* these days?" Charlie only had an older brother.

"They make *shows*," Hector said. "With feather boas. That shed."

Charlie didn't really hang out with us anymore. He attracted girls just standing still without doing anything. His chest and arms showed actual muscles. He reminded us his mom *liked* my sisters—they were her goddaughters—but maybe we could sleep at his house if we found someplace else to go before, say, ten. It ended up that Charlie's brother, Reed, was driving to Westwood and could give us a lift.

I opened the front door and saw Eli's two shoes, parallel, the way I had a hundred times. Maybe a bad person was entering our house, the thought flickered momentarily. He had his same grin as always, seeing me, with the ears sticking out. But bad people didn't think they were bad, probably. I remembered Eli's voice choking out that he'd give us seven thousand dollars a month. That made my mind close, like the first taste of sweet. I was aware of keeping my thoughts between blinders.

Charlie's father, Dale, had given Sare a necklace for her forty-fifth birthday. Dylan Land's mom had surprised his stepfather with a convertible for his fiftieth. Most of my friends had families like my dad's: everybody dressed up to celebrate big birthdays and anniversaries in the banquet rooms of hotels. My mom had one brother who still lived in Michigan. They talked on the phone sometimes, but he would never be here for something like this. He didn't know her friends. Marge was coming to the party at least. My mom's voice belled, listing the names. She still thought she was happy.

She and Eli disappeared into her closet. She came out looking better than she ever had, wearing the dress Eli had picked out for her in the Pasadena thrift store and big clear earrings. My dad had bought her a coat once that he showed us in a magazine, but now it seemed he'd been ordering clothes for a standard-issue store dummy. If Eli was a monster, he was a monster who understood my mother's body. He found a beauty the rest of us hadn't seen. I shivered, thinking why.

I have known *you, Irene Adler,* he'd written on that scrap in her drawer.

My father had been enamored; maybe he still was, but not that way. *There may be other people better-looking,* he'd once complimented her, *but no one smarter.* He'd meant that, and it was true. But she knew she was smart, so his saying so was just adding another penny to a pile of coins. Maybe she'd always wished to be beautiful and didn't quite dare to, because she could tell that people didn't say she was and more attention was given to other women, but she still had a frail hope that there'd been a mistake and she was after all. That was why, from years of living on intelligence alone, when Eli told her she already had what she hadn't been able even to admit she dreamed of—that must have acted like a drug, flooding her with irresistible relief. Boop Two wished she was prettier, too; she'd never say it, but I could tell. Maybe every single female, smart or not, couldn't help wanting that.

"Personal shopper," Eli kept saying, as if he'd found his true designation.

"Sometime before school starts we should take Timmy and the girls to Disneyland," she said. "I have those fast passes I won at the auction."

"Sounds great," he said, like a period.

I thought tonight he really might propose.

We squished into the back of Reed's car. I'd never been to Westwood without a parent before. I thought maybe we'd see a movie, but we ended up just following Reed and his friends into stores that sold candles and stuffed toys and electronic games and T-shirts with patented characters on them. The point seemed to be to run into people they knew but to pretend these collisions were a complete and not particularly desired surprise. They walked ahead of us, but when they stopped to talk to other kids we caught up. They acknowledged us with minimal shoulder dips. Reed bought us each a burrito. Near an alley, two girls stood in dresses and platform heels, one of them bending over, her hair almost touching the ground. She seemed to be barfing. Then I saw that it was Ella. "Hey, Ella," I said, and started toward her, my hands in my pockets, but one of the older guys reached around from behind and put his hand on her belly. That made me sick. She gave a little wave to me, her hand by her side. She didn't look happy or even okay. On the way back from Westwood I worried about her.

At Charlie's, we hung out in the TV room. I set my sleeping bag close to the door, so I could watch and still hear the adults. Reed put on *The Godfather*, which my dad continued to say I couldn't see yet.

"What if he proposes?" I whispered to Hector.

Reed's phone kept ringing. He finally answered. "What? I don't know. Call ya later." He had a girlfriend Sare hated, I knew from the wiretap, but now it seemed that Reed hated her, too.

From under the door, I heard Marge's long, rambling toast. I felt protective of Marge with Eli here. She thought they were friends. She started to tell a math joke. *What do you get if you cross a mosquito with a mountain climber?* When she said the answer—*You can't cross a vector with a scalar*—there was a little wave of polite awkward laughter because I'm sure nobody but my mom understood what she was talking about, but even that emboldened her. *How many number theorists does it take to change a lightbulb?* Oh, no, not a lightbulb joke! I wished she'd asked me. *This is not known, but it's conjectured to be an elegant prime.*

The joke wasn't funny. I loved Marge, but her timing was off. Even though she'd given me a one-hundred-dollar Amazon card for my birthday. She started another one. It was excruciating.

Two mathematicians are in a bar. The first one says that the average person knows very little basic math. The second claims that most people do. The first goes off to the washroom, and in his absence the second calls over the blonde waitress.

Okay, a dumb-blonde joke. A lightbulb joke and a dumb-blonde joke. All we need is a chicken crossing the road, I whispered to Hector.

He tells her that in a few minutes, he'll call her over and ask her a question. All she has to do is answer "One-third x cubed." She says, "One thir-dex cue?" He repeats, "One-third x cubed." She asks, "One thir dex cubed?" He tells her yes, that's right. The first guy returns and the second proposes a bet. He says he'll ask the blonde waitress an integral. He calls over the waitress and asks, "What is the integral of x squared?" The waitress says, "One-third x cubed," and, while walking away, turns back and says over her shoulder, "Plus a constant!"

The Mims couldn't have liked this. She would have wanted Marge to be sincere and say she admired her mind or something. The Mims had said that a lot of times about her.

Philip stood up and mumbled something I couldn't hear. These toasts depressed me. I wanted them to honor her. I guess every kid thinks his mother is better than other people. I wanted her friends to think so, too.

I was lying on my stomach, feeling the concrete floor through my sleeping bag, allegedly watching *The Godfather*, when Eli scraped his chair back and stood up. I heard the popcorn sound of gunfire from the TV. Just now they were shooting people in the back of a restaurant. I peeked under the door and saw Eli's feet in those hard shoes. "All of you love Reen for many reasons," he said. "But I, I love her, I love her because I, I can't help loving her. No matter what ever happens, I am and I will always be in love with Irene Adler."

"Sounds like a funeral," Hector whispered.

"I mean, of course he'll always love her. Isn't that what you'd expect?"

I tipped the door open a wedge. He'd sat down again, and the

Mims looked up at him dreamily, her hand picking at his jacket sleeve.

His speech had mollified me and shot me at the same time.

I didn't doubt that he loved her. But all of a sudden, love seemed a flimsy thing.

Later, after the adults left and Charlie's parents fell asleep, Hector sat up in the dark. He hugged his knees inside the sleeping bag, resting his chin on them. Boys around us breathed loudly. This must have been what it was like to be an animal in a barn.

"What do you think?" he said.

"I don't know. The party seemed small. Like for a forty-fifth birthday."

"What do you mean?"

"I guess, like for Sare's fortieth, Charlie's dad made a slide show of her whole life, pictures of her as a little kid, in college, all that. There were different tables with flowers on each one. But the Mims probably wouldn't want that. She'd say she wouldn't." My father wasn't even here. I wondered where he was. They were always saying how they were friends, and they did seem close. I thought all of a sudden maybe he didn't like Eli. I tried to think: I couldn't remember ever seeing them in a room together. Maybe once, the day we moved into the new house. But even if my father and mother were still married, my dad wouldn't have made a slide show. Philip wouldn't have either, for that matter. Hector's father couldn't have, probably.

"I know," Hector said. "My parents are like that, too."

I nodded. His life honestly seemed even smaller.

Does everyone want his mother honored? I understood that a lot of the other moms had qualities more credited by the world. My sister had said, "How'd I get you for a mother? A mathematician, a nerd." The Mims had cracked up. "You shouldn't laugh," Boop One said. "It's *not* a compliment." But I valued her. I wished I could take what I knew was inside her and show it around, like a mineral you could bring to class. It had a romance once for my dad. I thought of the weird guys sitting in front of computers in the math building right now. They understood. I loved Marge, across the table, her large freckled shoulders exposed. But Eli's speech. Hector was right: you would have thought he was talking about someone dead.

Hector and I weren't the only people up. On the other side of the room, Reed whispered on the phone, a slur of words, "Love-youtooyeahyeah wellyeah."

I thought of Ella, bent over puking, that guy with his hand on her silver belly, like the underside of a fish. I guessed that I loved her.

51 · With the Naked Ear

Sare gave me a ride home and all the way there I was hoping Eli would be gone. But when I banged in, my mom was serving coffee cake, and Eli sat there with Marge and Boop Two. Boop One stood on her hands, her feet wagging near Eli's face. Then, one by one, my sisters and Marge left. Eli's overnight bag waited, zipped up, by the door.

I went to my room and fell asleep. The few times in my life I've slept during the day I've had incredible consoling dreams. Not that I remembered them; I just woke up knowing I'd been restored. I rose gradually through strands of reality, one blindfold dissolving at a time. From somewhere else in the house I heard the Mims laughing and him egging her on.

This was happiness. I recognized it. Again. I felt sick before I even sat up in bed. I walked loudly into the living room, kicking a ball against the bookcases, in case they were embracing or worse. I pictured Eli's chest hair. I'd seen it poke out from his white shirt. I wondered how far down it went on his belly. It was disgusting to think of him naked. But I found them in the kitchen, fully dressed, only his sleeves rolled up, working at a problem with a pencil. She showed him where she and Marge had gotten stuck. I'd heard about this before. They were using an earthquake model; crimes followed a similar pattern, with predictable aftershocks. "Crime is not completely random," Marge had told me. But then, for mathematicians, or the wack religious, almost nothing was. Their idea of chaos was highly irregular behavior caused by laws.

"Like what?" I'd once asked.

Marge and the Mims had said in unison, "The weather."

Eli looked up when I came in. "Did you have a good rest?" he said.

"I'm sorry about your cat," I said. "How is it?"

"Thank you for asking," he said, and then told me there was almost no hope.

I poured myself a glass of milk. After Eli left, I asked her, "What was so funny?"

"Oh, he was teasing me about being in love with a woman who wears a dental splint. We woke up and discovered we were old."

I sure as hell didn't know what love was.*

Later, Boop One thundered in, loud even in ballet shoes. She looked like a princess—pink tights, pink slippers, hair in a tight bun with a pink snood—but she smelled . . . like whoa! We picked up Boop Two at the shelter, on the way to Charlie's.

"I *love* beets," Sare said with absolute authority, opening the door. I didn't see any sign of Dale. I'd had a hundred dinners in that kitchen and I didn't remember Dale at more than a handful, but you never had the sense that he was *missed* exactly. Those tall boys and that mother—they didn't need any more than themselves. We did need more. We still missed our dad. By ourselves, we weren't enough. That night I learned that Eli didn't give the Mims a birthday present. Only the expensive *cheese* platter, she joked. I'd heard her overthanking him for just that. He was mad at her, I gathered

---

* *You say you sure as hell didn't know what love was. I sure as hell didn't know what a dental splint was and I still don't.*

from what she and Sare were saying. So his not getting her a present was a takeawayment, as Boop One would call it. I stopped a moment, realizing how far they'd come from the beginning.

"You're never getting that suit." Sare's voice carried. That card with names of tailors was an IOU. It was shocking to hear her say *never*. "Dale's not big on gifts either."

"Eli did buy me that dress," the Mims said.

"So there was the fantasy gift and the real one. The piece I'd be concerned about is why he needed the myth. There's nothing wrong with a modest present or even no present. But that's different from a fake promise. Did he offer to take you to London?"

"I guess not really. He said he remembers my kids' friends' names. And he does."

"But that's like saying, *I made a promise I'm not going to keep, but you shouldn't mind because I give you other things*. He's the one who brought up suits in London. He didn't tell you that your present was him remembering your kids' friends' names. He could have said, *I'm not giving you a material gift, I'm giving you my attention*."

I thought of the suit again. He seemed to forget his promises. I remembered the silver forks and spoons he'd said he was going to buy us: they went shopping for them once and didn't find what they wanted. That was the end of it. That wasn't like the Mims.

He'd told her he'd planned two vacations for her birthday: one for just them at an inn in Big Sur and another for all of us, camping. But she wouldn't get them now, because he was mad at her. She thought she'd blown her longed-for family romance.

"Well, maybe you would have gone camping," Sare said, "but the Post Ranch Inn sounds like this year's suit."

If he didn't mean either, then why not offer two vacations? Why not five? My fear shot up in wild arcs, showering.

My mom sighed. "But I *luv* him." She was putting on that voice, that *luv*. But she felt a lot. I knew she did. And there was still that ex-wife—I'd seen her. The Victim, as I thought of her now.

That afternoon, when I was finally alone, I texted Ella. *Sorry you were sick. If you ever want to hang out, I'm around. Miles A-H.*

I didn't expect her to answer, and she didn't.

My dad came over later that night. He'd sent flowers on the Mims's real birthday. *All the little buyable things*, Eli had once said about my father's gestures. But they worked, judging by the envelopes slipped under his glass doors! Eli probably hated Valentine's Day. I flashed on the seven thousand dollars. I hoped that wasn't a bogus offer. If it was, we were tanked. I thought of the Victim. What if he'd promised her money, too?

"Your girlfriend glowered at me during Parent PE," the Mims said. A running joke between our parents: a divorced mom in the Boops' class flirted with my dad. He said he'd seen a table of moms in a restaurant. When he went over, one said they'd all decided if they ever left their husbands, it would be for him. My mom asked me to put the Boops to bed; she was opening a bottle of wine. They seemed to be enjoying themselves. This was all light, far above danger. I realized I breathed easier since Eli had left to go to LAX.

I told my sisters to brush their teeth.

"What if Daddy fell in love with somebody else?" Boop One asked. "Would that lady move in?"

So they'd been listening. It had never occurred to me that *they* could figure out how to eavesdrop! The Mims had to be more careful!

"Not going to happen."

"How do you know?"

"I just don't think Daddy's going to remarry. Go to sleep now, my dear." I'd heard our dad call the Mims that recently. I didn't remember him using those words when they were married. I'd spent all this time thinking about the Mims and Eli, but meanwhile, life was streaming by, and the Boops wanted our father to stay their dad and nothing else.

"Emma has a boyfriend," Boop Two said in the dark.

"Is that true?" I asked Boop One.

"Mm-hmm," she said, her one leg lifting in a right angle, toe pointed.

The doorbell rang: Maude Stern. People had nominated Hector and me to run FLAGBTU in the fall, and we said we'd only do it if she would, too. We needed her organization. The petition for the ballot proposition to eliminate gay marriage was gaining momentum. Maude wanted to bring Cottonwoods kids who had two dads or two moms to conservative Mexican-immigrant churches to talk about family. She stood in the doorway telling me that, out of breath. I was about to ask, *Why churches?* when she said, "How come you're in FLAGBTU? For me it's not—"

"Are you asking me if I'm gay?" I let her in and she followed me to my room.

"No, I mean—" Then she stopped. She wasn't really asking if I was gay—she was rooting around, trying to talk about feelings. She wanted to know if I *liked* her.

"If you're asking me, the answer is I don't have really any sexuality yet, I'm fifteen. I don't think I'm gay. Still, it's probably not a great thing to go around asking people."

"I didn't mean to," she said, flustered. Scolded. "That's not what I meant." She stood in my small room for the first time, looking around. She was almost a foot taller than me.

I wasn't sure if I liked her. I mean I didn't. There was no glow. But I could picture her, straight Maude Stern, sitting next to me on my bed, bending over and giving me a blow job, her hand cupped, the way she'd dutifully cup a candle flame. Her hand was small and fat. I couldn't really see Ella in my room. Ella wouldn't go down on me. But then I imagined a rush of things I didn't want to know: Eli's dick. I imagined it crooked, not straight-angled and circumcised like my dad's. I could see my dad's sex: physical and happy, the way he splashed in a swimming pool. Would I fuck like my dad? But I'd seen snapshots of my dad young. He'd never been fat. Boop One with her dancer legs. I could picture every single person in our family having sex, except me. Maybe not Boop Two either.

"Don't sweat it," I said to Maude. "You're not the first person to wonder." At the end of last year, the FLAGBTU faculty adviser called me in to say he was there if I ever wanted to talk. *O-kay*, I'd said, feeling like a fraud. I didn't think I was gay. I just wanted to yank my dad's chain.

"I meant I'm not in FLAGBTU because of me. I'm here because of my father."

"Your dad?" I didn't get it. Her father was one of those dads you rarely saw and when you did see him, even at Cottonwoods, he was in a suit.

"My dad's gay."

"Your *dad*? I didn't know that."

"Nobody knew. My mom didn't. I guess he didn't. Until last year."

I heard my mom and dad in the living room, laughing. They might have been talking about Maude's parents for all I knew. I could have told her about Eli, that would have been a fair trade, but instead I told her I started in FLAGBTU because of soup selling.

"I remember your soup." She laughed and I saw her a way I hadn't before. Usually there were red patches on her face, but with her eyes like this, everything aligned, and she looked down, intent. If I kissed her now, her face would open, and I thought, This is easy. "So you didn't join because of me?" I said.

"Of course I joined because of you," she answered.

But I remembered Eli and the seven thousand dollars we needed. I was still fat. And I thought of Ella bent over, throwing up. Later, I thought, I can have these things but not now. And that seemed okay, a city waiting, still asleep, and Ella one spire. The moment passed, and Maude turned away, looking embarrassed.

....

I hadn't planned on seeing Eli again anytime soon, but when I walked in one day after playing tennis with Charlie I heard two voices in the kitchen singing off-key. How could such a dork be a liar?

I heard her suggest that Eli invite a couple he knew along to dinner.

"People have plans; they have kids. They can't just drop everything because Irene Adler deigns to see them."

That wasn't nice. He wasn't always that nice. I must have looked at them strangely when I came in because my mom raised her eyebrows. But her voice stayed even. "Well, it doesn't have to be this visit. Just sometime."

"Sure," he said then, calm. Confident that he could shuffle *sometime* into *never.*

I hated hearing her like that. That was the worst part of it. The talking him down and the overthanking frightened me. I turned to face Eli. "Are you coming back after dinner?"

"No, unfortunately, I have to leave tonight. But I'm going to be here more. I rented an apartment."

"Really?" That stopped my heart. "Where?"

"On Wren Street. In Hancock Park."

"When are you moving?"

"Soon." He took out the key and showed us. For some reason, he handed it to my mother, and she passed it to me. We each felt its weight in our hand. We passed the thing back and forth. Then he worked it back onto his key ring, picking up a grocery bag of my old clothes, washed and neatly folded. "He loves that rainbow maker," Eli told the Mims again as they walked out.

My head reeled, as if the top inch would form a twister and spin off. I went to the medicine cabinet and shook out two Tylenols. I got headaches now.

I called Hector to tell him we had to see the PI.

52 · A Reconnaissance Mission

We laid our bikes on the spongy grass and rang Ben Orion's bell. He answered in socks. "Hey, how was camp? You guys look about ten years older."

Hector said, "Eli's back."

"I didn't know he left," Ben said. He sat down, hands latched in front of him, in his office. "So tell me."

"Now he's moving here. He got an apartment. He showed us the key." That key felt like a seed stuck in my teeth, an irritant of hope.

He sighed. "Well, I don't know much, but I learned some." He rolled in his chair over to a cabinet, extracted a file, and handed us a piece of paper.

Wisconsin Circuit Court Access (WCCA)
Case Search Results
You searched for: Party Name Lee, Eli J.;
Birth Date 11–10–1963
Your search returned no results

My first thought was, Maybe I got his birthday wrong. "What do you think this means?" I said.

"If they did get a divorce, it wasn't in Wisconsin. Either they got divorced in another state, or they're not divorced."

What if they weren't divorced? What if he and the Victim were just separated? I tried to picture the Victim in Wisconsin. I knew the shape of the state from the map. I'd learned from Wikipedia that Wisconsin made cheese and other dairy products. It was hard to imagine Eli there. Those suits! I pictured Wisconsin rural, with muddy fields and cows.

"I found an article about the writer of *The Other Woman*." Hector said. He unzipped his backpack and took out a folded paper. I was shocked that this was the first I was hearing about it. I took the paper and tried not to seem upset. But my hand was jumping without permission. It seemed to be an interview with the Victim on a blog called *The Romance Reader*. A librarian had interviewed her.

She talked importantly about how she made her male character believable. *I just asked my husband.* As Ben Orion read, he highlighted a section: *We recently bought a house because we got sick of having all our books in boxes in other people's garages! Now we have seven walls of books!*

"She likes exclamation marks," Hector said. We all sat there, quiet. Leaves fluttered outside the window.

"So maybe he lied about being divorced." The PI shrugged. "Or maybe he's even Steven. Wouldn't be the first ex-wife to say she's still married. Why don't you guys go visit that librarian. Says here she works in Glendale, California. You can take a bus. Ask her what she knows. She must have talked to the lady on the phone, at least." Ben Orion printed out a map of bus routes. We waited on the couch. In this room, there was no clutter. There were neat stacks, and on the wall, he'd hung his framed diploma. My parents had both gone to colleges and graduate schools I'd heard of, but I'd never seen one framed diploma.

Ben Orion was tracing his finger on a map now, explaining MTA routes and transfers, but my mind skittered around. I had no capacity to master the transit system. Almost any drawer in our house you opened, there'd be papers, keys, rubber bands, matches, a pencil, chewed on one end. I was like our house. Cluttered.

Before we left, I complimented the picture in his living room, of a woman going over a bridge in rain.

"It's a woodblock print," he said, lifting it down. "It's art I can afford." He told us about the artist. Kawase Hasui. He was farsighted, he said, so to sketch, he had to get just the right distance. He could not see clearly close-up. He'd traveled all around Japan, sketched outside, and then went back to his inn and added the color. He lost his home twice: An earthquake wrecked his print blocks, and he had to start all over. Then, during World War II, his house got hit during an air raid.

I asked if he was still alive. But he died in 1957. Ben took us to his bedroom to show us his most valuable print, by a different artist named Kotundo. He opened the door for us to see it, but he stayed back in the hall. It was a nude woman, stooping, combing her long Japanese hair. Maybe he had a thing for Asian women.

"You guys know a teacher at Cottonwoods named Zoe Fisher? Teaches art? She has a son, he'd be a year or two older than you?"

"Yeah, sure," we said. We knew her. We knew Ez. He was a friend of Charlie's brother. He played drums in a band.

I thought Hector had paid attention to the bus routes. But he hadn't. I avoided the whole thing for the last days of summer, and Hector, weirdly for him, didn't push me.

Finally, when we went, we decided to be the Westside kids we were and took a taxi we found in front of a hotel in downtown Santa Monica. We told the driver we wanted the Glendale Central Library, on Harvard Street in Glendale.

Hector was wearing a button-down shirt, his only one. We didn't talk much as we rode. I was watching the meter.

How far are we? I asked, on the freeway.

Still a long ways, the driver said. Already it was more than fifty dollars. I was holding the money. Hector's forty-one dollars, which hadn't grown since the day he'd unfisted them for Ben Orion, and my eighty, which had increased, via poetry and Hart relatives, to a hundred and some.

We were literally speeding on the freeway and the meter was ticking away, counting every mile. Something about money made me clear. I looked out the window at the unfamiliar, anonymous LA. Los Angeles was so big, I thought. Any other city, this would be three cities. "What are we doing?" I said. "We've gone crazy."

We were two rising high school juniors, underachievers, spending our entire net worth chasing down a rumor about my mother's boyfriend's ex-wife. We were spinning farther and farther away from our real lives. But we were more than halfway there, the man driving the cab said, and now the fare was approaching seventy.

"This has got to be the end," I said, to myself more than to Hector.

Hector had rolled down his window and had a hand out.

The meter passed a hundred before he took the exit for Glendale. I thought of asking him to just let us off. We didn't have nearly enough to get home. Now we really would have to take the bus.

When he finally stopped, we paid him almost all we had. I knew we were supposed to tip, but we only had eleven dollars left. We'd need that. I explained that Glendale was farther than we thought and more expensive, and looking back now, I'd have imagined he might have laughed at our pile of crumpled dollar bills, but he was immune to our charms. That seemed to have been happening more often. He turned around and roared off.

The air outside was crushingly hot. It felt like someone picked you up and squeezed the oxygen out. We hurried inside. The library turned out to be louder than I would have expected, with little kids and their moms draped over furniture, pawing through stained books. Homeless guys nimbly fingered DVDs. They felt too close to my situation. I was already obsessed with how we'd get back. We asked at the information counter for the librarian Joanna Greenwood and waited while someone pushed a square button on a telephone and then were told she was at lunch, due back in a half hour. We lolled around. Hector was hungry, and this library had a café, outside behind the glass doors, but we needed to keep our eleven dollars. Who knew how much the bus would cost? Hector dragged me then to the L shelf and found more books by the Victim. We turned to the dedications. Every one except The Other Woman was dedicated to Eli. "That marks a change," Hector said. "All those to him and this one to C." It must have been when he left her. Maybe C was a new boyfriend? Christopher? Carl? I hoped so. She sure wrote a lot of books. They all had covers with vividly painted skies. More than one took place in the mountains.

Finally, a tall, obviously pregnant woman with curly hair and humungous breasts tapped my shoulder. "I'm Joanna. You were looking for me?"

We explained that we wanted to ask about Jean Lee. We said as little as we could, but we kind of tripped over each other, explaining what the other one said, and it came out that we hadn't *met* Jean Lee, but we knew Eli Lee and he was my mother's boyfriend, and we were under the impression that they were divorced.

"What gave you that impression?" she asked.

"He told us," I said.

"He said that exactly," Hector added.

Her head moved as if she were looking for someone else around who could help, then she turned back to us. "I interviewed her for our Lunchtime Locals Series. I only met him once. He came here to pick up their son."

"What did he look like?" Hector said.

"Oh, he was a normal-looking boy. Cute. I think he had a stain on his shirt. Active, you know."

But Hector had meant Eli. He opened the tiny notebook from Kat and penciled a thumbnail drawing of him.

"Yes, that's him, I think. You draw well."

We asked if she knew who was C, the book's dedicatee, but she didn't.

She looked from one to the other of us as if wondering what it was all right to say. "I don't know what to tell you. She definitely *sounded* married. Everything was *my husband* this, *my husband* that." Then she lifted her hand to her mouth and right in front of us bit at a hangnail. It was awful to see a pregnant person gnaw at herself.

"Wait," Hector asked. "You said Lunchtime Locals. Is Jean Lee local?"

"I thought they lived in Pasadena," she said.

"Would you have a maps section here?" I asked. "With, like, bus routes?"

She led us to a computer, where we googled the MTA. She left us with that big screen open—it seemed we would have to go downtown, either on a 780 rapid or a 92, 93, or 94 to Broadway. We'd need to get off south of First, then take the 30 or the 31 to the MTA station at Pico and Rimpau. From there we could catch a Santa Monica Blue Bus, line 7, or Super 7.

"Looks like at least two hours," Hector said. "Maybe three."

As we were walking out, Joanna Greenwood came up to us again. "Here, I found this," she said. It was a Xerox of a clipping from the Pasadena paper.

PASADENAN PENS REVENGE TALE

After writing sixteen romances, including the best-selling *Heir-loom in August*, a Pasadenan scribe publishes a tale about adultery.

When we left the building, heat slammed into us the way a huge kid could, knocking our wind out. I didn't say anything. I kicked the debris by the curb, trying to orient myself to the bus stop.

"So what do we think?" Hector said.

That was the question. I really didn't know. The ex-wife, the Victim, whom I'd imagined in Wisconsin, stomping in rubber boots among cows and Nazis, with a sick cat and a stolen dog, now seemed to live here. With the kid, it had to be. What that meant about Eli, I didn't know. Was he pretending to be still married to her but living in Washington working for the NSF? Then why would she live here, though? And she hadn't dedicated her book to him this time. She must have known they were split up. But why had she said *my husband this, my husband that*? Had she *ever* lived in Wisconsin? When did she move?

But whatever was true, and it was all a storm in my head, I was pretty sure he'd lied to us. I hadn't heard anything about his kid moving here. That would have been a huge big deal! He couldn't have told the Mims, or I'd know. He probably visited his kid on the same trips when he saw us. I'd been told once to be careful touching a baby's head, because there was a part right at the top where the skull hadn't fused yet, and it was fragile, the brain swirling just below the skin. I felt like I could feel that drain at the top of my head now, pulling liquids down. And the air in Glendale was so hot and static that little specks of ash attached themselves to our skin.

We were walking to the bus stop. Even under trees, even in *shade*, it was murderously hot. The trees here looked dusty, half their leaves giving up and dying. "Do we think he never got the divorce he said he did, and that he's living with his wife and kid in Pasadena?" Hector asked.

"But he couldn't live here and work at the NSF. That's in Maryland. I know for sure. I mean, my mom and Marge have *been* there."

"He's got your mom thinking he's flying in to see her from DC. Do you ever see the plane tickets?"

"I never really looked." I should have. All the doors I'd listened behind, why didn't I check his bag? Eli living *here*! I hadn't thought of that. It never occurred to me once, even after I saw him that time in Pasadena. I couldn't believe it, really, even now.

"I think he has to live in DC. For his job."

"I wish we had a phone. We could call the NSF. See if he's there."

That made me feel awful, because I had a phone in my backpack. The dictators had finally broken down and gotten me one, for my last birthday. I hadn't told Hector. He and I were like the last kids in our grade who didn't have phones or smoke dope. I didn't want to tell him I'd defected. I thought of myself really wanting the phone but not being able to tell Hector and Eli lying and that that connected us. I made myself open the zipper of my pack, pull the thing out, and toss it to him.

"Oh, we do have one. Good," was all he said.

By then we were at the bus stop, a small ugly metal tent over an equally ugly bench with no one on it. We waited. Fifty minutes, and the bus still hadn't come. Hector finally called Ben Orion. I wouldn't have had the number on me. But he kept it in his little notebook. He explained that we'd met the librarian and that she'd told us Jean Lee lived in Pasadena. That Jean Lee had said *my husband this, my husband that.* I hoped Ben Orion would rescue us.

But Ben was in a car following a stalker who'd arrived the day before from Idaho. The stalker was in love with a nineteen-year-old singer my sisters listened to. He'd rented a car yesterday and checked into a hotel. He must have taken a shower and gotten himself something to eat, Ben said, and then, finally, hours later, he drove to her house—he knew where it was—and he walked straight up to her front door, carrying a bouquet of roses he'd bought from Vons. By the time he rang the doorbell, Ben had the house staff ready. A maid answered and told him the singer wasn't there and she wouldn't be back for a long time. It was true she wasn't home. She was hiding out in the Chateau Marmont. But then today the stalker drove to her manager's office and hassled the receptionist. Now he was heading toward his hotel, a low-rent Days Inn on Santa Monica Boulevard, where another car with one of Ben's guys was already parked.

We waited and waited. The MTA never came. I began to think we'd read the bus schedule wrong. Ben called back. "What's the story?" We told him, and he said to call our parents. We said they were working and anyway we couldn't reach them, and he finally said he'd get us. But he told us to leave messages. We said sure and then just didn't.

"Remember how she said in that article how *they'd* just bought a house?" Hector said while we were still waiting.

"She might've meant her and her son," I said.

"May-be."

Ben arrived at last. On the front seat there was a picture of a guy, younger than my dad probably but with wrinkles. Not good-looking. But not bad-looking either. He had on one of those cowboy ties. Ben said he'd lived with his parents most of his life; then the father died, and a month ago the mother got sick. Ben thought that set him off. He'd sent the nineteen-year-old singer that picture of himself and told her what flight he was coming in on. Poor guy was probably disappointed when she wasn't standing there waiting for him at LAX. The girl of his dreams who he'd never met.

Whom, Hector mouthed. I kicked him.

Then what'd he do? we asked. When she wasn't there.

"He did like you. He took the bus. For him, it came. He learned how to read a bus schedule."

That was a little dig. He thought we were spoiled. He was right. We were spoiled. And he didn't even know about the taxi.

But that poor guy, the stalker. He paid to fly out here for just his lonely dream. He must have understood, even as he hoped against hope, that the real girl wouldn't be standing there holding his picture at the bottom of the escalator where the arriving passengers came down to the luggage conveyors. There just wasn't any reality in it.

"What happens to him now?" I asked.

"He's in his hotel. He's got the little sign on his door that says don't disturb. So maybe he's taking a nap. Day two of his great adventure. We've got a psychiatrist on call."

"Who pays for that?" I asked.

"She does. The celebrity always has to pay the psychiatrist."

"Doesn't seem fair."

Ben Orion shrugged, driving. I looked at the glove box, imagining the gun. A Glock 9mm. I'd never seen a live gun. I wanted to. "I'll take you guys home. I've got to get back and jump on the computer." But when we were just a little past USC on the 10, his phone rang. It was one of those systems where it broadcast through the whole car. *0:400, the object is getting in his rental car and driving in the direction of the target property.*

"Oh, man. Okay. Meet you there. Keep him in sight. Let me know if there's any diversion." He told us, "I've got to make a detour. See, this is why I shouldn't have kids in my car."

We could have volunteered to jump out, but we just stayed

quiet. His car was comfortable. Air-conditioned. I thought if we were very still maybe he wouldn't do anything about us. He made two calls to a Dr. Gilmore. He made a call to someone who must have been in the house. And then he called the police.

The car went steadily but fast. Ben was gripping the steering wheel. We exited and drove north. When we finally slowed and parked outside a huge property, he told us to stay in the car. He opened the glove box, took out the gun. The real thing. He went around to the back of the car and put it in his trunk. Locked it.

"What does he think, we're gonna go Rambo on him?" I whispered.

There were two other cars parked in front of us. We couldn't see what was going on. There was a hedge all around the yard and a gate in front. Hector got out and looked through the trees. He said it seemed as if a bunch of guys were standing around in the yard, talking tensely. He said the way they stood looked like if you plucked them, they'd twang.

I asked if there were cops. "No uniforms," he said. "No badges." But when they finally came out of the gate, we had a glimpse of the guy, in handcuffs. He looked up around him wildly and then settled politely in the car parked two ahead of us.

Ben Orion slammed in. "You guys're gonna have to walk home from my place. The psychiatrist's already on his way there. There's a 9:03 flight to Twin Falls, and we've got to get him on that plane."

We didn't answer. At his house we just sat in the car. We said we were hungry. He told us we could hit his pantry but not to leave the kitchen. And cool as his house was, there was something dry about the pantry. On inspection, his snacks resembled ours. Bags that looked like chips turned out to contain dehydrated peas. The only graham crackers were certified organic. He had stacks of those foil-wrapped seaweed wafers Boop Two loved. We settled for the graham crackers. We had to. We leaned against the door trying to hear something.

"I wonder what'll happen," Hector said.

"I know. Me, too." I kept thinking about Jean Lee saying *they'd* bought a house and now had seven walls of books. I could see Eli with seven walls of books.

"What do you think?" Hector finally asked me.

"I don't know. I don't even want to know if Eli doesn't really live in DC."

Finally, we heard noise. We weren't allowed out, but the pantry had a window onto the front. We saw a slant view of four men, the guy in the center. He had his hands just hanging down in front of him. He looked at his hands.

Ben banged into the kitchen. "We're taking him to the airport. We're going to see that his car gets returned, and we'll put him on that plane. Let's talk tomorrow and we'll figure out what to do about your case. Wait till we're all out of here, and then you guys should head home."

Poor stalker. No sightseeing even. And after this, he wouldn't be able to use his worn, familiar fantasy. At least I wouldn't be able to, if I were him. Since Ella hadn't called me back, I couldn't work up the little scenes that I used to rely on to help me fall asleep. There just wasn't enough reality in them anymore. I didn't actually have a big imagination. Once I knew something was impossible, I couldn't use it, even for the pleasure of a dream.

On a table near the front door was a book called *The Sound of the Mountain*, with a picture of a flat-topped hill you could tell was Japanese. What was it with Ben Orion and Japan? I thought he probably did have a thing for Asian girls.

That night, Eli called. The phone rang, I answered, and it was him. That startled me like a gunshot. He told me his cat had died.

53 · Surveillance

The next day we rode our bikes to Ben Orion's.

"So you want to go to Pasadena?" he said. "Do some surveillance?"

I had to make myself ask him what that would cost. He waved me off. "Let's go." He opened the refrigerator and grabbed a six-pack of root beer in bottles. "Maybe we'll learn something. Settle in, guys. It's a long ways."

I felt glad for the drive. I wished I had Tylenol. I leaned against the car door and let myself drift. Hector asked what we were going to do when we got there.

"Well, first, we'll go to the city hall, department of records. See if we can pull a deed. See if there's really a *they* that bought a house."

Wilshire Boulevard rolled out straight and forever until it finally began to change, passing our desolate downtown. On the freeway, we passed close enough to see empty buildings, some of the windows glinting jagged silver. We were growing up in a city whose very own downtown had fallen to waste and windy debris, a place we were driven to in cars a few times a year with muffled automatic locks to hear music before the long ride home. Now there's a whole world there.* But then, as we passed through WPA tunnels and the fanciful bridge to Pasadena, we seemed to enter a different time. Pasadena had been built to be a city, the city, and now it was not a ruin like LA's stark, hulking downtown but a shrine, a beautiful place no longer central. Because of heat. Because of smog. Ben Orion said the air in LA was much better now than when he was our age.

"My mom says that, too," Hector said. "My cousins live here. In Mar Vista they had a nine-hundred-square-foot Ain house. They moved into a mansion in San Marino."

* *That's where I want to live. Maybe we'll get lofts in the same building.*

The trees bowed, with ancient trunks and leafy branches. We stopped in front of a bronzed municipal building that seemed to be made of sandstone and announced itself with a long pleat of stairs.

The heat, when we stepped outside the car, made my legs wobble.

I counted steps. Then, inside the refrigerated air, Ben led us down corridors and around corners. At the end of a maze, he spoke to a woman behind a high desk.

Fifteen minutes later, we held the document in our hands. Eli and Jean Lee had bought a house in August 2004. They paid one million two hundred ninety-five thousand. They put down three hundred twelve K. "So they've got a million-dollar mortgage," Ben said. A four-bedroom, three-bath house. Twenty-eight hundred square feet.

My stomach went. So he didn't live in DC? When had he moved? He'd told us he'd pay for half of our house if she ever let him move in. What now? I crumpled in the clean old tiled hallway and fell against the wall. I just needed a minute. Then another. I wanted to go blank. But I didn't quite.

They were talking above me. Then they were down, on the floor, their voices on my face.

"What about the key?" I asked. "That he showed us. Did he still get an apartment?"

"That key could belong to any lock," Ben said. "We have no way of telling."

I still pictured a building on Wren Street. Could he lie that much?

"There's a local Realtor listed. Should we look for her?" Ben asked.

Maybe he rented the apartment from her? I felt along for the ride. We were done with the world as I knew it. The real estate office doors were bolted. But Hector spotted a testimonial on the picture window.

Dear Carol,

You had a keen sense of the kind of house that would appeal to us as a family. You were a *SAVVY, SKILLFUL, AND ENERGETIC NEGOTIATOR!* I know we're going to be very happy living on Maybank!

—Jean and Eli Lee

The note was written in ink, with a flourish, the signature loopy and old-fashioned. Jean and Eli Lee! One generation down from Mr. and Mrs. The kind of couple I hadn't wanted him to be with my mom. My side cramped—but maybe she wanted to be that kind of *we*. Idiotically, names chimed in my head. Sarah and Dale. Eli and Jean. My parents had too many syllables. Cary. Irene. Nobody was the Dale. The Jean.

With Ben Orion's phone, Hector took a picture.

There could be nothing more good to discover. All I wanted was unconsciousness. I was ready to go home. But we were at the end of a string tending to a center. I wondered if I could fall asleep in the car that was nodding through residential streets. Finally, the string was spooled and we stopped.

"That's it," he said. "Their house."

It took me a moment to understand. It was white. Two stories. Way bigger than ours. And Eli and Jean Lee owned it. It looked a little like our old house.

"Not as nice as yours," Hector said, always loyal. "Your mom wouldn't have bought this house."

"More expensive than ours would be, if it was even for sale. And if it was, we couldn't afford it."

"Not as pretty." In all the years I'd known him, I'd never heard Hector say the word *pretty*. I've never heard him say it since.

Pretty or not, it was Eli's house, all right. I believed it because of a round chair, swimming-pool-colored, on the porch. That was why he'd been so mad when they fought about colors! She'd had no idea she was insulting his chair! And he couldn't tell her.

We sat in the car as streetlights magicked on, all at once. A woman stepped out to the porch. She had one pink curler at the top of her forehead. On her feet were those things women put between their toes for polishing.

"Can we get out and look around?" Hector asked.

"Didn't you say they had a dog?" Ben Orion said. "You'd need treats."

"Can we get some?" Hector asked.

"Seems risky," Ben said. But he drove to Trader Joe's, and we wandered through the aisles. Then he parked down the road from the house and let us wade closer. Two dogs sniffed and wagged at our legs, a lab and some kind of pit mix. We'd bought long bully sticks, and they settled, each working on a bone. Hector and I crept down the side yard near the back. Their neighbors had a fort built into the crux of a tree, the floor rotten, but little rectangles of wood had been nailed onto the trunk, and we climbed up. Light warmed the windows of a room that must have been the Lees' kitchen. On an old couch, a square-faced kid lay watching *Scooby-Doo*. The woman with the curler bent over an ironing board. Behind her was a rack with a row of white shirts, already pressed. I found myself following Shaggy and Scooby-Doo. I loved those old Hanna-Barberas. It was a sickeningly Rockwell-type tableau.

"What if they see us?" Hector whispered.

"I really don't care," I said in a normal voice. I thought, Pasadenan Pens Revenge Tale. This would be mine.

Then Eli stepped into the kitchen in sweatpants, no socks, and a T-shirt with a hole in the shoulder. He went to the refrigerator, took a carton of juice, and walked out, drinking from the triangular opening. Okay, I said, we can go. I jumped down, landing with a line of pain in one knee. We passed the dogs, who looked up at us, then returned to chewing.

"You know, he wanted to come Christmas Eve but he had to be there when his son opened presents in the morning. And my mom said, *You can't count on a plane landing in Wisconsin in the middle of the night in December. They have snowstorms!* He kept saying, *I'm not worried about that.* Well, now we know why. He lived *here.*"

"So he's pretending to be Superman flying through blizzards—"

"When he's got a clear empty road to Pasadena."

"You guys want to find out more, you should come out here one day early in the morning and check their garbage," Ben said. "You can learn a lot from people's garbage."

"Do you have a girlfriend?" I asked Ben.

"No," he said. "Not now. Why do you ask?"

I'd pretty much known that he didn't. I could just tell. I said, "Because it's Saturday night."

"You guys ask too many questions," he said, but then he told us during the long drive in that early dark that he'd lived with Zoe Fisher, the art teacher at Cottonwoods, for eight years when Ezra was small. He'd helped raise Ezra. That's why he'd perked up when we'd said we went to Cottonwoods. After that ended, he'd tried dating, but he wasn't really a dating kind of person. Like he told us before, he said, girls these days all hated cops. It had been six years since he and Zoe broke up. He said he'd like to get in touch with Ezra. He'd started letters to them. He knew Zoe was with some-body else now. She was happy. That was good. Oh, and she was who taught him about Japanese woodblock prints. They'd searched for them together at swap meets.

"Do you ever talk to Ezra?" he asked us.

We had to tell him no, not much. Ezra was older. This year, he'd gone to college. We didn't know where. I was sorry to tell him that. We were probably his blind alley. But Reed, Charlie's brother, had played in a band with him. I could ask Reed.

Ben nodded.

I wanted to go to my dad's and watch a movie. But when we called, my dad said no. Whenever my dad said not a good time, I always said okay. But tonight I pulled a Boop One. "Why not?"

"I'm going out with some people from work."

"We just want to be at your house," I said. "You don't have to be there."

"Your mother's expecting you. It's not going to work tonight, Miles."

Such a dick.

Ben Orion parked in front of our house. He said, "I can drive your bikes over later."

"Oh, maybe don't do that. My mom would freak. She doesn't know you."

"Wait a minute. You told your folks I was giving you rides?"

Hector and I looked at each other.

"I can put the bikes inside for the night. But your folks have to be informed where you are and who's driving you. I guess you're thinking that all this is going to be hard to tell her. Do you need help with that?"

"She wouldn't even want me knowing this stuff. How much do we owe you?"

"Nothing. Don't even think about it." He looked toward Hector. "You staying with him tonight?" Hector nodded. "Talk to you soon then."

But I wanted to pay him and be done. I pulled money out of my pockets. We only had eleven dollars. He said no again. I threw it at him and left the bills, curled like old leaves on the sidewalk. I promised more later.

He got out of the car and bent to pick them up. "I'm saving this! It's yours!" he called.

When we got inside the house, I remembered all of a sudden. I'd meant to ask on the way back. I'd wanted him to drive us through Hancock Park to Wren Street.

54 · Is Truth Necessary?

We'd already missed dinner, and the leftover chicken, in a glass box on the table, looked picked bare. The Mims was in the shower. I stuck a popcorn in the microwave.

On the blackboard: IN MATHEMATICS, WE CAN PROVE THAT SOMETHING IS IMPOSSIBLE.

"We could send her an anonymous letter," Hector whispered.

"But who would she *think* it was from?"

"The wife, maybe. We could mail it from Pasadena."

"She assumes the wife's still in Wisconsin." I couldn't think anymore. All I could focus on was the little jar, two Tylenols shaken out into my hand, and a glass of water. Then we watched *Airplane!*, which we'd both already seen a bunch of times.

The next morning, I woke up clear, wanting a cup of coffee. Hector still slept, the way he always slept in my beanbag, faceup, hands on his chest like a pharaoh. I was the first one conscious in the house. I dragged the wedding-present cappuccino machine from the basement and downloaded instructions from the Internet. Equations unfurled:

Those nice clean white shirts = that wife we'd seen ironing

In high school, Eli haunted thrift stores for white button-downs, which he *ironed* himself. When his mother was dying, he came home from England and *washed* her housecoat. He knew how to wash and iron; he'd taught *me* to do laundry. He'd promised to teach me how to press a shirt. He could do all that by himself. But maybe he liked the mothering. Then it came to me suddenly: money. He'd once joked about lending us millions. I could never figure out how he made so much. Jean Lee had written seventeen books + her family had a compound on a lake in Wisconsin = *the wife had money.*

The Mims entered the kitchen with her you're-in-trouble steps. Usually, she flicked on music in the morning so we heard flutes and frantic violins as we hauled out of bed. But today it was only the two of us and the hiss emitted by the cappuccino maker. A little puddle of black sludge had dripped to the bottom of the cup.

"Who dropped you two off last night?"

"Oh my God, Mom." The pedophile fear. She'd probably already called my dad.

"Tell me the truth. I wrote down the license plate number."

I told her he was a teacher at Cottonwoods and named the real film teacher, Nathan Henry. Just after I said it, I realized how stupid that was; now I could never take a class with Nathan Henry, because when she met him at parents' night she'd remember to thank him for giving us a ride home. She wrote down his name. Then the machine started shooting froth in a circle around the walls. She grabbed a dish towel and, after a few tries, plugged it up. "Milk is more difficult, I guess," I said.

"Take it back to the basement."

Hector slept another hour. Then he stumbled into the kitchen with a book, saying, "Read this."

They weren't happy, and neither of them had touched the chicken or the ale—and yet they weren't unhappy either. There was an unmistakable air of natural intimacy about the picture, and anybody would have said that they were conspiring together.

"Doesn't that remind you of the house? And *this's* the book he memorized. The wife has just run over the mistress."

For years, my entire reading life involved superheroes and villains. The Cottonwoods curriculum dwelled on the massacres of Native Americans and devoted disproportionate units to the Holocaust. We'd read Anne Frank's diary and both volumes of *Maus*. But until yesterday, I didn't really believe that a person I knew could be evil.

Did he plan to stop living in that house and move into the apartment he'd open with the key he'd given us to hold? But then, what about the Victim and the kid I'd seen?

All these years Cottonwoods had been drilling us. *Is it true, is it kind, is it necessary? Will it improve upon the silence?* Hundreds of times, it had been repeated to us that what was more important than grades, more important than test scores, more important than where we went to college, was kindness.

"He sure flunked that," Hector said.

After a childhood of games that had no winners or losers because we weren't allowed to keep score and years of making fun of touchy-feely, it had never occurred to me that I actually believed this shit.

Our mothers tended to deem people mentally ill, not bad. But Eli didn't seem crazy. He'd lied to us about where he lived. Nobody made him do that. Goodness and badness and insanity were going to be topics of conversation for my mom and Sare for months to come, I felt *sure*.

But how would we tell her? Should we even? Would it improve upon the silence?

Hector thought the best thing to do was send the printout of the Wisconsin divorce search. Or a copy of the deed.

"As soon as she gets any of that stuff, she'll call him. She might even fly to DC. She's talked about surprising him there."

"When did she say that?"

"I don't know, a couple times. She never did it. Probably because of us. What if she had gone there?"

"But he'd have just made up something. Remember the eclipse? I bet he keeps an almanac handy."

"Yeah. Another eclipse." We'd believed so much. Even when we half believed, we were still believing. More than we knew. Hector and I walked over to Ben Orion's to pick up our bikes. Ben thought I should tell her, too.

"But me knowing will make it worse for her," I said. The three of us stood talking a long time before we decided to stick the interview from *The Romance Reader* into a manila envelope. Then we fretted about where to send it from. We picked Los Angeles. It seemed big and anonymous.

"Remember how he was so jealous?" I said.

"The cheaters, they're the people who are jealous," Ben said. "They think everyone's as deceitful as they are."

"But it seemed like he really meant it."

"Do you ever get emotional about a game? You're screaming, but you still know it's a game. Well, he had a net." We rolled our bikes out the back door. "So I'll send it?"

"Not yet," I said. All the times I'd delayed, not calling back Ben Orion, avoiding Hector, those had seemed between them and me. And we were all inside a game. This was real. Once she knew, it was out of my head and in the world. "I'll tell you when."

"By the way, I looked up Wren Street."

"Oh yeah, I wanted to go there," I said. "Take a look around. Can we do that sometime?"

But Ben was shaking his head. "Doesn't exist. There is no Wren Street in Hancock Park."

Tomorrow was the first day of our junior year.

55 · Deployment

I saw Ella at my sister's piano lesson. The girl who'd vomited in an alley bent over double with an older guy's hand spidering her stomach played Chopin in the teacher's small living room. Everyone had secrets; I understood now that I did. With that one revelation, the world multiplied.

I thought of arrows. Dale loved Sare more than she loved him. Philip had loved Kat more. With my parents, I never knew. I'd thought Eli loved the Mims. But maybe for him it was all cyber.

I followed Ella's fingers. They were long and skinny, nimble.

Maude was less pretty than Ella, but she liked me and she would wait.

For weeks nothing had happened. Eli still called. I dug out the extension phone from my closet and plugged it back into the jack and listened for no good reason. It was like when a tooth hurt and I moved it with my tongue, waking pain.

"Our couple," she told him. "The Latin teachers? He's sick."

"Oh yeah, you always had a thing for them."

Before, *they* had liked the old couple. Now he'd dwindled that to just her. Why didn't she notice? I wished she'd figure things out by herself so I wouldn't have to tell her. But she let him off the hook. I was getting impatient.

She still thought she was happy. What if she never recovered?

Every day, Hector asked if I'd called Ben Orion to press the button.

There was a heat wave at the end of September, and Hector made me go along to Zuma. I knew how I'd look on the beach. They had wet suits they could lend me, he promised, but Hector weighed a hundred pounds. His legs still looked like bug feelers. I sat on my bed in trunks, holding the folds of my gut. I'd done this when I was ten. I liked the feeling. Ella wasn't a virgin. Maude probably was. Ella was way ahead in life skills.

Whatever made Kat a MILF, that day she was a MILF squared. Blonde curls sprung from the rubber band as we trudged over the dunes. The ocean looked like the Pacific in the movies. But Surferdude was old! He looked a generation older than Philip. His skin was like suede, from the salt, wind, and sun. We paddled out and waited for waves in the lineup. I clambered up to my knees and got pitched over, thrown into the churning mess, rag-dolled by the current and, flailing underwater, miraculously bobbed up again, salt in my mouth. I wished I were home in my room, with the sound of Gal scrabbling. Balancing on the thing was impossible. I wiped out every time. But Hector and Jules could wobble up to a stiff stand, knees bent, hands out to the side.

I lost track of time, lost track of everything. I paddled out, waited, and took the big ride that worked me again. The water felt old on our skin.

"I don't really see why you guys hate Surferdude so much," I said.

"I'm not sure either," Hector said. "But I really do."

Jules was standing by the lifeguard station with Kat and Surferdude. She was talking to him.

"That kid we saw in Pasadena?" I said. "He's got a life like, like Charlie's. He probably thinks his parents are happy." Once Eli's phone had rung, and we'd heard Jean Lee's voice—a teachery, lilting *Hi-eye*. "She sounds happy," the Mims had said.

"Well, that's all for Timmy," he'd answered.

" 'There's nothing deeply wrong with their marriage,' " Hector quoted. The Victim had said that in her interview, about the couple in her book. "But it's not true. They're not happy. There's a *lot* wrong with their marriage."

"Neither is Christmas *true*. But it was fun to believe."

"I like it better now. We get the tree; we put shit on. We make it."

"You're better at that," I said. "You have talents."

"You just want to believe in magic. So does your mom. So does that wife. But Eli knows there's no Santa Claus."

"I said I'd like to be his kid. I wouldn't want to be him."

"No. He's a marked man."

Late the night of the big Thomas Wolff lecture at Caltech, I heard talking in the kitchen. My mom and Marge slumped in ball gowns, drinking Ovaltine. I crouched in the hall against the heater grate.

". . . I went out and called him every hour. He seemed grateful. But then, I told him what the doctor next to me said about Dalmane and, well, you heard him."

"I heard him all right, I just about swerved off the freeway, he's screaming, *I don't want you talking about my life!*"

"I hadn't even said Hugo's name."

"He's crazy," Marge said. "Crazy and jealous." He was *still* jealous! Even now?

"You know, the doctor was talking about the Once Born and the Twice Born. People who are good just because they're raised that way he calls Once Born. Those who've struggled for some kind of faith in the world, they're the Twice."

"Stanley was definitely Once Born," Marge said. "Maybe not even."

"Cary, too. Eli's different, though. I guess that's why I put up with all this."

"You might be putting up with too much." Marge paused. "Philip's crazy, but he's not mean."

What did Philip have to do with it? Did Marge think my mom should date *Philip*?

Just then, the phone rang. The Mims asked Eli if she could call him back after Marge left.

All of a sudden, I thought, What if he proposes now?

I crept back to my room and called Hector, waking him.

"He might be a polygamist," he said.

"That's illegal, though, anyway."

"It's illegal, but I don't know how you get caught. I mean, those databases Ben Orion checks—do people who marry people have to check them?"

It was hard to think of priests and rabbis from faraway states calling Ben Orion to do background checks on their brides and grooms. That'd be a good business, I thought. Maybe better than reality shows even.

I finally texted Ben Orion to deploy. It wasn't any one thing. It was like finally turning in an assignment that had been due a long time ago.

56 · Then Came the Day

Then came the day. When Sare dropped me home after Specials, Boop Two was sitting on the porch. She looked up at me through her glasses and smiled the smile of a creature with no ambivalence. The house was quiet. I looked at the clock in the hall and went to find our mom.

She sat at her desk, the envelope torn open, her reading glasses on. It was getting dark, but the lights were still off. She just sat there, staring at the wall.

I stepped in. "How's about dinner?"

"We'll go out." She didn't turn to me. "I don't feel well. But I'll be back."

Back to what? Back to before the bad, before the divorce, before the Boops got born? "To when it was just us?" I said, my voice veering and cracked.

She swiveled in her chair. She'd had that chair longer than I'd been alive. When she'd been in graduate school, her adviser had found it outside the lab and given it to her. "Better than," she said.

I thought of her face in the picture when she was young and how she'd looked laughing with Eli and thought, You'll never be like that again.

"Call Jamie," she said. "We'll go eat."

"Where's Boop One?"

"At dance."

We went to the place Eli took us the first time we met him, Boop Two grumbling about a party she hadn't been invited to.

"You know what?" I said. "Life is fucking unfair."

"Language, Miles!" the Mims said. Then her phone buzzed, and she sprang up, the way our dad did during dinner, the thing at his ear. She was pacing when the waiter set our pizza on the table. We ate slowly so we'd still be eating when she sat down again.

At home, she said she had a work meeting. She'd say good night now. "Take a bath," she told my sister.

The doorbell rang. Then I heard a female voice behind my mom's closed door.

I snuck around the side yard and stood in bushes, smelling dirt. I recognized Dr. Bach's voice. Did shrinks make house calls? They seemed to be on speakerphone with Eli. He came through crackly, saying he was thinking of maybe reconciling with his ex-wife. Yeah, right, I thought, pawing a shoe in the dirt. They were so far behind us.

"I want to be with my son," Eli said, "but Irene rightly points out that I could be with her and be with my son, too."

"Eli, you are legally divorced, aren't you?" my mom interrupted.

"Of course, Irene." The tone he got! Stern, reprimanding!

"Well, in this article, Jean says, 'We have seven walls of books.' "

"I think she means she and Timmy."

I felt impatient. Why couldn't the Mims get up to speed? She mentioned the dedication to *The Other Woman*. So she'd found that, too. On her own.

"Is C the cat? Coco?" Jean Lee had dedicated her book to a dead cat!

"Well, Coco was very important to Jean, too." I detected a foreign strand in his voice. *Satisfaction?* He sighed then, sounding besieged. He said Jean was going to rent in Pasadena, but she ended up buying. My mom asked when he was going to tell her that. He said he didn't know how to tell her. Then there was a knock at her door. Boop Two! I skidded around the bushes, back into the house, down the hall. When I slid to the room, both women stood looking at Boop Two, in her pajamas, hair ridged from combing.

"I'm going to bed now," she said.

The standing green board in the bedroom had a long equation, slanting down. Graph papers fanned on the desk. But near her computer and coffee cup, there was an egg cracked open, the blue shell jagged. A real egg. The yolk just on the wooden desktop.

Boop Two mumbled good night and backed out. I stalled, bending down to pretend-tie my shoe. I no longer heard the staticky phone. They closed the door.

"Well, I don't know how you can believe a thing he says," Dr. Bach whispered. Hearing that from a doctor set off a shiver in my back.

I said good night to my sister, kissed the top of her head, then sat in the kitchen, staring at the blackboard.

YOU MUST SEARCH FOR SOME COMMON FEATURE THAT DOES NOT CHANGE WHEN YOU CHANGE THE ARRANGEMENT. AN INVARIANT.

I set the extension on my pillow. Sare said she didn't feel good about anything she was hearing. You had to love Sare. "He's hiding something," she said. "Maybe we should go out tomorrow and hire a private investigator."

My stomach clenched. What if they paid some PI to find out what we already knew? How much would that guy charge? I called Hector. He said he'd ride his bike over with our file—the deed, record searches, the real estate testimonial. I shoved out of bed and waited for him out by the garbage cans in our alley.

It was after midnight. We stood there, jammed all the papers into a big envelope, and walked around to the front door and shot it underneath, the way women had slid letters onto my dad's floor at all hours. A stone pinged my chest. Who would she think *this* was from? *Whom*, I thought. She'd want me to say *whom*. The fucking Mims. *May I please* repeated every time someone said *Can I*. She would probably assume the wife drove here, stalking us, when that woman, who looked like she'd been washed and put in the dryer too many times, probably slept soundly in Pasadena. My mom would call him as soon as she opened the envelope. She must have already told him about receiving the first batch. I hadn't heard their conversation in the restaurant.

Cell phones were a problem. She probably scared the bejesus out of him. He must have thought his wife sent that envelope, too.

We didn't sleep for a week of nights. I kept the extension next to me on my bed and felt it vibrate before the ring.

"I'm going to ask you again," she said. "And remember, this is a matter of public record, but I want to hear it from you. Are you legally divorced as you told me you were five years ago?" We hovered a long time, she and I, waiting.

Finally, his voice became someone else. "We had an agreement, but then Jean asked if I would do the right thing for Timmy." He sounded exhausted, even bored. "I just wanted to be alone this summer. I didn't want to be with any woman." It occurred to me that now, for the first time, we were hearing his real voice.

"Well, you can be alone then," my mother whispered, and hung up.

I kept waiting for—for what? Anger, maybe. She got furious with us and loomed like a smiting angel, right and strong, administering justice. But now she sounded stunned, as if she didn't want to find out more. And there was more. Lots.

A delivery guy arrived from Domino's, something she'd only allowed before on birthdays. She hovered around the table, filling our water glasses as if she'd forgotten how this part went. Dinner. After we put the dishes in the dishwasher, she let herself go to bed. This was new for me. Going to sleep after the Mims.

The phone rang. She picked up, but it was for me. Girls giggling, several of them. "Miles? Maude wanted to tell you"—a cascade—"that she's, she's, we're riding bikes by your house." Another blurt of laughter. "Wanna come outside?"

"Well, Hector's here."

It was silent a moment, as if they were conferring, someone's hand over the receiver. "He can come, too. We're just riding around."

Hector and I looked at each other. I couldn't be that way. Not now. "We're kind of busy here," I said, "but, yeah."

I thought I heard the whir of spokes.

Then, in the middle of the night, the phone trembled. My eyes felt strained, small tents pulled by stakes. It was 2:00 a.m.

"What's wrong?" my mom said.

"Oh, it's not important. A dog I was fostering bit my hand, and it's infected. They say I'll need surgery, and even then it'll never be the same."

I didn't care about his fucking hand. She never let us get away with excuses. *JK* got me ten dollars shaved off my allowance.*

Where was the wife with the curler when he called in the middle of the night? Why didn't he whine to her about his hand?

I knew what it was to be busted. Eventually, you sobbed and shook and said everything in the order it really happened. He wasn't coming clean. He was moving around the pieces she'd found into whatever shape he could to seem less horrible.

I went and stood in her doorway. It took her a while to see me. When she finally noticed, we flew into each other's arms. Her face, when she lifted it off my shoulder, was trapezoidal. "I was thinking about that Latin teacher," she said, pressing her temples. Maybe that's what adults did. She understood I could see: it was there, the egg on her desk. She couldn't hide it, so she was trying to give a bearable reason. Maybe that was the parent's job, to substitute a comprehensible sadness for the horror of random evil.

Eli was our chaos. I didn't believe there was any law to control it.

I wondered what correlation pain had with reality. All this had already been true a week ago, but she didn't know and she had still been happy.

* *At my house, Philip didn't even allow acronyms. I had to say it out. Just kidding.*

57 · A Place Beneath the Floor

The middle-of-the-night calls went on three weeks. I kept the extension on my bed, but I only woke up sometimes. Mostly, I turned the other way, the same as I did to my alarm.

He never apologized. He never came clean. He whined about his hand.

"Pretty early on, I'd told her I'd do the right thing for Timmy," I heard at 4:00 a.m.

"What about the shrink you were seeing?"

"I had to lie to her, too." *Had to!* "With her, I had to lie the other way. She didn't understand what I'd promised Jean."

Another night: "She asked me to reconcile, and then, I, then I asked her." He made it sound so polite. Dainty. Like the rounds of a dance. *Then I asked her.*

In the silence, I felt those words enter my mother, like four bullets. He'd told her he wanted to marry her. He'd said he'd give us seven thousand dollars a month. I'd heard him! But I'd heard him because I'd eavesdropped, and who else would ever know?

"So I guess we're really not going to end up together," she said.

She'd still thought they might?

"I've known that for a long time already," Eli said. "I kept telling myself, *I've got to stop stringing her along.*"

That jolted me fully awake. You don't string along someone you respect. Why didn't she know that?

At 5:00 a.m., his raspy whisper: "I've never touched her. That way, at least, I've always been faithful to you. I've kept your secrets."

"What secrets?" My mom laughed, a bad laugh. "My sexual fantasies? Eli, they're like the underwear you liked me to buy. Toys for adults who love each other."

Half asleep, I heard him talk about his hand; the infection was level 4, to the bone.

....

Mornings were worse. She looked the same but moved differently, as if pushing through mud, her spirit stunned. I went to check on her as soon as I got home from school. Every afternoon I found her in the same position on her chair. Marge was substituting her lecture class. One day, I found the room empty. On her desk a scrap.

2003–2005?
2004–2007 to Pasadena?
NSF?
Key?

Next to that, the picture from her forty-fifth birthday.

It could have been any key. Why did we fall for that? I was glad, though, that she wasn't home. She must have dragged herself up to teach her class.

In November, the Mims began to cook again. She served us meals but didn't eat. She used to love the food she made; she could never resist sneaking bites as she baked.

Boop Two saw her crying in the carpool line.

Great, I thought. This'll be the year the Mims bawls in public. I began to think like my dad. *How would it look to the other parents?* Boop Two had enough problems.

"Don't worry," I told her. "Adults cry sometimes."

"Over what?"

I shrugged. "Don't know. They just do. Try not to think about it. Worry about chipmunks." Her thing now was chipmunks. When the Boops had been small, we pushed them in a double stroller along the cliffs above the ocean with bags of stale bread to feed baby chipmunks in spring, when there were hundreds of the rodents, and in fall, for their second litter. *Sweets of chipmunks,*

Boop Two called them now, and the babies we could see tunneling through the sandy dirt that dropped down to the Pacific Coast Highway were being murdered. Our very own municipality poured poison down their holes with tax money. She'd protested at city hall.

Overpopulation was their excuse. The tunnels eroded the cliffs, they claimed.

Nights, Sare or Marge came over, sometimes both. With them, the Mims sounded alive. "I miss it all," she choked out. "I want what we had. I wish I could send it up again, but it's like a broken kite. Torn and dirty on the ground."

"You're not going to do that." Sare's voice was stern like a good doctor's.

They seemed to be talking her down from calling him or driving over there. It made me remember once standing in my crib, when my parents were dressed to go, bawling and trying to climb up the sides. A grim babysitter waited in the corner. Then the door shut, and they were gone.

Marge said, "This is a guy who lied about *where he lived*."

"I can't eat. I can barely walk." Her voice broke. "I cherished him."

"But you do walk," Sare said. "You're getting the kids dinner. That's all you have to do right now. I guarantee it will feel different a month from now. And in a year, he'll seem pathetic."

"I'm worried about the kids," she said.

"They're *fine*." I liked hearing Sare say that. Maybe we were! "And if you're not eating, well, I hate to say it, but your ass looks great."

I'd crawled into a spot in the basement under the Mims's room where I could hear. I sat cross-legged on the dirt floor. A big pipe touched my head. I couldn't really *move*.

"We have a plan," Marge announced. "Come to the kitchen."

I heard footsteps right above me. I climbed out then, brushed myself off, and went upstairs. Sare had the refrigerator open and was taking things out.

"Are we making something like cookies perchance?" I said.

"We're making something like lunches. You can help. And then, I've got the answer. Marge brought it."

Nobody asked for what. I'd noticed before that Marge Cottle kept multiple beverages going. She had a glass of wine, a bottle of iced tea, and water while making sandwiches. Then she pulled a boxed DVD set from her bag. The answer turned out to be serial television. "After Stanley died, this got me through," Marge said. "The first few you won't like, but then you'll be hooked."

We watched the first episode of *The Wire* on my mom's bed. I couldn't really understand the dialogue. She fell asleep before it was over. The next day she went running at dawn by herself and returned with her face glossed with tears.

"If you died," Boop One asked on the way to school, "would Esmeralda be my nanny?"

My one earbud was playing LCD Soundsystem.

"If something happened to me, your father and brother would take care of you."

"I wouldn't like that," Boop Two said.

"Neither would I," I said. "Dad, I mean I love Dad, but . . ." She couldn't die, I thought. I didn't want to be stuck with them. I had my life.

58 · Tampering with the U.S. Mail

I kind of missed Ben Orion. We called him and just got his machine.

"It's a bad ending," I told Hector. "Not like in Holmes."

"Our deduction was sound. We got the truth," Hector said. "We just don't like it."

"The reality Holmes uncovered seemed better," I said.

"Don't forget the guy was an opium addict."

Ben Orion returned our call a week later, from Arizona.

"How's your guy there?" I asked. "He still on the up-and-up?"

"No recidivism?" Hector said. *Show-off,* I mouthed.

"Yeah, he is, he definitely is," Ben said. "But there's a wrinkle. My guys were tailing him, and they followed him right into a Twelve Step meeting. That freaked them. So I flew there and attended undercover. The group turned out to be for codependence. His son had gotten into some drug trouble. Our guy was there to help his boy."

"Like in Shakespeare," Hector said. "Your kid pays for everything bad you do."

"It never goes the other way?" I asked. "From the kid's bad to the parents?"

I was thinking of my grades, which my mom didn't know about yet, because I'd intercepted the report from our mailbox. I'd been lucky; it had arrived when she was at UCLA. She tore through the mail every night now, probably expecting something from Eli, a refutation of all the documents that had already come to her or at least an apology. The way she grabbed the envelopes made me think she and Eli weren't speaking. Because of cell phones I couldn't be sure. But the house was quiet now all night long. Normally, she would have wondered where our midways were. I'd had to confiscate the Boops' too, because seeing theirs would have reminded her of mine. The only virtue of her misery was a loosening of her vigilance around the house, though every day she didn't wonder about our reports frightened me. Didn't she need to read them?

I thought I had to open the Boops', just to make sure nothing was wrong. Boop One's was perfect: Emma was a hard worker, a good student, and she was learning, the teacher wrote, *to be* consistently *inclusive.* The teacher worried about Boop Two's happiness, but said that her reading was improving and listed two books she'd completed. The Mims would have given her a reward for those two books, but I couldn't without arousing suspicion.

Our mom sat at the table with us now at dinner, but she still didn't eat much. I didn't notice at the time, but I must have eaten less, too. People began to say I was losing weight. Sometimes we looked at each other and said, *This will have to be a two-episode night.*

Hector doodled all day in school. He kept a pencil behind his ear. Even on tests, he drew in margins. One Friday night, he asked if I had a picture of Eli. He wanted to improve on the sketch we'd shown the librarian. I got the one Sare took at my mom's birthday party. Hector had already perfected the crenellated head of Bart Simpson. It wasn't a huge leap to Eli, whose head was the shape of a shoebox, with the shaved sides and hair straight up on top. His hair was already cartoon. That was the beginning of *Our Psychopath. A comic epic.* I thought maybe we could make money with it.

"Did you know that liars hide their hands? They stroke the backs of their heads."

"Eli did that. But my dad does it, too."

A week later, in school, Hector showed me a stapled flyer he'd taken down from a Co-opportunity community board:

Best Days for Surveillance to Catch a Cheating Spouse
We'll Give You Peace of Mind
Call: 1-800-94-TRUTH

- **The cheater's birthday**
- **Wednesday before Thanksgiving**
- **The Friday following Thanksgiving Day when claiming they have to work**

"Man. He came late for Thanksgiving because he was 'working in the shelter.'"

"He lied with lies that made him sound noble," Hector said. "He got *credit* for being with dying animals when he was at some big dinner with his wife and kid. You know what I found in that book? Lying isn't a means to an end. They're *in* it for the deception. It's a high. They call it duper's delight."

That bothered me more than anything.

You don't dupe people you love.

The next day, Hector hauled me into the computer lab.

"Look at this. A live psychopath! He wrote in to an advice column."

Dear Dr. Ambrose,

I am a moderate sociopath, and though part of me doesn't want to change, another does. It's entertaining to see how stupid people can be. They're so gullible. Yes, I am parasitic, but even so, there are some people I would like to stop hurting. I knew I was a sociopath before the age of ten but have only recently had it officially diagnosed. I have been lying and destroying others' sanity for a long time. So, please post some tidbits that might help sociopaths resist the sweet urges we get when we encounter weak human beings. Sociopaths, though born that way, are people, too.

"He's Shakespearean," Hector said. " 'Sweet are the uses of adversity.' "

"I wish I knew some uses."

59 · Retroactively Chumped

I developed rituals. As soon as I got home from winter tennis, the first thing I did was pick through the mail. I found a catalog of cookies the Mims ordered every year and put that on the top of the pile. I found a letter she had written to Eli Lee, at 4201 Wilson Blvd., Arlington, VA 22230, stamped NO ADDRESSEE. RETURN TO SENDER. I tore the thing open. It was a thank-you note she'd written him months ago for flying out to her birthday party. It didn't mention the cheese platter. I'd one-clicked a book called *Blankets* the guy at Neverland told me about, and I was watching for that Amazon package. One day, I picked up an envelope, addressed to

Irene Adler, no *Miss* or *Ms.* or *Mrs.*, and a blank where a return address would be, postmarked SANTA ANA, CA. I thought I recognized Eli's penmanship. I hid it in my sock drawer until Hector arrived. We knew to open it with steam. We boiled a pot of water. I didn't realize, though, that the envelope would ruffle. That would show.

> Dear Irene,
>
> This letter is the most difficult I've ever had to write. Literally. I know I must write this by hand, but my hand is always so wobbly I can't make out my handwriting. And right there, in that first sentence—by focusing, as I always have, on my feelings rather than on the difficulties and pain that I've caused and am causing you—I've added to the obscenity of what I've done. What I find myself muttering and have been muttering to myself for so long is that I'm sorry and that I never meant to hurt you.
>
> My connection to you and the small ways that I've been able to help you have been so central and addictive to me.
>
> You will ask why I've done this.
>
> I deeply wanted to be with you.
>
> Many people experience great calamities and overcome them. I've never been able to overcome, really even slightly, my mother's death, and it's left me in need of connections to her. I know almost no one who knew she ever lived. Those connections now amount to Jean and my brother. My memories of her and of Coco are stained completely by their terrible illnesses—that's really all I think about when I think about them, and I think of them hourly. And I don't know where to put this, but I wanted to make sure I was with my dog when she was died. She's old now, too. More important, toward the end I knew there was no way you could be with me after I revealed what I'd done.
>
> For a time I convinced myself that my deception was not so

bad. Then I realized that I'd have to reveal to you my terrible deception, one that soon became monstrous. I cataloged my lies. Those lies are deeper and fuller than I've ever told you—and even now I can't send you the catalog. Every day I tried to summon the courage to tell you: I always failed. I couldn't bring myself to reveal these bad things because I prized your esteem. I imagined I would extricate myself, we wouldn't talk for a year or eighteen months, and then eventually I could start to try to get you back.

I will always be available to help you. You can trust me to listen, to keep your confidences, to advise, to help me find the right teakettle. But you must not trust me to give you an honest view of myself—my self-loathing and readiness to lie are too deep.

I knew long ago that you had given me the greatest happiness, and that I have repaid that with actions that bring me (again—me) profound shame. I will carry both with me forever.

A teakettle! I put the thing down. My hand was shaking. "A teakettle!" I started to laugh, but the shaking grew. I'd never cried in front of a guy before. Eli hadn't even proofread. He wrote *me* when he meant *you*. That's how unimportant we were. When I finally looked up, I saw Hector's face. All this time, Hector had gone bad cop on Eli, but now his features were drained, and his bones stuck out.

"She's banked her life on him, and he offers to help her select, not even buy, a teakettle," he said.

"He said himself that he was monstrous." He didn't even mention my sisters or me. "Do you think we should glue the envelope and put it back in the mail?"

"She'd probably feel retroactively chumped off. Maybe we should burn it."

We rode bikes to Ben Orion's house. We didn't even call first.

Just as we slowed, our shoes sanding the sidewalk, a woman with a ponytail dashed out of his gate and into a white car.

"You guys look different again," Ben said, opening the door. When he first met us, we'd worn shorts. California kids stay barelegged for years. Then, overnight, they start wearing jeans. It happens around the time you switch from baths to showers. Boop Two still wore shorts. But one day soon she'd come out of her room and it would be over. Forever.

"New girlfriend?" I asked.

"Oh, no, that was the lady I told you about. After this last trip, she finally decided to fire me. Was kind of emotional. We've been doing surveillance together nineteen years."

"After that guy, did she ever find someone else?"

"For a while she did. Now she's on her own with a kid. How's your mom?"

"Every day she makes an X on the calendar," I said. "We're on week nine. But we got this letter."

After he read it, Ben put the folded paper down. "Well, the guy has a way with words. I couldn't of written that."

"You'd never have to," I said.

His finger traced over the paper, picking out traps and lures. "See, he's laying out a scenario. Eighteen months. He's setting her up to hang on another year and a half. People who get out, get out," he said. "They get out tonight. I see it all the time."

"Too bad he didn't send that catalog of lies," Hector said. "I'd like to see it." I knew Hector: he wanted it for our comic book.

"He didn't make any list a lies," Ben said. "He's grandstanding. People who do inventory, they're deep in. He's still just spinning cotton candy."

"You can tell from just this?"

He picked up the envelope. "He doesn't even give her his address. Doesn't know we already have it."

"Should we burn the thing?" Hector asked. "She hasn't been doing so well."

Ben Orion shrugged. "We're not God. It's her letter. Let her open it or not."

I stuffed it back into the ruffled envelope, glad to be told what to do.

"I've got bread rising," Ben said. "You guys know how to knead?"

"His mom does," Hector said.

He handed us aprons that looked like bibs. "Really? I thought mathematician. Head in the sky."

He took the puffy dough out of an oiled bowl. It was like a stomach. Kneading was fun at first, then work. You had to keep going. My hands hurt.

"People at UCLA probably still think Eli lives in Washington," I said.

"Sure," Ben said. "They're in the 'Irene' column."

"Why did he have to find *us*?"

"Con artists are canny judges. They find good people," Ben said. "*He's* not going to be taken. Be a lot worse if she'd married him."

"But her happiness," I said, "it was all fake."

"Was she happy, really?" Hector asked. "Maybe it was just hope for happiness."

"Hope for happiness *is* happiness," I said.

Ben shook his head. "Love. It's the one thing you should never lie about."

"That woman we saw," I said. "How did she finally get over the guy?"

"I don't know that she did."

"Well, then how did you talk her into firing you?"

"I didn't. It was our guy in Arizona. I told you he's in Twelve Step. As part of that, you have to make amends to everyone you've wronged. He sent back money he'd taken from her, with the interest compounded."

Ben showed us how he'd put bricks inside his oven to form an open box. The kind of thing Sare was always complaining our dads didn't do. But I couldn't exactly imagine our moms with Ben Orion either. It had something to do with Sacramento State College and the way he talked, what I recognized but wouldn't have then called class.

He walked us out to our bikes. The moon hung low, close to the rooftops, a huge ball.

"Sure you guys don't want to wait till the bread comes out?"

But we had to get home. "Hey," I said. "What happened to the stalker you sent back to Idaho?"

"That's all quiet. He's living with his mom again. We've got somebody in Boise checking up on him. Make sure the old lady doesn't die. Still the same job, but he joined a group at the local library that meets once a month to talk about *American Idol*. All the studies show just being a member of a group, any group, makes people happier."

"What Eli did should be a crime," Hector said.

"It was, once upon a time. You could sue a man for harming a woman's marital prospects. But your mom'll have plenty suitors."

"How do *you* know?" I tried to say that in a nice way.

"I saw her once. Going into your house. She was carrying a bag of groceries." So he thought she was beautiful, too. Maybe Ben Orion had a crush on the Mims from afar. Maybe *that* was why he'd helped us for free. "You think she's okay for money and everything?" he asked.

I really didn't know. She'd been counting on Eli's seven thousand a month. I didn't tell Ben or Hector that. I was ashamed we needed money.

60 · Flushing Drugs

I glued the envelope, but it still looked tampered with. I tried to iron it smooth on the ironing board in the basement. I browned a corner, then just slid it back into our mail, between two bills. The next day, when Hector and I loped in, Marge stood in our kitchen mixing batter, her arm like a ham. "Bundt," she said. My mom bent over chopping walnuts. I checked and found the letter still unopened. I'd buried it too well. The bills weren't opened either.

The Boops sat on the Eli-sofa, decorating tags: *From the Adler family.* Cakes cooled on mesh racks. Hector asked how many they were making.

"Hundred, hundred ten," Marge said. "It's everybody at your school and all the departmental secretaries."

"Nothing like this ever happens in our house," Hector said. "I don't even think our oven works."

The oven too now! I knew the washing machine was busted. He didn't tell me these things. And he knew everything about me! Why didn't Philip just call a repair guy? I felt bad about his oven. Once, a long time ago, his mom had made jam with us in their kitchen.

When Philip arrived to pick up Hector, Marge poured him a glass of wine. "Not too shabby," he said, the glass in one hand, a small cake in the other. For him, this was ebullience. I felt like asking him about his broken machines. My sisters tied their tags onto red-cellophane-wrapped cakes for the teachers, janitors, parking patrol guys, secretaries, and the school nurse. The assembly line reminded me of all the other years, but the Mims stood like a zombie, doing her job with blank eyes. I worried about money.

Hector herded his dad to the door. "I've still got Latin and my book's at home."

School was all of a sudden hard. While we'd been busy, we found ourselves dropped into the time when everything *counted.* I had a paper due, but I kept thinking of presents my mom had given Eli. She'd bought him a digital camera once to take pictures of his son. She'd given him cuff links and what should have been my watch. I assumed the parties he attended, where he wore cuff links and the four suits, took place far away. At least we'd found out before Christmas; she wouldn't buy him anything this year. Did he wear that watch with the Victim? Did *she* ever ask where it came from?

"Leave a list of your teachers," my mom said, "and who should get cakes."

I wrote down every teacher. I figured I'd need the help.

By the weekend, the letter was gone from the mail basket.

She still took us where we needed to go. She signed our permission slips. She gave off a feeling of trudging through an obstacle course with no appetite or hope of pleasure. Even Pedro, the security guard at our school (who earned hardly any money, she'd once told us, which was why we had to look at him and say his name when we said good morning and why she'd stayed up baking him a miniature Bundt cake, to go along with the twenty-dollar bill), *he* asked me, "Everything okay your family? Your mom look like she be sad." I worried about all those twenty-dollar bills, too.

In hac spe vivo. Now what didn't seem a question anymore. We would go on like this for months, I thought. Years, maybe. My dad put Post-its on his glass doors. *Tell Malc to send cases of pinot to Susan, Jeff, Adam, and Bailey.* People he worked with and his bosses. My mom baked cakes for janitors and secretaries.

No wonder he made more money.

Our mother slept. In our family, we all looked like my dad, but though he woke up at four in the morning and cycled through frets until it was light, the three of us came out true great sleepers. Nine hours was nothing to us. I could do fourteen. The Mims had always loved to sleep. My dad had joked that they'd have a fight, he'd stomp out to let off steam, and when he came back, she'd be sleeping. *Soundly,* he'd added for the laugh. Since October, though, I'd woken at odd times in the night to her crying. I never told that I heard; a measure of her despair was the fear that she was failing us.

I hadn't known that happiness was a requirement for parenthood. I didn't know how I'd ever manage. But now, the noise had stopped: she went to bed early, and we had to wake her in the morning.

"I bought pajamas at lunch," she told me one day, coming in with a bag. She seemed to live for sleep. I'd seen her computer open to a consumer page, comparing mattresses. Maybe I'd have to go to college nearby, I thought, if things didn't improve.

Twice, Sare drove us home from school. Those days, my mom pushed up from bed and made supper in her pajamas. She slept, burned food, cut herself with the knife slicing an Asian pear. She'd become less capable, overnight.

"Remember the Christmas lights?" Hector said.

"Fucking Christmas lights."

"You got ladders from the gardener. Every year, you kept thinking Eli would do it."

"He probably put up lights on that house we saw with his kid."

"We could go look. We could appropriate the bug. I can drive, remember?"

I let him spin out the adventure in my small room in Santa Monica. Pasadena was thirty-some miles away. When his mom was out, we'd have to drive off without her or his aunt seeing, in Kat's old powder-blue VW.

"But what if we got caught?" I said. "Like by police!"

"They're only allowed to stop you if you're breaking the law. My dad said that."

We google-mapped the address, planned a route without freeways, but I didn't think we'd ever use it.

My mom showed us pictures of puppies from a breeder. The one she said had poodle hair, apparently good for allergies, was butt ugly. Hector thought so, too. Sare, when she came by, said it looked learning disabled. You had to love Sare.

"I don't want that dog," I said.

My sisters chorused me. Only Philip thought he wasn't so bad. He and the Mims talked on the porch. Hector and I climbed up to the roof to hear.

"You can't yell somebody into loving you," she said. So she must have told Philip. I liked knowing that they talked.

Philip knocked on his old briefcase. "Eighty student interpretations of *Hamlet*."

"I worry that you're not liking this enough," the Mims said.

"I worry about that, too," he said, and then called Hector.

We hugged the eave spout, then dropped to the ground, our hands smelling of grass and the cold smear of mud.

One Wednesday, I came home to the box of cookies we'd ordered waiting on the porch. I hid the red tins under the Mims's bed so the Boops wouldn't consume them before the holidays. I peed in her bathroom then and, for no reason, opened her medicine chest. I found a bottle of pills still in the pharmacy bag. Xanax. I googled it and learned it was a tranquilizer, then opened the small plastic bottle and lifted out the cotton. The pills were tiny, innocent-looking.

I called Hector. "They're sleeping pills. But she already sleeps all the time."

"Are you worried she'll hurt herself?"

I remembered the night of keening outside our old house. I guess I thought it was possible. "I don't know. She's on day seventy-four. But she doesn't seem much better. She might even be a little worse."

"We could go to CVS and find vitamins that look like the pills. Then we can switch them." It occurred to me again that Hector was the smartest person I knew. Philip forbade him to leave on a weeknight, though, so I had to wait for his sister to fall asleep so he could shinny out their window. Two hours later, Hector knocked at my back wall. He'd come on his bike. We rode to the all-night Rite Aid. I'd brought a Baggie of the pills. They were white and oval, with XANAX printed on them in tiny letters. I worried about the writing. It was hard to tell in the pill aisle what the vitamins looked like. We couldn't open the jars without getting caught. "But wait," Hector said. "Will she even remember what they look like? Probably not. Let's just get vitamin C. She'll never think somebody's swapped them out on her."

I emptied the Xanax pills into the toilet and flushed them down, filled the jar with vitamins, and stuffed the cotton back in.*

"Miles!" my mother called later that night. "Were you in my bathroom?"

My heart went stone. "Yeah."

I waited, suspended in the stretched air.

"Please remember to put the toilet seat down."

Another thing my vexing report said, besides the grades, was that I was behind on community service hours.

"Same," Hector told me. That had to be wrong. So we went to see Mrs. Fisk. Even though we'd done tons for FLAGBTU, since it was a club, she said, it didn't count. Same with Specials tennis. Specials didn't count *because* I'd done it for so long. Mrs. Fisk said if I wanted to do something new, like run a bake sale or a raffle to benefit the Specials, *those* hours could count, because they'd represent a *dif*ferent activity. I asked the Specials director, and he said, "Well, city supplies rackets and the van. They buy balls." He shrugged. "They don't really need money."

"So community service isn't actually to serve the community," Hector said. "It's for us to develop 'new skills.' The way scholarships here aren't for the recipients. They're for us to 'experience diversity.' "

Philip made him do Clean Up the Beach. Charlie said you just put trash in a bag, and you could claim eight hours' service. Philip

---

* *Then I come to this thing about you* flushing *the Xanax. I didn't remember you did that. What were you thinking! The point should have been: she gets the vitamin C, we get the Xanax. Win/Win.*

dropped us off at the bottom of the California Incline, which was kept intact by murdering chipmunks.

"Was your grandfather a psychopath?" Hector asked me as we trudged over the sand. "Women are supposed to fall in love with men like their fathers."

"I don't think so. I mean, she saw him like four times her whole life."

We had to sign up at a table, set in sand. They gave us each four huge garbage sacks and balled-up litterbags for dog poop.

"I thought animals weren't allowed on the beach."

"They're not," the woman said, "but you know. People."

"My mom got a four-hundred-dollar fine," Charlie said, walking with us; his head was already pointed toward the clump of standing girls, who held their sandals. I looked at their legs, wondering if I was like any of their fathers. Maude Stern's legs were shaped like scalene triangles.

I tied my laces together and hung my shoes around my neck; Hector stuck his flip-flops in his shirt pocket. We headed south toward the pier, bending down every few minutes for garbage. It was amazing the shit people dropped. You kind of expected pop tabs and candy wrappers, but we found condoms, barrettes, a green sparkly high-heeled shoe, cigarette butts, two combs, one stray earring, and pennies. People left food, too: sanded watermelon rinds, gritty French fries, a whole carrot.

"My aunt is back in the hospital," Hector said, wiping the carrot on his shirt.

"Oh. That sucks," I answered, the surf roaring at our backs. What could you say?

"Don't tell anybody."

I wouldn't. "You want to know something bad?" I wanted to give him a secret of my own, to prove it. "My mom thinks she's not a good person." There was no one else I could tell this to, not even the Boops. Hector loved my mom a way you couldn't love your own mother. "Remember Eli told her if she was crippled that would be better than what was wrong with her because a bad leg wouldn't get in the way of a relationship?"

"Like having a wife didn't get in the way!"

"She believed him when he said things like that, though, because she's always wondering: Is she good enough? Could she *improve*? She wants to improve us, too."

"But she's a really good person. She's my favorite. Of the moms." Hector kicked sand. "Eli wasn't very worried about improving. If he had any conscience, he would have committed suicide by now."

I shrugged. "I heard her say once that if two people like them were lucky enough to find each other, there was a God. They said they were going to join a church. And they were going to become birdwatchers."

"Him with his two wives. That'd go over well with the congregation. Maybe it's only good people who worry about being bad."

"And her crimes, like forgetting his birthday. They go flimsy against *his*." I'd been mortified when the Mims forgot his hometown. I'd felt guilty about my not wanting Eli to move in. Not anymore. If he was evil, did that make us good? We seemed better to me now. It was a relief, in a way.

We heard the highway, where headlights staggered on, smearing the fog.

"I'm jealous of you," Hector said.

"Me? Why?" I was truly dumbfounded. Why would anyone be jealous of me?

"At least you got rid of him. I wish I could get rid of Surfer-dude." Hector picked up a whole apple from the sand, wiped it on his shirt, and bit into it.

"I'm not sure we're rid of Eli forever." Sometimes, when I was falling asleep, I imagined that he'd come to our door with a stack of wrapped presents and a long, long story that would make all of it forgivable, like in a book.

....

When Philip picked us up, he invited me along to see Jules playing Nurse in *Romeo and Juliet*, but I thought I'd better get home. Then, once I was there, I snapped at the Boops to clean their room.

The house had loosened its angles. The kitchen floor felt sticky and slanted. I swept every night after dinner, but that didn't keep it clean. Mail piled up in random stacks on all the surfaces. The Boops' beds stayed unmade until I yanked the scrambled sheets up before I said good night. Boop Two still didn't like to read. "Boring," she said about *To Kill a Mockingbird*. "Scary" was her excuse for stopping *Harry Potter*.

I checked the Mims's medicine cabinet. Every couple days I counted the vitamin Cs in the Xanax bottle. There were still thirty.

After the play, Hector's dad dropped him off. They worried about us now the way we used to worry about them.

The last day before vacation, we stayed after school to collect the jackets and scarves from the cardboard boxes we'd set out around campus for the FLAGBTU cold-weather drive. Through the glass of a door, I glimpsed Maude in a school desk, facing a wall, her shoulders heaving. I'd been at Cottonwoods since kindergarten, so I'd seen most people cry. But not her. Whenever Maude had any emotion in my presence, it felt off. As if it were an act. What she really meant was *Like me*. And what I had in me was *I don't. Can't.* But this was different. She didn't know I was watching.

I stepped into the classroom and she looked up.

"We're probably going to put our cat to sleep," she said.

"Wait, didn't you have two cats?" They had one they kept in the house, I thought, and an outside one that tormented it.

"Tomcat and Mittens. I'm talking about Tomcat."

Hector burst in, then. "Oh, hi, Maude. How did you like the math test?"

"Not bad," she said.

Hector and I looked at each other. "I thought it was effing impossible," I said.

"Did you study the supplementary problems?"

Instead of answering—I mean, it was pretty obvious we hadn't studied the supplementary problems—I told Hector about Maude's cat. She said he'd attacked the neighbor's maltidoodle.

"Has he ever bitten a person?" Hector asked, with that weird intensity he got.

"He did!" she said. "Oh my God, this three-year-old was toddling along, with my brother's friend, and he jumped up and bit his knee."

Maude's mom wanted to give the cat away, but no one would take him. Hector was following this story so intently I wondered, all of a sudden, could *he* like Maude? She was mine, kind of! Even though I hadn't decided I really wanted her.

"If you bring him to the pound," I said, "they'll kill him. Cat adoptions are way rarer than dogs." I knew from my sister that they put down eight or nine cats a week.

"Tomcat has issues, but he doesn't deserve to die. We're trying to find him a home. There's an organization that places animals, but they have a long wait list. My mom asked what would get them to for sure take Tomcat. They said fifteen hundred dollars."

"We'll do it for three," Hector said.

"What?" I said. "How do you think—"

"Ask your mom," he said to Maude, interrupting me.

61 · A Revenge Plot

Maude told us the next day that her mom would pay three hundred dollars, but she needed to be certain nothing bad would happen to Tomcat. They wanted him to have a good life.

"This couple we know," Hector said, "they *love* animals. Even difficult ones."

The mammal was huge. It must have weighed half as much as Boop One. Maude's brother handed us a crate. "Now, I'll be happy to call the new owners," their mother said. Maude stood there, barefoot in a skirt, holding Mittens, the fluffy indoors cat. Her legs were very, very long, her feet small. "Can you manage?"

We carried the heavy thing, me in front, Hector in the rear. Maude walked us to the edge of her lawn. "Where's his new home?"

"Pasadena," I mumbled.

Then, when she cartwheeled, her skirt dropped open so I saw tight hot-pink shorts.

I hissed as soon as we turned the corner. "How're we going to transport this oversize vermin to Pasadena?"

"It won't be as heavy without the crate."

"We need the crate, dumbo. You can't tie a cat to a doorknob. What if they're not home? We've got to leave it with food and water. Probably at night, so they don't see us. You haven't thought this through. Are you planning for your dad to drive us?"

"He'd make us tell your mom. Do you think she wants revenge?"

Confucius had appeared on the blackboard: BEFORE YOU EMBARK ON A JOURNEY OF REVENGE, DIG TWO GRAVES. "She's not there yet," I said.

"I'm there," Hector said.

The car sputtered and then spurted forward like a go-kart. "See, I'm not a bad—"

"Look where you're going!" My hand hovered in the air, ready to grab the wheel. Not that I knew how to steer. "Don't talk." I stayed mad. The vehicle wobbled and veered too close to the parked cars on my side. I ducked in toward the middle. Before we passed under the 405, something changed, and the motion felt different, as if we were sliding on ice. Then the car sputtered to a stop.

"What? Whoa. You're out of gas, man! I can't believe you!"

"Kat is such a flake."

"Don't blame your mom. She probably would've filled it up the minute she took it out."

We bickered like a long-married couple. I said he had to call his dad. He wanted to try the Mims. "She'd be kinder," he said. We blamed each other. Finally, Hector dialed Ben Orion, who sounded extremely annoyed. Forty minutes later, he arrived carrying a can of gas with a spout like the Tin Man's, still angry. We saw the police side of him. He unscrewed the cap and poured it in. He nudged Hector out of the driver's seat and silently steered us to a Union 76, where he filled the tank and paid.

"You guys realize you've broken the law," he finally said.

We tried to explain about the cat and Pasadena. His mouth stayed in a straight line. "I don't like this at all."

"No," I said. "I didn't expect you would."

He started driving. We stayed quiet. Finally, I asked where we were going.

"I'm driving this car back to wherever you found it."

"What about your car?" I said.

"I'll have to get a taxi. This time I'm going to let you pay me."

We tried to argue that Hector could drive now, but Ben wouldn't hear of it. In the Palisades, we had to tell him where to turn to get to Hector's aunt's house.

"What about the cat?" Hector said.

"I suggest we take a taxi to my car, then I drive to where you got the cat, you tell the truth and give it back."

"But it'll die otherwise!" I explained.

Ben Orion just shook his head.

"He likes the girl," Hector said. That was a cheap shot.

I started to object, and we talked for a while sitting in the car outside Hector's aunt's house. Ben Orion wanted us to put the psychopath behind us. "The mystery's solved," he said. "Case closed. Now it's just life. Next time I see you, we won't even talk about

Eli Lee. And, *and*, you'll have each read a book on a new subject. You've gotta develop hobbies." Hobbies! That word seemed to belong to another era.

But we agreed. When the taxi he'd called arrived, he stepped out. "You sure you don't want to get a ride and return the cat?"

We shook our heads.

"You're going to try to deliver that thing, aren't you?" he said.

I didn't answer one way or the other. I shrugged. I didn't want to lie.

"I don't like this," he said. "I don't like this at all."

By the time we got off the bus in Pasadena, the sky was deep blue with one visible star and a bright crescent moon. When we found the street again, the house looked like it had before. No Christmas lights. Only a sad wreath on the door, the kind you bought at Ralphs, with a fake paper-velvet ribbon.

We lifted the crate with Tomcat balancing inside and hauled it to the edge of their lawn. We'd planned to put Tomcat on the porch, but now that seemed risky. Maybe they'd hear the thing meowing in its crate. I slipped in a treat from my pocket. When we turned around and started walking, Tomcat made a sound like nothing I'd ever heard from a cat. Then we ran.

I felt relieved that Eli's house had no lights. He must have promised lights to his own kid if he'd promised *me* lights. I was glad he'd been bad to that kid, too.

"Hey, what happened with the puppy?" Hector asked, on the long ride home.

"She came back with more pictures on her phone. But we're not getting a dog. She just likes thinking that we're the kind of family that could. We can't afford a breeder dog anyway."

"Want to make a mutant when we get home?"

We dug out the bag of half-ruined animals, cut and sewed in a desultory way, like we had for days and days in middle school, but we'd lost the heart for it. The next time Zeke came over, they went home in the grocery bag to his house, and we never mentioned them again. For all I know, they're still there. His mother is an artist and doesn't go on rampages to throw things away. She keeps household odds and ends, believing they'll come to some eventual, higher use.

Hector didn't go away that year for break. His dad was stuck grading finals. And his aunt was losing it. "Christmas is the worst time of year if your boyfriend's married," Hector said. "She should break up with him. But he woos her back every January." Hector sussed out the Bundt cakes in our kitchen. I was sick of them already. "We should give one to Ben," he said. We rode our bikes, with a red-wrapped cake in the front wire basket. But Ben wasn't home. He hadn't called us either. We left the cake in his mailbox.

62 · My Sin

I told Boop Two she could stay up late. *It's vacation!* But she wanted to go to sleep. And then the house went quiet. I puttered, wishing my mom would get home so we could watch an episode of *The Wire*. It turned eleven, then twelve, and I began to search on her computer.

In the drafts folder I found an unsent e-mail to Sare.

I can't even kill myself because the kids

That stunned me. No period. *Because the kids* what? Or did she mean because *of* us. I'd once heard Eli wail like an animal. I thought it was him, anyway. I googled *suicide*. There was a hotline number, but that was for if you were about to jump off a bridge, not if you were scared about your mom. One in the morning, and she still wasn't home. I paced. I called her cell phone. Her mailbox was full. She hadn't said where she was going tonight, only that I was babysitting. I thought of calling Marge, but now it was really late. I tried to make myself pray, but I didn't know how; we'd been raised without religion. Fucking mixed marriage. What was I supposed to do? I started counting. Prime numbers and then number chains. I thought of calling the police, but I'd have to say her name, and I didn't know if they kept records. I didn't want it to affect her job. I dialed my dad and got his machine. I kept counting. I worked myself into a weird state. I counted and rocked; maybe this *was* praying. I never told anyone, even Hector.*

Finally, I heard tires bite up the drive.

I dived into bed, turned the light off, and pulled up the blankets, still counting to myself when I heard hangers in her closet. She walked down the hall and opened the Boops' door. Then mine. I closed my eyes, pretending sleep. I still had clothes on, even socks and shoes, under the covers. She walked to my head and pulled the comforter up to my chin. I tried not to move. I felt her breath on my face. Then she rose, but she didn't leave; she collapsed in the chair at my desk. We stayed in the dark, Gal scrabbling on wood chips in the terrarium where she'd lived her whole life. My mom stood and opened a window. She cried evenly then, not loud. After a while she stopped. Then I was asleep.

But the next day I woke up hurting in my shoes. When my mom left with Boop Two to deliver presents for a poor family the school had assigned, I dialed Eli on his home number we weren't supposed to have.

He answered the first ring. He probably had caller ID and saw our number.

"It's Miles Adler," I said. "My mother killed herself."

For a moment there was silence.

Then his voice caught on a sob—I recognized the animal cry

---

* *You were too spooked to tell me you prayed! You could have told me that. I did bath salts. I did LSD. I had a conversation with Jesus on 'shrooms.*

from that night long ago. I hung up and stared at the phone, afraid something would happen. Certain he'd call right back. Horrified at what I'd started. But he didn't call. Not then. I couldn't believe myself. I'd been afraid for a long time. My mother was harmed. She was worse. Less. I assumed the change was permanent.

All day long, everything held still, our life again. The trees outside looked dense, pulled into themselves. The air felt like air after a storm, new clear.

A reprieve. My sisters clomped back in, and I liked them. We moved slowly. I brought the Mims a coffee and played a game of Trouble with the Boops on the floor. The doorbell rang: I froze. But it was Marge. Marge! I hugged her. She looked surprised but game and grateful. That afternoon, even with the Mims not up to speed, I felt patient. I trusted her to return to us. I didn't mind, right then, my life away from the eddying bright hormones that flashed at school. Away from the whorl of chaos, in our small house, we could mend and grow.

I didn't want to think about what I'd done. But it had accomplished something: we would live far away from him. If I'd learned that the Lees had moved to another continent, Australia, for example, I could have almost wished him well.

Every year, the Mims volunteered us at a food bank. We stood in line freezing outside the big airport hangar, jumping to warm ourselves, but I was glad to be there. If Eli showed up at our house we'd be gone. I'd been sure to turn off the lights when we left. We ran into the cavernous, high-ceilinged warehouse, and it was still as cold as outside, but there was room to move. We joined up with Charlie's family at their long table. Rock music from our parents' era boomed in, the Stones pounding, as the Boops counted out carrots. The Grateful Dead. "Box of Rain." The Mims and Sare measured scoops of dry corn into ziplocks. Maude's mom gave me a box knife to slash open sacks of potatoes. So many times with community service, it seemed that the community served was actually doing *us* the favor. But there was work here for real: every family would receive a crate with four dozen potatoes, twenty apples, bags of grain, vegetables, and a turkey. Maude's mom ran the show, standing next to the open back of the hangar where the trucks parked, with a whistle around her neck. She bent down to hear people above the noise. She had red hair, too, but the red was mixed with other colors and her curls were loose. Her hair was long, longer than Maude's. I didn't think I'd ever seen that before. A mother with longer hair than her daughter. Charlie and I did more than we had last year. Maude's brother let us unload a truck bed of turnips by ourselves.

Finally, at midnight, our shift ended, but the music was still going. I wasn't tired, and I never wanted to go home. My mom and Sare stood shouting, their breath visible. None of us had really eaten. We ended up standing at the Slice, biting pizza on napkins, them talking about how next year, they'd plan. "A thick barley soup," Sare said.

"How about not," I mumbled, and Charlie laughed.

I bolted out of the car and ran up to our porch in case Eli had left a note or slid a letter under our door. But no. Nothing. No phone calls that night either; I half slept. I got up a few times to check outside; no cars moved on our street. This was evil: an absence—just wind, the place where guilt would pool. I turned over and tried to think of something else. I didn't want Eli to come. I was afraid of him because of what I'd done.

After my bad prank I waited days, and nothing happened. Eli never knocked at our door. I didn't see another letter. I checked CID on our phone. It was as if my lie lived suspended in a nether zone. What if the Mims *had* died? I wondered. He thought she had, and he didn't do anything.

Once, he couldn't live without her. Now he could, apparently. Did. I remembered an old humiliation. I'd sat, knee against bare knee, with Charlie, and he said Zeke was his best friend. My head weighed on the stem of my neck. *I was your best friend and you changed your mind but didn't tell me.* I didn't protest that someone could stop loving me. The only complaint I thought I had a right to was that he didn't tell me *when. What to make of a diminished thing.* A line from a fifteen-dollar poem I couldn't remember the name of. Since then, Charlie and I had been good, but we'd never been really close again. Maybe he didn't want that. And anyway, I was fine with Hector. But the Mims didn't have her Hector.

What I'd done felt imaginary; the fallout was so silent. Still, I'd really called him. If the Mims found out, she'd be disappointed. I understood uncaught criminals who walked through the world trembling. I was glad no one knew. That was probably the way Eli felt every day.

For a while, in the shade of his crime, I'd felt we were simple and good, trying to walk in ordinary sun. Now I'd blighted myself.

I was ashamed to have loved someone who didn't care about us. For I had loved him. Even aside from her. I didn't think I'd ever see him again. I hoped I wouldn't. I held my mind, as if I couldn't trust it, and pointed it—this way, not there. I wanted to avoid the things I didn't want to think about: clusters of wind, unformed and horrible, like a dead near-birth, a tooth grown inside hair.

Holidays didn't happen in 2007. My dad bailed on Hanukkah, and the Mims gave us only okay presents for Christmas. "I don't want to sound greedy," Boop One said, "but is that all there is?"

I remembered the year when, after we'd opened presents, she'd shown me the tree house. I liked thinking of the Rabbits' Pad now. Even if we still lived there, I probably wouldn't go in it anymore.

My mom disappeared for a few minutes. I thought maybe she'd gone to a hiding place to get more loot. An Xbox 360 with Guitar Hero. But where would she have it set up? I heard a car door, and then she came in carrying a dog tucked inside her sweater. "He's deallergic," she said, looking at our surprised dad.

The girls shrieked.

"Don't think I'm going into this with you fifty-fifty," my dad whispered on the porch. "Don't think I'm going into this with you at all! I think it's a mistake."

"Merry Christmas to you, too," I said loudly. But when he left and she came back inside, I said, "I can't believe you gave us a living thing." The Boops were shaking its paws. An hour later, they'd gone into the boxes the Mims kept of our baby clothes. (*Theirs* were intact; the monster had only a boy.) They stuffed the puppy into a dress.

Hound was no mistake.

He jumped all over Hector when he arrived. "It likes males," I said. "The bad news is it shows affection by peeing on you." We were crate training him, but he didn't seem to be getting the message. My dad thought he wasn't all that bright.

Hector sketched a sign.

PET OUT OF CONTROL?

UNTRAINABLE ANIMAL?

WE'LL FIND YOUR INCORRIGIBLE A GOOD HOME.

"Remember when he was whining about his hand? That the dog bit his hand?" Hector said. "We'll make him an honest man."

"Would take a lot more to make that guy an honest man."

"If a dog bit off his dick, maybe," Hector said. "When I tell a lie, it comes true. Like when I said I was sick to stay home, by the middle of the day I had a fever."

I shivered. My lie. I thought it would stay in me, a needle in a wet organ. What happened to Eli? For years he'd called every day; he'd come bounding up our steps, and now nothing. "Remember when he called Charlie's mom that time?"

"Or when he flew out after the quote 'brain operation'? Quote 'flew out.' "

That was the thing, though, about uncaught lies: I still believed he'd had that operation, sort of. But didn't he miss us? He'd loved us. I'd thought I knew that. It felt like a real thing in my body. Either that was wrong, or love could dissolve. Maybe he got tired of us. They'd talked about my grades for hours. And Boop Two's reading. The one time I'd heard the wife's voice, it was dancy, lilting, like a dog keening for affection.

"I'm an idiot," I said. "Who borrows dogs?"

63 · Our Idea of Art

He adored her.
  She was *eh* about him.

He was a card-carrying member of PETA.

A rotary-phone receiver.

HER BUBBLE:

HIS BUBBLE:

A handshake with an old man.

PSYCHOPATH: I'm sorry, sir, for leaving your daughter.

OLD MAN: I'm sorry for you, son. You have no character.

A turkey baster. I'll give you another baby, if you want Buster to have a sibling.

It didn't feel like falling in love.

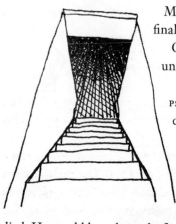

More like a stalled train at last finally moving.

Or: Steep stairs leading down to an unfinished basement.

PSYCHOPATH (*kneeling*): I'll always call you on your birthday.
HER: (bubble) Well, duh ...

"He had a thing with birthdays," Hector said. "It would have been perfect for him if she died. He would have brought flowers to her grave."

That made me shiver. Hector said his own lies came true.

Eli had told her that her work lacked vibrant romantic hope.

"How can geometry have hope?" Hector said.
"I can kind of see it."

HER: Were you ever going to tell me?
PSYCHOPATH: I was going to tell when you turned fifty. Because
    by then you really would be too old.

Hector drew them in a bed, covers up to
their clavicles, with a fantasy bubble: her
at fifty, hair up, in a regal dress, him
kneeling, giving her a jewelry box with
the typed fortune: *I'll always love you.*

"I gained four pounds over the damn holiday," Marge said.
    "We'll resume training," Philip answered.
    "Well, we got through Christmas," the Mims replied.

64 · A Message in a Bubble

"Down, boy, down. You're not a pound dog at all, are you?" Marge
said. She looked at the Mims. "You know this dog is proof that
you're over Eli."

She wasn't, though. This was late January, day 125. Marge came
over nights to work on grant proposals. Their first collaboration
was going well; they had two more ideas they were applying to
fund. The Mims couldn't stand to work alone now, she said. She
told me that back in the days of Euler and Gauss nobody distin-
guished between pure math and its uses. Euler worked on the
arrangement of ship masts and also on elliptical integrals. We

know Gauss for number theory, she said—Speak for yourself, I mumbled—but he also computed the orbit of the first known asteroid, conducted geographical surveys, and invented the telegraph.

The Mims looked thinner than she'd ever been.

I was, too. I knew because I needed belts for the first time.

"I'm the one who shouldn't be eating," Marge said, opening the refrigerator and taking out a wrapped wedge of cheese. On the table was a bowl of Asian persimmons. She sliced one paper-thin.

The Mims said people asked her what diet she'd been on. She and Marge laughed.

"Might as well take advantage of it. Drive into Beverly Hills. Buy a new dress." Marge said she'd read that the more subjective the discipline, the better dressed the faculty and the more illicit sex they had. Mathematicians, by that theory, had few affairs.

I doubted that the Mims would drive into Beverly Hills to go shopping. Whenever I went to her room at night, she was working numbers with a pencil. I noticed her hands; they looked like mine.

One evening Marge came over after dinner and said, "I've got something." I listened from the hall, against the heater. "He's not at the NSF anymore. Look. I e-mailed to tell him we wouldn't need him at UCLA spring quarter, and this bounced back."

They bent over a piece of paper.

"When somebody leaves under good terms, that isn't what they say. He must've been fired," Marge said. "But I wonder when. He couldn't have been living out here and working for them. I'm going to ask around." I wanted to see the paper but Marge put it back into her bag.

Then I hurried to my room and e-mailed Eli. Just a blank e-mail. A form came back.

The person you have e-mailed can be reached by personal e-mail at the following e-mail address: EliLee5@gmail.com. If you would like to contact someone internally at the National Science Foundation, please reach out to: AndreaCullens@nsf.org.

Philip started running with my mom every morning in the dark. They picked up Marge for the last mile. Now, when the Mims woke us, her face was glossed with sweat. Weekends, they nabbed us out of bed for dawn hikes, with headlamps. After, the Mims dragged us to dog obedience school in the parking lot of a church. We stood like drunks wavering from exhaustion, holding Hound on the leash. She carried around a puppy-training book written by a monk. It seemed as if he'd never learn to go to the bathroom outside, but then, on day 148, he did. He still chewed things. We put our shoes up on our desks. Not one of us, except the Mims, used a desk for anything else.

In March, a stranger who'd seen our flyer on the community board called. After two obedience classes and a shock collar, her pit bull still attacked. For a biter, I told her, we'd have to charge three fifty. Hector stuck his foot near my face to show the holes in the bottom of his sneaker. We promised to fetch the pit on Friday. It lived near Hector's dad. But when we arrived, it was obvious that we weren't what the owner had expected. She sat at her desk writing the check very, very slowly. "Your parents will help with this?" she asked, some shred of compunction battling her desire to get rid of the dog. Hector nodded. Then she led us to a pen where the dog stood, ears up, and handed over the leather-and-chain leash.

That fib came true. We tied Moto to a tree in Philip's backyard, putting out food and water in their lost dog's bowls. We told Philip we knew of a family in Pasadena that would take him. Philip assumed this was part of the animal rights club at Cottonwoods, and we didn't say anything to dispel that notion. After two nights of howling, Philip stuck him in the car. Jules butted against me; Moto took up most of the seat.

We got out a few doors down from Eli's house. Everything was pitch-dark.

"What if they're out of town?" I whispered to Hector, yanking the dog. The dog just sat on the sidewalk, so I pulled, scraping his bottom along the cement. We'd brought Rebel's bowls for food, which we carried in a Baggie, and water that we would pour from my thermos. I had a pocket of treats, too. If they were out of town, though, then what? Maybe Moto would die. I thought of Tomcat all of a sudden. I hoped I'd see him.

The house stood still and closed. We hooked the leash around the doorknob, knotted it. When we started walking away, the pit barked, and then we scrammed.

All the next day, I kept thinking about that dog hooked to the doorknob. I pestered Hector to skip seventh period. After two hours and three buses, we still had to walk a long time, Hector in his shoes with the holes. Their street was hard to find, even with Google Maps. We had my thermos full of water and another bag of dog food in my backpack. We'd googled the Pasadena pound, too. If worse came to worst, we could drag Moto there. Once we arrived, though, the porch was swept. No scattered kibble. No bowls. It was as if we hadn't tied a dog there the night before.

"I told you it'd be fine," Hector said.

"But we couldn't know." Walking back toward the bus, we passed a mini-mall with a sports shop. I elbowed Hector in to buy shoes. We had three hundred fifty dollars. We threw his old shoes into a Dumpster. We bought a six-pack of socks, too. "You know what I just thought of?" he said. "I bet they have a dog door. We could've shoved him in. Shut it from outside with a stone."

That night the moon hung low and enormous. "It's a super-moon," Hector said. "We're at the perigee. It's thirteen percent bigger and way brighter than usual." These were the kinds of facts Philip and Hector just knew.

Our house stayed quiet. We kept to our rooms.

We finally finished the last *Wire*.

Sare maintained a discussion with the Mims about whether she should ask Eli to return the watch. The Mims didn't think so; it was a gift, she said.

"Still. A good watch." Sare probably felt guilty: she'd talked the Mims into giving it to him in the first place, instead of to me.

They listed items, as they remembered:

Cuff links
The watch
A pen
The string bracelet*

She forgot those father-son synthetic mitts from Canada. The camera. My baby clothes. For the next few months, I checked my mom's drawer for the note Sare had drafted, and I always found it. *Please send back the gifts which were chosen with love for a person who turned out not to exist.* She never sent it.

Underneath was the corner scrap of yellow lined paper: *Yours is the last face I'll see.* I always covered that right back up.

We scrawled the list inside a bubble in *Our Psychopath*, like a message in a bottle. Maybe someday, I thought, I'd receive a package with no return address, and there would be my watch.

The running, the hikes, the obedience classes, the applications

---

* *Seeing that list we put into the book again was weird. "Cuff links. The watch. A pen. The string bracelet." We should have added: + 6 years.*

she and Marge wrote at the kitchen table, her renewed preparation for classes—they were all efforts, and maybe they helped. But happiness—I didn't see that returning. A light had gone out.

"Okay, I found something," Marge said, walking in briskly one night in April. "He was fired over a year ago. People think it was something personal; he was difficult. Moody. But I got the name of the woman he had the affair with. Lorelei Bruckner."

Marge had already looked her up. It had been easy: the woman had given the NSF a forwarding address. She lived in Northern California now. She'd left science altogether. I remembered what Eli had said about her. He'd said it was just an affair. He hadn't told her he loved her. He said he couldn't be with her because she didn't read. I remembered hearing that and thinking, What, she's illiterate? Oh, and she'd said unpleasant things about his wife.

"Well, she's no slouch," Marge said. After the NSF, she worked at the Smithsonian and then at the National Gallery, in their design departments. Now she was a potter, with her own business. Marge showed the Mims her webpage.

My mother and Marge flew up to Marin County to meet the potter sometime in the next few weeks. They must have left and come back the same day. I didn't know they'd gone until I heard them talking about it with Sare one evening around the kitchen table.

Apparently, Lorelei—the potter—told my mom that when she and Eli worked at NSF they'd *both* been married. He'd pursued her *very aggressively* in the office. Everyone knew. They'd moved in together, and one night they'd come home from dinner and found Jean sitting on the steps of their place, chewing the ends of her hair. Eventually, they each got their own apartments. The affair went on another two years, but he always came to her house; he never let her come to his.

When my mom told her what had happened to us, Lorelei shook her head. She said she was sorry to hear that he was still up to that; she'd hoped once he and Jean reconciled and had the child, he would have made that his life. They'd asked if Eli had ever said *I love you*. She laughed a little. She said she had a box full of letters that would answer that question.

So he'd lied at the very beginning, the Mims said. That seemed important to her.

The potter offered to send them the box of letters; her husband always said she should throw it out. She liked the idea of it finally coming to some use.

"I'm glad at least she *has* a husband," Sare said. "No children?"

My mom murmured no, no kids. After Eli, Marge said, she'd been alone years before she met the man she married. Eli had cost her the chance to have a family. Something about the way Marge said that made me remember that she didn't have kids either. That seemed a serious thing. Like a lack of money.

Marge and the Mims had each bought a pot from her studio. Sare picked up the vase and complimented it. That was what had made them start talking about Lorelei in the first place. A while before, the white vase had appeared on our table, where it always stayed. I hadn't thought to wonder where it had come from.

The Mims had already placed orders for Christmas. Every year, from then on, we gave small white vases instead of cakes.

65 · Busted

Then the doorbell rang on a Tuesday night and the Audreys stood there, Jules swaybacked against her dad, elbows hooked in his arms. He unlatched her and sent her to the Boops' room. "Sit down, guys," he said. By now, the Mims had shuffled in. Philip took a piece of paper out of his pocket and handed it to me and Hector. "Could you please explain this?"

A laugh slipped out of me. It was one of Hector's signs. His picture of monstro dog and electric cat. He must have left a copy in the printer at home. But no, there were staple holes. Could Philip have unhinged it from the Co-opportunity community board?

"Did you get *paid* for the pit bull I drove to Pasadena?"

My mom's neck jolted at the city name. I mumbled that we had expenses. Animal treats. And what with soup selling prohibited . . . We didn't say that the yard where we'd left the pit belonged to Eli. I was listening carefully to detect any hint that they knew. I didn't think they did.

"Could you please explain who Ben Orion is," the Mims said.

My eyes and Hector's found each other. "What is this, the Inquisition? How do you know his name? No, Mom. I really want to hear where you got that."

"Is he someone from FLAG?" Philip asked, never having attached the *BTU*.

"Did you meet on the Internet?" the Mims asked. The pedophile fear! Now she'd infected Philip. I looked around as if my father might jump out from behind a chair.

"He's not a pedophile, Mom. He's just a friend of ours."

"He's a man in his thirties, Miles. That's not a normal age for a friend of yours to be."

"How do you know this person?" Philip asked.

We looked down. Neither of us broke. Then Philip asked Hector to walk around the block with him. Watching them go, I noticed how Hector put his left hand in a back pocket, just like his dad. They had exactly the same gait. Hector was close to his father. I knew that. I didn't envy it exactly. It was more complicated than that. I loved Philip, but I knew, without even forming the thought, that for me, I would always pick my dad.

"Ben Orion is a perfectly decent guy, Mom. You want to meet him? I'll call him right now and ask him to come over."

"Please do that, Miles."

Ugh. I hadn't expected her to say yes. She stood there while I began to dial. I hoped he wouldn't answer. The last few times we'd called we'd gotten his machine. He was still mad at us from the day with Tomcat, when the VW ran out of gas. He'd never thanked us for our Bundt cake. Then again, we hadn't put a tag on it. He might not have known it was from us. Please, please don't answer, I thought. *Be gone.*

"You know this thirty-nine-year-old man's number by heart!" my mom said.

How did she know his exact age? We didn't even know that.

"Ben Orion here," he answered.

"Oh, hey, Ben? Yeah. It's Miles," I said. I explained that my mom wanted to meet him. It was okay if he couldn't make it. I mean, I knew it was last-minute, I said.

But he offered to drive right over.

Philip returned with Hector shambling behind. "Let's let the boys do their homework," he said.

"In other words, you want to talk about us." That was all right. I needed Hector alone anyway. "She made me call Ben!" I hissed when he closed my door. "And he's coming!"

But Hector wouldn't look at me. All of a sudden, I understood: he'd caved.

Why? My face dropped into my hands. We had been working on this mystery together a long time; Hector was so close; he didn't feel like a completely other person. It was nearly as if I'd been doing it all alone. We'd moved in complete secrecy, almost as if we were playing a make-believe game in our own heads. Now our mutual figments were being lifted out of the water into air for everyone to see.

"The pill thing," Hector said. "That night I snuck out and we went to Rite Aid, I got in big trouble coming back. And I was scared. I thought the Mims might get addicted or start drinking or something.* That seemed more important than a secret."

---

* *That's ironic. That that would be my fear.*

"Did you tell about soup selling, too, then?" I felt ashamed all of a sudden. I'd thought we were in this together. Maybe everyone felt sorry for our family.

He swore that he'd only told his dad about my mom being depressed that one night in December, and now he told him that we'd researched Eli and transferred pets. *Two separate things.* He hadn't told him we brought the creatures to *Eli's house.* Philip was going to make us give the money to my sister's animal club.

"Ohww. Not even to FLAGBTU?"

"He's a homophobe," Hector mumbled. "They all are." The doorbell rang. Hound barked as if the enemy had landed.

It was Ben Orion. Standing in the kitchen, he seemed cut from a glossy magazine next to our pale parents, who belonged on thin comic-book paper. Wearing jeans, a black T-shirt, and a blazer, he looked literally sharp, his colors more saturated, his hair a true black, his teeth whiter. I wondered if he actually did resemble a pedophile. "I thought I'd seen you before," he was saying to my mom. "I guess it was somebody else." So he *hadn't* seen her. I thought he had a crush on the Mims as a damsel in distress. But she turned out not to be the damsel he'd seen. Perhaps distress, by itself, wouldn't cut it. It shocked me again: maybe my mother was plain. From Eli I'd learned where to look to find her symmetries. Maybe no one else could. Maybe we really were pitiable, I was just beginning to understand.

"I'm a private investigator," Ben said, "and once upon a time these two found me in the yellow pages." He took out his reserve police badge, which wasn't actually a badge at all but a card in his wallet, with a drawing of a badge. "And I'm familiar with Cottonwoods kids, because I lived with Zoe Fisher, the art teacher there, and her son, Ez. When these two first came to me, I couldn't decide what to think."

I realized he was going to tell the story of us.

"I thought they were probably imagining things that weren't there or that the adults already knew about. I tried to talk them out of it. But then I slowly got the sense that they were beyond their depth—"

Philip interrupted. "Guys." He looked to my mom, who was nodding in agreement with him. She unhooked the dog's leash from the peg. "Walk him to the beach and back," Philip said.

As we passed through the living room where Boop One and Jules were choreographing a dance, I shouted back, "Why do *they* get to stay?"

"Because *we're* very good," Boop One said, a leg diagonal in the air. "And you're in trouble!" Then she folded herself around the dog. Boop One annoyed me, though I could see her same shapes in Ella, and *she* didn't annoy me at all. These girls—I suppose you'd call them the girly girls—had bodies that could fold and unfold again. Smoothly. Boop One slid down from standing to the splits. "She's more of a leaps girl than a turns girl," I heard as we left. "I'm a turns girl."

I actually didn't mind being banished. A wind from the ocean cuffed our faces. Maybe for the first time in our lives Hector and I didn't have much to say to each other. I was mortified that he'd been talking about us to his father. I'd taken it for granted that we were partners. Hector was probably the most important person in my life. I loved Ella; that was a sharp, narrow, painful feeling. But Hector was way more central. In my life then, someone could be insufficiently imaginary, like Maude, and someone else, Ella, insufficiently real. Hector was the only person who was right.

But maybe it wasn't the same for him.*

We let the dog lead us. Philip had said to go to the beach, but when we came to the street where we'd turn for Ben Orion's house, Hound pulled in that direction. Like a Ouija, maybe he felt our prompting. We followed. Ben had left lights on inside, so the windows glowed. The Mims always yelled after us to turn off our lights.

"I wonder if we'll ever come here anymore," I said.

---

* *It wasn't the same. But it was a lot.*

"I kind of doubt it." Then we were quiet. "Kat got a job," Hector finally said.

"You mean, besides working for Sare?"

"Yeah. Some people hired her to make their kitchen."

"Oh, she can do that really well." Kat had had a breakfast restaurant once, called Jams. After all the times Hector had referred to her as Charlie's mom's gopher and Sare's slave, good news sounded odd coming from him, but of course I knew that all kids really love their mothers. "They tore out a picture from a magazine and said they wanted it to look like that. She told them, 'Fine, it'll look like that if you let me take the pictures.' "

We fell quiet again. "How's your aunt?" I asked, trying to make conversation. We'd never had to do that before. "Is the married guy still being all nice? Or was that just right after the holidays?"

"You know how she doesn't have kids to spend money on? Well, my dad told her she didn't have to pay our tuitions anymore, and she had a meltdown. It turned out she *liked* being necessary. She says her life is going to have to change."

"So wait a minute, why *isn't* she necessary? Because of your mom's new job?"

"I guess that and my dad teaching and with Marge."

"What do you mean, with Marge? Are your dad and Marge getting together?" I hadn't meant to say that the way it came out, kind of shrill, but I'd never thought of Philip with Marge. The Mims and Philip had talked on the porch so much this terrible year, I'd hoped—I didn't know what I'd hoped. I'd started to wish they would decide they liked each other, but then I worried that Hector would have to move into my tiny room and we already had too many girls. Now I wanted that option back.

"I *think* so. She bought a frying pan."

"For your house?"

"Yeah."

"Oh. Then it sounds like they are." My organs sank. We still stared at Ben's windows. What now? I thought.

"But my aunt, though?" Hector said. "She gave her boss an ulti-matum to tell his wife. He said his wife *knew*, she knew and she didn't know, she knew as much as she wanted to know. But Terry said she had to be able to call him at home. 'Cause the way it was, if he was in the hospital, she couldn't even go see him."

"And *did* his wife really know?"

"Well, she does now, and she wants a divorce."

"That's good, right? Is Terry happy?"

"I guess." He said that a way that made the word disyllabic.

We finally shuffled into the house as if handcuffed. My sisters skated around the table in socks, slapping down napkins. It looked as if we were going to get dinner.

The Mims poured pasta into a colander, then mixed it with gar-lic and parsley. She stared down at the food.

"They did research and deduction," Ben Orion said. "They were ob*sessed*. They'd make good cops."

My mom's half smile fell a millimeter. Boop One called out, What side do the knives go on again?

I couldn't settle down at the table. My fingers and toes jumped. Hector and I had kept this to ourselves for so long.

"Miles said you didn't know he was married," Ben said. "I didn't believe him at first."

"I'm an idiot," the Mims said.

I never stopped watching her face. I couldn't tell if she'd been crying. I wondered what Ben Orion had told them.

"We thought there was some madwoman sending that stuff about Eli from her attic," Philip said. "And all along it was you guys." For Philip this was effervescence.

I was amazed that they weren't furious. Maybe they would be furious later. Still, it was exhilarating for them to understand what we'd done and have it be all right. I'd joked about coming out as gay to my father, but this was a truer confession. I felt an urge to lead them downstairs on a field trip and show them the wires and the phone from Hector's garage we'd rigged with Silly Putty, but I kept scanning my mom's face, and I could see she didn't want to learn more. She seemed fragile and embarrassed, as if she could barely hold the new information she'd gained and stay herself. I just then remembered she didn't know about me calling Eli. No one did.

"Did *you* think the guy was lying?" Ben Orion asked her. I wished he hadn't, but her face didn't avalanche. He had a nice voice. He was sitting next to her. His hand touched her elbow.

"No. But . . ." She stopped with a laugh through her nose. "But one time he talked to me about his eighth-grade teacher. She was the one who told him to read a book a day. Eli read a book every day. I loved that about him."

"If it was even true," Ben said.

"I think *that* was." She was doing it, too. She believed everything Eli said except what we knew for sure were lies. Eli didn't really read a book every day, I bet. How many people did? Hardly any. Not even teachers.

"She had him over to her house after school," the Mims went on. "She gave him cake. He said that once the teacher's husband came home, and she rushed him out the side door. He said nothing ever happened, but I thought he was trying to tell me something. That same year, he moved down to the basement, away from his mother and brother."

"I thought they lived in an apartment!" I called from the refrigerator, where I was getting milk.

"I guess it had a basement," she said. Our basement and the one beneath Dr. Bach's office had dirt floors. You couldn't really *move* there, like with a bed. My dad's house didn't even have a basement. Holland had told me a lot of California houses didn't.

"So, what, you think he lost his virginity with his eighth-grade teacher?" I said to her in the kitchen. I'd brought in plates.

"He'd told me it happened at that age with an older girl. He said it was strange."

"Doesn't sound so strange to me," I said.

She hit me with a dish towel. A flash of the old, real her.

Hector shook his head. "What Eli did was worse than just ordinary lying. Remember how he flew around all the time? Where did he get the money for that?"

"Maybe he was just in Pasadena."

"I think Ben Orion should run a criminal check," he said.

I remembered that little sketch Hector had made of Eli that we'd shown to the librarian. We'd put it in *Our Psychopath*, WANTED printed above the picture, like a mug shot in the post office or the Doors album Philip kept. But wanted for what? For breaking a promise to love? That happened seventeen times a day in just our class at school. That wasn't criminal enough for Hector. He felt unsatisfied. It seemed too small. He'd thought we were missing our high school life to do something big and important, to chase down evil.

Eli had promised us money, though. And a future. I still thought he was terrible, even if that was all.

I wanted everyone to leave. It was a school night. But the grown-ups stood talking on the porch. Hector and I lurked around the bushes on the side of the house. I still felt weird with him. He'd told his dad, and all this time I hadn't known.

"Well, case is finally closed," Ben Orion said. "Done."

The Mims sighed. "How can you change the way you feel about someone after six years?"

"You're loyal," Philip said.

"There's such a thing as loyalty to the wrong cause," Ben Orion said. "And he's a wrong cause if I've ever seen one."

" 'I'll always love you,' " the Mims said, her voice with a sarcastic curve I'd never heard before. "Is that just something people say?"

"Some people," Ben Orion said. "Charmers."

Snake charmer, more like it.

"It's like 'Let's have lunch,' " Philip said.

"Oh my God. Philip told a joke." I felt like calling my dad.

Just then Kat's VW pulled up to get Jules. "I thought Miles was yours," Ben said when she was introduced. So he thought the Mims was Kat. No wonder he had a crush!

Then, as the Audreys were leaving, a buzz came from Ben's pocket.

"Another client?" my mother asked. "A better-paying one, I hope."

"Not a client anymore. Used to be. For a long time." It must have been that woman who'd finally fired him. I felt a twinge: Ben Orion wouldn't be going out on any dates with the Mims. That woman we'd seen was an ex-actress.

He waved good-bye, walking down to his car with the phone to his ear.

The Mims stood in the kitchen, whisking warm milk with cardamom, a star anise floating on top. I wanted to talk. When I'd woken in the night and heard her crying, I understood because I'd *seen* Eli tickling her on the floor, his face in big clowny exaggeration, softening to her fleeting expressions. Can you fake that? I wanted to ask. But I guessed *he* could. I said, "Do you think he lied about everything?" She just shrugged. She still didn't want to talk to me about this. She didn't talk to our dad about it either.

This is what you got growing up, I thought. You lost your closest person. I'd entered a new, uncertain feeling with Hector. But at the end of that long night, I realized, nobody had said anything about the animals being delivered to Eli, so we could probably keep the business. I called to tell Hector. "I noticed that, too," he said. We needed the money. We'd have to take the flyers down from Co-opportunity and Whole Foods and put them somewhere else, he said, somewhere Philip and the Mims didn't shop. Then Philip came into his room and made him get off the phone.

I ambled to the Mims's closet, found the camera, and looked at the pictures in her trash. She didn't know how to empty her trash. "It's the same dog, isn't it?" I said, carrying the whole contraption out. "Hound is the ugly puppy Sare thought was brain-damaged."

"Well, would you rather have a different dog?"

I got down on the floor and set Hound on my chest. "Not now."

"That's what you do. You find the best angle. You crop. You edit. That's not cheating. That's love."

"Dad's family sure does that," I said, "up to and including bragging."

My mom sighed. "I remember when I met them. They seemed a whole better world."

66 · Flunking

I had a small bad worry, always with me, but never precise: my grades. I'd been confiscating our assessments the whole year, and I felt guilty about it. Final reports would be sent the first week of June. I had a wild hope that I'd yanked up my scores the last few weeks. The day Hector got his, mine didn't come. Hector, who truly was the smartest person I'd ever met, had turned in work as late as humanly possible all spring and still got A minuses. The next morning, I told the Mims I needed a mental health day. When I heard the mail drop I ran and ripped open the verdict.

Bad. One B minus and three C's. For my junior year. When it counted. That night, after the Boops went to sleep, I handed the paper to the Mims and stood there as she read. She was never one of those parents who paid for A's, but I understood that she'd had hopes for me.

"I know you wanted me to do better," I said.

"Miles, I expect you to try your hardest. You know that."

"Maybe I did. I'm not as smart as you always thought."

"Not everything shows in grades. Come on, let's take the dog." She unhooked the leash, the clamp ticking on the floor, and we followed Hound out into the dark. The world smelled more at night. A brush of pine wet my face. I thought of Eli. He'd loved his mother, too; through his lies you could hear that he cherished her: an undereducated secretary who read history books. Yet she'd failed: she'd made one son who had no friends and another who lived his life as an impostor. Her momentary happiness, when her boys got into better colleges than the sons of her employers, turned out to be only a short-lived blast of promise.

"Look." My mom nudged me. In front of us a family of deer stood straight-legged, tentative, all pointed in one direction, about to spring.

Hound went stiff too and started barking to call in the Marines.

The deer turned, their knees synchronous, and leaped off, down the hill of brush.

"I'll get my grades up," I said. "First semester senior GPA counts, too."

"We had a hard year," she said. "My student evaluations weren't great either. One said, *Professor Adler's mind seems to be stumbling. She keeps dropping chalk.* None of this is your fault. But I need to start focusing on what matters, and I want you to, too."

"Tutu," I said, did a twirl, and tripped.

67 · Life Goes On, Especially for Other People

Hector and I didn't do much that summer. We woke up around noon and then began to figure out how to get to the other's house. His house was better because Marge left food around, but ours was because no one was home. We puttered lackadaisically, but then, in the late afternoon, we started messing around on our comic book and stayed at it until ten or eleven. I couldn't completely get rid of the embarrassment I felt from him having told his father what I'd thought was our secret, but we both had a new quiet excitement for our project. Hector got the idea to go to the comic-book store and check out titles like ours. So we made a field trip to Neverland. Locking our bikes, we remembered the library across the street.

So our schedule developed. We met at twelve thirty, worked in the library until two, and then bought sandwiches for lunch. We had cash from the 20 percent we allowed ourselves of the animal profits. Then we moved across the streets to Neverland. Hector read the good books the length of ours with the same split between text and drawings, and I sought out the bad ones. Whenever I found a really lame story, I read it through. The guys and one girl with a nose ring who worked there teased us about turning the store into a library. At the end of each day, Hector showed me the best book he'd read, and I showed him the worst. Then, invigorated, as much from the worst (ours seemed at least as good as *that*) as from the best, we rode our bikes home and kept on working. After three weeks, the shame I'd felt from that awful night when he'd told his dad began to dissolve. We started joking about it. Maybe this was the way we could get back to ourselves. Even better, because with this project we didn't have to wait for discoveries.

It was too bad we weren't gay, I thought more than once that summer, because there was no chance either one of us would ever find anyone else as compatible again. Hector was still undeclared. But if he were gay with someone else, I'd have been offended. We'd gotten lucky. For the rest of the time we both lived in our parents' houses, we were best friends, and the comic epic we were trying to make together was the most important work we'd ever done, more important than school. It lingered in us long after tennis and surfing became occasional sports and pastimes.

Hector had the brilliant idea of showing the double lives on different-colored backgrounds. But once the kids busted the Villain, our story seemed to peter out. Then what? The characters on the light background just went back to regular life, which doesn't really fly in comics.

"How about sex?" Hector said. "Maybe we should put that in."

I shook my head.

Hector had changed the signs we'd posted to say we accepted animals under twenty-five pounds and that larger mammals could be handled only by special arrangement. On the phone, we explained that oversize animals had to be brought to the outside patio of Peet's in Pasadena, where we'd take possession. We'd located the Lees' dog door. Twice, we shoved pets in and then obstructed the flap with a fallen branch. The night they busted us, Philip had made us agree to give the money we'd already earned to the animal rights club, but he and the Mims never exactly forbade us to continue. We took down our signs from Whole Foods and Co-opportunity. We didn't go to Pasadena often, only once a month or so. We carried treats to quiet the barking dogs. Twice, the house was completely dark. Once, a car slid to a stop in front, its door slammed, and Eli carried a suitcase up to the porch. He opened the mailbox, took out envelopes, and then let himself in with a key.

The Mims and Philip ran mornings; she ate now, but she still seemed too thin. For Marge, on the other hand, weight loss helped. I found a book, open on my mom's desk.

> *O Western wind, when wilt thou blow*
> *That the small rain down can rain?*
> *Christ, that my love were in my arms,*
> *And I in my bed again!*

So she still missed him, I guessed. Maybe she hoped he'd return. But how could he? Wouldn't he have to start all over at the beginning and tell us the real version? He'd have to get a divorce first off. I didn't think impostors came back. What would they come back to? He hadn't ever been *known*.

And Eli had a real life in Pasadena. I'd seen it.

But I supposed that real life wasn't enough for him either.

Hound liked to roughhouse. He'd push up next to me and bite the end of my pants when he craved exercise. I threw the squeak toy into the yard. He bounded to get it, but he hadn't yet learned how to bring it back to me. I had to fight it out of his mouth to throw it again. I tossed it too far into the side yard and he wouldn't go into the bushes, so I climbed through the untended margin between our house and the fence to retrieve it and heard my mom talking in her room. I'd promised myself not to eavesdrop anymore, but this had to qualify as a complete accident.

"I didn't get a chance to say good-bye to him," she said.

I stood in the mess of unidentified growth holding the squeak toy and thinking, But what did it even mean to say good-bye to someone who wasn't all real? I felt discouraged. It had been such a long time. In high school people got over people faster.

"He fed me at restaurants," she said. "I thought he loved me." *That* made her think he loved her!

"He did love you," someone else said. "Remember how he came to my office hysterical? You can't put that on." Her office! It was the old doctor, the psychiatrist who made house calls. "He loved you, but he's crazy. He's just too crazy."

Then what were feelings worth? Like currency, their value depended on a sound treasury, so love from a liar was pretty worthless. "He's just too crazy," the ancient doctor said again, her voice light, as if insanity were a joke. My long-ago impression had been that she was a party girl, just a very, very old one. But was she good at her job? I wondered, with a shiver, if my mom was improving at all.

At the edge of the perimeter, Hound growled.

"Philip says I should call his wife. He thinks the two of us would have a lot to talk about."

I thought of that wife we'd seen ironing. The Victim. I'd watched her swoosh her boy up in the park. She'd stepped onto her porch with a curler in her hair, a frill of paper between her toes. The idea of her and my mom talking seemed as impossible as the Mims having a conversation with Olive Oyl, Marge Simpson, or, for that matter, a figure Hector had drawn.

She sighed. "What am I going to do for the rest of my life?"

"Have you thought about online dating?" the aged doctor said.

I crawled back to Hound, who stood stiff-legged at the edge of his known world.

The old doctor seemed to think love was a laughing matter, a question of who asked you to dance at the big, long party. Sare didn't believe in love at all. She understood that the Mims was working through her days with no particular hope. *Welcome to the human condition* was pretty much her point of view. But not Marge's.

"I just don't think I can live without him," the Mims had said to Marge one night while they sat at the table working.

"Well, maybe that'll change. And, if you can't get over it, we'll just have to get him away from Jean somehow."

I'd liked hearing that, even though I knew better.

"Kat's getting married," Philip said during one of the dawn hikes he and my mom still dragged us on, as we stood looking at the vast detailed carpet of LA.

"She really is now?" the Mims said.

"They set a date."

I turned to Hector. He looked down. *You don't tell me anything*, I thought.

At the bottom by the cars, Philip mentioned, "They offered me a job at Cottonwoods. Teaching drama. But they put on a musical comedy every winter. I've never even seen one."

"I own every musical comedy recording there is," Marge said. "I can tutor you." She started a shuffle ball change, hands flat and parallel to the ground, so she looked like a bear dancing. Even thinner, you could still see her big.

When we were alone again in our house, Boop Two asked the Mims if she was ever going to remarry.

"She can't," Boop One interrupted. "You have us. And that's enough for you. I don't think Marge and Philip will really get married either."

"Why not?" I said. Hector had told me on the way down the mountain that they'd had a new washer/dryer installed.

Boop One shrugged. "I just don't think so. She doesn't look like a second wife."

My mom said she hadn't heard anything about a wedding. But Marge had picked someone from the architecture department to draw an addition to Philip's house. Hector and Jules would each get their own rooms. She was probably too busy to plan a ceremony, the Mims said. Marge warmed to the *project* of it all, the sad house with its broken machines, the children whose mother lived with a fragile sister. I could see her happiness: a contained excitement, a private, satisfied calm.

"So you think it's a good thing for Marge?" I asked.

The Mims sipped her coffee. "Yes. I worry about her work. But she wants this."

So both of Hector's parents had found someone.

Mine remained single. And still, the Mims was too sad.

68 · The Unnecessary Lies

Maude Stern had the good-student habit of reading the newspaper every day, even in summer. When she dropped by flyers against Prop 8, which was on the ballot for November, she told me three or four things, and I spaced out. She followed me to my room, still talking. Whenever she came into my lair, she started picking up papers from the floor. Maude loved busywork. "What is this?" she asked.

"Just leave it," I said, the way I did to my mom.

She was starting SAT boot camp. She said I should do it, too. She always moved frantically the first minutes alone with me. She circled the room, making neater stacks, collecting old homework from the floor, balling the paper and throwing it into the basket.

She told me that her mom was putting together family photo albums. Her life was worse than mine: the bad guy was her dad. She looked at me, her hands hanging ready, and I could see—this time in my room; it wasn't the same for her. It was more. Maybe this was how you kept someone hanging on. Had Eli seen us the way I saw Maude?

I thought I understood what was supposed to happen. I could pat a spot next to me on the bed, like I did for Hound just before he jumped. I was even attracted to her that afternoon in an easy way, like a door one inch open. She wore shorts and a sleeveless blouse. I didn't feel even one percent nervous.

I wanted sex. I thought about it all the time. I jerked off every night. Except for Hector, the other Rabid Rabbits were having it. Charlie had Laura; Simon had Cait. For all our trying to prove what good divorces we were, the Rabid Rabbits who had intact families were the ones who got girlfriends and sex. I'd lost weight, but I wasn't buff like Charlie. Ella had never returned my text. I could smell Maude's shampoo or something, the chemical spray of it, astringent, maybe orange. But the air held no charge. I turned my face away.

Instead of patting the spot next to me, I stood.

In a little while, she left, her head bumping on the square paper hanging light.

What did other people feel? Was it what I'd passed up the chance of with Maude or what I still longed for from Ella?

....

When Neverland closed to do inventory, Hector and I counted and shelved for two days. We took cash, made change, and bagged the comics at the Saturday-morning crate sale in the back parking lot. "Wish we could hire you guys," Hershel, the owner, said, "but we'll give you the staff discount. You earned it."

The Mims drove the Boops and me to see an old table in a warehouse. She asked, did we like it? We said, Well, yeah, I guess, but what for? It was too tall to eat around. Or for a desk. She said it had been made that way because people worked at it standing. It was a Chinese counting table. But Sare knew someone who could chop the legs down. She wanted to use it as a dining table.

Later that day, Sare and Reed met us there with an SUV. We spread packing blankets over the roof and tied the table on top.

We went bowling with Ben Orion and he asked us what books we'd read. He offered to take us to a conference on forensic induction.

"Do you think Eli ever separated like he said?" I asked. "He told my mom once that he apologized to his wife's father."

There was a look Ben got now whenever I brought up Eli. But I hadn't said his name the whole first hour at the bowling alley!

"When your mom asked if she could see his divorce papers, the guy said *sure*. His saying something doesn't get you any closer to the truth. You guys need to remember that the case is closed."

"But you have to admit," Hector said, "it wasn't a very good ending."

"Not a good one, maybe, but it's the end. We know he's a bad guy." He knocked out the remaining pins. A spare.

"Miles'd like to be done. He can't help it," Hector said. "He loved him." I felt grateful to him for knowing me.

"I didn't understand that." Ben sat on the edge of the chute, hands clasped. The clicks and rings of a strike in the lane next to us clattered. "What do you still want to learn?"

The things that really bugged me now were the unnecessary lies. Eli had accepted our gifts for his kid. Why?

"He pretended they were from him," Ben said. "Saved him some money. And they helped his guilt; he could tell himself his kid was getting something out of this, too."

"Who did he say my old clothes were from?"

"He probably just threw them away."

Those tiny garments she'd carefully laundered and folded, that had once been saved for our children—they were gone forever.

"And he wanted to be the only one she talked to. But knowing what he knew, shouldn't he have been glad she had friends? If he cared about her at all?"

"Here, your turn," Ben said. My favorite ball had choked up the chute. It was purple and marbleized. "You're hoping for some kind of honor among thieves. The only place to find that is at the movies. You know, the longer you work in criminal justice, those stories begin to seem like fairy tales."

"So that's just all?" Hector said. "Nothing happens to him?"

"Here's what we can do. We'll tune in every so often and watch the show. We can't lock him up, but somebody else might. We won't lift a finger. We'll just see. And call it God or karma or whatever, usually these guys get it in the end."

I looked up at him, surprised. "Do you believe in God?"

"I believe in good over evil," he said. "Of course. Don't you?"

"No." I shrugged. "I'm half Jewish." Hector and I didn't pursue that further. Neither of us wanted to find out Ben was some wack religious. The age we were, with the education we'd had, any religion seemed superstition.

"He'll probably never send back that watch," I said. I thought he kept all our gifts in one place, like the Mims's drawer. His presents to her were all promises. For a tattoo, a suit, loyalty on his death-bed. All except *Irene Adler, I have* known *you*. Someday, maybe, he'd give my watch to his own kid.

"It's likely in some Pasadena pawnshop by now," Ben said. That shocked me. But Eli had thought she was dead, and he hadn't called us.

I could live without his loot.

At the end Ben asked how my mom was doing.

I told him not so great. Not the same as before.

"She hikes with my dad," Hector volunteered.

"Well, 'cause of the puppy. Hound needs exercise."

"It peed on my dad."

"Hey, you told me Eli was a big animal rights guy? Well, I put out an alert on the address. Turns out they rented their house to McDonald's. That tells you they're hard up. Those commercial shoots wreck a place. And how does McDonald's square with animal rights? Tell your mom that. Maybe it'll help." When he dropped us off at our house, the Mims waved at him from the porch.

Hector and I were waiting in line at the Aero when a guy with a ponytail came out. "Sorry, people. The kid who does the concessions didn't show. I had to start the popcorn before I opened the doors. I'm the only one here, so I'll collect tickets, and then we'll move to the refreshment bar." I offered to help. He showed me how to tear the tickets and drop half down a slot in a wooden box. When the movie started, I said I'd like to put in an application. By the end of the night I had a job.

From then on, four evenings a week I took tickets, swept, sold popcorn and Cokes. I let Hector in for free. My dad stopped sometimes on his way home from work. He snapped a picture of me in the outside booth and made it the wallpaper on his phone. For some reason, the movie theater didn't scare him about pedophiles. Or maybe he'd finally outgrown that fear. Thinking so made me nostalgic.

69 · The Sex Journal

By the time school started, Hector and I had reputations as do-gooders, because of the money Philip made us give to the Animal Rights Collective. Our donations had benefits: quite a few good-looking girls apparently cared about animals; they'd learned our names and voted to fund FLAGBTU's fight against Prop 8. They elected Boop Two as vice president. And just from the handed-over money, we'd completed our community service hours for the first time in our whole academic lives. The only bad thing was that the pretty girls assumed we were gay.

We vowed to quit the animal-transfer business; we needed better grades, especially I did, but we still had one schnauzer to deliver. Then that would be it.

Boop One hipped into my room, a leg pointed in the air. "Can I have ten dollars for the In-N-Out truck? Mom's not home and I'm going to Jules's play."

"How're you getting there?"

"Philip."

"I'll look in the Mims's drawer." I found two fifties and some curled ones. I started flattening the dollars. My sister discovered a stack of old baseball cards with her mug on them that she couldn't stop cooing over ("Look how little I was! Aww!"). I had nine dollars when she gasped. She'd opened one of those cardboard FedEx envelopes and taken out a picture of our mother naked.

"Give me that." I grabbed. Queasy. A yellow Post-it was stuck to the cardboard: *I want to get frames.* I shoved the photograph back in the envelope and returned to counting, all business. "Okay, I'll give you nine and change. That enough?"

"Yes," she said, her hand ready for the money. "Why would she do that? Get pictures taken with her booty like that?"

"Medical reasons," I said. Good save. A car honked in front. She ran out.

"What time will you be home?" I called after her, trying to sound parental.

"Later," she yelled back.

I opened the cardboard envelope. There were more, five in all, taken in our old house. It's strange to look at nude photographs of your mother. They made me feel exposed. As if I would never be attractive. They were odd pictures. Her face looked pretty, her smile like an open fan. Her body looked too pale and bare—shy, as if it wanted to put on clothes. She wasn't as thin then. I recognized Eli's penmanship on the Post-it. He must have taken the pictures. I felt like burning them. I'd leave the one of her back; in it, she looked like she could be anyone or even a smooth rock. Someday my sisters would want this, I thought, their mother beautiful at forty-something. Her back. But I slid the black-and-white photos between the cardboard so nothing looked different. It was her property. She wouldn't want me touching it.

I had the feeling again that I'd had when I was afraid there was more bad to find.

But what could be left? I rummaged in the drawer. I found his letter, in the envelope with no return address, and a small black Moleskine notebook, closed with a rubber band. I slipped the band off, opened it, and inside the fly read, *Our Sex Journal.* Then snapped it shut. It was what Hector had once guessed. A prank! I thought, Hector planted it! The idea spread with relief, but no, I realized, Hector would never have taken the risk—not to put this in my mom's room. Hector came over less now anyway. This was a Friday, and he wasn't here. On the first page, I recognized Eli's small, spidery writing.

Where are my arms?

What did he mean, *Where are my arms?* Sex again. Liquids swirled in my gut. I put the rubber band back around the Moleskine and closed the drawer.

Boop One asked me later, "What ever happened to Eli?"

"That's over," I said.

She nodded, absorbing the information. "Is he still in Washington?"

"I don't know where he is." I shrugged. "Not in our life."

My bad. The Mims would have said something like *We're friends now*. I thought of all the trouble our parents took with the divorce, the *We still love each other*s and the *as a family*s. Parents don't want kids to think people just fall off into anonymity. And they don't normally. My dad was coming over for dinner the next night.

Boop Two sluffed in with a friend. I'd noticed before that Boop One's friends looked like her—they wore sweats and leotards and always seemed to know where their legs went. They kept their hair in neat buns or brushed it out long and shiny. Boop Two had her peeps, too. This girl wore hiking boots and fleece. One long thick braid swung on her back.

I heard our mom in the kitchen and thought of the Moleskine. Eli had remembered Zeke's and Simon's names, my daily class schedule, for Pete's sake. With his memory, I shuddered to think what was in that notebook. I hated that the thing existed in our house. Hector had hounded me about sex for our comic. I'd put him off. Even now, I didn't tell him about the Moleskine, though I wanted to talk about it to someone. But I thought he'd zero in on it for other reasons than just me and my roiled brain. And there was no one else to tell.

After a week, I finally stole the thing and handed it over to him.

His jaw actually dropped, and this time his eyes fell more open, too.

"Did you read it?" he asked.

"No," I said. I had an aversion.

The way Hector held the small notebook, a finger on the cover, I could tell he felt a tingle. He wanted something for our comic.

"Read it fast," I said, "so I can replant it before she notices it's gone."

In school a day later, Hector showed me a picture. A made bed, the cover nicked in under the pillows. One window. A Canary Island pine outside. That all seemed okay. He gave the Moleskine back. "Finished?" I said, and he nodded.

"Anything I need to know?"

He thought a minute. "Most of it wasn't even about sex." They'd had conversations running and on the phone. They'd talked for years, before anything. The monster had written that their relationship rested on a long, deep friendship.

"Right," I whispered. Not like any friendship I ever want.

I slipped the Moleskine back into the drawer, never to be opened by me again. I rummaged around and in the back found a small leather pillbox, inside of which was *the Ring*.* I wondered what the Mims was going to do with it. She never wore it anymore. She had two daughters; she could hardly give it to one of them. But I was glad it was still here, in with the scraps of paper, promises from Eli, and our baby teeth.

Boop Two rallied the Animal Rights Collective to carry signs against Prop 8 with us in front of the polling booths. So it was animal activists in fleece, bunches of girly girls who were also members, and our weird gang from FLAGBTU. A guy in a Cadillac rolled down his windows and called my twin sisters lesbos, ten feet away from real lesbos. Maude thumped the front of his car.

But we lost.

* *That hit some spot and settled me. We still had that.*

After the polls came in, Hector and I waded through a crowd of girls to my room and closed the door, with a chair hooked up under the knob so they couldn't enter. This house always seemed fuller than our old one. Hound whimpered against the door, knocking his tail. I finally asked Hector about the Moleskine.

In the beginning, Hector said, the Mims told Eli she had problems. With sex. Hector asked me how much I wanted to hear. Less than I'd heard already, I said.

Eli had made her talk about it. Talk some more, he'd said. Just blab.

It's pretty bad, she'd told him. *I think of my mother.*

What was so bad about that? I'd known my grandmother. She'd run, pushing my tricycle, wearing a long scarf, the times we'd visited Detroit.

Hector opened his notebook and showed me a sketch of a woman yanking up her T-shirt.

I have to show you. From breastfeeding.
One smaller than the other.

"He cried the first time," Hector told me.

Eli *cried*! What was I supposed to do with that?

And after, he sent her a list of ideas. That seemed to involve pillows.

"Maybe I don't need to hear this." You've heard of dry humping? It turned out there was also such a thing as dry retching.

We were quiet for a while.

He showed me a panel.

Pitched up on his arms, in a bed, Eli asked, *Where are you?*
And so I told him. Where I was, was not with him.

Tell me where you are, Eli said a lot. He wanted to climb inside
her thought bubble, join her there.

I had a headache starting. Rounded brains throbbed against my
skull. I shouldn't know this. She wouldn't have told me. This is why
you shouldn't break into people's privacy.

She needed to imagine ugly things.

I gagged, feeling sick, maybe permanently unhappy. If this was
where all our investigations led, I understood: Ben Orion had been
right. We'd gone too far.

Hector said Eli found porn on his computer, postage-stamp-
sized pictures of young girls. Eli thought a certain type of girl
excited her. He said he could tell she was aroused.

A word a person should never hear about one's mother.

Hector showed me another frame.

A couple in bed.
Most of the time we're having sex, you're not even with me, the man
said.

"We can't use any of this, you know." I stood up.

Eli talked about getting a real live girl for a threesome. The
Mims had freaked.

She tried to explain to him that wasn't what she wanted at all.
He begged her to tell him what she imagined doing to the girl or
the girl doing to her.

I put a hand up to stop. But Hector kept on.

She said neither. I imagine *being* the girl, she said. Something
had happened in that small apartment in Dearborn. With her

brother and her and their mother in two small rooms, there wasn't privacy. Sometimes her mother brought home men. I recognized flecks of the story: the working mother, two kids, in the immigrant enclave outside Detroit. Maybe her dials were set then, she told Eli. But she wanted to be with him. Eli. No girl. No one else.

In Hector's drawing you saw only the gray outline of a couple under covers in bed, their dialogue in bubbles.

Some things happened when I was young and now I have to think of them.
Why have to?
In order to come.

In the end, it was a small sad story of accommodation to damage. Not my business. I thought of my dad. He couldn't have followed her where she went with her eyes closed. My dad was a happy camper. A Once Born. A firstborn. I wanted to be him.

Another panel:

The same made bed again, one window, a pine outside.
Vibrant romantic hope, read the caption.

"We're almost done," Hector said.

THE SEX SHOP

He'd drawn a young immigrant guy behind the counter; he looked too much like Apu from *The Simpsons*.

So this is all it is, read the woman's thought balloon.

"That really happened?" I asked. "They went to a sex shop?"

"Just to see." Hector nodded. "They didn't buy anything."

The last drawing was a spoon with a fortune-cookie fortune in it: *the family romance.*

He fed her dreams, read the caption.

"I feel bad for your work, man," I said. "But we've got to throw all this out."

We'd been villains stealing this stuff she wouldn't want us to know.

Maybe Eli had ruined me.

Hector nodded, respecting my verdict. "We could do a more fantastic version," he finally said. "Give ourselves superpowers."

70 · The Last Dog

I accepted my life as it was. I didn't worry anymore about whether the Mims could make dinner, but I had no big hopes for happiness either. She and Eli had mixed themselves together in a way I didn't understand. Sometimes I thought there had been good in it, too, strands of care along with the deception. I'd seen behind a curtain something small and human, a misshapen child with a smear of dirt on its shin. I was done trying to discover anything. What I didn't know, I wanted to keep that way.

I turned my attention to school for my senior year. What my dad regularly harped on was true: this was my last chance at a decent college. While Hector and I had messed around all summer, Maude had manually lifted her SAT score another hundred points.

And we still had to deliver a schnauzer.

This last dog fit into my backpack, but he scratched at the fabric, frantic, a biter and a yapper. Even mean dogs spooked, apparently; madness provided no protection from terror. We went on a Friday and had to make three transfers. On the final leg, we sat at the back of the bus, and I lifted him out. MAX, the tag said. I unlatched it. They couldn't have a number to call that might trace back to us. Max climbed up my chest as if clawing his way to air from underwater. He ripped my shirt. *It's okay, Max, you're going to be safe. This guy loves dogs.* Outside the bus windows, the world streamed green and blue. But the word *love* had tripped me. People said *love* all the time. What if Eli had lied about this, too? We knew now that the holidays he said he worked at shelters he was probably just eating. What if he'd really been eating a turkey, that had had a face?

That idea revealed a cliff. He could have taken our pets to the pound and let them die. I told Hector, wanting him to talk me down. But he sank back against the seat as if shot.

"You're right. He could have been lying. Like the quote-unquote 'operation.' "

The thing's skull, under its fur, felt paper-thin. The past summer, I'd made a hierarchy of least favorite animals. I hated schnauzers. Hector's most reviled breed was poodles. "Maybe we shouldn't release him." We were almost to our stop.

"We already left a bunch of animals," Hector said. "You think we're like those Polish Catholics who delivered up Jews to the Nazis?"

"That once I saw Eli hold dying kittens. He knew how."

"But what are we thinking believing this when he lied about everything else?"

"Maybe it was his one sweet spot." Ben Orion would say I was *makin' fairy tales.* I held Max, shushing him. He was an incredibly nervous animal. We passed long grasses blowing against a chain-link fence. Finally we arrived at our stop. So far we'd left them:

Tomcat
The pit bull from Mar Vista

A chihuahua named Pretzel

Two geese from Cottonwoods Elementary that had been
   hatched from eggs. We did this one gratis for the Animal
   Rights Collective.

A pug that couldn't be trained out of peeing inside

A spaniel that barked all night long

A dominant, pecking ancient parrot

It was December and warm, in the high sixties. Some of the
trees had changed color. I had to admit: it was beautiful here. We
were walking this route for the last time. "The Mims wrote him
that contract once to move to Pasadena. If she didn't have us, this
would probably be her life." An old shingled house. Drowsy roses
planted in sand. Mountains outside dormer windows. "I think that
was before they bought their place."

"And she'd be with a psychopath!"

"True. Good save." I'd been marrying my mom off to a villain
because I felt lulled by trees. We'd lost our house. He gained one.
She still wouldn't drive on our old street.

Max was up on my shoulder and trying to climb higher. "Let's
go around the back," I said. "We should be able to see some of the
other animals. You can't keep a goose in a living room."

In the alley, I tried to jump up to grip the fence. But it was
smooth new painted wood, hard to scale. I had to stand on Hector's
back. From the top, the yard looked landscaped, with a rectangle of
gravel and a pink-flowering bush. But I saw our geese, their wings
folded in, two ovals on the lawn, and dropped down hard on the
pavement.

"I don't hear barking," Hector said.

"But if you were going to get rid of any animal, wouldn't it be
the geese?"

"Maybe they plan to eat them. Maybe he's not really a vegetar-
ian! For all we know the pound doesn't accept waterfowl."

"Should we bring Max back home?" He now seemed to be scaling the side of my face. Reaching the top of my head and finding just air, he jumped and started running. We chased him down the alley, around a corner, and across a block of sloped lawns, running harder than I remembered ever running in cross-country, my heart gonging in my chest. Hector sprinted. I felt fat again, even though I wasn't. Max ducked under a hedge, and we followed through prickly bushes, but then he disappeared. We zigzagged the neighborhood for the next two hours, hollering his name. We lost Max.

In the end, we put his bowl of food and water on the south edge of Eli's lawn. Maybe Max would smell it and think he was home. Just as we were leaving, Tomcat streaked across their grass. I lunged to grab him before he flickered away. Now that we'd admitted doubt about Eli's commitment to animals, I wasn't going to leave without him. And he proved catchable.

"So maybe they really did keep them all," I said. "If he's still here."

The sky was dark blue. I looked up at the house. A light was on in a room on the top floor, a sewing machine silhouetted in the window.

"We'll never know," Hector said, and in his voice I heard distance. He'd come to an end. For so long, he'd been the rabid one.

I held Tomcat. He didn't recognize me at all. "We sure botched our last mission."

"Ben Orion's right. With this many lies, there's no bottom. We have to forget the whole thing."

"I'll try to," I said, and meant it.

That night, I forced myself to ring Maude Stern's doorbell. I couldn't bring Tomcat home, with my allergic sister. Maude's mom opened the door. I started to explain, the cat in my arms, and he leaped down heavily. I offered to pay her back for the crate and everything else. Maude appeared at the top of the stairs in a nightgown printed with rosebuds. I promised to turn over my paychecks from the Aero until the debt was clear. Tomcat had settled under a table. Mittens, in Maude's arms, stiffened.

Maude's mom herded us to the kitchen. She asked questions. She hadn't known my mom had had a boyfriend or a breakup. When I told them that we put the animals on the villain's lawn, she started laughing. The three of us sat on their stools laughing a long time. I remember that night, Maude petting the small white cat in her arms.

I never did fall in love with her, and she forgave me.

The next day, I slipped a rubber band around my wrist. Every time I thought of Eli, I snapped it and made myself turn to something dull and good, like school. A strange thing happened. I finally began to like some classes. I figured out that I cared about history. For the first time, I received a midway report I was proud of, but I understood the fact my father hadn't admitted to himself yet: that it was already too late.

Hector and I changed our comic. I smoothed down the story—a lot of the real details didn't fit. We made the discovery of our villain's perfidy just background, the scale of Batman's childhood. We gave our boy heroes superpowers that worked everywhere but in their homes. They moved pets around the city when lives were imperiled. Every heartbroken woman found an animal smuggled into her bedroom. We got interested in making good. Little kids built scaffolding on cliffs to prevent erosion for community service hours. The Villain was only a small part at the beginning, so now *Our Psychopath* didn't work for the title anymore. We had a terrible time finding a new one; all we could think of was *Two Sleuths*. But the Villain's darkness was what made our ordinary nerd lazy boys think they had a chance to *be* good. In the part that says that resemblance to anyone living or dead is coincidental, we substituted: *Some of our story was based on tales told by a liar, so the authors have no idea what, if anything, may be true.* We gave our panels to the guys at the comic-book store to read. I let myself believe that because I thought about Eli almost painlessly now, the Mims did, too.

One day, after Hector had been telling me that his aunt Terry had rats in the attic of her old house in the Palisades, I had an idea. I went and asked Maude's mother if I could borrow Tomcat. The first night he did kamikaze rat busting in the attic, Terry discovered him at 2:00 a.m. with a flashlight. Her boyfriend the architect, who climbed up to the attic, too, thought he was the best-looking cat he'd ever seen. Tomcat had one blue eye and one green eye, they marveled. They had a groomer come to the house every other week. Eventually, Tomcat slept on the end of her bed the nights she was alone.

I stayed obsessed with Max. For the next months, I went to Pasadena every third Saturday, to check two shelters and a rescue place until the people there knew me and promised to e-mail when any schnauzer came in. I received pictures of seventeen schnauzers that year, but I never saw Max again.

I didn't mention those Saturday trips to Hector. I understood: he was finally free. Not only of our perpetual half-solved squalid mystery. But of me.

71 · The Inevitable Day

In April, the inevitable day came when people found out their acceptances and announced them in the middle of class. Maude stood on top of the desk and said, "I'm going to New York City!" Hector got into Bard. Ella was moving an hour northeast to CalArts. No one asked me anything. They must have been able to tell from my face. Finally, Hector cornered me and asked what happened.

"Nothing," I said.

"What do you mean, 'nothing'? You couldn't have gotten rejected everywhere. Even the idiot counselor said you'd get into UC."

"I wasn't rejected."

"Okay. You weren't rejected. Are you wait-listed?"

"No."

"I was on the phone with you the night you did your Berkeley app, I know you finished it, you read me what you wrote, all you had to do was push the button." I still didn't say anything. "You couldn't have not pushed the button."

I was silent.

His voice shrieked up. "Not there or not anywhere?"

"B."

"Wait a minute, your dad wouldn't have let you get away with that. You had those fights with him over your essay for the common app!"

"He doesn't know," I said.

"What're you thinking, man?" Air came out of him in a whine, like a balloon emptying.

"I have a job. I like it." This was turning out to be scarier than I'd thought. I really didn't want to be home with only the guys at the Aero while my friends walked over tiered velvety lawns. I hadn't thought things through very well. "I was worried about the Mims, maybe."

"Your mom's *fine*. Marge says they've got two patents."

"Her work's going okay." She was going to freak. She'd been fretting over the UC system, which operated on a firm grid, with no special privileges for professors' kids with so-so grades. "There's still Santa Monica City College, the best community college in the country." We'd always said that but never meant it. We'd both wanted to go away.

"Your parents don't know anything?"

"They thought I pushed the button. Like you thought. I almost did."

Hector had gone pale under the freckles. He looked gaunt. "Remember how it seemed like my parents couldn't pay for college? It's like we switched places."

"Yeah. You ended up with Surferdude and Marge. I drew a psychopath who put a spell on my mother that turned her permanently sad."

"You're making that worse than it is."

I'd managed to skip one tiny thing, like a hundred other omissions and passive infractions. I hadn't realized that this one would turn out to be such a big deal.

My parents screamed. My parents met with the guidance counselors. No city college seemed to be in the cards. My dad—who'd never wanted us to see shrinks—insisted I "talk to somebody." *He* talked to plenty of somebodies and, from them, got the idea to ship me off to Uruguay or Israel or anywhere that could make it look like I'd done this on purpose. "Look like to whom?" I asked. To colleges? To his friends? My dad was the one losing his shit the most, but he couldn't stay mad long. He didn't have the concentration. Mondays, he went back to work.

Hector remained disappointed. "Why didn't you tell me, man?" he kept saying.

Worst of all, what I'd done, or not done, made my mom sadder. She blamed it on herself.

After he got into college Hector got into drugs. Almost overnight, he found a new obsession. We were still close, but it was different. And even with my rubber band, I wasn't done. I was looking for a schnauzer, one part of my mystery still at large. Though with typical perversity, second semester senior year, when it no longer mattered, I got straight A's.

Our phone rang on a Saturday. The Mims answered and shot me a look. But she already knew Ben Orion! He came over now to walk the dog with her. And I had no other secret liaisons. It turned out to be Hershel from the comic-book store. He'd finally read our floppy and liked it. He really liked it! Some guys he knew from Comic-Con and he were starting a press, called Emerald City, and they planned to publish five books a year. They'd publish ours. They were still working out distribution, he said, but their stuff would get on the front table at Neverland at least.

"Do we have to pay you?" I was about to ask how much. I had money now, from ticket taking.

"Nah. We pay *you*, maybe four hundred to start with, then, if we earn that back, a percentage of profit. It's just three of us, putting in our own savings."

Hershel promised to have it out in time for Comic-Con.

My first thought was that this could lure Hector back.

And he did draw me a card that said wowza on the front. I turned it over. KAZAM.

I still saw Hector, but seldom enough that I looked forward to every time. In June, all of us attended Philip's doctoral hooding. In a medium-sized room with a balcony on the third floor of an old building at UCLA, thirty people milled on a blustery, wet day, warm inside the wind. Philip wore a hat with a tassel. When the chairman of the department called his name from the podium, he walked up and bowed his neck. The man moved the tassel from one side of Philip's head to the other. It was a solemn thing.

"This was a long time coming," the Mims whispered to Marge.

"Remember yours?" Marge said.

"Yes." My mom nodded. I could see in both women's faces the memory of something they'd once wanted badly, then obtained, and now still valued.

I stayed working at my job. Hector hung out there some summer nights; he brought his stoner friends, and they watched the movie, then slumped against the wall while I swept and cleaned the popcorn machine. I gave them free candy but then put my own cash in the register for it. In July, we both went with Hershel to Comic-Con and sat behind a table with stacks of *Two Sleuths* on it. By August, Hector was packing to go.

It was hard to say good-bye. I admitted that he was the most important person in my life, and he said, Same. I worried again that I wasn't gay but I should be, because I loved him more than I'd loved any girl yet. He still hadn't had a crush of any kind. I thought of Ella all the time, but I hadn't seen her this summer. I kept checking her Facebook page for updates. Maude and her brother came a couple nights a week to the theater, and they stayed to help me clean and close up.

On a windy day in late August, after they'd all left, I lay my bike on our porch, yelled hello, and no one answered. "Yoo-hoo!" I opened the Mims's door. She sat at her desk, on the phone.

"I'm talking to Eli," she said.

My heart shocked, going heavier and small. Then: *He knew she wasn't dead.* Had he called to tell on me?

Her arm, on the desk, seemed calm and permanent, with an intelligent hand, veined, not young. But her face looked back to full color. I suppose I should've known it was Eli. Once, in the middle of the night, I'd thought we were hearing his real voice for the first time; I wondered if he was using that voice now. Open on the desk was the letter folded in three that she'd received two days ago. *The Field Foundation is pleased to* . . . The prize. She, Marge, and two young biologists would outfit a lab on South Campus. Seeing that, I remembered how I'd been worried about our finances for a long time, and now I wasn't anymore. I noticed a small card near the letter.

Congratulations,
Yours, always, always.
Eli

Guy has a way with words, Ben Orion had said. So Eli was up to his old tricks. Three little words. Who knew what they would do to her? *Never really ever* was more like it. He must have read about the prize and figured out that she was alive.

She shooed me out of the room. I couldn't listen by the door. One night on our porch my mom and Ben Orion had made me promise no more eavesdropping.

When she finally slid into the kitchen and started slicing zucchini, I shuffled in like someone about to be hanged. "What did he say?" I asked.

"Oh. Well, he said that what he has with Jean is an arrangement to raise his kid."

"An arrangement, not a marriage?"

"I said, 'Eli, what were you thinking? What if you'd been at the movies with your wife and run into us?' He said that never would have happened. He said they don't go out. He kept saying, it isn't like that."

"They never go to movies?"

"I asked him if they ate together, and he said, 'Not really.' "

"Meaning: she fills my bowl every night."

"He said, 'You're my most important relationship, and I still did this.' He said he's been having convulsions. He didn't want me to see him like that." I pictured Eli shaking on a cement floor. Maybe that was his "surgery." No wonder it left no scar! I'd begun to use analogies to understand the logic of his substitutions, to try to excavate some fucking particle of truth in the rubble of lies.

"You know how his brother is addicted to that terrible drug—"

"Dalmane," I interrupted.

"Well, Eli's taking Dalmane now. He says it's the only thing that works. He wanted me to go to his doctor with him. He said I'd have a lot of questions."

He hadn't busted me, it sounded like. A feather of elation passed through me: *Maybe it hadn't really happened.* But I'd called him. I had. I knew I didn't imagine it.

"Will you please set the table? He says he lives in the basement, and Timmy sleeps there with him sometimes. He offered to take a picture and e-mail it." She filled the pasta pot.

In those days, I still mixed up the knife and the spoon. "Can I see?"

"Oh, I told him not to bother. I don't doubt that he *has* a basement." She shook her head. "Why didn't he just tell me? He said he still feels romantic about me."

Romance! What was it, even? I sure wasn't going to bank on it. It seemed worthless, like those thin Christmas-tree balls that shatter so easily. I thought of the presents she'd given him—even if he kept them as his little shrine, he still went barefoot to his kitchen where his wife stood ironing his shirts. Romance had done my mother no good; it probably didn't help that ironing wife much either. Still, that day in my bedroom, in the real light, I'd turned my head away from Maude. I'd wanted something more.

"I asked him if Jean knew about me. He said she didn't know the scope of 'the deception.' "

" 'The deception.' As if it were an accomplishment. An algorithm. A concerto." I suppose it was what he had. His great deception. He hadn't told her about my lie, though. That seemed pretty obvious. I supposed I owed him one.

I hated that.

"He gave us the sofa." She shrugged. "Good sofa."

"Your personal shopper." I asked if I could go along to Eli's doctor. "I mean, *I* have a lot of questions."

"Honey, I'm not going. I can't see Eli."

"Ever?"

"Probably not. We may have seen him for the last time already."

"But we didn't know it was the last time."

It wasn't my last time, though, as it turned out.

The door slammed. My sisters ran through the house and gathered near the Mims. She nudged them to the sink to wash hands. We stopped our conversation. It seemed strange to be talking to her like this in the kitchen. No more need for eavesdropping. I had the sense of time passing.

I rode my bike to Ben Orion's. "You want to take a walk?" was all I could think of to say. "I know I didn't call or anything."

He slipped on clogs by the door. "So what's up?"

I told him that Eli had called my mom, that he'd told her *This is the most important relationship in my life!* "I'm sure he tells his wife *she's* the most important relationship." I wanted relief. And it helped to think we'd mattered. But if we really were important to him, he wouldn't have done what he did. "So why does he keep feeding her this dope?"

Ben Orion sucked up a breath. "Because she knows too much."

I felt socked. I hadn't thought of that. I'd assumed he was going to say because he does care about all of you in the way he can or something like that.

"You mean, so she'll shut up?"

"So she'll shut up." He sighed. "The Dalmane was a nice touch. You've almost got to admire it."

72 · I Touch a Breast

School started again, but not for me. With everyone gone to college a quiet boredom fell. I kept working at the Aero. I changed the marquee every night, spreading the letters out on the pavement, then hooking them up one by one on the grid, using a long pole. I returned cans of film to distributors. After the screening I counted bills, sealed the ticket stubs in a ziplock Baggie, marked the numbers on a ledger, and took the cash in a cloth case to deposit in a bank chute. I pedaled fast those minutes I carried all the money in the front wire basket of my bike.

By day, I took driving lessons. My dad made me, so I could

drive myself to SAT prep. My grades were the problem; my SAT scores were fine, but now that I'd joined the ranks of the unmentionables, he thought they had to be not just good but fucking incredible. I didn't expect one week to be different from another anymore. I had a permanent life. *I can see distances*, I texted to Hector, *like someone living on a great plain.* In October, Hershel hired me to work afternoons at Neverland. Sometimes people I knew called, but I didn't want to go to their high school parties. I started mucking around writing a movie script, but it sogged in the middle. I couldn't even imagine an ending. Ben Orion had been right. I needed hobbies.

He came to the Aero Sunday nights, sometimes with the Mims. Once, he brought Ez, who'd been almost his stepson for a while. I bit the inside of my mouth when I saw them, thinking, Fucking Eli. *Don't you want to just go to the movies with me?* he'd said once to my mom. After all the sex and declarations and pain, maybe it all came down to *Don't you want to just go to the movies with me?* And we could never go to the movies with him now. "I thought he loved me," the Mims had said to the ancient doctor. But I'd thought he loved *me.* The night Ben Orion brought Ezra, I kept my distance. But the next Sunday I sat with him after the concessions line emptied and watched *In a Lonely Place.* We'd also seen *Chinatown* together. He wanted me to know the great vanished LA neighborhoods of his youth that now existed only on film. He waited while I closed up, and we walked down the street for hamburgers. He still wouldn't let me pay. Sitting across from each other in the dim bar, we were watching another show, waiting for Eli's demise, the way in movies we hoped ahead for the heroes to best the villains.

This plot was moving much slower.

The Mims still took detours not to pass our old house.

I called Sare once in her MSW soon-to-be-therapist capacity and asked if she thought my mother was still sad. "Well." She laughed. "Your not going to college hasn't helped."

I was working on that, I told her. My dad was working on it even harder.

I passed my driving test and arranged my work hours so I could pick up my sisters and take them to their activities. My dad and I split the price of Malc's old car. I added a morning job at Krispy Kreme I went to right after I dropped them off. Once I'd been driving for a while, I drove one Saturday all the way to Esmeralda's house. She fixed me an enormous lunch. Her son's baseball team had won the league championship. In November, they were going to play in Japan. She showed me pictures of all her kids, asked about my mother and sisters. She gave me a bag of pig chips to take home. I thought of sending them to Hector but I ended up eating them myself.

By then, I had almost three thousand dollars in my account.

I took my sister to Beverly Hills, where her piano teacher lived with who knew how many family members crammed into a house that looked like it hadn't been remodeled since 1957. You went through a gate to the dead-looking backyard. Two sliding glass doors opened into a studio where a poster on the wall read:

WE ARE WHAT WE HABITUALLY DO.

Eli habitually lied. He'd made promises to two families that canceled each other out. A con artist of love. The teacher conducted lessons at an upright piano in a silk dress, high heels, and the clear-colored nylon stockings that marked her as either irremediably old-fashioned or foreign to LA. On the other side of the room, there was usually a girl wearing headphones silently practicing on an electric keyboard, and three or four other kids sprawled on the floor, filling pages of theory worksheets. There was always at least one waiting student. The teacher, a Persian woman my mother's age, ran her lessons over, and by late afternoon, she was often an hour behind. It was a place of intent concentration, not really an atmosphere I loved, though today Ella was the pupil at the upright Yamaha. We'd heard her as we rounded the corner. Music gusting. Boop Two, who wanted to quit piano, moved differently under her sound. It was Beethoven. Even I knew that. I felt something trampling branches in my chest. I hadn't seen Ella for a long time.

Her hair looked normal again. Straight. Light brown. The time I'd seen her retching in a silver dress, it had been Kool-Aid-dyed, red at the ends. The teacher stood and gave my sister stapled-together pages of key signatures to identify.

I sat in the armchair where the moms and dads waited. With all her troubles (vomiting, the older boy's hand spidering her belly) Ella could still make this—a shape that dissolved as soon as it touched air—and I felt that rampage through me, destroying all the principles I'd used to talk myself out of her. The hundreds of ways I'd noticed Maude—Maude organizing my papers, Maude looking up at me—she couldn't make this.

Finally it was over, and Ella turned around—just herself again, a girl.

The teacher beckoned the next in line. Ella hoisted her backpack and stepped outside. *Hey*, she mouthed through glass. I thought she said that. She stood like a feather. Small shoulders. No hips. A hand clipped in her back pocket. My sister lay on the floor, marking notation. I went to the yard and followed Ella.

Behind the shed, she turned to face me, leaning on a rusted wheelbarrow filled with ancient water and decaying leaves. It smelled like dirt and worms. "This is where I come. It's the only place without a bunch of little kids."

"Need a ride somewhere?" I asked.

"No. I'm getting picked up after my brother's jujitsu."

"I remember your little brother. George."

She took out a cigarette and lit it. She offered me one. I refused, though the smoke in the air smelled good. Stirring. But all these years, it had been pretty clear, she didn't like me *that way*. Could people change their minds? The insult had felt permanent.

"I heard you raised a lot of money for animal rights."

"Well, yeah, kind of, the summer before last. With Hector."

"That's cool. We're never here over the summer. I miss everything."

"I mostly stayed in my room." I didn't know what else to say. "I work at the Aero now."

"I heard that, too." She knew about me, as if she'd collected random facts the way I kept any detail about her. Could I have been wrong? Could she have liked me, even before? My hopes swung wildly, a bird trapped in a room. She'd always had an odd smile; it started as a frown and then went up more on the left.

"You want to kiss me?" she asked.

"Should I?"

She set her hands on my shoulders—she was as tall as I was—and her lips touched mine, exactly. It was something I'd imagined so many times, and now it was real, a color, transposed over another color to make a third. The smell of half-decayed leaves came from the wheelbarrow. Then she pulled off her T-shirt! She hung the rose-cotton top on a bush, then reached back to unhinge a light green bra. I glimpsed her small biscuit-colored breasts, like my sisters'.

She knew I liked her; she had to. Everybody knew.

I thought this might be happening because she'd heard something about Maude. Maybe she didn't want to lose me as her permanent admirer. But I didn't want her to kiss me for that. "If you're interested now because you heard I was with Maude," I said, "we're, we're just friends." I wanted to let her off the hook.

Great salesman, I could hear Hector say.

"Anyway, she's gone," I said.

Ella shrugged her shoulders, the small bones going up and down. She stood looking at me. I looked at her, too, our mouths smeared from kissing. I put my hands on her breasts the way I'd first touch an animal, and they were like that, warm, as if they could each act back.

"You don't have to do this," I said. "I'll still like you anyway."

She pulled me to her again, and this time we fell down. Okay, now I get it, I thought. The drug of this. The power. So this was what all the fuss was about. For years, I'd gone to sleep every night in Ella's arms. Now I was there. It was different. *More*. Once you'd felt this, you'd never want to go back.

Then the gate creaked. The au pair with her brother George. She reached back quickly, fixed her bra, and pulled her shirt on again. "How's college?" I asked.

"I didn't like it there, so I moved back home. I'm only taking five units."

Maybe that was why. We were the ones left. The remainders.

The circle of wrought iron clanked. I moved to stand in the place where she'd been. I wiped my hand on my face and it came back red. My nose was bleeding.

I wasn't gay, I supposed.

"Do you like Ella?" Boop Two asked in the car.

"I love Ella," I said, telling the truth a way that seemed just talk. "We're friends."

I fully expected to wake up from this shimmery aftercalm and find all the sparkles fallen through my fingers.

"I meant as more than friends."

"She doesn't think of me that way." I knew it wasn't the same for Ella. But what was it for her? I kept picturing her breasts, the reddish-brown part around the nipple slightly bigger on the right. Still, I didn't know if I'd talk to her again. We didn't have school together anymore. And I remembered that time I'd texted her and she'd never texted me back.

....

"You should tell your father you're heterosexual," the Mims said that night. Boop Two must have ratted something. "Because if you don't, I will." Our father was coming over for dinner. "You're using this to yank his chain," she said.

"I'm using it to get his attention."

Hector and I had stopped talking about our parents' marriages a long time ago. We never really figured them out, and Hector had stopped caring. I thought I understood our divorce. My dad had wanted to give the Mims a safe, easy life. But that life had felt too soft to her. After the Boops were born he'd wanted her to quit. "You care about math, not teaching," he'd said. "You hate faculty meetings." A lawyer by training, my father litigated, never discussed. At that point, she'd taught four days a week, as an assistant professor. She earned seventy-one thousand dollars a year. By my father's accounting, that sum was not worth her exhaustion or complaints, most of all not worth her nagging *him* to help more.

She'd grown up poor but *necessary*. She couldn't find a way to be that with him. He really didn't need any of us. She'd worked in a Detroit hospital when she was young, as a Candy Striper; she'd described the feeling of smooth time, the paddlewheel of days, where despite the construction-paper cutout decorations, Christmas was never Christmas, Sunday was not Sunday, and the rounds remained the same.

But she was the guilty party. She'd loved Eli and hoped to marry him.

My dad had still never settled on anyone else.

But he finally had his hit show. More people have seen *Happy Never After* than any single one of Shakespeare's plays. He still handed my mom garbage from his car window, but often she asked him in for dinner, and when he walked up the lawn Hound went wild. Dad hadn't wanted Hound, but the dog loved him.

And Dad had more pictures of himself with Hound than any of us did, and Hound lived in our rented house. Rented or not, our house felt permanent now. We knew our landlord, Einar Nelson, a ninety-year-old Swedish widower who lived up the street. When Marge and the Mims baked, they made one extra and had the Boops walk it to him. At Christmas, he got a Lorelei vase, too.

My dad helped himself to seconds before he brought up my future. "Your SATs matter now, Miles," he said. "But once those are done, I'd like you to find something educational. An internship. A volunteer program abroad. I don't see that taking tickets at a movie theater will expand your perspective."

"You guys cost me hundreds of dollars I could have earned selling soup."

"Cry me a river," my dad said.

"I ate soup every day for a year!"

When I went in to say good night to the Boops, they were looking at a baby book, a Berenstain Bear. Dad had annotated it, adding a *Twin Sister Bear* to the drawings. Our dad was a master of scribbles found years later that made a child's book permanently *personal*, theirs and his. The Mims seemed to be okay with just the evaporating present. Those nights Dad stayed for supper the Boops whispered in their room in the dark.

Our parents were laughing together in the kitchen.

"We *are* close, Irene," he was saying. "We've been talking for forty minutes."

"You're not the only one I told," she said.

"I know I'm not the only one, but I'm in the rotation."

That was love, I supposed. Not romantic love. But a kind of love we still had. Leave it to my dad; he'd found a way to earn his A in Divorce.

When I went to say good night, he had to keep his mouth in check: it wanted to smile; you could sense his muscles pulling the edges down. "If I'd known heterosexuality would make you this happy," I said, "I'd have told you in time for soup selling." The long joke was over (no coming out for April Fools' Day), but they didn't say anything more about my ticket taking. I kept my job.

As my dad was walking down to his car, Ben Orion was loping up to take the dog for a walk. He and the Mims set out. When she returned with Hound, I asked her if she and Ben were ever going to date. She got that smile. *The* smile.

But then she said no. She said she wanted Ben to have the whole shebang: a wife, children, all of it. And she was too old.

"He's your same age, almost," I pointed out.

Just then my phone buzzed. Ella.

73 · A Noise in the Night

A noise woke me in the middle of the night, and I made myself shove up. I thought it was the Mims, crying again. Marge said that it took half as long as you were with a person to get over them. And the Mims had been with Eli six years. He'd bought that house with his wife in the middle of it. Buying a house was a huge deal, even I knew that. He must have made his decision then and put off the ugly duty of telling us.

I found the Mims on the back porch, holding Hound. "He was whimpering," she said, her face dry, a cup of tea next to her. I rummaged on the cluttered kitchen counter, found a tennis ball, and threw it across our small backyard. He ran, leaping in the dark. He could *fetch* but still not *retrieve*. We watched him together. Our delight.

Open cookbooks were strewn on the porch next to a small shoebox. She told me she'd been reading recipes as bedtime stories. Now that I was up, I didn't feel tired. She talked about work. She and Marge strayed in and out of each other's offices every day. After lunch, they walked down to the lab on South Campus. They had invitations to fly different places around the world. Mostly, she said, she wanted to just stay home and keep working.

"What's this?" I finally said, knocking on the shoebox. "Love letters?"

I'd been joking, but she nodded yes. She told me the potter had finally sent the box of letters, and she didn't know what to do with them. She said she would have sent them back, but she had the feeling that Lorelei, or at least Lorelei's husband, wanted to get rid of them.

"You could send them to Eli and his wife," I said.

I took the lid off. There were about twenty-some letters still in their envelopes. The potter had tied them into a little bundle with plain string.

I took one out, glanced at it quickly, then folded the stationery into a paper airplane. I flew it. Hound bounded after it but lost interest once it landed; the paper was too flimsy for satisfying mastication. I kept folding and sending them up, though; he liked the airplanes while they were still in the air.

The Mims asked if I was seeing a girl. She said she thought I was. She could tell. I asked how.

Showers, she mentioned. Also, a comb seemed to have been involved.

I told her yes.

"Oh, good." She sighed. "I worried that things with Eli turning out the way they did may have . . . I wasn't wary enough," she said. "But I don't want that to make you too suspicious."

I had been too suspicious. Hector and I both. And for all our suspecting, we didn't really know anything until we saw hard evidence. All our suspicions hadn't protected us from the bad truth.

She told me then that she and Ben Orion had decided, more than once, that it didn't make sense for them to get involved, but that it seemed they'd begun to anyway. She shrugged. Sometimes things didn't make sense, she said, or at least the sense isn't immediately apparent.

That same morning at dawn, I walked over to our old house. I'd been thinking of the Rabid Rabbits' Pad. Since we'd moved, I hadn't seen our house once, even from the outside. When I got there, I stood on the curb. It looked the same. Nothing had been painted or changed that I could tell. I considered creeping around to the back and just climbing up the rope ladder. Or waiting an hour, then knocking and asking the people who lived there if I could sit in my childhood tree house. But I had to get back to drive the Boops to school. I didn't detect any motion through the windows. The people who lived there must have been asleep. Still, I could feel that the life in the house wasn't ours anymore. It was like visiting a strange future; I knew all the walls but not the people. I stood there awhile and then went home.

I called Hector and woke him, even though it was three hours later in New York. He said he'd discovered something called rogue taxidermy that was like our mutants but made with real dead animals, patched together. There was a museum of it in Canada. One day, he said, we'd drive up to see it. "Inspiration," he said. It was almost ten there, but he was just getting up, and I could hear him drawing on a joint and coughing.

Hector had turned out to be right, though. As the year wore on, the Mims didn't seem so sad. She had a taut energy for work; she and Marge were busy in a happy, contained way that involved many lists. I didn't think she pined for Eli anymore.

The only thing she still seemed sad about was me.

74 · A Hummingbird in the Yard

One ordinary afternoon in Neverland, Hershel told me they'd been receiving orders for our book, fifty a week, steadily, from indie comic-book buyers all over the country. "It's word of mouth," he said. "It's been happening for eight, nine weeks, but I didn't want to tell you, in case it was just a blip. But people respond to these kids redistributing pets." They had to reprint *Two Sleuths*. They would pay us fifteen hundred dollars! But it took a day and a half to get Hector to pick up his phone so I could tell him. He was glad, but not like I'd expected. He sounded really stoned. I felt a little superior to his new friends and a little inferior at the same time. Fifteen hundred dollars would have once made him swoon.

"We should write another," I said.

"Maybe. But what about?"

"I'll think of something," I mumbled. He was doing a lot of drugs. He told me he ate junk food with his roommates for dinner. They slept through breakfast and lunch. He didn't go to classes. He stayed in his room. I started to think I wasn't meant for college. I felt old. When Ella and I went out, I paid for dinner. We got into the Aero for free.

I banked an extra hundred and fifty taking my dad's online traffic school course, twice. "What did you do *before* when you got tickets?" I asked. He was watching the news as I ripped through the sections.

(Fact: In the fifties Japan outlawed hula hoops because the swinging hips proved to be too distracting for motorists.)

"Malc did them, but it's better to keep it in the family. I'm not *proud* of getting tickets."

One morning, our mow-and-blow gardener knocked on the door just as we were leaving for school. The Mims was already gone. The gardener had a hummingbird in his large palm and explained that he'd found him on the grass. I didn't even know the gardener's name. Boop Two ran back in the house. She googled hummingbirds and then tried to feed him water mixed with sugar from an eyedropper.

"Come on," her sister shouted, her backpack hanging off one shoulder. "We're gonna be late."

Boop Two had the eyedropper in her hand and the phone against her ear. She was talking to a woman in Orange County who kept forty injured hummingbirds in her kitchen, feeding them every twenty minutes. Boop Two wanted me to drive her with the bird to Orange County, but Boop One had to get to school. The hummingbird rehabilitator on the phone told us to put the bird in a strawberry box on a bush or somewhere off the ground. Its mother would find it, she said, or he'd learn to fly. His pinfeathers were already grown, Boop Two explained. Just as we were getting in the car, we saw him try to flap his wings and then leverage himself up into the air.

He learned to fly right then, while we were watching.

"Miles Adler-Hart, yeah, I know Miles Adler-Hart. Sure, I know where to find him. He's right here." Hershel had the phone to his ear behind the cash register.

He handed me the receiver on its sprongy cord. A professor from Princeton said he was teaching *Two Sleuths*. He wanted to invite me and Hector to come there and talk about it! He'd pay for our plane tickets! He seemed shocked to find out we were actually nineteen. I told him Hector was in college. "What about you?" he asked.

I found myself sounding like my dad. "I'm taking a gap year. Working here and at a revival movie theater." I didn't say about the doughnuts.

He offered to pay us each five hundred plus transportation. I said yes right away. He asked if I was considering Princeton. I said sure, but I didn't know if Princeton was considering me. He said he'd make sure it did. I cleared the days with Hershel and the Aero and Krispy Kreme before I mentioned any of this to my folks. They didn't know about *Two Sleuths*. Since soup selling, I didn't like to tell them about my businesses. I wasn't 100 percent sure I could get Hector to go. I thought it would take a delicate negotiation to get him out of his dorm room.

I added Princeton to my college list. I applied to Bard, Berkeley, and Princeton, early action. Professor Tin recommended that. This time, I pressed buttons.

Before Hector and I visited Princeton, the Mims received a diagnosis. The news stabbed me. I thought I'd caused her cancer. Right away, I blurted out that I'd called Eli two years ago and told him that she'd killed herself. My lips moved against the fabric of her shirt. Eli would have nothing on me now; I could purely hate him. But even that didn't matter anymore. My face was in her shoulder so I couldn't see. Finally, I lifted my head. She didn't ream me out, she just looked incredibly sad, as if Eli had deformed me, me, her favorite.

When I got the letter from Princeton, I waited three days before telling them. I didn't know how to explain. My test scores were high—purchased 800s, as my dad called them—but there was still the matter of my GPA.

When Hector and I had received the precious first copies of *Two Sleuths*, we'd talked about showing our parents. We wanted to, but great as the book looked, we wished it was about something else, something entirely made up, or at least from our lives, not my mom's. We only had the Villain in a few pages at the beginning and his house as the place of last resort for the incorrigible animals whose lives were endangered and who needed a home. I'd hidden my copy under a mountain of comic books. For the first days, I took it out and held it when I was alone in the house.

I told my dad about Princeton and the book first. "Does your mother know about this?" he asked, sitting in the car, leafing through *Two Sleuths*. "It's mostly a fantasy, but she might object to the notion of boys flying errant pets to a bigamist's yard. I'm assuming you never did actually put animals on his lawn." I'd had to tell my father the whole story of Eli. He hadn't known. I was surprised. "I never trusted him," he said, shaking his head. "I didn't like his hair."

In the end, after the Mims read it, her only question was, "You got into Princeton because of a comic book?" She shook her head and laughed. "I stayed up reading it with the windows open, and I laughed and laughed."

It took me years to understand that that was a generous reading of our book.

The Superboys wondered how the Villain's lies were different from lies everyone told. And why his broken promise to love was worse than their own mothers' and fathers', who'd stood at altars and vowed to love each other until death did them part.

When I left, Ben Orion promised to take the Mims to treatments. He slept in her room sometimes. I guessed that she decided to lift her scruples about the future, probably for the obvious reason that there was none. I didn't ask.

75 · The Woman Who'd Been Washed and Dried Many Times

That summer before I tried Princeton, Ella and I drove to Pasadena together. She waited in the car. I walked up Eli's lawn alone, my chest fluttering. I didn't know what I'd say. The wife opened the door. She looked middle-aged, not so different from my mom or Sare. She stood in a housedress and old-fashioned pointed white Keds. Her legs were bare, shaved only a few days ago so that five-o'clock-shadow bristles showed on her muscled calves.

"Is Eli here?" I asked.

"No, he's out of town," she said. "Can I help you with something?"

"I'm Miles Adler-Hart. Do you know who I am?"

She first kept her public face, but when I said I was Irene's son, she motioned me to sit down on the bright blue porch chair. She didn't invite me inside. I'd glimpsed the living room, though; it had a blue-and-green color scheme, and a mod Escher-looking skewed plaid rug.

"What can I do for you?" she asked. It didn't occur to me then that she might have been scared. She kept her hands folded together in her fabric lap.

Six years, I thought. I hadn't prepared anything. I told her about the cabin her husband had taken us to. The Mims's *family romance*. My Christmas lights. That key he gave us each to hold. The talk about rings and marriage. The delivered sofa.

"Did you know all this?" I said.

For a while she didn't answer. Then she said, "What can I tell you? Marriages are complicated. They have long, deep roots. No one but the two people in a marriage can ever really understand. We have a fine marriage, but I know that there are places I can't follow. Eli had a problem with lust."

A problem with lust! "I'll say," I muttered. Just then, Pretzel the chihuahua ran through the bushes chased by the barky spaniel.

"Eli and your mother don't have anything to do with each other now. There's no other way that can be." She stood up. "I have to pick up my son at football."

"Does Hugo live with you?" The question just burped up.

She looked at me, startled. "No. He lives far away." I noticed she didn't tell me where, even the state. But Ben Orion had found Hugo's address in New Jersey. For all I know, the Mims had sent him a white vase.

I told her about Eli's last note, signed *Yours, always, always.*

"I'm sorry if Eli made promises to your mother that he couldn't keep. He shouldn't have. But I have a little boy who needs his father. You have a father, don't you?"

"Yes," I said. "I have a great dad."

"Well, be glad of that. You're what, eighteen, nineteen? My son is twelve. I'm not going to say anything to Eli about this visit. He won't contact your mother. He wouldn't. He's past all that now. And it sounds like you have what you need already. Try to be grateful."

She opened the front door again to go inside, and I saw our parrot in a cage at the end of a neat hallway. A dog I didn't recognize nudged against her hem.

"You sure have a lot of pets," I said.

She smiled. "My husband calls me Saint Jean of the Animals." *My husband!* Who says that? All the moms I knew called their husbands by their first names.

But the woman was right: I did have what I needed. Could the cure for suffering be the person picked instead of you? Jean seemed okay; she was prettier than she'd looked at a distance, and she loved her kid, I was sure, but she could live with someone who called her Saint Jean and let that make her happy, knowing that he'd harmed other people. She could forget about the uncollected promises he left littering the world.

The Mims couldn't have, I didn't think.

And Jean wasn't who the Mims would have wanted to be. Marge was that. Marge, whom Eli had never appreciated. *What exactly is there to preserve?* He could keep his Saint Jean of the Animals.

I'd take Marge any day.

76 · The Right End

I bagged Princeton after seven months and came home. I didn't tell anyone ahead of time. One day in winter, I took the shuttle to the Newark airport and bought a one-way ticket in cash. The most romantic moment of my life will always be that March Tuesday when I walked into the gold-lit playground of the nursery school where Ella worked in aftercare. It had been snowing gray sleet when I left that morning. It was a good thing I went to Ella first. I had two parents in two houses and not one of them was glad to see me home. The Boops didn't care either way. Only Hound was happy. Later on, guys at the Aero threw a party. I felt like telling all the people walking around numb and bundled back in Princeton, *You know, you don't have to live like this!*

For two years then I worked and racked up money. Ella's parents kept on her to get a degree. I had mine worried about my sanity. When the Boops were graduating, I thought I'd better get my shit together, and so Ella and I and Boop One all drove north to college in my car. We dropped her at the Farm and kept going to Berkeley, where Ella and I started like freshmen, three years late. We found a house to rent just over the Oakland border. The Aero people had already set me up with a job at the Pacific Film Archive, and so we began the life we're still living today.

But I saw Eli—"my husband," as I thought of him—once more when Princeton was already ancient history. I'd driven down to LA to help move Hector out of the sober-living place he'd been in for eighteen months. I'd had a key made for our house. I thought it would do him good to live in the room where he'd crashed half his childhood. He'd been happy there. Boop Two was living in her old room with a bunch of animals. She was planning to go up to UC Davis for vet school in a year and then we'd need somebody to look after the place. Our mother had bought the house from Einar Nelson. He'd given her a good price.

Hector had become very clean. He woke up early his first day there, a Sunday morning, and scrubbed the whole kitchen with lemon and white vinegar. He told me those were the kinds of things they drilled you on in rehab.

I gave him these pages and told him he could do what he wanted with them. I'd talked to Kat and Philip and arranged with Hershel for Hector to take my old job. *Two Sleuths* was still selling; Hershel said he could promote Hector to manager if he liked the work. He could have gotten hours at the doughnut place, too, but he actually found work with a real bakery that he had to get up at four in the morning to go to and knead.

And with his fancy degree, he started school all over again at Santa Monica City College, the best community college in the country. And he told me he'd been lucky and found the right teacher the first time out. A cartooning class. At night. He walked in late to a room where a woman who looked like a guy from behind was writing on the blackboard:

The only tools required for this course are:
Paper
Pencil
Life

Those and these pages from me. He said he's been reading them. He's made notes and amendments. He changed all our names. He's made private jokes. So it's a collaboration again.

He told me, Remember how Sare used to say with a kind of

rueful grin that was so Sare, *Yes, beginnings are hopeful*? Well, this beginning feels hopeful.

When I was leaving to drive back up north, I stopped in Westwood at a Whole Foods parking lot where a bunch of cages had been set up to give away rescued pets. Boop Two had told me she thought she'd seen Eli there.

And sure enough, there he was. *My husband.* His wife wasn't with him or his kid either, though by then Timmy would have been at the end of high school or in college. Eli sat on a foldout chair on the sidewalk. He looked older, small and fidgety. His khakis were frayed, washed too many times and yanked up with a belt. I felt guilty all of a sudden for the lie I'd told him. I wanted to keep walking. He probably wouldn't recognize me, I thought. I could get away. Still. I stuck my arm out and said, "Miles Adler. Eli?"

He stood up to hug me and held on, pressing me hard. I wondered if he knew it was me who'd delivered animals to his yard. Then I thought: I never found out who ratted on my soup selling and I didn't care at all anymore. I must have been the distant past for him. Maybe his son had read *Two Sleuths* along with a hundred other comics without a flicker of recognition. Hector and I had written *Two Sleuths*, we'd put mean scared animals on his lawn and watched the shadows of his family move inside the windows, but we couldn't make him give the Mims the dream that he'd conjured and she treasured. *You and your family romance.* Dreams had expiration dates, too.

I couldn't help but stare. His hair was still black. My father had told me that anyone his age who didn't have gray in his hair was dying it.

"How are you?" he asked. We stayed standing there in the sun.

"I'm sorry I lied to you that time I said she'd killed herself. She never would have done that."

"I understand," he said before I was even finished. He was rolling up the sleeves of his white shirt. He said he loved this weather and shuddered—you could see him literally feel the sun on his arms. The Mims wasn't like that at all. I doubt that she'd ever even noticed warmth or light on her skin. Maybe together they'd had that kind of slow pleasure, on the few days she had away from us. I knew a little by now about the way time bends for two people in a room.

"Did she, did she," he stuttered. "Did she find—" Then he stopped again.

"Do you mean happiness?" I asked.

He nodded, gulped, as if he couldn't get the words out.

"Yeah. She found a guy who cherished her. She died in his arms."

He nodded, absorbing that.

"I suppose she hated me."

"I think she was grateful. Eventually."

He opened his battered, creased wallet. He had two pictures and a license in it, and a few dollar bills. The kid looked like a normal-enough kid with acne. From behind that, he pulled out a picture of my mom. "Hers will be the last face I see."

We exchanged phone numbers and e-mail addresses, but that was the last time I saw Eli. I never heard from him, up until now.

That felt like the right ending, though I'd lied to Eli again. Sort of.

Ben Orion remained my mother's constant friend, through five years of chemo and remission. They never talked about marriage, so far as I know. There was a fizzy summer quality to the Mims during that time. It's hard to explain, but some of what she got from Eli, that wide smile, a way of turning up a sleeve, wearing skirts and canting her leg, she kept. Every few months she came home carrying shopping bags, one dress for herself and one for each of my sisters. When she first had chemo, she didn't wait for her hair to fall out; she shaved it. She told us on the phone from the salon and Boop One cried. But when the Mims walked in the door, Boop One said, right away, *Oh, I was wrong. It looks amazing.* Our mom, she claimed, had a great-shaped head. After the chemo, when her hair grew back, she kept it very short, half an inch at most.

She laughed with Ben Orion and picked at his shirts. She and Marge said more than once that they were giving each other the best years of their working lives. I never heard anything more about a family romance.

What I learned from those months of grave illness was the smile. She had a smile. Before, of course, the Mims had smiled, but when I try to remember her face in joy, it wasn't the same; the expressions I could conjure were quick, fleeting movements, a tight-lipped *See*.

This was different. It was a gift. Her whole face was in it, like a nodding sunflower. She'd look at you and smile and keep holding it there, for you to take in all of her. She gave you her face smiling for what seemed stopped time; it must have been two or three slow minutes. You wouldn't forget. And that had an ending, too, a soft ending that was an apology for leaving. A regret for the inevitable.

The last day wasn't like anything I'd expected. We laughed. We ate on her bed, watched all of *Star Wars*, which she'd never seen before. Ella brought us food. My mother died at home, of metastasized breast cancer, with her three children, two friends, her ex-husband, and a dog.

Acknowledgments

Without Michelle Huneven's wisdom and humor, my writing life would be too solitary and much less fun. I'm grateful to Lorin Stein for an early reading and central, valuable advice. Marina Van Zuylen, Sally Singer, and Jeanne McCulloch helped me immeasurably, tinkering with sense, scenes, and sentences. Yiyun Li read the book deeply and productively, following the voice and gently identifying its wrong turns. Alexander Quinlin, Eliot, Sam, Ezra, and Lucas have left their vocal fingerprints everywhere on these pages. Andrea Bertozzi was incredibly patient explaining the romance of math and the steps of an academic career. I used Ian Stewart's *Letters to a Young Mathematician* shamelessly. His ideas are strewn throughout. To learn to cartoon, I studied *Cartooning: Philosophy and Practice*, by Ivan Brunetti, and I've lifted his blackboard message and given it to a female California professor. I talked to Mike Miller, a Los Angeles private detective, mystery shopper, and loss preventer, and his line "Everyone loves the firemen" started the character of Ben Orion. I'm indebted, as always, to my family—Grace, Gabriel, Richard Appel, and Elma Dayrit—for our peaceful household.

I'm grateful for the honest advice and spot-on suggestions—for my books and my life—from my agent, Amanda Urban. And I'm steadied daily by the abiding friendship and collaboration with my quietly brilliant editor, Ann Close.